SPI
EGE
L&G
RAU

ALSO BY ADAM MANSBACH

Angry Black White Boy

Shackling Water

genius b-boy cynics getting weeded in the garden of delights (poetry)

A Fictional History of the United States with Huge Chunks Missing (editor)

THE END OF THE JEWS

A Novel

ADAM MANSBACH

SPIEGEL & GRAU
New York
2008

PUBLISHED BY SPIEGEL & GRAU

Published in the United States by Spiegel & Grau,
a division of Random House, Inc., New York.
www.spiegelandgrau.com

SPIEGEL & GRAU is a trademark of
Random House, Inc.

Library of Congress Cataloging-in-Publication Data
Mansbach, Adam, 1976–
The end of the Jews : a novel / Adam Mansbach.—1st ed.
p. cm.
1. Jews—United States—Fiction. 2. Authors—Fiction.
3. Family—Fiction. 4. New York Region—Fiction. I. Title.

PS3613.A57E53 2007
813'.6—dc22
2007019465

ISBN 978-0-385-52044-7

PRINTED IN THE UNITED STATES OF AMERICA

1 3 5 7 9 10 8 6 4 2

First Edition

THE END OF THE JEWS

I

CHAPTER ONE

Tristan Brodsky jogs across the block, toward his building, sidestepping the rotten produce the fruit-and-vegetable men pitch toward the gutters as they close up shop. He is late for a dinner table he will be the first to vacate, but Tristan's ears still perk, listening for the slaps and shouts that herald stickball. Tristan is a two-sewer man. If a game is being waged against the wall of Moishe's Delicatessen, he can cut the line and step up next to bat on neighborhood respect alone, take his two broom-handle swings at the pink rubber ball. No matter who is pitching, the fielders will retreat to the second water grate—the greatest compliment in life.

If eager dice tumblings and tough, anxious murmurs waft through the coal-smudged autumn air, Tristan can follow them into the brick-walled alley and extend a math-filled hand and be given the cubes as soon as the shooter makes his point or craps out. He can wager his train fare and win enough to buy himself breakfast tomorrow, or else lose his nickel and be fucked and miss tonight's class: yet another setback for the Jews.

The neighborhood is quiet, though, of boys his age. Only the old men are out tonight, standing three and four beneath the failing butter-colored shafts of the streetlamps, each group very close together, many hands moving in English, Yiddish, German. German, Tristan likes best, though he understands it least. He and his little brother,

Benjamin, have a game in which they pretend to speak it, the joke being that each word is incredibly long and articulates a concept or circumstance so complex or specific that it takes a paragraph of English to define. Their father, on the street, invariably joins a Yiddish-speaking cadre. He will not teach Tristan the language, even though it's all around. Jacob's face darkened and he shook his head the one time Tristan asked, as if embarrassed to speak the tongue of the old shtetl or scornful that his American son wanted to know it. Tristan was unsure which was unworthy, he or the language. Regardless, the desire disappeared.

The apartment is three flights up, twelve mingled dinner smells away, and Tristan breathes through his mouth as he ascends. Everyone cooks the same food the same way in this tenement, this part of town. The thick-waisted matriarchs pick through the same piles of pale vegetables at the same wood-crate markets, filling sad cloth bags with potatoes and turnips and wilting cabbages and waddling down the street to haggle over stringy gray beef. Undernourished chickens dangle from the butchers' rafters on bloodstained lengths of rope, as if they had lost patience with the mundane gore of ghetto life and flung themselves to their demise. Every mother in the neighborhood culls dignity from her ability to sate a growing brood on water, chicken bones, and withered carrots.

It seems sometimes that the Jews think only of food, that for all the ritual and history and custom Tristan has endured in Hebrew school and seen dimly reflected at home, for all the professed sanctity of knowledge, all his people really care about is sitting down to a full table—what it's full with doesn't even so much matter, so long as the platters overflow.

Tristan's parents, everybody's parents, chase one foot with the other all day long and come home to a bowl of hot stew and a hunk of crusty bread to dip into it, and talk to their children about education with their mouths full. They buy two sets of dishes, buy the more expensive kosher meat, buy shul memberships, buy into the notion that the Jews are smarter than everybody else and that things are improving for them all the time, even if the country as a whole is in the shitcan and half the Bronx is on rent strike. For three months last year, Jacob kept a homemade blackjack under his bed in case goons came to collect, and Tristan's broomstick stayed close at hand for more than just stickball.

Already some of the most prominent men in America are Jews. Already we have Bernard Baruch, Felix Frankfurter, Groucho Marx, the good half of Mayor La Guardia. Already we have Hank Greenberg, the best first baseman in the history of baseball.

Already we have Tristan Brodsky, cutting past the rising smells of soup pots and gefilte fish: fifteen years old, the sum total of five thousand years of Jewry, one week into City College, a mind on him like a diamond cutter. Here is hope and proof incarnate even if he has not been to shul since his bar mitzvah and often skips dinner entirely, subsisting instead on five-cent apples bought from one of the six thousand vendors who have decided that hawking fruit is more dignified than joining the waiting list for city relief.

Tristan opens the apartment door and steps into the dim, grease-stained kitchen, where his father, brother, and two sisters are arrayed around an overburdened card table.

"Sorry I'm late," he says, picking up his fork.

His mother spins from the sink with a big woman's grace and waves an arm at Tristan's back. "Late for dinner is no problem. Late for opportunity, Jacob, that's what I worry about. They give him a scholarship, and already he's fooling it away."

Tristan stabs a bite of boiled beef and cabbage and squints across the table at his old man's wristwatch. He has five minutes to eat, if he wants to make it on time to the address printed on the postcard in his pocket noting that due to special circumstances the first meeting of Professor Pendergast's Contemporary Literature seminar will be held not on the City College campus but on Fifty-second Street, and it will meet not at 11:00 in the morning but at 9:00 P.M.

"What kind of a class meets at night?" Rachael adds when no answer is forthcoming, and returns to the suds-filled basin and the bobbing cookware. She has not yet sat down to eat; her food sits steaming on the table. When she's indignant, Rachael cleans.

When she is tired, which is most nights, responsibility for the dishes shuffles between Liza and Pearl. Tristan is expected to return to his room, his halo of yellow light, his studies. The wisest men in the country where Jacob and Rachael were born and raised, where they met and married, were nurtured in this fashion: sustained with meals and solitude, shielded from the trivialities of life, left unmolested to contemplate the Talmud. The same reverence for intelligence persists here and now, in the Brodsky household in the East Bronx in 1935, but the appropriate vector for it is no longer so clear. Except to Rachael.

"Law classes he could take, Jacob. Or medicine. Even science. Your son could be another Albert Einstein, with a brain like his. Will you not talk to him?"

Tristan's father dabs his mustache with a napkin and cuts his eyes at his elder son. With his mouth concealed, Jacob's expression is reduced to ambiguity, perhaps censorious, perhaps bemused. The napkin falls onto his empty plate, where it lands like a tepee.

"Tristan," he says in lumbering English, "how about being the next Einstein for your old mother here?"

"Sorry, Pop," says Tristan. "I don't think so." He is named not for the Celtic myth or the German opera, but a line of ladies' sweaters, Bertram & Tristan, that his father once peddled from his pushcart. Elias Tristan Brodsky is the full appellation, a salute to his maternal great-grandfather, but Tristan has not answered to his first name since the day he began school and found three other boys named Eli in his class alone.

Jacob drops his elbows on the table, interlaces his thick fingers, and rests his chin atop them. "Tough break." He winks at his son—a coordinated twitch of cheek and eyelid so quick, it might go unnoticed. All four children smile.

"He refuses," Jacob reports. "You want I should ask again?"

Rachael brandishes a soapy wooden spoon. "You two think you are funny. Ask why he should waste a whole class, instead of studying something that will help him get ahead."

Jacob's great square head swivels back toward his son. "Your esteemed mother wonders why you do not take up something of more utility, such as maybe ditch digging, or clock repair."

Rachael slaps her husband on the shoulder with the spoon, then points it at Tristan. "We are here," she says, "to survive. Adapt to the surrounding and you survive, as Mr. Darwin said. You don't adapt, you have to leave. Or die." She tucks the spoon beneath her arm. "We have to stay focused."

"It's just one class, Ma. I think I'm entitled to study something just because it's interesting. Besides, aren't we supposed to be the People of the Book?"

"That book." Rachael lifts a finger to point at the gilded Torah lying closed atop the highest cabinet, swathed in six months' worth of dust. "That book." She indicates the Midrash next to it, a tome Tristan cannot remember ever seeing open. "Not—what was it you had your face buried in last month?—Kafka. Not *The Great Gratsky*."

"It's *The Great*—"

"Whatever it's called," says Rachael, triumphant, and Tristan peers again at his father's cracked timepiece. Somewhere between Kafka's shadowed villages and Fitzgerald's glittering West Egg, he thinks, lies the Bronx.

Jacob scratches his beard and watches his wife. When she turns on the water, he cups Tristan's cheek in his hand, gives it a light pat. His fingers smell of street grime, of the sweat he's wiped from his forehead. "I won't tell you what to do," he says. "What do I know? At your age, I was working in my father's shop. If not for your mother, I would hardly have picked up a book." He lowers his voice, just far enough to pretend his tone is confidential. "As for her, she used to read I. L. Peretz until I thought she would go blind."

"Only after I was done with all my work and had a few minutes for pleasure." Rachael twists at the waist and looks at each child in turn. "You can read all the novels you want, after you have made yourselves successful."

"The real brains skip a generation in this family," Jacob announces, not for the first time. The outstretched palm again, reaching for Tristan's cheek. The pat, harder than before. The refrain: "Better you than me, boy. Better here than there." He points toward the air shaft and, presumably, Poland.

"Right." Tristan spears the final chunk of meat on his plate, swipes it through the thin gravy, and plucks it from the tines with his teeth, chewing as he pushes back his chair and rises from the table, swallowing as he kisses his mother on the cheek. From atop a three-foot stack of browning *Jewish Daily Forwards* he snatches a cardboard-bound notebook and clamps it in his armpit, then steps around his father and makes for the door. Benjamin's clear light eyes dart after Tristan, drinking in the brusque departure of his elder.

Tristan slams the door, lopes down the stairs, and hits the pavement. The elevated tracks rumble across the street, and he reaches the platform just in time to slip on board the last train car. He stands by the window, staring at warm kitchen-window dioramas, cutouts in the soldier-stolid buildings, and marveling at the whole stalwart notion of living within the cramped enormity of stone and brick heaped on this island. Paving the roads: How on earth did they do it? How long did it take? How was the water separating Brooklyn from Manhattan bridged?

He wonders if there were any Jewish architects or city planners, and decides not. Jews would still be debating the precise shape of Central Park. Tristan imagines a great gaggle of them, shouting and pointing compasses and slide rules at one another while teeming immigrants stand in an endless line outside the office window, freighted with suitcases and babies, waiting for their homes to be built. Across from the immigrants loiters a row of construction workers with broom-bristle mustaches, tools at the ready, thick forearms crossed over their chests. They roll their eyes at one another.

And just like that, Tristan's exuberance peters away. The world fills up again with striving Bronx dwellers, recasts itself in wan, selfish hues, and pulls him in. He thinks of Mr. Jennings, the best teacher he had last year in high school if not the most appealing, the one who impressed upon Tristan that to appreciate the beauty of Latin you must think like a Roman—understand the words in the order they are written, rather than transplant them mentally to their Germanic homes.

One day, Tristan was partnered with an exacting, watery-eyed fellow by the name of Sammy Fischer for a writing exercise. After class, Jennings detained Tristan, looked up at him with his small hands laid flat on his desk and said, *You don't like Fischer, do you?*

Jennings had no way of knowing it, but Fischer was the boy with whom Tristan shared his bar mitzvah day, as well as the spate of lessons leading up to it. They are a week apart in age, two buildings apart in distance.

I like him fine, sir.

No you don't. Jennings smiled. *Go on, Brodsky. You may be frank.*

Tristan shifted his weight. *I suppose I don't particularly care for him, sir. No.*

Jennings raised an index finger. *That, Brodsky, is because Fischer is exactly like you.* The teacher leaned back in his chair, appearing quite pleased with himself.

The train doors open on Fifty-seventh and Tristan trudges the length of the platform, eyes fixed on the downtown skyline and the proud, hollow trunk of the structure known as the Empty State Building. Over a hundred floors, and rents so high that most of them have never been occupied. It must be the quietest place in New York.

The station at Fiftieth would have brought him closer to the address in his pocket, as would have transferring to a West Side train back at 116th. But Tristan hates backtracking and lacks the patience to stand still, and he likes walking. He buttons his jacket, smoothes his hands over his chestnut hair, and cuts a path southward, darting west when traffic blocks his way.

A thousand little things are different down here. Newsstand rags blare HITLER'S LOVE LIFE REVEALED! and KINGFISH KILLER INNOCENT? WITNESS SAYS LONG'S BODYGUARDS TO BLAME in bright, crisp letters, with nary a gnarled Hebrew character in sight. Men's suits seem cut from a more cunning fabric, somehow, as if they'll never wrinkle, and ladies' dresses are soft and light about their calves. Clothing speaks elaborately on the wearer's behalf, doesn't mumble *go away* with downcast eyes. People are on their way out and on their own time; no one will be where they are now at this hour tomorrow. There is perfume in the air, perfume and possibility.

Perhaps the postcard was meant to say 152nd Street, for here Tristan stands before 201 West 52nd, and it is nothing but a bar, Oswald's, with front windows tinted so dark that Tristan can see himself in them: a lanky, perspiring kid sporting a cheap Bronx haircut, faint concentration furrows already lining his forehead. He looks as though he doesn't know his ass from a hole in the ground, this future doctor/lawyer, the pride of the Jews.

Tristan approaches the black glass door and pulls it open. On the other side is an unexpected density of conversation, vibrations he feels all the way down at the bottom of his balls. Clinking silver and glassware punctuate an unseen symphony of trills and murmurs around the corner; whiffs of liquor and calligraphs of smoke roll toward him. Tristan has never been anywhere like this before, and in his mind he edits the sentiment for clarity: he has never been *anywhere* before.

Perhaps he never will. Sitting on a stool in front of him, at the edge of a luxurious burgundy carpet, is a thick, bald troll who appears to be contemplating whether to break Tristan's jaw with a swipe of his hairy meat hook. A cigar lolls from side to side in his mouth, like a log in the ocean.

"You gotta be eighteen, kid. You eighteen?"

"Is this two oh one West Fifty-second?" asks Tristan, a staggeringly obtuse query, since the numbers are stenciled on the door's outside glass, right above the handle.

"Don' answer a question with a question," the troll growls, sliding forward on his stool so that one black-shod foot touches the floor.

"I'm looking for Professor Pendergast."

The troll chuckles through broken teeth and eases back on his haunches. "Oh. Yur wunna his. I shudda guessed. Alla way back, in frunnada stage. Two drink mimum."

He jerks a thumb, and the cigar follows it. Tristan nods, ducks, passes. He half floats, half stumbles to the back of the room, gaze bouncing off the dark plush walls, the high ceiling, the carved mahogany bar stocked with mysterious bottles. Even as his legs carry him forward, Tristan twists back to look longer at the crisp white-shirted bartenders and scan the smooth sepia faces mingling with the pink ones. For a moment, he is mesmerized by the sequined red dress of a woman leaning in to laugh at her man friend's joke, a long unlit cigarette cocked in her hand. A gleaming lighter emerges from behind the bar, cleaving the air with perfect timing, so that she notices it just as she reaches the summit of her lean-in and begins to rock back on her splendid ass.

Tristan's footfalls grow heavy. His tongue and fingers engorge to the size of uncooked sausages. The shirt he's wearing changes from light blue to mottled shit brown; his hair grows a foot and mats over his ears. A gnawed woolly-mammoth drumstick appears in his left hand, a Torah in his right. Tristan is a swarthy Jewish caveman, eyes twitching in the sifted light. The thought that he's smarter than any son of a bitch in here is little consolation, and while the floating part of Tristan's brain continues registering delight, the stumbling part sizzles with resentment of his parents, the entire Bronx.

By the time Tristan reaches the long table laid out in front of the stage, he's had time to compose a future fantasy, a return-in-triumph reverie in which his entrance turns heads and freezes words in mouths and his topcoat alone is stylish beyond the aggregate of every stitch of clothing in the place. The daydream is pathetic and he casts it off, but not before noting that a doctor/lawyer could never galvanize such a response.

The table is full of other cavemen, dressed as carelessly as he. A dozen of them sit straight against the backs of their chairs, rigid in this house of curves, heads cocked, listening. Some have notebooks like his. They look to be Tristan's age, which means that really they are eighteen, nineteen. There is one empty chair, at the foot of the table, and at the head, speaking, is a man who can only be Professor Pendergast. Tristan sees the glossy black back of his hair first.

The teacher pauses, turns, and smiles. "Brodsky, is it?" he intones with a hint of melody, clearly the master of his own voice. Tristan nods. Pendergast is dressed for a night on the town. Even his thin mustache looks exquisitely groomed, as if a tiny luxurious animal, perhaps an infant mink, has crawled onto his face and stretched out for a nap. A cigarette smolders in the ashtray at his fingertips, and the pack of smokes lying by his other hand, next to a burnished gold lighter, is a brand Tristan has never seen. He is beautiful, in a way no man Tristan knows would ever allow himself to be.

"Welcome to Contemporary Literature." Pendergast gestures to the empty chair and checks his watch as Tristan takes a seat. "Let's begin, shall we? No—wait—a thousand pardons. Not until we procure Brodsky a drink." He spins a finger in the air before Tristan can consider protesting, and a moment later a glass of amber liquid is deposited by Tristan's elbow. The other cavemen have been similarly feted.

Tristan lifts the heavy glass, takes a cautious nip, pulls back his lips and twitch-winces casually as he has seen men do in movies. Now Tristan understands why. The scotch burns, and he holds it in his mouth a moment, waiting for it to mellow before swallowing. His form, he feels, is excellent. A small warmth ripples through him.

"As some of you gentlemen have no doubt taken note," says Pendergast, "this is not a conventional classroom." A pause as the class chuckles and the professor smiles indulgently. He is younger than his bearing would suggest. Thirty, Tristan would guess.

"Nor, I regret to inform, will we be meeting here at the redoubtable Oswald's again. Tonight is a reward which I hope, over the course of the semester, you will earn." He halts once more, this time lowering his face to browbeat them. "I am a new breed of teacher," Pendergast declares, raising his eyebrows, "and this, with your cooperation, will be a new kind of class." He straightens, magisterial again. "You will read no contemporary literature this semester. Rather, gentlemen, you will write it."

Pendergast taps the ash from his cigarette and waits, as if expecting the students to turn to one another and begin stage-whispering in excitement. Instead, they sit with the air of undecided jurors, and Tristan almost laughs. Cavemen they may seem, here at Oswald's, but City College kids are far from dumb. These are the choicest members of New York City's bumper crop of underprivileged Hebrews, and their reputation is for aggressive intellectualism, for educating themselves and one another when the school's instructors prove unequal to the task.

You can find any debate you like being waged in the dining alcoves of the school cafeteria, passionately and at maximum volume. The Stalinists of Alcove One and the Trotskyites of Alcove Two go home hoarse every day, whether they've been arguing among themselves or against one another. Politics is the new religion. Tristan listens to the sermons as he wolfs down his homemade sandwiches, but he remains an atheist, believing only in himself.

For a moment, faced with the table's silence, it seems that Pendergast has prepared nothing further. Then: "Here is life," he proclaims, raising his arms like a king at a feast. "Here are men and women, drink and song. I wrote the first words of my novel in this very room, sitting in that corner, listening to the sounds you hear right now and some you will hear soon. I want all of you to find that spark, to feel the urge to press pencil to paper and invent."

So this place is Pendergast's muse. It is a cheap trick, trying to inspire them by showing them his lair, cheap and self-serving. And yet Tristan has to force himself not to fall for it; the ease and glimmer of the life Pendergast is putting on display are that seductive. Only the professor's satisfaction with himself prevents the siren song from taking hold. The scotch glass is in Tristan's hand again, and when he takes it from his lips, he finds it empty. He wants more.

"Montaigne said, 'I write to compose myself,'" Pendergast announces. "Writing creates us, gentlemen, even as we create it. Certainly it can calm, as Montaigne suggests, but believe me when I tell you, lads: it can also inflame."

Tristan flags the waiter himself, using only his eyes. A slurred energy is beginning to fill him, and it's not the booze. If anything, the fresh drink in Tristan's hand will mitigate against the expanding desire to squeeze Pendergast's words into paper balls, set them on fire, and watch them shrivel. From some unspelunked chamber inside Tristan a righteous fury is beginning to well, in defense of things he didn't know he held so holy. Pendergast cannot be a real writer. He's too comfortable, too handsome, too much on the inside of things, and what's more, he's a fool for laying all this Let's Be Writers drivel out before a tableful of kids who signed up for a regular three-papers-and-a-final-exam English class.

Only a phony would bandy such ideas so carelessly, attempt to baptize everyone immediately in what should be sacred, hidden waters. Who the hell is Pendergast to throw open the temple doors? Tristan thinks of his mother's grandfather and her stories of the old craftsmen's guilds, the years of toil and apprenticeship a man endured before he attained even Journeyman status. Pendergast, you wileless schmuck, has your race no such standards?

He sips his new drink, blinks back his thoughts, and finds the professor has stopped talking. Pendergast is sitting with his legs crossed at the knee and his chin lifted to the stage. The other cavemen, too, have turned toward the narrow bandstand. Two colored men in suits are up there; one sits down at the piano bench and plays a nimble snatch of melody, then turns and looks into the room, making an arcane gesture at an unseen accomplice. The other clasps the neck of an upright bass with one hand and runs two long fingers against the strings with the other, loosing a low, pleasing thrum.

Tristan watches the class watch them, and sees in the students' eyes a childish vacancy. They cannot define this in the language they know. It is not prelaw or premed or pre-anything; it is fully formed and alien, and they are unequipped. The sight should not surprise him, but it does, and Tristan clasps his hands in his lap and tightens them until the bones of his fingers ache, as if to compress the ambition surging through him into as small a space as possible.

He surveys the room and attempts to think in words, not sensory impressions, mind sprinting to translate what he sees, hears, feels. He can't do it, not at all. The failure fills him with resolve. He thinks of the lunchroom politicians, shouting at one another, trying to bore their way into hearts and minds, and of the lawyers- and doctors-in-training laboring to master their small portions of the world. They have their limits, all of them. But a writer can strive to know anything—can tell his own story as if it is another man's, another man's as if it is his own.

Tristan's thirst returns, but there is not a waiter in sight. He notices the drink at the adjacent caveman's elbow; the glass is still full, and the fellow's head is turned. Tristan swaps their glasses, takes another sip, and reflects. A writer can wrestle with the snarled, mystifying whole, with the fact that nothing is simple, that no answer is right, that life is twinned and layered and everything contradicts everything else. A writer, if he is good, might do justice to the complexity of the truth—reconcile, for instance, the simultaneity of Tristan's desires to punch Pendergast in the face and to be him.

The problem with this firecracker string of epiphanies is not the rending of expectations or the sloughing off of everything Tristan has been told about himself. The problem is that they have come in Pendergast's presence, and could even be said, by one with a muddled sense of cause and effect, to have been inspired by him. Tristan resolves to borrow the professor's novel from the library tomorrow, read it, and despise it.

Pendergast is banging his hands together for the saxophonist, who has now mounted the stage and stands with his back turned, conversing with the bassist. "This cat is going to be famous soon," he tells the class over his shoulder. Immediately, Tristan doubts it. Cat?

The man hears, and turns. "Lady Pete," he says, bending at the waist to shake Pendergast's hand.

"Lady Les." The professor clasps the musician's palm in both of his.

"This your class?" Lady Les surveys the table with a dimpled smile, and Tristan grins back like everyone else. Pendergast could not be more pleased at his friend's attention; he's still holding on to Lady Les's hand, as if he wants to make certain everyone sees the embrace before consenting to end it.

"Thanks for making the scene tonight, y'all," Lady Les says, reclaiming his hand and tucking his thin, casually knotted tie more tightly into the vest of his rumpled charcoal suit. "I'm glad to have you here. You prick up your rabbits at what Lady Pete lays on you, now. This is my main man right here." He tugs the brim of his porkpie hat in punctuation, or perhaps irony—and here it is, camaraderie and disdain together, the one beside the other, stratum upon stratum, the full weave of life revealing itself for an instant—then straightens and nods to the band. Behind him, the drummer counts off the song, and then a lushness spreads over the room, washing over conversation and eroding it to whispers: soft cymbals and piano, soft chocolaty bass, and then the most intimate, softest sound of all coming from the man's horn, a tone so sweet and warm and light and airy that it feels as if he's breathing right in Tristan's ear.

It is astounding that such a contraption as Lady Les's saxophone can produce these tender notes—softness from hardness, the full weave visible for an instant more. The song makes Tristan want to move very slowly with a girl he loves hard, pressed as close to her as possible. Lady Les stands with his eyes shut and his eyebrows prancing, immobile from the neck down except for his strolling fingers on the metal pedals. His arms are rigid, holding the horn away from his body like a first-time dance partner, and the instrument curves up and connects with the corner of his mouth like a forgotten toothpick.

The band does not pause between songs to share the titles, just swings into the next tune, as if playing only for itself. Pendergast is right: this man is something special. Tristan knows only a thimbleful about jazz music, but that only fortifies his certainty. He's heard Benny Goodman on the radio—a Jew, a Jew, the Bronx jumps to its feet—and seen Louis Armstrong's impossibly white teeth glinting from advertisement posters. His high school band played an arrangement of a Fats Waller novelty hit once. But this is nothing like any of that.

Even the Benny Goodman stuff, nobody's all that affected by it. Music isn't so important, unless it's the cantor singing in shul. *Such a voice*, the women say, touching their fingertips to sternums. Plenty of kids suffer through piano lessons, but only about three adults in the whole neighborhood play instruments, guitars and bugles. Whenever the bugler tries to practice, he is shouted into silence within minutes, from four directions. Tristan imagines living in a neighborhood where music thrives, where men like these emerge from their apartments at night and stand on the corners playing songs instead of craps.

The whole room flares into applause when the band calls it quits, and Lady Les and his partners bow and step offstage, still unintroduced. Pendergast cautions his brood that class is far from over, that they will reconvene in five minutes and discuss the aims of fiction, and he leaps up from his chair to follow Lady Les backstage and wring his hand some more.

Tristan, too, would like to speak to Lady Les, or any one of the musicians, if only so he doesn't have to sit there like a fan. The drummer is onstage still, packing his trap set into its cases. Tristan stands, pockets his hands, and ambles over.

"Thank you."

The drummer glances up from the leather strap he's fastening across the top of the bass drum's box. "Our pleasure." He is a small, lithe-limbed fellow, perhaps twenty-five, with skin the color of teak and a long scar over his left eye.

"They make you pack the drums?" Tristan asks, bracing to be indignant.

The drummer chuckles. "They're my drums. I gotta haul 'em uptown now, to play a rent party."

"Y'all"—Tristan tries to say the word sharp and quick like Lady Les did, but his tongue can't make it work—"y'all are playing again?"

"Yessir. This was just to warm up."

"What's the name of the place?"

"Ain't no name. We play and the cat who owns the pad charges some bread at the door so he can pay his house note. We jam as long as folks wanna dance. His wife be cookin' up a hurricane, too, man. Plenty of food, plenty of liquor, plenty of women."

"Are you leaving right now?"

"Soon as I can. Matter fact, if you want to tag along, we can split a taxi. The cats always stiff me, 'cause with these drums there's only room for one more in the car. They split a cab three ways and leave me dangling. Never no girls left neither by the time I pack up. I'm telling you, I'm gonna do like Lester did and switch over to horn. I already got a tenor I been practicing on. So what do you say?"

Tristan fingers the change in his pocket, yesterday's craps profits, and wonders what the ride will cost. "I'm with you—as far as thirty cents will get me."

The drummer flashes him a smile, hands over a case. The cavemen gaze at Tristan as he walks past them, as though he is carrying the choicest slab of flame-charred mastodon on which they have ever laid eyes. Not until he's clear of the table does one of them pipe up, a prodigiously nosed fellow who might be Sammy Fischer's older brother.

"Dropping out to join the band?" he calls.

Tristan spins, heat rising to his face, and almost floors a passing waitress with the snare. The cavemen are all smiles, and it takes Tristan a moment to understand that the attention is friendly.

He sets down the drum case, lifts a hand to his upper lip, and smoothes the tips of an imaginary mustache. "I am inflamed," Tristan declares. "By men and women, drink and song." The cavemen erupt in laughter. The sound is loud enough to dominate the room, and all around Oswald's, heads turn.

"Godspeed," says Fischer's double, and Tristan nods and hefts his parcel. The troll opens the door for him, and Tristan exits the club and stands on the corner, guarding the drum. The name stenciled in white on the black box reads *Albert Van Horn*.

"So why is the saxophone player called Lady Les?" Tristan asks him when they're both wedged into the cab, drum cases atop and between their knees.

Albert shrugs. "Just Lesterese. He calls everybody Lady. Reefer is ettuce, like *lettuce* without the *l*, cops are Bob Crosbys, the bridge to a tune is a George Washington, anything depressing is a Von Hangman. Just keeping up with his jive is a job in itself. Sometimes I be figuring junk out weeks late. Les always used to talk about his people after a gig, like 'Boy, my people were smooth tonight.' One time, I said to Paul, 'I didn't see Les talking to anybody. What's all this about his people?' Paul told me, 'Man, his people is what Lester calls his finger pedals.' "

Albert shakes his head. Tristan stares out the window, turning over the idioms of Lesterese in his mind and enjoying the ride. He's been in a cab only once before, the time his brother broke a wrist playing street football and had to be rushed to the hospital. *Medical bills are a luxury this family cannot afford,* Jacob had lectured the kids afterward, pacing back and forth before the dinner table with the hospital release form rolled in his hand like a diploma. *From now on, I expect all you kids to be more careful.*

Harlem slides by outside the dirty windows, block after block of artful brownstones, snatches of angry noise and melody, dark liquid silhouettes. Albert taps his hands against the flat top of the drum case on his lap, reprising the rhythm of the set's last tune.

"So can you dance?" he asks.

"No, but I can eat." The cab pulls up to a four-story building on a leafy residential street, a block down from the bright commercial strip. The third-floor windows are a shadow theater of backlit bodies, and as he steps from the cab, Tristan can already hear a thump piano, the clamor of conversation.

Between the two of them, he and Albert manage to haul the trap set up the bald-carpeted stairs. A man with shoulder muscles that must earn him his living greets them at the top of the third landing. The sleeves of his white crewneck are pushed to the elbows, and one of his leather suspender straps keeps slipping down his arm. He holds a floppy newsboy hat in one hand, a wax-paper cup swishing with some kind of liquor in the other. "Al Van!" he says, draining the cup and donning the hat. "Our prayers have been answered!" He relieves Albert of his burdens, leads the way inside.

Tristan follows, lugging the snare and the leather cymbal bag, and finds himself in a small living room dense with people. An L-shaped sofa beneath the front windows is crammed tight with couples leaning forward to talk over the notes and voices. Two tired-looking women, one old and one young, bookend the couch, fanning themselves against the rising body heat. The old woman uses her hat, the young one her hand.

Plates, drinks, and the ghosts of drinks litter the coffee table, and everything jumps when the portly, sweat-soaked man sitting at the piano by the opposite wall, a personal cemetery of crushed paper cups and empty plates around his own feet, digs in and starts swinging fast and loose and the dancing picks up. Young men in their shirtsleeves stand close to women, whether dancing or just talking, and everyone is shouting and drinking and half-hearing one another. Gumbo and bottled beer and cayenne pepper and fried chicken and whiskey and gin and cologne and sweat and almond cake and cigarette smoke funky up the hot air but the smell is good.

A big woman is jitterbugging to the music as Tristan struggles through the room, toward the alcove where Albert is unpacking the drums. "Uh-oh," and "Watch out," people exclaim, stepping back as much as they can to make room as the heavy dame and the pianist lock eyes and he ratchets the tempo skyward. Tristan has never seen such a large woman move so well. There are plenty of them in his neighborhood, his mother being one, but they all walk arthritically and act as if they went to grade school with Methuselah, and he can't picture any of them cutting loose.

Tristan mutters a stream of *excuse mes* as he walks, but after the first few fellows hear him, an awareness ripples through the crowd and folks clear a path, smiling and nodding and lifting their drinks as he passes, saying, "Right this way" and "All right, now."

Tristan smiles back. Beneath the fear and excitement of being here—alone, alive, half-drunk, useful, unique—there lies, in the pit of his stomach, an unprovable suspicion that these people are like him, or like he wants to be. He feels a wrenching lust for a life like theirs, a life lived in the present moment, an American life. The Bronx shadows Tristan, staggering like a golem, a motley amalgam of old customs, new realities, the bargains and concessions forged between the two. The people here stand with both feet in the here and now—for horrible reasons, to be sure, but it is brave and wonderful. Or perhaps, Tristan thinks, recoiling from his own certainty, that's a load of bullshit and there is no freedom here in which to immerse himself, and this kind of broad fantasy is just what a writer must reject. Or both.

Albert takes the drums from Tristan, sets them down, shows him how to undo the taut leather cords. Tristan fumbles at the task, his awkwardness becoming harder to bear.

"Hey," says the drummer, "meet Charles, our host. Charles, Tristan." Albert winks. "My valet."

"Pleased to meet you." The man who let them in pumps Tristan's hand. "I'll set 'em up if you please, Al. You know I know how. You fellows go grab yourselves a plate and a drink."

"Don't forget a woman," says Albert, and strolls off toward the brightly lit kitchen. Tristan stays where he is, hunched over the equipment, hoping he can continue to look useful for a moment longer.

"You a musician, too?" Charles speaks over his shoulder, unfolding the tripod legs of Albert's cymbal stand.

"No," Tristan says, apologetic. "I'm in school." A pause, and then he summons the courage to add, "I'd like to be a writer."

Charles steals a backward glance at him. "Yeah? Good for you. You know who was up in here last month? Langston Hughes. I know you've read some Langston. No? Man, before you leave, remind me to show you one of his books."

The drums are ready to be played. Charles folds his arms, surveys the room. "Never know who's gonna show up here," he says. "Wouldn't surprise me none if I looked up and saw Joe Stalin standing in my living room, holding a plate of pigs' feet and doing the shake with

Miz Clarke." He points at the big woman with his chin, then shoots Tristan a look that seems intended to put him at ease, and thus doesn't. "That's why I didn't bat an eye when I saw you comin' up my stairs." He chuckles. "Who knows, maybe you'll write about me someday."

Tristan smiles for as long as Charles does, then says, "I think I'll get something to eat."

"Sure. Go on in and fix yourself a plate. Don't be shy. Have a drink, too. No Bob Crosbys here."

The pale green kitchen is full of people, mostly women. The window is open to the fire escape, where three men in suits are standing and passing something back and forth, and the room is cooler by far than the other. In the center squats a card table like the Brodskys', every inch covered with serving trays and pots, ladles and tongs. Albert strolls over from across the room, where he's been leaning up against the counter, ankles crossed, chatting up two pretty young things. He corrals Tristan and walks him through the menu as if his charge has never eaten before. Soon Tristan's paper plate is buckling beneath the weight of all the chicken, macaroni and cheese, heavy-dressed salad, buttered corn, and string beans Albert has piled on "for starters." The girls watch the whole thing, shaking their heads as the heap of food grows.

"Now honey, you ain't got to eat all that," the taller of the two assures Tristan when Albert finally hands the plate over.

"But if you don't," warns Albert, "no dessert." The four of them laugh, and Tristan freezes the moment in his mind, breaks it apart. They are all laughing for different and numerous reasons, he thinks, thrilled that he notices. The girls' laughter is hospitable, but also mocking; they are in on the joke of his oddness, getting a kick out of how a misfit makes them feel more vibrantly themselves. Albert—whose laugh is wild-eyed, raucous, leaves the rest of them behind—is showing off for the girls. Tristan is his pet and he knows he must strike the proper balance between care and disregard; too much of either will make him appear unmanly. Tristan, for his part, laughs to please and to connect, to communicate his willingness to play his role and because he is relaxed and tense and wildly delighted.

Albert snaps his fingers and takes Tristan's elbow. "I got somebody I want you to meet," he says, lifting the plate from Tristan's hands and setting it down atop the stove.

"You better let that child eat," the shorter girl protests.

"Got to work up an appetite first," Albert calls back, leading Tristan down the dark hall that connects the kitchen to the rest of the apartment. "Down here is the card game," he explains as they near a doorway, but Tristan doesn't need to be told. Gambling sounds the same in Harlem as it does in the Bronx.

The air above the table is blue-gray with smoke. Three of the five players grip plump cigars with their teeth, the other two puff cigarettes. On couches in the dim recesses of the room lounge others, studying the game and waiting for a vacant chair. A serene girl who could be Tristan's age sits on a stool in the far corner, next to a makeshift bar. No one looks up from the cards for longer than a second when Albert and Tristan enter.

"Dolores." The drummer beckons. "Come here a second, sugar." She walks over to them, and Albert lays an arm across her thin shoulders. Dolores is every inch the schoolgirl: petite, with big brown cat eyes and obedient hair tied back into a ponytail that just brushes the collar of a blue cotton blouse. "Last call for food and drink, gents," Albert announces. "Dolores's going on a little break."

"Thank you for taking such good care of us, honey," says one man. He stands, wobbily, and bends across the table to hand her a folded bill. Dolores takes it quickly, slides it into her skirt pocket. "You know Dee's my lucky charm," he tells the others. "I was smart, I'd cash out right now."

"But you ain't smart, Earl," somebody calls from a couch.

"No, I'm not," roars Earl, lifting his glass. "Sling the cards, Doc, sling the goddamn cards."

Albert shuts the door behind them. "Tristan, meet Dolores. Figured the two of you might like some company your own age."

Dolores flicks her eyes at Tristan and then crinkles her forehead at the drummer. "How old is he?"

"Don't ask me, girl, ask him." Albert struts off toward the kitchen, leaving them alone.

Dolores drops her hands to her hips and gives Tristan the same impatient yet resigned look his cousin Gerty used to wear when she came to baby-sit.

"Well? How old are you?"

It's a fight-or-flight scenario. He's a nuisance and a fool and it is time he got back home. But Tristan draws himself up and says, "Old enough."

Dolores giggles. "Old enough for what?"

Tristan is stumped. A Yiddish phrase his mother uses when she scolds the young ones jumps into his mind and then right out of his mouth.

"Old enough to know better."

"Better than me?" Dolores folds her arms over her chest in a posture of aggression, or mock aggression. Tristan is not sure which, and he doesn't want to make any assumptions.

He raises his palms chest-high. "Old enough to know when to give up."

"You give up pretty easy," she replies with a wicked smile. "So what are you, anyway?"

"Well, I want to be a writer." Saying it is easier this time, but no less exhilarating.

"No." Dolores leans forward at the waist without uncrossing her arms, as if he is dumb or hard of hearing. "I mean what *are* you. Irish? Italian?"

"Oh." Isn't it obvious? "I'm Jewish."

She raises her hand to Tristan's face, so close that his cheek tingles in unfulfilled anticipation. "But you haven't got those curly things."

"That's only if you're very religious," he explains, charmed by her ignorance. This is the dream of every boxed-in kid in the neighborhood: to be around people who know nothing of him. "I'm hardly religious at all."

The hall is empty save the two of them, and Tristan feels the space acutely after all the bodies he's brushed up against tonight. "I never go to synagogue," he continues in the silence—in the noise, rather, which is loud and just around both corners, but in the silence of her voice. "I don't think I even believe in God. Not the Jewish God, anyway, the one who cares whether you eat meat and milk from the same dish." A nervous laugh snorts from him. "I mean, the milk touches the meat when they're both part of the cow, right? And whose fault is that?"

It's an old joke, but not to Dolores. She laughs, and Tristan wonders what else he can reveal or retell to impress her. The joke about the *alta kocker* stuck on the desert island is a good one, but he doubts she'd understand the punch line about the guy building two shuls, one of which he prays in and the other of which he wouldn't be caught dead in. He imagines her repeating it to her friends at school on Monday, thinks about how the joke would change shape in her possession, and puts it from his mind.

"So this is your job?" he asks.

"Only once a month. The rest of the time, I just live here."

"Oh. So Charles is your . . ." He waits for Dolores to fill in the blank with *brother, uncle, cousin*. Charles is too young, too agile and untrammeled, to fit with Tristan's conception of *father*.

Nonetheless: "My dad." She narrows her eyes. "You know him?"

"We just met."

"Oh. Can I ask you something? Is it true that Jewish people have to do it through a bedsheet with a hole cut out?"

With the exception of Leah Krasner, who lets boys touch her for money, no girl Tristan knows would ever say anything so bawdy in mixed company, and hearing Dolores ask the question so casually, so easily, is enough to make his dick stiffen. Tristan clamps his notebook under his arm, slides both hands into his trouser pockets, and tamps himself down, firing off a quick volley of cover-up laughter.

"Where in the world did you hear that?"

"It's not true, then?" He can't tell whether Dolores is relieved or disappointed. What else does she think about him? Then again, until a minute ago, the only folk Dolores recognized as Jewish were the Hasidim. A little imagination a few moments back, and Tristan could be a goy right now, footloose and fancy-free.

"Maybe if you're extremely, extremely religious. And by extremely religious, I mean crazy." Dolores gives him a strange, sad smile.

"You're very curious," he tells her, wanting to wipe the pity from her face.

"If I want to know something, I ask. What about you? Isn't there anything you want to know about us?"

The truth is, there is plenty, but nothing Tristan can put into words. Instead, he is surprised to hear himself say, "Can I see your room?"

It is not what Dolores expects, either. She gives him another of her odd, bemused looks, then says, "Sure," and leads him down the hall. They stop before a narrow, unlit staircase. "It's up here."

"You have two floors?" Another idiotic question from the young ambassador, but such luxury is so foreign to Tristan that he cannot stop himself.

The steps creak with each footfall, and Tristan is compelled to silence. There is a sweet sneakiness to this mission, this escape into private, and Tristan emboldens himself by remembering that he initiated it.

The upstairs is smaller, all bedrooms, and smells faintly of dampness, mold. Dolores leads him through the hall until they reach the end, and the only closed door. The floor buzzes with the noise of the party downstairs, but the click of the doorknob turning in Dolores's palm echoes through the corridor. Tristan stands behind her, trying to get a whiff of her hair, but it is saturated with the smoke of the gambling room, and he can only imagine the sweet haze he's sure encircled her before the guests arrived.

Tristan does not have to imagine for long, because as they enter the room, he is met with a blast of just the kind of womanly scent he's been trying to conjure. A little tray table full of cosmetics sits in one corner of the room with a plastic-framed vanity mirror atop it, tilted against the wall. It is so low that Dolores must have to kneel to see herself. The rest of the room, too, is almost miniature. The mattress is narrower even than his bunk bed; it lies on the floor below a down-sloping plane of ceiling, against a window covered with pink paper blinds. The bureau is stuffed with clothes, the open drawers jutting out almost halfway to the opposite wall.

It may be a glorified linen closet, but it is hers alone. He folds his hands behind his back and turns in a slow, appreciative circle, as if in a museum.

"My sister Lillian got married last year. Before that, I shared a room with my little sister Ida, down the hall."

"How many kids in your family?" Tristan notices some pictures taped up by the bedside, clipped from newspapers and magazines. They are all of colored women. The only one he can identify is Josephine Baker, smiling coyly from beneath her feather plumes.

"Six. Seven, but my brother Michael died when he was a baby. You can sit down if you want." Dolores is perched on the edge of the bed, her legs jutting out in front of her and her hands in her lap. She pats the place beside her and Tristan tosses his notebook to the ground and folds himself into it.

"Thanks." He crosses his legs, rests his hands on his thighs. It is the only option the space offers.

"You know," Dolores says, "I'm older than I look. I'll be eighteen November first. I'll bet you thought I was younger."

Some neighborhood putz, quite possibly Sammy Fischer, once told Tristan that women always want to be mistaken for younger than they are. He wonders if that applies now; it seems doubtful. And anyway, you could fill Yankee Stadium with what Fischer doesn't know.

"I hadn't really given it much thought."

She turns and grabs his hand. "My cousin Freda in Chicago is twenty-one. She has her own apartment and everything, and she said as soon as I finish school, I can come out and room with her. She's got a job as a cigarette girl in a supper club, and she's going to get me one, too, and introduce me to all the stars she knows."

"That's great," says Tristan with all the gusto he can put forth. The simple touch of her hand is wreaking havoc on his bodily self-control, and the last thing Tristan wants is for Dolores to notice what's going on beneath his strategically placed forearm. "What stars does your cousin know?" he asks, determined to keep Dolores's mind on the glitzy midwestern future until his dick realizes, as he does, that this girl is merely being friendly.

"Well, Freda told me that every weekend—" she is saying when the doorknob turns. Her voice cuts out abruptly, like a radio when the power fails, and her hand snaps back into her lap. Both of them stare at the rotating lump of brass for a moment, and then, as the door swings open and slams against the wall, Tristan and Dolores leap to their feet and stand as far apart as possible.

Standing at the threshold, with an unlit cigar wedged between two thick fingers and a woozy shimmer playing in his eyes, is one of the gamblers, a stout man with a pumpkin of a head. Perspiration beads where his hairline would begin, if he had one.

"Earl!" Dolores crosses her thin arms. "What do *you* want?"

It is no invitation, but Earl begins to shamble across the tiny distance between the door and the bed anyway.

"Thas jus' what I was gonna ask yo' friend here," he drawls, the words soaked in liquor and a sluggish southernness. Earl pokes the cigar at Tristan and then parks it in his mouth while he retrieves a handkerchief from his back pocket and sops the moisture from his brow. "Little late to be collectin' the rent, ain't it?"

Earl is smiling as he says it, so Tristan smiles back. "The rent?"

"Thas what you're here for, ain't it? A nigger's money?" He turns to Dolores. "They like to wipe they ass with it. Own every damn building in Harlem and don't never repair shit. Just come around on payday. Tell her, Hymie."

Tristan's hands clench and flex by his sides. Only the persistence of Earl's smile keeps them there.

"I think you've got the wrong man. My name's not Hymie, and I don't own a thing, pal."

"Yeah, sure." Earl splays a hand over his belly, rubs a small circle. "My mistake. Must be yo' daddy, owns this place. And I guess Charles fell behind on his payments, so your pa send you over to have a little fun with my niece here."

He grabs at her elbow, but Dolores pulls away. "You're drunk, Earl. And I'm not your niece. Go downstairs. I'll bring you a coffee."

Instead, Earl steps closer: right in front of Tristan, nose-to-nose—a distance that, in the Bronx anyway, in every schoolyard and on every street corner Tristan has ever known, implies the imminent failure of diplomacy. Tristan's stomach tightens and a lone drop of sweat eases its way down the curve of his armpit. Earl's face is still plastered with that fool's grin, but his eyes have changed. Or perhaps Tristan has failed to notice, until now, that there is something sharp and probing underneath the glassiness.

"You like colored poontang, huh?" He leans forward even farther, halving the space between them. The *p* pops, spraying Tristan with moisture. "You sheenies chase the dark meat every time." Earl eye-checks Dolores, then rises to his tiptoes and hisses in Tristan's ear. "Think on what your daddy'd do, he caught me with his daughter. Cuz thas exactly what's gon' happen to you."

What? Tristan thinks deliriously. My father would shake your hand, then go into his room and slam the door and scream at his wife about *schwartzes* and how she raised the kids wrong, until he keeled over on his face with a heart seizure.

"My father," he says in a low voice, filled with pride and shame, "wouldn't do a thing."

Earl throws back his head and cackles. Two flecks of gin spittle jump out of the fat man's maw and land on Tristan's lip, and the pride of the Jews thinks, Enough. Taunting he can handle, but to be cat-and-moused, fucked with for sport, is something else again.

"Your father—" Earl starts up, and when his hot breath hits Tristan, Tristan hits back: lifts both palms to Earl's chest and shoves, hard. The fat man careens backward, unprepared, and stumbles against the vanity tray table, flipping it end over end. Lipsticks and compacts sail through the air.

"Motherfucker!" He throws his saliva-soaked cigar to the ground and charges forward, right hand already cocked by his ear—a ridiculous posture, and a clear indication that Earl has not fought in years. He might as well send over a telegram detailing his plan of attack.

The fat man's arm uncoils with surprising speed, obvious power, but getting clear of the blow's trajectory requires only the simplest of sidesteps, and before Earl can regain his balance, Tristan's own fist is in motion and then a painful sting is surging through his hand as his knuckles slam into the hard bone of his antagonist's blubbery cheek.

Earl staggers. Dolores lets loose with a piercing scream, and Tristan glances over at her—foolishly, since another quick blow might have dropped Earl and now, instead, he's ratcheted himself into a boxer's pose, bent at the knees, protecting his face with his forearms, remembering whatever he once knew about scrapping or maybe just doing his best Joe Louis impression as blood pools beneath his nose.

"Come on, boy." Earl beckons with a fist. "You ain't no Maxie Baer. I'll—" But his agenda goes undivulged, interrupted by shouts of "*Dolores*!" and stampeding footsteps on the staircase, and then the room is filling up with men and Charles is pushing through them, striding straight for Tristan, seizing him by the shirt, pinning him against the wall. The back of Tristan's skull thuds into the plaster, and exploding lights spangle his vision. He blinks himself toward clarity, each blink a stroke against a current that wants to pull him out to sea.

As he comes within reach of the shore, Dolores's screams sound in his ears like seagulls' caws. She is flailing at her father's rigid arm, his hand now clamped around the base of Tristan's throat in a near choke-hold. The mere anticipation of being strangled robs Tristan of breath. Charles begins to shake him back and forth. Again and again, Tristan's head hammers the plaster. Flakes fall from the wall like snow, dusting the ground.

Tristan stares back at his aggressor bug-eyed, wondering what the fuck Charles thinks is going on and whether he is mad enough to kill, snap Tristan's skinny neck like one of those dangling shtetl-butchered chickens.

"You just calm the hell down," Charles growls, giving Tristan a final shake and then shoving him against the wall and letting go. "I don't know where the hell you come from, but nobody fights in my house, understand?"

Before Tristan can wheeze a breathless assent, Earl lurches into view behind the host, hand cupped to his nose. "He was tryna put the make on Dee, Charles. If I hadn't got suspicious and come up, who knows what—"

Charles's eyes snap over to Earl, silencing him, then back to Tristan, who opens his mouth to defend himself and finds he cannot muster words. The looped internal protest of his innocence. *I did nothing! I did nothing!* pounds through his head, blending with a deeper, contrary, wholly unexpected rumble of understanding for Charles—sympathy even, because in some strange new crevice of his soul, Tristan understands that he can be guilty of everything and nothing all at once.

Tristan's guts, tormented with alcohol and terror, knot and rebel. He stares into Charles's livid, searing eyes for an instant, and then Tristan buckles and a torrent of vomit gushes out of him and splashes onto Charles and the carpet.

"Goddamn it!" Charles darts back too late, raises his hands to his shoulders, and grimaces down at his ruined trousers. Tristan peers up, doubled over, his hands on his knees, a tendril of drool still connecting him to the reeking puddle. He closes his eyes, takes a deep breath, waits for a blow to explode against his jaw and drop him to the floor.

Instead, there's a commotion, and a commanding male voice says, "Charles. Get ahold of yourself." Tristan opens his eyes and sees feet, bodies, a man dragging Charles backward by the waist, and then Dolores's stockings planted between himself and her father. Tristan stumbles; the wall catches him and he straightens against it, stomach clenched with nausea.

There, sure enough, stands Dolores, her face streaked with tears. Behind her is Charles, wrapped up in a pair of suit-jacketed arms, violence glowing in his eyes.

"Take it easy," counsels the man behind him, working to lock his hands around Charles's broad, heaving chest. Not for a second does it look like he is any match for Charles if Charles will not allow himself to be restrained. "Don't do anything stupid."

Tristan knows the voice. He has been rescued by Peter Pendergast.

"Get off me," Charles says through his teeth. "This is none of your damn business. You're in my house, Peter, and I'll do what I want with this son of a bitch." He twists at the waist, shakes free of the professor's arms.

Pendergast takes a step back. Tristan sees a flash of something like fear cross his face, and then the professor regains control.

"I think you ought to let it go, old man."

"Let it go? Man, where the hell do you get off? He was trying to—" He glances at Dolores, who has turned toward him now to plead with her eyes, and Charles cannot utter the words. He looks the other way. "Trying to—"

"No he wasn't," Pendergast says, edging forward. "Ask her yourself. They were only talking. You don't have to like it, but it's certainly no grounds for murder."

"Murder? What the hell you talkin' 'bout, murder?" Charles stares at Pendergast as if the professor is crazy, but Peter doesn't appear to notice.

A tall man emerges from the shadow just outside the threshold. "All right," he says, brushing past the others in the room until he reaches the host's side. "Come on, Charles. Let's get you into some new clothes, huh?"

"Good idea," says Pendergast. "And while you do that, I'll get this son of a bitch out of here."

"You do that." The tall man reaches for Charles's elbow, and he allows himself to be led away.

"I see you again, your sheeny ass is dead," calls Earl by way of farewell as he, too, is escorted from the room, flanked by two more men.

Dolores throws a final inscrutable look Tristan's way, then follows the procession, pulling the door shut behind her. Only Tristan and Pendergast remain in the room, the moat of vomit between them.

Pendergast spreads his legs, sweeps back his suit jacket, and drops his hands onto his belt.

"I'm willing to let it go this time, Brodsky. But if you leave my class early again, I'll have no choice but to mark you absent."

Tristan forces a smile. "Won't happen again," he promises, and swipes his sleeve across his mouth.

"Good man. Now then. Let's get you out of here, shall we?"

"Shouldn't we clean this up?" The smell of Tristan's own breath makes his eyes water. He stares down at the floor. "We can't just leave it here."

The professor's forehead wrinkles. "How thoughtful of you. No. Come on. Someone will take care of it."

Reluctantly, Tristan high-steps the puddle. "Where's Albert?" he asks. "I'd like to say good-bye."

"This is no time for pleasantries. And anyway, he was embarking on an errand when I arrived. Seems the party had run low on some of his favorite delicacies." Pendergast studies him. "You keep fast company, Brodsky. Hurry up."

A minute later, they are standing on the curb. The tonic water Tristan guzzles splashes cold into his empty stomach, powerless to wash the bitterness out of his mouth. Pendergast sucks down another fancy cigarette, blinking up at his smoke as it curls in the beam of the streetlamp, as if enchanted by every single thing that comes out of his mouth.

As soon as he polishes off the drink the professor was thoughtful enough to grab on their way out, Tristan will have to look him in the eye and thank him. The bottle pops off his lips and Tristan takes a deep breath. "I want to—"

"Don't bother." Pendergast glances out into the darkness from within his shaft of light. "Charles is my friend. I came upstairs to help him, Brodsky, not you."

Tristan mulls this over, wondering if Pendergast even knows how close Charles came to taking a pop at him, too. "Well, at least now I'll have something to write about," he offers.

In one incredible motion, Pendergast flicks his cigarette into the shadows and spins on his heel to point the flicking finger at his student. "Quite right. If you want my advice, you'll find someplace quiet and empty your mind into a notebook."

Tristan feels his chest swell up with hope again. His head throbs harder, not just from the pain but the fresh blood coursing to it.

"Yes, sir. That's just what I was thinking about doing."

"Good. Keep my name out of it." Pendergast wags his haircut at the ground. "I am not wholly unimpressed with you, Brodsky. I hope tonight's events have not soured you on . . ." He pauses, and Tristan hears the professor's lighter, in his pocket, click open and closed. "On adventure."

Pendergast slides another cigarette from his pack, taps it. The sizzle of a cymbal escapes the house, and both of them look up at it. "I'd better head back in. You'll find your way home, I trust?" Tristan nods. "Of course. Until Tuesday, then." Pendergast cups his hands, lights his smoke, and strolls back toward the house, untouched by any of this.

Tristan's hand flutters and he remembers something.

"Professor?" Pendergast stops but does not turn around.

"Brodsky."

"I left my notebook upstairs. By Dolores's bed."

"One moment." He lopes up the steps. The building bulges with people, music, laughter, and Tristan thinks of Moses standing on the mountain overlooking the Promised Land, forbidden entry as punishment for his sins. A minute passes, and then a notebook and a pencil sail out of a top-floor window and fall to the ground, paces from Tristan's feet. He picks them up, drifts toward the subway.

For hours he rides, down through Brooklyn and back uptown again, with his pencil clutched and poised over the page. Tristan's brain pulses in its sheath, and his entire throat is tender to the touch, beginning to bruise. It is an act of great willpower to avoid thinking about what his mother will do when she sees him, but Tristan manages. The darkness of the night grows dilute and he stumbles off the train, walks through the silent streets of the neighborhood until he reaches his building. He sits down atop the stoop, wedges himself against a wall, and finds his fatigue burned away, his mind clear, his frustration with himself acute.

There is so much he wants to write, but Tristan does not know what any of it is. He feels as if ghosts or elves or angels are following him, flitting in and out of shadows, cackling, and every time he stops and whirls around, he's too slow and they disappear. The world feels heavy with life, the air thunderstorm-electric with a potency that won't last. He leans against the cold stone and feels the desire to capture everything overtake and erode all he has ever felt—his protector love for Benjamin at its strongest, the most intense, restless, disgusted claustrophobia that's ever gripped him at his parents' dinner table, the lift-and-crush-the-world-and-let-its-juice-gush-down-your-chin rush of elation he's felt at the moments when his brain and body have best served him.

The only thing that has the power to endow existence with meaning is the very game of trying to transcribe it, and nothing has ever sliced through Tristan like not being able to play. He blinks in the dawn light, rubs the goose pimples from his arms, and catches sight of a ghastly future: a lifetime of sitting here, incapable of filling these pages and unable to stop trying, until he is catatonic, frozen on the outside and still burning uselessly within.

CHAPTER TWO

The aria playing on Czechoslovak National Radio is turned up loud enough to dominate the kitchen, where Nina's mother rolls fat sausages in a pan and her father tends to the sizzling eggs, an unlit pipe clamped in his teeth. It is the famous 1982 recording of José Carreras singing *La Bohème* in New York; Nina has heard it at least a dozen times since last year's live broadcast and knows it is supposed to be great, but it doesn't do much for her. Miklos catches his daughter padding into the room, spits the pipe into his palm, and belts a brutal, off-key accompaniment, throwing out his arms as if he's hugging a barrel to his chest. Twelve-year-old Nina giggles.

Her father is a stout, thick-handed man, with a trim brown beard she likes to rub her cheek against. People often say he's full of life, but Nina has never understood the phrase. It makes more sense to say that life is full of him. Wherever he goes, Miklos *presides*. Even at dinner tables not his own, he is seated at the head. Nina watches him solicit opinions and conduct stories with jabs and sweeps of his fork, and waits to return the winks he throws her way.

Her father is frequently furious, but his ire is directed only at phantoms, serves only to delineate the *us* of family and friends from the broad, dull *them* of government officials and corrupt policemen, closed-minded fools and blind lackeys and the majority of Miklos's colleagues in the philosophy department at Univerzita Karlova. Most of the time, when he is angry, he is also very funny.

Today is a day Nina has looked forward to for weeks. She is skipping school and coming to work with her parents. She and her father pass into the school's gated cement courtyard and stop before the enormous fenced-off statue of the university's founder, Emperor Charles IV. He is green with age, severe and bearded, and he stands bearing an outstretched scroll Miklos says symbolizes knowledge. The other hand hovers near the hilt of his sword, as if he'll cut off the head of anyone who fails to accept the proffered wisdom.

They bid the emperor farewell, and Miklos settles Nina at the back of a high-ceilinged classroom musty with the smell of books. From ten to twelve, she watches her father meander back and forth before nine graduate students, seven blanched young men and two mouse-faced women, none of whom ever look up from their gyrating pencils. Nina follows very little of her father's speech, but she observes intently. Even in this austere place, he's unafraid to shoot a few quick winks her way.

Professor Hricek, as the kids call him, is more the man she recognizes during the final hour of class, which begins when he rocks back on his heels, folds his hands before his stomach, and says, "Well, then?" Hands flutter up on willowy arms and Miklos jokes with his brood, draws them into discussion like a set of dinner guests. Nina is sure he knows the answers to the questions they ask, but her father does not give them. Instead, so cleverly that she can hardly bear it, he hints and kneads until the class, and sometimes even the man who asked the question, arrives at an answer. It reminds Nina of playing charades, only with words.

She and her father sit down to lunch in the drafty, spartan faculty mensa, its bronze chandeliers set so near to the ceiling that the light they cast loses its way before reaching the tables. Miklos leans over his tray, smiling in a way she has never seen.

"You want to hear something funny?"

Nina nods, knowing it will not be funny like a joke, but funny in that other way.

"This is the only place in all of Prague where anybody cares about the things we talk about in my classroom."

She frowns. "Why?"

Miklos shrugs as if it doesn't much matter, but Nina is not fooled. "Most people, they only want to bring home enough food for their families, perhaps a black-market video machine for Christmas. They have enough to think about without really thinking at all. And who can blame them, in an environment like this? Can you imagine, Nina, what it would be like to live in a place where—"

She must look scared or lost or both, because her father waves his hand and drops the subject, whatever it is. He asks her if she wants dessert, gets up without waiting for an answer, and returns with two servings of chocolate pudding. "Sometimes I forget how young you are," he says, handing her one. "We'll talk about this later, as a family. Let's get you to Abnormal Psych, shall we?"

He hands Nina off to her mother at the lip of a cavernous, tiered lecture hall, so big that Rayna speaks into a microphone. Nina seats herself at the very top, amid students who squirm and whisper like kids at her own school. She understands a lot of what her mother says, follows along as Rayna points out parts of the brain on a slide screen projected behind her. The only questions here are asked by the professor, and they are answered through the consultation of a seating chart, the calling of a surname. Nina decides that when she's old enough, she will choose courses like her father's.

That night, after they have cooked and eaten supper, Rayna brews a pot of tea and turns off the radio. They settle into the living room, three in a row on the overstuffed couch. Nina sits in the middle, hot mug cradled in her hands.

"This is an in-the-house discussion, Nina," her father says. "Okay?"

She nods, solemn and thrilled. Nobody else she knows has a house in which to keep secrets. All her friends live in apartments or in houses shared between two families, even three—and if Nina understands correctly what she's overheard, her father paid someone a lot of money to keep this house unparceled. It was his grandfather's, and then his mother's.

The list of subjects that can be broached only at home is long, and sometimes confusing, but the main things Nina knows never to tell anyone else, or even mention to her parents in public, are that her father is trying to obtain a travel visa and that her mother, and thus Nina herself, are something called Jewish. Both facts she learned a year ago, when the in-the-house rule was instituted and life started to grow heavy with secrets.

There were once hundreds of thousands of Jews in Czechoslovakia, according to her parents, but most of them were killed, or left before they could be. Today, the number is perhaps as low as three thousand, or as high as ten. It is hard to know, because being Jewish is still dangerous, illegal, something to conceal—but then again, Nina tells herself, practically everything is something to conceal. Many Jews don't even know that they are Jewish; their parents spared them the knowledge that they were different, vulnerable, in an attempt to remove them from peril or to forget the fact themselves.

It's a religion? Nina asked when they first told her, unclear on what Jews were besides hidden, persecuted.

Yes, her mother said. *Well, partly*.

But we're intellectuals. Aren't we?

Her father laughed. *You can be an intellectual and also a Jew, Nina*.

Being Jewish isn't like other religions, Rayna explained. *You don't have to believe in anything—I've never believed. You're Jewish by birth, like being Czech. If your mother is a Jew, you're one*.

Do I have to do anything?

Not unless you want to, Miklos said. *I can try to get you some books that explain more, if you like*.

Nina shrugged. Books were his answer to everything. *What about Deda? Is he one?*

Her mother's father lives in Bratislava. Every time they see him, he tells Nina the same gentle jokes, and she pretends they're new. When he exhausts his repertoire, Deda goes quiet, smacks his lips together, stares at nothing she can see. The skin beneath his eyes sags; fascinating bushels of hair sprout from the valleys of his ears. Once, she asked him why he was so sad. Deda looked over Nina's shoulder, at her mother, and didn't answer.

No, Rayna said. *Your grandmother was Jewish. Her name was Eliska*. She got up from her seat on the couch, squatted before Nina. *She died giving birth to me, as you know. When the war started, a year later, Deda sent my sister and me to live in an Anglican convent, to hide us from the Germans. He was afraid that even though he wasn't Jewish, they would find out we were. And take us away.*

How long did you live there? Was it scary?

Until I was six. It was very scary. But Lenka was with me, and Deda would come visit. Rayna smiled. *The nuns were not very nice, but I don't want to think about that now. And you don't have to be scared, Nina. All that was a long time ago. It will never happen again.*

A few weeks later, Miklos brought her a book, wrapped in the ubiquitous brown paper that concealed any item one might wish to hide from the public eye, anything bought on the black or gray or pink market, anything purchased with foreign currency or subversive intent or from a vendor whose storefront was unmarked and locked from the inside—all in all, about half the items tucked under the arms of people scurrying through the Staromák at any given moment.

It was called *The Story of the Jewish People*, and Nina opened it reluctantly. It looked babyish, with its cover illustration of rosy-cheeked children sitting before a row of burning candles in a holder. She flipped through it, growing more and more perplexed. Jews lit candles every Friday night and prayed. They didn't eat pork. They read Hebrew, believed in God, maintained that somebody named Moses split open the sea and led them out of Egypt when they were slaves, then went up a mountain and came down with laws that God wrote down on huge pieces of stone—although in the illustration, Moses was carrying one in each hand, so it must have been a very light kind of stone, something they had only in the desert outside Egypt.

It was like one long fairy tale, with holidays and rules added, and not even a good one at that; the collection of Greek myths her father had given her the month before put it to shame. Nina hid the book deep in her closet, so none of her friends would find it. Most of the time, she forgot she was Jewish. When she remembered, it filled Nina with fear, and she had to convince herself that it was probably one of those things adults made a big deal about for no reason, like skateboarding.

Tonight's in-the-house talk, though, has nothing to do with religion or heritage or whatever. Miklos has finally succeeded in securing travel papers, and he will be leaving next week to attend a philosophy of language conference in San Francisco, California.

It is easy enough to visit one of the neighboring Communist countries, Yugoslavia or Poland, but if you want to venture outside Eastern Europe, you have to be everything her father is: well educated, prosperous, entrenched. Even so, getting this visa has taken him a year. Owning a home was what finally did it. The government, he tells Nina with a bitter laugh, considers property as great an incentive to return as family.

The three of them take the bus to the airport together, Nina making use of the long gray ride to recite, one last time, the list of toys and clothes she wants her father to bring back for her. They walk him to his gate, hug and kiss him good-bye, stand before a huge window and watch the plane taxi, ascend, vanish. Nina misses her father pleasantly for two weeks. Then the whispering begins.

"I have a surprise for you," Rayna confides, tucking her into bed. "We're going to go to San Francisco and meet Daddy. We might go very soon, so I want you to say your good-byes to the house, okay my love?" Nina gasps, kicks her heels against the mattress in delight, then sits up and clutches at her mother's arm. Questions tumble from her lips, each one erasing the last: "Will we stay in a hotel with a swimming pool?" "What if my English is no good and everyone laughs at me?" "How far is San Francisco from Disneyland?" Before Nina can get any answers, her exhilaration proves too much for her small body to sustain and she falls giddily asleep.

The next night, because Nina insists on hearing all of it again, Rayna renews the promise of America. She does so every day for the next month, and Nina bounds through life in a constant state of near delirium, bursting with anticipation and the burden of keeping the trip a secret as instructed.

"Today?" she asks each morning—in English, all she speaks at home now—and each morning her mother, a coffee mug hiding her mouth, head-shakes a no.

"Tomorrow?"

"I don't know, baby."

Every evening, Nina practices filling her small suitcase, meticulous and artful in her conservation of space. The thought of any of her stuffed animals missing out on the trip distresses her, but Nina considers herself too old to sidestep the dilemma by asking if there is any extra room in her mother's luggage.

It is during a packing session that Rayna tells her they aren't going to be leaving as soon as she thought.

"There have been complications," she says in a voice taut as piano wire, and bends at the knees, palms resting on the trim thighs of her olive slacks, to come face-to-face with Nina. "Did you tell anyone that we were going?"

"No," Nina whispers. "Of course not." Her mother continues to look at her, so Nina shakes her head from side to side.

"You're sure? Not even Beta?"

"I kept the secret, Mama."

Rayna drops her head and rubs her eyes, then squeezes Nina's hand. "I'm sorry, child. I believe you."

"What happened?"

Her mother stands. "Someone has informed on us."

"Who?" Nina asks, aghast. She knows, from listening to her parents and their friends, that informing is a terrible thing, the reason one must always be careful around whom one speaks. Anyone could be an agent. Miklos sometimes made light of it, carrying on in that grand, farcical way of his, which, if it went on long enough, made Rayna stop laughing, reducing her mouth to a thin line. *Your auntie*, he'd boom, pinching Nina on the nose and moving past her through the room, *she's been eyeing your teddy bear collection. Your best friend, he follows you home from the pub to see whether you talk to anyone seditious. The old grandmama at the bakery is bugging your bread.* By this point, his audience of dinner guests would be awash in pained hysterics, and Miklos would draw himself up for the denouement: *For if we help the government to rob our comrades of their freedom, it is sure to reward us with our own!*

Despite her father's rhetoric, and the schoolyard gossip of her classmates, who huddle together during recess and discuss politics in the same hushed tones they use to talk about sex, Nina's understanding of the plague of agents is thin. She knows to hate and fear them, but these things she has known since kindergarten. Agents are the bogeymen of the Prague playground, the source to which any misfortune or inexplicable phenomenon is linked. If a classmate is mean to you, the cruelest revenge is to float a rumor that his father is an agent. The child will be shunned, and by his best friends most intently.

And yet Nina has never bothered to understand what kinds of things these agents listen for, or say, or to whom they say them, or what consequences follow. Is agent a job, or does reporting something make you one? Do agents really take over the homes of their victims? Why would an agent not want her to see her father?

"It is wrong to leave the country, Mama?"

Rayna smoothes the top of Nina's straight brown hair with a dry palm. "It's not wrong. But if you don't plan on coming back, leaving is not allowed."

Nina looks up at her. "But we are coming back."

Rayna sits down on the bed. "No, sweetheart, we're not. I didn't want to tell you this yet. Your father has a new house for us in America. We've been planning this for years. And now that he's gone, he can never return. They'd put him in jail."

"But I don't want to go." Nina bursts into tears.

Rayna studies her, just long enough for Nina to register her mother's distance, her hesitation, then gathers Nina into a hug. "Don't you want to see Daddy?"

Nina sniffles into Rayna's shoulder. "Yes."

"Well then, we've got to go."

Nina steps back, out of the embrace. "But we *can't* go."

Rayna's mouth opens, then shuts, and Nina recognizes the new emotion flickering across her mother's face. Panic.

Now Nina feels it herself: a fluttering rush of knowledge, overwhelming as a flock of bats. Her family has been attacked, betrayed by an enemy whose identity remains unknown, who might be watching them right now. They are impotent and stranded and the plan has failed. Her mother is as scared as she, and can't even pretend otherwise.

"We'll find a way," Rayna tells her. Nina nods, but not because she believes it.

Before exhaustion claims her at 4:30 that morning, she begins and abandons a letter to her father, indulges herself in two long, pillow-muffled bouts of sobbing, spends an hour in systematic but fruitless contemplation of the agent's identity. Sometime around two, Nina starts to feel herself anneal with resentment for her parents, for their incompetence in carrying this off. She wakes up headachy, grouchy, in no mood to sit through class, but Rayna claims it's crucial that they go on as if nothing is wrong. She brings the girl a mug of hot chocolate, flings the bedroom windows wide.

They walk together toward their schools, weaving through cobblestone alleys that seem newly dark and narrow. Nina remembers Miklos explaining that the Staromák was built this way on purpose: if Prague's people are its blood and Staroměstské Náměsti its majestic heart, rimmed with sky-piercing Gothic church spires and baroque terracotta-roofed hotels and beating to the rhythm of its famed astronomic clock, then quelling an uprising is as simple as blockading the veins. And thin, winding streets are easier to cordon off than open boulevards.

The autumn air is cold enough to icicle the tips of Nina's just-washed hair. Rayna wears a scarf around her head. She hasn't showered. "What we talked about last night we shouldn't talk about again at home. Only outside."

Nina glances over, full of scorn and fear, and finds her mother staring straight ahead.

"Why? Is someone listening? Can they do that?"

"I don't know. They're watching very closely now. We must be careful. All right?"

Nina nods, endures seven interminable hours of lessons, learns nothing, returns to a house that has changed completely in the time she's been gone. She cannot trust it anymore: imagines microphones in the walls, cameras in the bathrooms, ripe-smelling men huddled in vans, watching her shower. She begins to do her homework at Café Vasek, a small restaurant owned by a friend of her father, heading home only at dinnertime.

The meals that await her are simple and bland, as if Rayna has forgotten how to cook, or no longer cares enough to season anything. The only topic worth discussing is forbidden, so they eat in silence—

broken only by Rayna's inquiries into the mundanities of school, and restored by Nina's monosyllabic responses.

Nina tries to be encouraged by the hardening of her mother's features. She tells herself Rayna is preparing for battle. But it's hard to believe. There are skirmishes. One night, the doorbell rings and Rayna rises from the dinner table as if she's been expecting it, runs her napkin across her mouth and drops it on her chair, then stalks out of the room. The visitor penetrates no farther than the hall, where he and Rayna exchange muffled words; the only phrase loud enough for Nina to make out is "traitor to his socialist homeland," and it ruins her appetite. Within minutes, the door is closed behind him, and her mother is back at the table, hands shaking. She pushes her plate away and pours herself a shot of vodka.

"God only knows how he heard about us," Rayna says the next day on the way to school. "But he won't be the last of the vultures."

In the weeks that follow, Nina grows accustomed to dinnertime visits and the low tones of StB agents and counteragents, all of them unseen, distinguishable only by the degree of body odor lingering behind them. They come calling with cagey proposals of assistance and facilitation: offers to guide exorbitant sums into the correct pockets and thus usher the woman and the child onto a train, a bus, a plane. They proffer visas, just as costly, guaranteed to be accepted at the airport for brief windows of time. In return, they want the house.

The agents remind Nina of the suitors waiting for Penelope to make up her mind—occupying the royal palace and feasting on her food and demanding her hand in marriage when Odysseus is really alive, clawing his way back toward Ithaca to set his kingdom right. It is her favorite story in the book her father gave her, and more so after Miklos explained that among the classical heroes, Odysseus alone was a man of cunning rather than brute strength, a modern man in ancient times. That only he was descended not from the line of Zeus, but from that of Hermes, patron god of travelers and thieves.

"Why don't we just give them the house and go?" Nina demands one morning as soon as she and Rayna step outside. Part of her has come to hate their home, to blame it for the insomnia she and her mother share. The only thing worse than wandering the dark house, wide-awake at two in the morning, is running into Rayna in the kitchen. "We'll have a new house where we're going anyway, won't we?"

"This house has been in your father's family for almost a hundred years," says Rayna, glancing back at it. "I'll be damned before I hand it over to the likes of them. Besides, there's no way of knowing whether a visa will work until you're standing at customs, and then if you've been cheated, it's too late. We'd be in jail and they'd be sleeping in our beds. Are you willing to risk that?"

Nina pauses to consider this. "What's he doing over there anyway?" she asks as they pass through the racket of an accordion player who has been busking for tips on this corner for as long as Nina can remember.

Rayna dons her sunglasses and looks into the distance. "Let's hope he's found a job."

How would they know if he has? How will they ever hear from him? His letters, if he writes any, will be intercepted. His calls, monitored. For all they know . . . Nina stops short of completing the thought, afraid to fill in the blank. It feels disrespectful, somehow, to imagine too minutely what her father is doing. She gives herself over to vague ideas instead: Miklos is in New York. Miklos is in Hollywood. Occasionally, momentarily, Miklos is dead—and then he is even more vigorously in New York or Hollywood. Nina watches American movies whenever she can, knowing it's silly but hoping to catch a glimpse of her father in the background, shuffling along in a crowd scene, puffing on his pipe and looking out of place.

As the first year since his departure nears completion, Miklos begins to grow hazy in Nina's mind, and she has to appeal to her mother for reminders. At first, Rayna provides them with enthusiasm, pulling photo albums from the bookcase and narrating the moments immortalized within. Nina listens primly, hands folded. She concentrates on remembering, tries not to notice how much the turning pages and her mother's recitations remind her of the clicking slides and lectures Rayna gives at school. Better is when Rayna merely tells her husband's jokes and apes his mannerisms, brandishing an imaginary pipe and patting her poked-out belly as she mocks a very real professor of moral philosophy, a man who was Miklos's favorite target.

The memory sessions invariably end in tears—sometimes Nina's, always Rayna's. "It's okay," she smiles, wiping her cheeks with the back of her hand, "I like talking about him." But the evidence says otherwise, and Nina initiates the sessions less and less. They're of little help anyway. Her image of her father is being replaced by the image of her mother playing him.

At the two-year mark—the time Miklos should have gained citizenship, with an American university as his sponsor, and been able to come back for his family, divorce Rayna and then remarry her as an American—Nina's mother decides she's no Penelope. She takes on a heavier course load in hopes of earning tenure and begins leaving Nina money for dinner rather than cooking. The doorbell still rings in the evenings, but even if Rayna happens to be home, she doesn't answer. One day, Nina returns from school and finds a selection of bras laid out on her bed, price tags still attached. Rayna runs her eyes across her daughter's chest the next morning, confirms that Nina is wearing one, and nods.

The memory sessions come to an end when Rayna snaps a curdling "I don't want to think about him right now" at the sight of Nina standing at her bedroom door with a photo album in hand, the first time she has taken one down off the shelf in months.

"Sorry," Nina whispers, the word catching in her throat. She slips off, flips idly through the first few pages, then shoves the book away and spends the rest of the evening wondering whether it is Rayna's rancor that has grown, or her own maturity in her mother's estimation, to the point where Rayna no longer feels an obligation to pretend. Such things go undiscussed, like the bras on the bed or the fact that Rayna has abandoned English, and thus conversations between mother and daughter are conducted in disjointed, lunatic fashion, with each one speaking her preferred tongue.

"He could have contacted us, you know," Rayna says one night as she and Nina cohabitate her study in silence, Nina reading her history textbook and Rayna flitting from one task to the next, grading papers and sorting laundry and writing in her diary, as if no one chore is sufficient to hold her interest.

"But, Mom, if he tried, they could—"

"There are ways of doing things." Her mother drops the bedsheet she's been folding back into the basket and stares at Nina the way one gunfighter might another in an old movie. "Your father has abandoned us."

Her tone is not that of one sharing a revelation or breaking painful news. It isn't sharp or soothing, but weary, and the words are all the uglier for it. "He's probably found himself a new family in America, while we suffer in this miserable place."

"Don't be ridiculous," scoffs Nina, but she, too, has caught herself imagining a new wife, a new daughter—no, a new son. All she can bring herself to object to is the most trivial part of Rayna's statement. "Besides, it's not so bad here."

"How would you know?" Rayna snatches the same sheet up again, clamps the middle underneath her chin, and folds the corners together at arm's length. The action gives her jowls; Nina looks away. "You've never been anywhere else."

"Not yet."

"And what is that supposed to mean?"

"It means I'm going to college in America." She waits for a reaction, but all Rayna does is purse her lips, grab hold of the reading glasses dangling from the chain around her neck, and bend over her desk.

"Sooner if I can."

"Now you're leaving me, too."

"No, but I'm leaving here."

Speaking it out loud is an act of such portent that Nina almost expects magic from the universe in return—as if the declaration might make the Iron Curtain rise, revealing a stage set for the second act of her life.

Instead, Rayna tightens her fingertips around the neck of her red grading pen. "At least you've told me."

She begins to sort a sheaf of papers, and Nina watches with the special, studious disgust children develop for the mannerisms of their parents. Rayna's posture is meant to constitute dismissal. She expects her daughter to shuffle from the room and go feel guilty and wretched in some distant corner of the house, and so instead, Nina wanders over to the office closet and opens the door.

A forgotten smell meets her: the apple tobacco and sandalwood blend of her father. The deep-set shelves are full of things she hasn't seen for years, objects Rayna has spirited away lest they remind her of the man she can't stop thinking about anyway. There are pipes, unopened pouches of tobacco, cardboard boxes of his correspondence, a triple stack of thin philosophy journals stretching up from the floor. On the highest shelf, barely within reach, sits a tall box packed haphazardly with the contents of Miklos's home darkroom, and next to that his gleaming camera. Nina reaches for it.

"What are you doing?"

"Taking Dad's camera."

"Put it back."

Nina holds her prize to her chest, feeling the instrument's bulk and heft, its cool metal and hard plastic.

"No."

Rayna springs to her feet. "Fine! Take it! Here! You can be just like him." Her hand shoots into the closet, grabs Miklos's felt fedora, and slams it onto Nina's head.

"Here, why not smoke his pipe, too? The two of you can go crazy together in America, you and your fat liar of a father and your new stepmother from California, with her red lipstick and her big fake tits." Rayna rushes from the room and slams the door, leaving her daughter huddled against the wall, shielding her face and camera.

By fifteen, Nina is as dark and beautiful as her mother in old pictures, carrying the camera everywhere and beginning to recognize a vigor in herself that makes her surge with hope. She begs a job at Vasek's café in order to afford film and contact paper, the only things she buys. Anything else—food, makeup, clothing—is a waste of money.

She is gloriously alone, attached to others only by thin tendrils of biology and friendship. So much younger, the girls at school seem—unseasoned by tragedy and difference and handling their new powers, their new womanliness, by acting more like kids than ever. Nina feels a tenderness for them; they are the girls she grew up with, or at least around, and they are nice enough. As she disappears into herself and her darkroom, they are merely cold, when many girls would be mean. She wonders who they'll have become in twenty years, and reflects that satisfying her curiosity will be as easy as returning to Prague.

It is the boys, and the men, who are unbearable. On the streets and in the school hallways, they fondle her with their eyes, peer through even the loosest, thickest fabrics, spin in her wake to gawk at her ass. Some girls develop ways of walking that make their breasts bounce up and down; others learn to carry themselves so that nothing moves. Nina cannot be bothered. She walks the way she walks. Nobody asks her out. She imagines they call her a stuck-up bitch, a snob. Fine. Her parents—when they were her parents, instead of a dissipating memory and an unpredictable Fury with whom Nina chances to share a house—had been elitists, too. She isn't going to apologize for believing in the hierarchy of the mind. Not to a bunch of beery Communists.

Nina's refuge is the university library. She updates her journal in the reading room, browses the English-language and photography sections of the musty stacks. The weak yellow lights are set to fifteen-minute timers for energy conservation, and often when they wind down Nina doesn't bother to reset them, but sits and peers into the darkness, spine pressed against dozens of others, and contemplates escape.

For all her resolve, the country is a lockbox. Photography is a potential key should she become sufficiently excellent; one reason Prague is so dismal, despite its ancient beauty, is that the virtuosos have all been clever enough to get themselves anointed cultural ambassadors, pack up their paints and typewriters, and go. It's as if a neutron bomb has exploded in the center of the city, leaving the architecture intact but wiping out the artists.

After three years of relentless effort, thousands of wasted exposures, Nina is finally comfortable believing she is good. The exhibition that Vasek, an amateur photographer himself, threw her at the café last year attracted an art teacher from the university, who recognized her surname; he told Nina she had promise, encouraged her to apply for an arts scholarship when she was old enough. She placed third in the school photo contest as a sophomore, won it as a junior.

Each victory, each accolade, is one more step toward nothing. Nina lusts for a project worthy of great expenditures of time, great sacrifice. She begins attending every concert and lecture the university and city have to offer, shooting any visiting scholar or musician reputed to carry the tinge of greatness. She streamlines her darkroom process, starts taking her photos to *Lidové Noviny*, the newspaper she grew up reading. The arts editor, a man named Zdenek, buys nothing for a year, but he looks at everything, explains the difference between what she shoots and what he wants, tells her to keep coming by. The week Nina turns sixteen, he purchases a photo. Instead of taking payment, she asks for a press pass; the laminated card grants free admission to any cultural event in town. The editor hesitates, and Nina throws in the next six photos he wants, free of charge. Zdenek lifts an eyebrow, but agrees. With the increased access her new status affords, it takes Nina only two months to earn out on the deal.

The demands of shooting prevent her from digesting much of what is played and said by her subjects, but it doesn't matter. The images, when she coaxes them into visibility, tell Nina what she needs to know. She trusts her camera to reveal all, trusts it further than her ears or brain. But nothing of majesty appears on Nina's contact sheets. Legendary white-haired violinists do not move her no matter how crazed the looks in their eyes. Nor do esteemed Czech men of letters expounding on Nezval, or troupes of Russian acrobats. A year passes, and Nina considers giving it up. The only image she is really proud of is a shot of four doll-faced American ballerinas in full stage regalia smoking cigarettes in the wings of the Prague opera house—deemed unprintable, naturally. Standing below the stage, her lens trained on the stars above, Nina begins to feel like a lowly sunflower, face turned toward the streaking sun.

"I finally figured it out," Rayna greets her, sitting at the kitchen table in her colorless ankle-length nightgown, a plate of toast and a coffee cup before her. Nina rummages through the cabinets, pretending to be in a rush so she can consume her morning meal of bread, cheese, and black tea unmolested in the school courtyard. "It came to me last night." Rayna's voice is oddly chipper, the bags under her eyes heavier than ever.

"What did, Mom?" Nina is half-listening, working the cheese slicer, her back to her mother.

"It's so obvious." Rayna shakes her head.

"Spit it out already, Mom. I'm running late."

"Your father is the agent. He planned it all, Nina. Everything." She takes a dainty bite of toast. "Extremely clever of him."

Nina marches up the stairs without so much as a look at Rayna. She knows exactly what to pack.

"I'll be at Vasek's," she says as she cuts back through the kitchen, a week's clothes folded in the duffel bag over her shoulder and no force she can conceive of capable of making her stop moving until she is out the front door. Her mother sips her coffee and says nothing. The serenity in her eyes is too much to bear, and at the front door, Nina changes her mind, spins.

"You're out of your fucking mind. I hope you know that."

Rayna replaces the cup in the saucer. "He threw us to the wolves. A woman and a child. Helpless. Jewish."

Nina's hand flies off the doorknob. "Oh, for God's sake. Now this? Look, we don't do anything Jewish, we don't believe in anything Jewish, and nobody knows we're Jewish. We're not helpless and we're not fucking Jewish. You're crazy."

Rayna is about to respond when Nina decides she doesn't want to hear anything else her mother has to say.

"I'm through," she declares, and slams the door.

All day, Nina refuses to think about Rayna's words. She has a concert to shoot this evening, some American orchestra in town for three nights, the theater sold out weeks in advance, the way it always is for anything American. She will use Vasek's darkroom; it is set up all wrong and will slow her down, but it beats going home. She used his place once years before, when Rayna padlocked hers for two weeks to punish Nina for staying out until dawn photographing vagrants in the dismal Soviet-built suburban housing projects. Vasek will chastise her for leaving home, but he would never deny Nina anything: not his darkroom, not his couch. Which she intends to sleep on until she can find a room to rent.

She arrives at the theater early, hoping to catch the sound check. This is the best time to shoot. She can climb right up onstage while they're rehearsing, get as close as she needs to. And she can chat up the artists, build enough of a rapport to be allowed backstage and in the dressing rooms.

As always, Nina begins by finding Jiri. The night manager is mild and middle-aged, with a slight limp and the habit of constantly smoothing down his long gray hair. He makes it his duty to introduce and praise Nina to the performers, which is a tremendous help, and to steal quick glimpses at her breasts several times a minute, which is not. Nina reciprocates for the intros by bringing him a stack of contact sheets and a red wax pencil from time to time, and printing whatever he circles. His taste in her work is abominable, but so be it.

She finds Jiri behind the soundboard with the engineer. He steps around to greet her in the aisle, and they walk backstage together, toward the laughter booming from the dressing room. Jiri raps on the door. The sounds inside abate.

"Who *is* it?" coos a falsetto like the voice of a cartoon princess.

The manager clears his throat. English flusters him. So do musicians. "It is Jiri."

The voice inside drops several octaves. "Come on in, bruh." He doesn't sound like a conductor. Bruh?

Jiri turns the handle and they enter a room full of men in suits. Young black men in gorgeous sleek-fitting suits, some fingering shiny brass horns and one bent over a giant mahogany bass. *Jazz,* Nina thinks with a thrill. It is a music she has hardly heard but loves to watch; the photographs of William Claxton, Chuck Stewart, and Roy DeCarava are burned into her mind from frequent library-floor perusal. Only in these books of images from the 1950s and '60s has Nina encountered black Americans.

"It is my pleasure introduce," says Jiri, making a slight, stiff bow, then indicating Nina with an open hand, "very good young photographer for tonight."

"Oh yeah? How good?" asks the man closest to the door. He is slim, round-faced, grips his trombone with one large hand. He's speaking to Jiri, but he locks eyes with Nina, smirking and raising his eyebrows so high that his entire forehead ripples.

"How young?" somebody in the back responds, and the room fills up with laughter.

"She is," Jiri continues doggedly, smiling all around to acknowledge a wave of mirth he seems to suspect might be at his expense, "is Nina. She want to know is all right she take some picture in dressing room. For newspaper."

"I don't know," calls the same heavyset joker in the rear, the one clutching the double bass. "She might see something back here that scares her." Two or three of them snicker.

Nina stands and smiles, enduring the megawatt scrutiny of all their eyes, willing Jiri to leave so she can get to work.

The man with the trombone glances censoriously behind him. Fake censoriously, perhaps. "Yeah, sure, that's cool." Jiri nods, shows himself out. The musician shifts his weight from one foot to the other, passes his instrument from right hand to left, and offers his palm.

"How you doing, sis?"

Nina takes it. "I'm fine, bruh. How are you?"

The trombonist's look of surprise turns quickly to delight, and without releasing her from his dry, loose grip, he twists backward to look at his bandmates. "Damn, bruh, you heard her? Sound like she from Baton Rouge, right?"

His arm relaxes at the elbow and he swings her hand in a low arc, as if they are dance partners about to begin a routine. "Where you from, sis?"

"I'm from right here, bruh," she says, enjoying herself, swinging back.

"Naaaw, come on now. You look like you Creole or something. I know you got some black folks in your family someplace. I can see it in your face." He implores the closest man for affirmation. "Right, bruh? At least a drop. A great-granddaddy. Something. She's too soulful not to."

Nina laughs, flattered and confused. "And what about you?" she asks, rather than let the genealogical speculation stretch on. "I don't even know your name."

"Heh," says the bass player, "she said, 'Leggo my hand, motherfucker, I don't know you from Joe Bazooka.' "

The trombonist deadpans him, eyes cutting a broad swath through the chorus of guffaws. "If that's what the sister wanted to say, Conrad, then that's what the sister would have said. She speaks better English than you."

He turns back to Nina with mock ceremony. "Terribly sorry, sis. Please forgive my manners, or lack thereof. My name is Devon Stafford Marbury, Jr., and if my band starts behaving like gentlemen, then perhaps I'll introduce them, too. Until then, you'll just have to converse with me. Shall we?" He leans forward and pushes open the door. Nina glances uncertainly at him and Devon beckons her ahead, then follows her into the hall and lets the door swing shut on the band's noise.

He can't be more than thirty-five, Nina thinks, appraising him out of the corner of her eye as they stroll across the stage. But even in Devon's smallest gesture, the way he rubs two fingers against his lips or eases the buttons of his jacket into their eyelets, there is confidence and style. This is a man who understands himself in relation to something larger: a tradition, a purpose. She wonders if he treats all women with the same flirty, mischievous regard he's been so quick to make their lingua franca, then stops herself and wonders why she is so eager to analyze a man she met all of two minutes ago.

"How long have you been shooting?" he asks as they walk up the slight grade of the aisle.

"About three years. How long have you been playing?"

"Twenty-six, twenty-seven. My daddy teaches music, so he started me off young. I'd like to see your work, sis. I've got a feeling about you. You got a portfolio or something?"

He has a *feeling* about her? What feeling is that? Who says such things?

"Not here. But maybe after the show I can go get it. Or you can come see it. I live not so far away."

He hits her with that cruel smirk. "Only if you guarantee me it's some bad shit. You gotta swear on your Negro great-granddaddy that you won't have me looking at no bullshit."

Nina laughs. "For all I know, you might be about to play some bullshit." One of the theorems that have long sustained her in her resolution to leave Prague is proving itself now: the company of other artists is a mind-expanding drug. If it weren't, if new neural tracks weren't being laid this very second to accommodate new trains of thought, she would never be able to hold up her end of this conversation. It's not some restless, darkroomy Czech girl bantering with Devon, but a cool, bemused Creole sister. Even if she's not quite sure what Creole means.

Devon shrugs. "Yeah, I probably will play some bullshit. But what else is new? There he is." Devon cups his hands toward the balcony. "Sparkplug! Come down here a second, bruh, you gotta meet somebody."

The precarious side staircase emits a descending scale of squeaks, and then a man in his late forties is walking up beside them, handsome and scholarly in wire-rimmed glasses and a khaki shirt. A thin white beard sets off his light brown skin; a gleaming Nikon and a light meter dangle from his neck.

"Presenting Marcus Flanagan," says Devon with one arm held wide, and Marcus strolls into the shoulder-squeeze embrace. "Better known as Uncle Sparkplug. Also known as the Big Greazy, Old Man River, and Cherokee Slim. Official photographer of the Devon Marbury Octet, Global Youth Jazz Orchestra, and Life. Marcus, this is Nina . . . Jenkins. Nina 'Pigfoot' Jenkins. She's in your line of work, bruh. Supposed to be bad. We're going to her crib after the hit to check her work out."

Marcus shakes her hand and smiles. "Are you shooting tonight?"

"Sure is," Devon answers for her. "Big shoot-out at the opera house tonight. Old Doc Holliday and little Annie Oakley. The future of photography versus the past."

"You can ignore him," Marcus says. "He's used to it. May I see what you're working with?"

Nina unstraps her shoulder bag, glancing at Marcus's state-of-the-art machine as she hauls out her dinged-up camera. "This was my father's. Equipment is expensive here, and very hard to get."

Marcus hefts it. "I had one of these once. It'll dig a hole in your shoulder, but it gets the job done."

The trombonist watches them a moment, then announces, "I'm going back to warm up. You coming, Pigfoot, or staying here and talking shop?"

"I think I'll . . ." She pauses, playing the phrase back in her head to make sure it means what she thinks it does. "I'm gonna talk shop. I'll catch up with you in a few minutes."

"That's cool." Devon turns on his heel. "Give the cats a chance to talk you over." He steps into the shadows and is gone.

Marcus hands her camera back. "You a jazz fan?"

"I've never heard anything but 'Take the A Train' and 'Hello, Dolly' and a Czech group that came to my school when I was ten. My parents played classical at home, and American tapes are hard to get. But I know the photos—Claxton, DeCarava."

"Huh. Well, you're gonna get a crash course tonight. Devon talks a lot of junk, but he's the best trombonist since J. J. Johnson. Not that that means anything to you."

"How long have you been shooting him?"

"I shot Devon's birthday party when he turned two. Known his old man since the fifties; used to shoot his band. Devon senior's a pianist—used to play with Albert Van Horn?" Nina gives an apologetic shrug, and wonders how many more names she'll have to confess to not knowing.

"Been traveling with Junior almost three years, on and off. Done Africa, Japan, whole lot of Europe. We're working on a book together—kind of a travelogue slash photo essay."

"Why does he call you Uncle Sparkplug?"

Marcus snorts. " 'Cause I'm the only one out of all these mugs who knows how to fix the bus when it breaks down. Which it invariably does in the middle of the night, in the pouring rain, two hundred miles west of nowhere. And how did you get to be Pigfoot Jenkins, may I ask?"

"I have no idea what it means. Should I be insulted?"

"Naw, flattered. That's some down-home stuff. Means he's impressed. Of course, you're also very beautiful."

Nina stiffens. He had to say it. In the midst of this totally unrelated conversation, he had to find a way. And she's supposed to smile like it's just an aesthetic observation, not a come-on.

She looks into the wings. "Thanks."

Marcus studies her. "I'm sorry." He tilts his head sideways, puppy dog–style, to catch her eye. "I didn't mean to make you feel uncomfortable."

"No, no, it's fine." Nina takes a deep breath, prepares to forget about it. "I guess I'm no good at taking compliments." The smile she gives him is so brief, it looks like a facial tic.

Marcus nods. There's a softness to his eyes, like maybe he understands. "Well, Pigfoot, if you start hanging around these jazz musicians, you'll have to get better at it. That's a fact and a warning. Listen, I'll tell you what." He lifts the camera strap from his neck. "Why don't you take this for tonight? Give you a chance to try out something new."

"Really?" Marcus has wiped the slate clean, and from the look on his face, he knows it. "Thanks. That would be great."

"No problem. I'm shooting from the balcony, so I gotta go get ready. You're welcome to come see my setup, but I've got a feeling you'd rather go backstage and get busy."

"I'd love to see your setup later."

"Sure. We're going to your pad after the gig anyway, right?"

"Right."

"Well, all right. See you later, then."

"Get some good ones, Doctor Holliday."

He laughs and bows. "You, too, Miz Oakley. And hey." Marcus takes a step closer. "If you go back there and Devon plays you kind of cool, don't take it personal. Sometimes he touches down to earth, but most of the time he lives up in Devonland." The photographer taps his temple.

Sure enough, Devon barely lifts his head to acknowledge her when Nina enters the dressing room. Even with Marcus's warning, she struggles not to see it as a snub, retaliation for her failure to heed his summons.

The other musicians take their cues from the bandleader and ignore her, too, but being invisible is to Nina's advantage. She stashes her own camera in a corner and burns through thirty-six exposures on Marcus's machine as the men chat, graze a silver platter of sandwiches, and look over mimeographs of a song arrangement the leader wrote on last night's flight from Budapest.

"Not because I didn't think Pipe Man's charts were working," Devon is careful to explain, laying a hand on the rotund saxophonist's shoulder as the pages are passed around. "Just because I wanted to hear some different things."

Nina is trigger-happy, heedless of her weekly film rations and determined to emerge from this evening with at least one perfect image. She reloads, then shoots their preperformance prayer circle—a solemn departure from the lascivious loudmouthery of just before, and a ritual so seemingly natural and heartfelt that it makes Nina pang, if only momentarily, for some spiritual life of her own. The men stand silent for perhaps a minute, holding hands, before Devon intones, "Let's go out and heal some people with our music, brothers. Praise be to God. Amen." And they disperse, heading for the door.

Nina lights out first, wanting to capture the procession moving toward her. They pass onto the stage, and she slips down into the empty orchestra pit. From there, she can move in and out of the wings, even travel a circuitous back route up to the balcony.

The music tells her where to go, dances Nina in a way she's never been danced before. Devon's agility on that big, unwieldy, military-looking instrument astounds her—as does the realization that nothing in all that technique is the least bit gratuitous. Even the slightest flick of his wrist serves the sound. The fact that all of them are *making it up*—within some kind of structure, obviously, she can tell that much, she isn't completely ignorant—strikes her as wildly heroic.

Shooting this music makes explicit the relationship between camera and subject, formalizes what Nina's been doing all along. Everything and everyone she's ever shot is negotiating time and space, charting a course along dual governing axes. These men dramatize it—stand up there and try to say what they have to in the time allotted by life and by one another, in the space their instruments are capable of occupying and the space they carve collectively away from silence. She can see from their faces that it is a joy and a struggle, no metaphor for life, but life itself. And while they try to get it, her job is to get them getting it. It's just like everything else, only more so. Nina feels her thoughts begin to jumble and congeal, and she puts them aside and joins the other seven hundred members of the audience in clapping as the members of the Devon Marbury Octet take their final bows and file toward the dressing room. Her entire film reserve, hoarded over months, is almost gone—vanished without her noticing, like the last hour and a half.

Devon is the last to leave the stage. He takes a solo bow, and when he walks into the wings, Nina is waiting.

"So, Pigfoot? What's up? Was I bullshitting?" He does that little weight-shifting thing of his again, then brings the horn to his lips and puffs his cheeks against the mouthpiece without making a sound: another twitch, or perhaps an exercise. Nina watched him do it half a dozen times before the show.

"No. You weren't bullshitting."

He blots his lips against the back of his hand, shifts again. On another man, such body language might suggest the need to find a rest room. On Devon, it seems to bespeak an equally urgent desire to find some form of mental engagement.

"Yeah? I felt like I was bullshitting big-time on 'Green Chimneys.' The ballad, too."

She wants to tell him how his music really makes her feel and think, but that would be giving him too much. "If you were, you fooled me."

"Come on now, Pigfoot," he chides her, beginning to walk. "You're supposed to know when somebody is bullshitting."

"Wait till I develop the film," Nina says, keeping step. "Then I'll be able to tell."

He glances over with a smirk. "Yeah, that should reveal plenty about who's bullshitting."

Devon grabs a cup of coffee and a sandwich backstage, then spends the next hour receiving every visitor lined up in the opera house aisle. He shakes every hand, autographs newspapers and programs, squats eye-to-eye with every child musician who's been brought to meet him. "He is studying piano," or guitar, or trumpet, their fathers declare in fractured English, and Devon nods and smiles at the kids, asks questions about what they've learned. Nina is amazed to see him allow several older children identified as brass musicians to actually hold and blow into his horn. He gives them little tips, corrects or compliments the way they hold their lips, pats his foot delightedly and hollers for any band members within earshot to gather round as a twelve-year-old trombonist struggles gamely through a few choruses of "I Got Rhythm."

Marcus appears halfway through the meet-and-greet routine and stands by Nina's side. "Ambassador Marbury," he says. Devon, about to pose for a photo with three sleepy-looking children, glances over, grins.

To each youngster with whom he confers, the trombonist gives a shrink-wrapped cassette tape from a small blue duffel bag embroidered with the words *Antibes Jazz Festival 1985*. Nina assumes it is his latest album, but when she looks closer, she sees that Devon is disseminating copies of an album called *A Love Supreme*, by a troubled-looking man named John Coltrane.

"You might not like it right away," he warns the children, their faces reddening with shy elation as they turn the unexpected gifts in their hands, "but keep listening to it, okay? Get your whole family to check it out." Nina translates the sentiment when she sees that it is going unfathomed, which is most of the time, and the parents nod to her and then to Devon as they take hold of their children and back gratefully away.

"Can I have one of those tapes?" Nina asks when the last fan is gone. She, Devon, and Marcus are waiting outside for the opera house van, which will shuttle them to Nina's.

He rubs his hands together in the slight chill. "You never heard *A Love Supreme?*"

"I keep trying to tell you, I don't know anything about jazz. I live *here*. I have a can of Coke in my bedroom that I saved when I was twelve."

Devon shakes his head. "We gotta get you outta here, Pigfoot. Back to your Creole roots."

"Tell me about it."

"You sure it's gonna be cool with your old lady, you bringing home a couple of Negroidal strangers at one in the morning?"

"I really don't care."

The men exchange a look, a chuckle. "Watch out, now," says Marcus, shaking his head. "Pigfoot, Junior. Pigfoot."

"Pigfoot, Uncle Sparkplug. Little Sister Pigfoot."

Nina is enjoying their back-and-forth too much to remain merely a listener. "Hey, pardon my Eastern European ignorance, but do people really still say 'Negro'? I mean, didn't it go out of fashion with George Wallace and Bull Connor?"

Devon arches his back and claps his hands; laughter and breath twirl toward the sky. Marcus turns to Nina. "Hold up now, Pigfoot. Just what could you possibly know about Bull Connor?"

Nina pretends to scan the cobblestone street for signs of the van, so they won't see her smile. "I read. There's nothing else to do. I've been through every *Life* magazine from 1953 to 1968."

"No shit. You've seen my work, then."

"Have I?"

"I shot Miles Davis for the cover of *Life* in—what?—'66 or '67. He's in profile, playing his horn, with Herbie Hancock in the background." Marcus models the pose, and Nina glimpses something childlike in his playacting, his desire to be known.

"I don't remember that. But some are missing from the library."

The van arrives. Nina directs the driver in Czech. Fifteen minutes later, they disembark, and she leads Devon and Marcus up the path to her front door, noting with some trepidation that the light in Rayna's study is still on.

"Damn," mutters the trombonist. "Pigfoot got a serious pad, Sparkplug. We might have to move the band up out of that sad-assed hotel and bunk down here."

Nina settles them in the living room with glasses of red wine, then tiptoes upstairs to fetch her portfolio, shutting every door between them and her mother on the way back. When she returns, Devon is browsing the floor-to-ceiling bookcase covering the room's longest wall, head cocked sideways to read the titles. Marcus is sunken into the plush, dusty couch, swirling the liquid in his glass and assimilating his surroundings with quick, fastidious eyes.

"So, uh, here it is."

The photographer sits up, tabling his wine, and Nina slides in next to him and drops her portfolio atop the newspapers littering the coffee table. Devon lingers at the bookcase, long enough for her to begin thinking he is being very rude, then seats himself on Nina's other side, knee touching hers.

She looks at each of them in turn, bends forward to open the cover, then straightens. Marcus and Devon lean into the vacant space. Nina clasps her hands, tries to distract herself by noticing the way Devon's close-shorn hair spirals out from a point at the crown of his head like a whorl-pattern fingerprint.

"Mmm." Marcus studies the image. It is a low-angled portrait of an old woman silhouetted against a troubled sky, her head framed between the storm clouds gathered on each side. Her eyes are closed and she looks totally asleep, except that Nina has caught her in the midst of drumming her weathered fingertips against the top of the wooden table at which she sits.

"Mmm," he says again.

Devon holds his chin in his hand. After a moment, he reaches out and flips the page.

"Damn," he mutters, stealing a glance at Nina. She pretends not to see it, and he turns back to the picture. In the foreground is the back of a stout schoolmistress, hair a sloppy bun atop her head. Facing the camera are thirty girls of about ten, looking up toward her or sideways at one another or down at the ground. Two stare directly at the camera. A panoply of sentiments plays on their uncreased faces. Each set of eyes is perfectly in focus.

"Do you crop?" asks Marcus without looking up.

"Never."

Devon turns the page. They work their way through the portfolio's forty images in near silence. The men's respect, once she is certain that is what it is, makes Nina want to cry.

Devon closes the portfolio with a care that seems almost ceremonious. His cheeks puff quickly, then deflate.

"How old are you?"

"Eighteen," she says, adding a year without even planning to lie.

Devon's eyes dart to Marcus's, then resettle on Nina. "And nobody ever taught you anything about photography?"

She shakes her head. Devon opens his eyes wide, expels a huge column of air, and looks again at Marcus. "Well, Sparkplug?"

Marcus frowns down at the portfolio. He seems to be choosing his words with care, as if he's afraid of embarrassing one of them. "Pigfoot is nice," he says finally, meeting her eyes for a fraction of a second and then turning to Devon. "She should be studying with a master."

"Like you, for instance?" The bandleader flourishes a hand, and the words run into it like a question mark.

"For instance."

"I wish I could. But there's—"

She snaps her head in the direction of the stairs. Rayna is walking down them in her nightgown, cardigan, and slippers, reading glasses bouncing off her chest with every step.

"Mom." Nina stands. Her guests are on their feet already.

Rayna gives the men a tight smile as she reaches the landing, then addresses her daughter in Czech. "Nina, it is two in the morning. Who are these people and what are they doing in my house?"

"Mom," Nina replies in English, "I'd like you to meet Devon Marbury and Marcus Flanagan. Devon is a jazz musician and Marcus is a photographer. I met them tonight at the opera house. Devon, Marcus, this is my mother, Dr. Rayna Hrlcek." She switches to Czech and adds, "They're very famous artists, Mother."

Rayna studies her daughter for a moment, then seems to come to some conclusion. "Good evening." She offers her hand to Marcus and then to Devon. "Please, sit down. Can I offer you something to eat?" Despite years of disuse, her English has lost none of its fluency.

Marcus and Devon remain standing. "No thank you, ma'am," says Devon. "We ate after the concert."

"Well, I see you already have drinks." Rayna drifts into the kitchen and pours herself a glass of the same red they're drinking, then settles herself in an easy chair. "How long will you be visiting our city?" Nina lowers herself back onto the couch, watching her mother with suspicion.

Devon has moved to the other chair. "Just another two days. We're finishing a tour for the State Department. Before this, we were in Budapest; next are Sofia, Dubrovnik, and Zagreb, then back home. I wish we could stay longer. Prague is very beautiful."

Rayna crosses her legs, stately even in her sleepwear. The conversation hits a momentary lull, and Marcus leans forward, elbows resting on his knees, hands clasped. "Your daughter is exceptionally talented, Dr. Hricek. As I'm sure you're well aware."

He has the air of a man getting at something, and they all wait for him to go on. "She just showed us her portfolio. It's quite remarkable. The fact that she's achieved so much without the benefit of formal training is all the more impressive."

Nina cannot think of anywhere to cast her gaze. She is afraid to look at Rayna's face and find out just what level of turmoil her mother's placidity masks, too shy to watch Marcus praise her, and reluctant to find out where Devon's eyes have wandered.

"We were just discussing what she might accomplish given proper instruction."

Rayna weighs the question with a sharp sideways nod, as if dislodging water from her ear, and takes a sip of wine. "If she has achieved so much without schooling, isn't it possible a teacher would ruin her?"

"I don't think so. Nina is coming to a point, it seems to me, where her skills need to catch up to her talent. She needs to learn the technical side of photography—that and go into the field, find a project about which she is passionate."

"I see. Well, why don't you take her back to America with you? There's no one who can teach her here."

"Mom!"

Rayna looks at Devon. "I've read about you, Mr. Marbury. You discover young musicians all over the world, no?" She turns to Nina. "He started an orchestra in New York just so he could give them all jobs," Rayna says matter-of-factly, then continues with her guests. "If you think Nina is that talented—and I am not surprised, although I have not had the honor of viewing her portfolio—then I want you to help her, Mr. Marbury. Mr. Flanagan. If you can."

Nina stands and forces herself to smile. "Why do you tease me, Mother?" she asks, hoping the question sounds passably cavalier despite the strain in her voice, the heat emanating from her eyes. "She's joking. She knows leaving the country is impossible. And I know Marcus is only talking, not planning my future."

Nina steps nimbly around the coffee table and into the middle of the room. "I'm sorry about this," she says with a laugh that's almost a sob. "For years, my mother has been warning me against America. I don't know why she's suddenly so eager to imagine I can disappear with you two."

"When your child dreams of leaving, you do not give up so easily on finding her a way," Rayna says almost to herself. "But perhaps Nina is right and I've misunderstood. After all, my daughter is not a musician. There is no work for her in your Global Youth Jazz Orchestra, Mr. Marbury."

"Not in the orchestra, no. But you're right, Dr. Hricek. When I see talent, I make room. And right now, I'm going to make room for an assistant photographer."

"Jesus Christ! Is anybody listening? I can't leave this fucking country, Devon." Who is this woman masquerading as her mother? Who are these strange men, so unperturbed by the notion of carrying her across the world to start another life?

Rayna looks into her lap. "It is perhaps not so impossible as you think."

"What does that mean?" Nina demands.

Rayna sighs, blinks long.

"Mother . . ." Nina says, her voice a gathering storm.

"I have a travel visa for you. For the airport. It's a forgery, of course, but if you go with them, I think it will work. No one will doubt American musicians from the State Department."

Nina walks across the room and sits before her mother. Questions blow through her mind like wisps of cloud, dissipating before she can mold them into words. With her eyes, she implores Rayna to explain, and as they stare at each other, the hardness into which Rayna's features have set looks suddenly heroic. The message in the lines etched on her face blurs and revises itself as Nina watches, perplexed by this creature about whom she now feels she knows so little. And about whom, she realizes with a stab of raw alarm, she may be losing the chance to learn.

Rayna blots her eyes with the hem of her sweater, gives a forlorn chuckle.

"Is this always how it is?" she asks Devon.

"Sometimes."

"Mom?"

Rayna raises her eyebrows. "Yes?"

"How long have you had it?"

She reaches to take the handkerchief Marcus is holding out to her, looks up at the ceiling, and pats the corners of her eyes.

"About two years." Rayna wraps the cloth around her hand as if it were a tourniquet.

Nina makes her voice level, inflectionless. "When were you going to tell me?"

"When the time was right. When something happened."

Nina looks over at Devon and Marcus, sitting as invisibly as they can so as not to intrude, and the blankness of her future swells before her like an unexpected mountain coming into view on the horizon. How can she do this—put her faith in strangers when she's been taught to trust no one? When even family has betrayed her? How can she even consider it?

"Where will I live?" she blurts.

"We'll work something out," says Devon, and for the first time since Nina opened her portfolio, that smirk is back in place. Relax, Pigfoot, it reads, I got you covered. Nina finds her sense of adventure, of absurdity, of faith, suddenly and thoroughly bolstered—perhaps because she can't help but believe in Devon, and be thrilled that he believes in her, or perhaps because his smirk is intended to both fortify and challenge. Not to buck up and smile back means she's not taking up the gauntlet.

"Make me a promise," her mother says, and Nina's eyes cut to her. Tension has reclaimed its rightful place in the set of Rayna's jaw; she looks once again like the woman Nina has learned to avoid. Rayna's gaze flickers over Devon and Marcus, and Nina realizes her mother's dilemma. Whatever she wants to say is too private for their ears, but she cannot ask them to step into the kitchen.

"What is it?" Nina asks in Czech.

Rayna relaxes slightly upon hearing her own tongue. "Promise me," she answers in the same language, with the air of someone who knows she asks too much, who understands that distance can corrode the hold of any oath, "that you will not look for your father."

Perhaps this is why the visa has gone unmentioned, hidden in some secret crevice of the sagging house. Rayna has not known how she could hope to extract such a pledge from her daughter, tried to imagine what leverage she could bring to bear, come up with nothing. And yet here she is, setting her daughter free anyway. Nina can see no option but to love her for it.

Enough of Nina is already drifting toward the future that she pauses before answering to wonder what Devon and Marcus might think is being discussed. Do they flatter themselves that Rayna is begging her daughter to vow not to sleep with either of these charming, eminent gentlemen? Or worse, do they assume that she is counseling Nina to maintain some kind of racist wariness of their motives? Or perhaps her new patrons are too understanding to be curious at all?

If it is what her mother asks, it is what Nina must grant.

"I promise," she says, wondering.

CHAPTER THREE

RISK ONE bends at the waist, hefts a stolen supermarket crate onto the jutting shelf of his hip, and prepares to climb the basement stairs of 19 Algonquin Road. An unwieldy system of conveyor belts once ferried this crate from the checkout counter of the Fairfield, Connecticut, Stop & Shop to the minivan-jammed parking lot, where patrons claim their groceries by matching the numbers stenciled on the sides of the sturdy plastic-bodied units, reinforced with metal corners and wood crossbars, to those printed on their receipts. Six months ago, local b-boys noted that the crates were perfectly sized to hold LPs. They have been disappearing ever since.

It was RISK who set off the crime spree, ending an hour-long stakeout by springing from the shotgun seat of DJ Zone's mom's Buick to yank crate 808, specifically, out of orbit as it shuttled toward the bowels of the store. The numerals reference the vaunted Roland TR-808 drum machine, a small push-button appliance that produces a tremorous and celebrated simulated kick drum. It is the sound anchoring the classic recordings of the mid-eighties, the period during which RISK first discovered hip-hop through late-night radio, *Style Wars* on cable access, and black kids with cousins dwelling fifty miles south, in New York City.

It is the fall of '89 now, in more ways than one. Professor Griff has given his infamous anti-Semitic interview, setting off a shitstorm of protests and boycotts. Chuck D has announced Public Enemy's breakup, retracted that statement, retreated from that retraction. A year ago, the Hip-Hop Nation was surging unstoppably forward, but now the future of the world's most important group is in doubt, and nostalgia blues the air.

Even the new Boogie Down Productions album, which dropped two months late and forced RISK to spend all of June and July running hopefully to, and walking dejectedly from, the record store: he loves it, already has it memorized, but he can't front. It's no *By All Means Necessary*. Everybody's come up short, by inches or by yards: *It's a Big Daddy Thing* isn't as good as *Long Live the Kane*, *Walking with a Panther* sucks compared to *Bigger and Deffer*, *Unfinished Business* lacks the butter funk of *Strictly Business*. '88 has calcified into a fist-size fossil that sits in RISK ONE's belly. You could sharpen a knife on it, if you had one. It's almost funny, the way his b-boy generation—seventeen like RISK, eighteen like Zone, nineteen and twenty like their mentors—cops a collective creak-kneed squat to genuflect before a past so recently departed that the Nikes they were wearing when they met it still aren't scuffed. Not beyond some cursory toothbrush-and-bleach repair work, anyway.

RISK's shoulders ache as he half-times the shag-carpeted staircase like a toddler, foot meeting foot, lugging what must be fifty pounds of vinyl. He surfaces in the hallway, where the air is always slightly hotter and thicker than in the cement basement, as if the house is breathing right in your face.

Before he can even set his burden down, his mother calls his name—like a hunter sighting the first, whatever, *duck* over the bluff and squeezing off, thinks RISK, suddenly tired behind the eyes. From the sound of it, she's upstairs, in her bedroom, where she'll remain through the impending interrogation. The members of RISK's family address each other face-to-face only if circumstance happens to place them in proximity. Otherwise, they shout through the thin floors, walls, ceilings of a house that has seemed unbearably small since RISK was ten.

"What?" he rumbles back in a voice he hopes is either too low-toned to be heard across the distance or hostile enough to put her off. Crate 808 thuds to the linoleum floor, rattling the twin Gemini decks stacked there—199 bucks for the pair in J&R Music World's mail-order catalog, the lowest you can go if you want pitch control and a flashy S-shaped tone arm. They're mockeries of the real thing, quarter-priced knockoffs of the Technics SL-1200. Try to cut without laying a nickel atop the cartridge and the record's guaranteed to skip like a schoolgirl. But on the flip side, as Zone likes to point out, if you can get reasonably busy on a pair of Gems, you'll murder Tech 12s. Should you ever get the chance.

This could be the first RISK-seeking missile his mother has launched, or the fifth. The basement is semisoundproof, a bunker, which is why RISK annexed it. Between the cement walls and the humming furnace, the Colorado River burble of the washing machine and the white noise of the dryer, you can hear nothing from above save footsteps. RISK sleeps down there now, on a foldout couch across from his turntables. On occasion, he even chances getting high: perches on the couch before the top-latching window buttressing the ceiling and blows his smoke through a sheet of fabric softener affixed to a cardboard paper towel tube, thinking all the while of the teddy bear who capers in the fabric softener company's TV commercials. The sellout cousin of the Grateful Dead's menagerie, no doubt.

"Come here," Linda demands—perhaps having heard his answer, perhaps not. This game. What is she, Jabba the Hutt, incapable of locomotion?

"What?" RISK parries. "I'm running late." Accurate as a kind of general life summary, if not in terms of his current timetable.

"Come here."

He sighs, gallops up the staircase, presents himself at the jamb of her door. Linda sits propped against the headboard of her bed, legs crossed before her, one slip-on sandal dangling from her foot. A folded rectangle of newspaper obscures her face: last Sunday's *New York Times* wedding section. The sunlight streaming through the windows is supplemented by forty or fifty thousand watts beaming from a bedside lamp. You could perform surgery in here. Linda doesn't believe in mood lighting, or any activity it might imply, and she delights in liberating others from the bonds of dimness. How many times in the history of their history has she entered a room for the sole purpose of upgrading the visibility—declaring "Have some light" in the same chipper tone she might use to tell a starving child "Have some pizza," flicking every switch and then departing, leaving RISK awash in so much luminescence that he half-expects a crackly bullhorn voice to tell him he's surrounded, order him to throw his weapons down and come out with his hands up?

"What?" he says once more. His mother lowers her paper, lips already pursed. RISK feels his own face tighten, despite the fact that he's been trying to thwart this bit of genetic carry-over before it can settle—training himself to wiggle his jaw from side to side when he feels anger mounting, blow out his cheeks instead of sucking them in.

RISK would like to steel himself for the fight her expression heralds, slap together a few bullet points of self-defense, but he doesn't know for which crime he's on trial. Linda may reach into her nightstand drawer, flick a sandwich bag of weed at him, and demand, "What the fuck is this, Tris?" She may march him downstairs, out the kitchen door, and into the driveway to point out a month-old, heretofore-undiscovered two-inch scratch running along the rear passenger door of her Chrysler Caravan, etched there by a sapling branch RISK grazed while backing out of a clearing in the woods near his high school.

She may inform him, calm and furious, that she's just had a call from the police. Even then, RISK will have to stand mute, worrying the carpet with the toe of his shoe, and wait for further details, not knowing if the criminal substance in question is beer or spray paint. In the last six months, his twenty-one-year-old state ID card–holding doppelganger, one Justin P. Mayfield—so christened because RISK believes imaginary people should sound inconspicuous and vaguely Waspy—has purchased ten or fifteen cases of beer and resold them for a buck a can at a series of otherwise-unmemorable parties.

Meanwhile, the elusive aerosol bandit known as RISK ONE has inflicted several thousand dollars' worth of damage to property both public and private, from the juicy shoe polish mop tags afflicting the town's mailboxes to the RK throw-ups lining the Harbor Road Bridge to the burners splashed across the tennis practice walls of all three of the town's junior highs.

To say nothing of the heist of crate 808, which, for all RISK knows, may have been captured by the Stop & Shop security cameras and sent straight to the FBI's Quantico crime lab for computer analysis.

"You know you're still not allowed to use my car" is what Linda has subpoenaed him to say.

"Why?" RISK knows why: a series of blown curfews, plus a missing hubcap. He doesn't need the car anyway, as Zone should be arriving any minute. The response is automatic.

So is the way it makes Linda tense up. This game, she thinks: Why You to Death. Her son is amazing, really. He questions her more in a day than she questioned her parents in the eighteen years she lived with them. He cannot win, but Tris seems to believe that refusing to relent is not quite losing. He follows her from room to room, demanding, "Why? Why? Mom! Why?" until she loses control, spins toward him, screams like a banshee. And even then, Tris reacts like a knight fighting a dragon, sidestepping the blast of fire breath and parrying again.

No justice, no peace.

Her son the burgeoning activist, who makes Abe—when he, too, is not fretting about all the stupid shit Tris does, the beer and the vandalism and Lord knows what else—so proud. Who's been working his way through his father the newspaperman's shelf of sixties paperbacks, digesting Alinsky, Cleaver, Thompson, Didion. Who stays up late now, refusing to go to bed at Linda's command, writing political poems on the family IBM. Scary verses full of heroic dead musicians and fiery revolutions that incinerate white middle-class people like herself, judge them guilty of a shallow liberalism and post their heads on sticks to decorate the perimeter of some new sanctified land where Amiri Baraka seems to be emperor.

How Tris can possibly have the energy to pay attention in school all day, Linda cannot fathom. She lies in bed listening to the familiar clack of keys—it has followed her, seemingly, throughout her life—and worrying that her son's irresponsibility will catch up with him in the worst way, and he won't live to see his graduation. That he will hop into a car with some drunken asshole classmate she used to watch play weekend soccer when he was eight years old, and that will be it—blood and gore, tragic six o'clock news coverage, game over. That one of these protest rallies he's started to take Metro North into the city to attend will get busted up by cops, and her son will have his head bashed in, or end up in a jail cell. Try explaining *that* one to the college admissions officers.

She tries to support the activism—certainly, it's better than the other outlets Tris has found for his free-floating rebellion. Didn't she let him skip class to go see his favorite rapper give a talk at Yale, the one whose name sounds like a *Star Wars* robot? That was only a month ago, but Tris has already forgotten the favor.

Linda's problem, everybody tells her, is that she takes things personally. Tris's failure to do his dishes, or move his shoes, after the ten-thousandth reminder? It means he doesn't care about her, that her feelings don't matter. Abe shakes his head, doling out some of his infinite patience, and tells his wife it's just carelessness; he was the same way as a kid. Linda knows better. It's a statement. Tris is informing her that she is petty, concerned with trivial bullshit, and that he refuses to lower himself to her level of care.

Linda will fight him on this to her last breath. There is no way she's letting her son turn out like her father, even if they do share the same name, in defiance—or, rather, total ignorance—of Jewish custom. That was mostly Abe's idea anyway; he spent the last trimester of her pregnancy entranced by *Blockbusters*, the last novel Tristan had published before what the rest of the family refers to privately as the Slow Down. Twelve years separated that book from its ill-fated 1973 successor, *The Organist*, and now the count is sixteen and running. Linda acquiesced to Abe's suggestion as a kind of private peace treaty with her father, who, of course, had no idea she was even upset with him.

She will not admit it, even to Abe, but Linda cannot help feeling that Tris's growing social conscience is a direct repudiation of her. *All forms of oppression are linked*, as he once said. Tris is marching against her, well equipped to fight the good fight by years of outrage, years of "It's not fair." Years of "Why?" He's come to realize that the world is no different from his own life, brimming with the same injustice he's long railed against.

Why. The word alone now makes Linda want to shut down, fall asleep. Tris crosses his ankles, folds his arms over his chest. He might as well pitch a tent; he's digging in. Or maybe her son feels as trapped as she does, like a lawyer—which is what he'll surely become, a great one, if he lives that long—objecting purely for the record.

"You know why," she tells him.

Beep beep.

"I gotta go." Tris disappears, leaving Linda to contemplate how much of her life she spends yearning for various noises, car horns and telephones and doorbells, to intercede and send the two of them stalking back to their corners like boxers at the end of a round. It is this moment, though, the one directly after the bell sounds, that Linda finds least bearable of all. In it, their conflict—which is at least honest—morphs into silent conspiracy as they prepare to face the world. How many times have the two of them wiped rage and tears from their cheeks, becoming hard new people by the time they reach the phone, the door, the car?

She glances out the window to see who's picking Tris up, and finds Malik Courtney's station wagon idling in her driveway, trunk jacked open and latched with fraying twine to accommodate the two huge speakers jutting halfway out, looking as though one pothole might send them toppling into the street. A nice kid, but she doesn't trust Malik; he's a year older and he smells of cigarettes. She watches the two of them load the backseat full of records, record players, a mysterious small silver box that glints in the sun, then glances at her watch and smiles. It's Saturday, twelve noon. They must be on their way to synagogue.

RISK flicks the power strip, runs ground wires from the decks to the mixer, and clips on the battery-powered fan they hope will keep the ancient amp from overheating and cutting out, the way it did last week. He's doing all of it as fast as possible, because Risk Zone Productions has arrived at Temple Beth Israel a scant ten minutes before they are scheduled to play, as is their trademark. Guests are already streaming into the synagogue's huge function room, finding their seats and casting eager glances at the laden buffet tables.

Thanks to the half blunt Zone sparked as soon as he pulled out of the driveway of 19 Algonquin Road, Risk Zone Productions is operating from beneath heavy eyelids and feeling ambivalent about the prospect of spinning for yet another gaggle of timid suit- and party dress–clad thirteen-year-olds and smug professional/parental Jewish types. As is also their trademark.

The father of Jamie Siegel, the Bar Mitzvah Boy, turns sideways in his head-table chair, away from the lavish flower bouquet and the murmurs of proud aunts, and beams a vaguely threatening brand of concern at them across the polished parquet dance floor.

"Okay." RISK bends to flip through Zone's crate, number 420, although he knows exactly what's in it. "You brought the 'Chicken Dance,' right?"

"Yeah, sure. If you've got the 'Electric Slide.' "

"Of course. *Sinatra's Greatest Hits? The Big Chill* sound track?"

"Check. 'Brown Eyed Girl'? 'Stairway to Heaven'?"

"No doubt. 'Oh, What a Night'? 'Twist and Shout'?"

"Naturally, homeboy." They're both laughing now, at their own sheer, stubborn incompetence. The Risk Zone Productions catalog consists of little beyond rap records and breakbeats, plus a few old soul joints of the Al/Marvin/Aretha variety borrowed weekly from Vanessa Courtney's living room stereo cabinet. They've got none of the new Top Forty pop radio horseshit for which the Bar Mitzvah Boy and his large cadre of colleagues will surely clamor, nor a single traditional favorite. Not even the dominant rap songs of the epoch are represented: no "Wild Thing," no "It Takes Two," no "Supersonic." But RISK and Zone charge $150 per bar mitzvah, and the competition asks six times that.

The competition is Steve Goldman Productions, owned and fronted by the eponymous tuxedo-clad ex–lounge singer and staffed behind the boards by underpaid high school kids from two towns over. RISK attended about fifty Goldman parties in his thirteenth year, when everyone but him was memorizing Torah passages and Becoming A Man to the tune of major cash infusions. They are slick, corny affairs featuring smoke machines, oversized plastic sunglasses, an endless supply of neon glow sticks, and an arsenal of audience-participation games that provide the little hormone balls with a sanctioned form of boy-girl contact. Steve Goldman, moreover, plays cassettes. For this alone, the words *Sucker DJ* should be branded across his forehead with a white-hot iron.

"Sweet! I was hoping it'd be you guys." RISK looks up from the wires he's dejumbling to see Zone extend a hand. Apple-cheeked Adam Silverberg, coolest kid on the bar mitzvah circuit, slaps him an enthusiastic five.

"Whaddup, Ad Rock?" inquires RISK.

Adam shrugs. The red knit tie he wears to every bar mitzvah is stained with something pinkish, probably last week's salmon cream cheese. "You guys need anything?"

"My man!" says Zone. "Can you hook us up some plates?" With Adam in attendance, they can eat without looking like derelicts for abandoning their station. He's thrilled to be the kid who gets to hang out with the DJs, more than happy to run errands to the buffet tables and even the bar. Under the quiet tutelage of the senior half of Risk Zone Productions, Ad Rock has become a proficient, gleeful thief of alcohol. His reward, aside from the satisfaction of a job well done, is exemption from the dumb-ass games the kids, brainwashed by the Goldman Agenda, will eventually cajole RISK and Zone into orchestrating. Adam is small for his age, and pudgy; he's waiting on the growth spurt that will turn him into a ladies' man, and until then he's content to bide his time taking DJ lessons and getting schooled on hip-hop. He jogs across the empty dance floor, untied shoelaces flapping, and joins the just-forming lunch line.

Zone back-cues Risk Zone Productions' theme music, nudges the volume on the mixer up to two, the proper volume at which to blend it with the buzz of conversation, and lets the record play. A six-note minor-key piano riff falls over heavy drums, and RISK smiles the way he does every time they set a party off like this, with the most wildly—yet subtly—inappropriate bar mitzvah platter in the crates: "Why Is That?" off the new BDP album, KRS-ONE's chapter-and-verse breakdown of biblical lineage in service of the argument that Moses was black.

Nobody but Zone, RISK, and Adam is listening to the lyrics, but something in RISK needs to perform this ritual, mount this unreceived challenge. His place is here behind the turntables, with Zone, and no matter how many of his parents' friends might come over to say hello, RISK will never step out from behind his barrier to greet them. He is hired help, and Moses was black. He scans the room for signs of recognition, disbelief, outrage, waits for someone to stalk over and argue the point. No takers. Ha. Another victory. Complacent dickheads.

If only Hyman Pearlmutter could see him now. Agnostic to the core but resolute in the belief that their son should possess at least a half-assed understanding of his cultural roots, RISK's parents enrolled him at age ten in the Sunday School for Jewish Education. It met at a community college twenty minutes from their house; at first, RISK hated going because it meant missing his weekly fix of televised professional wrestling, but soon he found better reasons for enmity. The other students were lame, off-brand versions of the kids he knew, and RISK was the class dummy. If the holiday wasn't Hanukkah or Passover, he couldn't name it. He was sure his parents couldn't, either, and it pissed him off that he had to waste his weekends learning a bunch of shit they didn't care about themselves.

Hebrew class was the worst of all, and when the chance to opt out and take Jewish Cultural History instead presented itself in his second year of study, RISK jumped on it. The teacher was Mr. Pearlmutter: two hundred years old, a staunch Zionist, the kind of guy who spent his Sundays educating the youth because he liked the idea of a captive audience.

Jewish Cultural History should've been called Pearlmutter's Pride and Prejudice. Between monologues on Hebraic Heroes—Shlomo Ben-Yosef, Meir Kahane, Sandy Koufax—the teacher held forth on the differences between the Jews, a great people because they never turned their backs on their communities, and the blacks, not a great people because they did. All around RISK, kids sat nodding their heads, while RISK's was practically exploding, his brain incapable of assimilating what he was hearing with the parental maxim that Your Teacher Is Always Right.

The third week of class, RISK stood up and told Pearlmutter he was wrong, that plenty of black people didn't abandon their communities when success came calling. Pearlmutter, 118 pounds of spiritual authority draped in a seersucker suit, challenged his student to list them. The first names that came to RISK's mind were those of his favorite rappers. *Run-DMC*, he said. *UTFO*. *Kool Moe Dee*. The jumble of nonsense syllables did little to change Pearlmutter's ethnographic worldview. He told RISK to sit down and shut up, ignored his tears, taught on.

RISK left school still crying, clambered into his dad's car, and told him what had happened. Abe's face glassed over with fury. He drove straight home and called the teacher. RISK stood next to his father, watching how tightly he gripped the phone, listening to the choke in his voice as he demanded, *Did you tell my son . . .* RISK felt a surge of vindication. Surely, confronted with his crimes, Pearlmutter would crumble into a pile of dust, like an evil sorcerer on TV.

Instead, Abe slammed down the phone, and RISK heard his father use the *F* word for the first time ever: *goddamn fucking bigot!* Thus ended young RISK's formal religious education, and with it the promise of a culminating ceremony and an accompanying financial windfall. The only money RISK would make off bar mitzvahs would be in $150 increments.

Adam returns, a plate in each hand and a cloth-napkin-and-silverware roll poking from each trouser pocket. RISK sets his rations to one side. Zone digs in. He adores bar mitzvah food.

"It's your turn to do Coke and Pepsi," RISK informs him preemptively.

Zone shovels down a hacked-off chunk of noodle kugel, shakes his head. "I did it last time."

"Bullshit. You did not." Unspoken between them is the fact that Zone has much more cool to spare, but the acknowledgment comes a moment later, in the form of Zone's agreement to sacrifice some of it by emceeing the contest.

He is something of a folk hero on the bar mitzvah scene. The more aggressively liberal father types make a point of coming over, one by one, to shoot the shit with him, crack a few jokes, and Zone delights them by being just a regular guy. The bejeweled, pantsuited women inquire as to whether he has had enough to eat, and Zone charms them with his enthusiasm for the spread, tells them he's eaten so much already that he's half Jewish. If he's feeling especially gregarious, he might even toss off a couple of mazel tovs, blow everybody's mind.

The kids vie for his attention, dashing over to slap him five and then retreating triumphantly into their edge-of-the-dance-floor gaggles. Zone ushers them into the circle of his hipness, dubbing them "homeboy," "homegirl," "my man." Everybody sneaks quick fascinated looks at his pencil-thin shoulder-length dreadlocks. RISK watches it all, happy to be left alone but jealous of the attention and his partner's comfort.

"Coke!" Zone shouts into the Radio Shack microphone forty-five minutes later, as RISK hits the turntable's stop button. Thirty full-bellied adolescents sprint the length of the parquet to sit on the knees of their crouched, waiting partners.

"Pepsi!" Everybody races the other way.

"7Up!" Sixty kids reverse direction halfway across the floor, lurch back the way they came. Eventually, the field is narrowed to one winning couple—two dudes who take the contest way too seriously, so seriously that they don't realize the whole point is to partner up with a girl. Particularly since Risk Zone Productions, as is their trademark, have forgotten to hit the toy store, have nothing whatsoever to offer in the way of prizes, and eventually award the winners a small battery-run fan suitable for pointing at an overheating amplifier. The taller of the victors informs RISK that at a Steve Goldman party, you get to choose from an array of cassette singles. RISK considers telling the kid, in retaliation, that it's time to borrow his old man's razor and get rid of the dark fuzz bracketing his upper lip and giving him the air of a sleazy French rat. But he does not.

Twice, elderly women ask Zone to lower the volume, claiming their conversations are being impeded. Thrice, RISK is forced to apologize for not having "Hava Nagila," the song to which the hora is danced. Finally, getting into the make-do spirit that sustained their forefathers through forty years in the desert with nothing to eat but manna and more fucking manna, the revelers organize themselves into a circle anyway and find a chair on which to hoist the Bar Mitzvah Boy, those footing the bill, and the parents of those footing the bill. Zone throws on the instrumental B side to Eric B. & Rakim's "Microphone Fiend"—a proven substitute, because it has hand claps—and the partygoers pause, palms poised in ready-to-clap rigidity, then cock their heads and don complainy faces.

RISK nudges Adam. "Set it off."

Adam nods through a couple of bars, getting his bearings, then bangs his palms together and bellows, "Hava nagila, hava" to the beat. The crowd joins him on the second go-round, drowning out the record. The circle spins, the chair is raised. Zone pats Adam on the shoulder, turns his back to the dance floor, and pours himself a glass of straight Bacardi from the half bottle the kid liberated from the bar. He downs a slug and passes the cup to RISK, who opens his throat and drains it.

"Have you been drinking?"

RISK flinches and wakes up, but catches himself in time to avoid opening his eyes. He tries to play the spasm off as part of a dream, pretend he's still asleep. A feeble strategy, but worth a shot.

He can practically see his mother through his eyelids, standing at the foot of the couch with her arms crossed. RISK sighs, turns onto his side, and buries his face in the cleavage of the love seat, executing the move with as much oblivious, somnolent languor as he can muster.

It's four in the afternoon, and his crates and turntables are stacked ten feet away, by the kitchen door. RISK, in his infinite stupidity, couldn't summon the energy to carry them downstairs and pass out properly, on his own bed. Instead, he's lying here in public, right smack in the middle of Linda's domain, and the moment he opens his mouth to speak a mighty gust of rum fumes is going to escape and swirl around the room like a tornado, flinging newspapers and *People* magazines every which way and pinning Linda, screaming, to the wall.

"Tris? Hello?"

He feigns waking up: flutter-blinks his eyes, stretches his arms above his head, the whole tableau. He drapes the crook of an elbow over his mouth before speaking.

"Hey."

"Have you been drinking?"

He hates this, the way his mother and father have forced him to become a liar by disapproving of everything he does. The bottle of Bacardi is buried in RISK's bag of stereo cords now, two mouthfuls left. Perhaps Linda has already seen it. If so, he can hide behind the—what, Fourth Amendment? Whatever. The right to privacy. Flip the argument on its head and go on the offensive, tell his mother she has no right to snoop through his things. Ask her if she's listening in on his phone calls now, too. Throw some final line about the Gestapo over his shoulder as he slams the basement door, then wait to see if he's rendered Linda's evidence inadmissible, earned a mistrial. His father might grant one. Historically, Abe's household voting record has been characterized by strong support for the Bill of Rights. Although not as strong as his support for his wife.

RISK twists his face into a look you'd give a crazy person. "No," he tells Linda, and then adds, "I was at a bar mitzvah," hoping the invocation of old Yahweh might set a mood of righteous indignation.

He watches his mother's jaw edge forward, her lips bunch and jut into what looks almost like a kissing posture. You could bounce quarters off her cheeks, they're so taut. RISK possesses the sheer dumb tenacity to hold on to his lie forever, and he knows Linda knows it. His guess is that she's doubly pissed off because she holds an unplayable trump card—eyewitness testimony she can't mention without compromising its source. The town's full of her spies.

So what's her move? An unsupported, talon-pointing accusation, just to relieve the tension? Dismissal, to be followed by consultation with cocounsel when cocounsel returns from laying out the newspaper at two in the morning, until which time she will maintain her current rigor mortis–like carriage, somehow prying that face open long enough to feed herself dinner?

Instead, Linda turns and walks three steps. She lifts the telephone from the wall-mounted cradle, jabs at its soft belly.

"Don't bother Dad at work, Ma," RISK says by way of free advice, like a chess player tapping his queen. Hasn't Linda figured out yet how pathetic this gambit is, how powerless it makes her look and feel?

She turns her back on him. "Hi, Dad. Is Mom there?"

RISK spins on the fulcrum of his ass until he's vertical.

Linda speaks into the phone. "Oh. Well, I'm bringing your grandson over. . . . Because he's driving me crazy, and I don't want him in my house, that's why."

Tristan, on the other end, mounts what must be an objection. He's working, probably.

"Well then, Dad, you know what? You can take a few hours off. Do something for somebody else for a change." She slams the receiver back in place, or tries to; it doesn't catch, and falls onto the countertop, prone.

Linda looks at her son. "Get in the car."

For once, RISK does as he's told. He sits there for five minutes, watching Mr. Cassell wax his yellow Lotus in the passenger-side mirror. The Freedmans have gone through three across-the-street neighbors during their tenure at 19 Algonquin Road, all of them youngish Anglo families captained by men who devote their Saturday afternoons to maintaining the never-driven luxury cars cloistered in their garages. RISK has spent countless mornings chewing cereal and studying these energetic automobile enthusiasts, unable to discern the slightest similarity between them and his father, who's driven the same blue Toyota as long as RISK can remember and faces spring thundershowers in a raincoat he bought in college. *Stole from a hobo in college*, as Linda likes to say.

She climbs aboard, yanks on her seat belt, slaps the shift into reverse. The twenty-minute trip to New Haven is wordless. RISK checks off familiar landmarks as the minivan closes in on the house; when he was young, every ride through this neighborhood had been a guided tour, whether the driver was his mother, dropping him off, or his grandmother Amalia, taking him home. Linda would regale her son by pointing out the crucial sites of her childhood: the empty lot that had once been a candy store, her still-standing elementary school with its small concrete playground, the immense yellow Victorian in which Marcy Pontis and her darling black Lab, Grendel, had resided.

Amalia's tours were grander in scope, cultural surveys of an area dense with writers, scientists, and historians, most associated somehow with Yale, where she's taught writing since 1969, the year the university began admitting female undergrads, and with the Brodskys. She graded their importance on a scale of epithets: the *well known*, the *prominent*, the *famous*, the *esteemed*, the *great*. It was during those drives that RISK began to grasp the level of accomplishment that was the cover charge at his grandparents' parties. He never would have guessed. Nary a guest ever breathed a grandiose word—not that RISK could understand, anyway. Nor did they dress their parts. These were first-generation American successes, men and women who'd traveled the well-tramped path from Brooklyn or the Lower East Side or the Bronx to City College; Hunter for the women, not Amalia's alma mater, Vassar. They'd never learned to spend money on clothes.

The minivan pulls up before the Brodskys' house, and Linda barely allows her son to shut the door before hitting the gas. If she intends to pick him up tomorrow, or let him find his own way home, or have the locks at 19 Algonquin Road changed and his belongings piled on the curb by sundown, she makes no mention of her plans. RISK does not inquire.

His grandparents' door is unlocked, as always. RISK crosses the foyer, sidestepping the blast of mothball air that rolls toward him like tumbleweed, and appraises himself in a brass-framed mirror suspended above a table cluttered with tins of lemon candy, unopened mail, two shrink-wrapped VHS copies of *Blockbusters*, and his grandmother's students' manuscripts in their manila folders. A stack of books abuts the wall, topped with a gift-wrapped, ribboned rectangle that can only be another one. It has been sitting there since Christmas. At least the attached envelope is open.

"Hello," RISK calls, not expecting an answer. He heads for the kitchen, pours himself a glass of cranberry juice, and grabs a container of mixed nuts from the snack cabinet. The household's only television is enshrined here, a dusty wood-grained model squatting on a countertop above the breakfast table. RISK slumps before it, jiggle-sifts the tin until two almonds breach the sea of peanuts, pops one in his mouth.

He flips twice through the mundane alphabet of channels before settling on MTV, in the hopes that he might witness the miraculous: a rap video aired outside the daily hour to which the music is confined, boxed in on either side by endless whiteboy crap rock. No such luck. He takes in a Madonna video and a string of commercials, then rises when he hears his grandfather's chair roll across the floor above. RISK positions himself at the foot of the front staircase and waits to greet him, but nothing happens. Tristan is probably standing before his typewriter, evaluating his last page, or crouched over the machine, banging out a final paragraph before calling it a day. Or before granting himself a bathroom break, then pressing on. There's no particular reason to believe he's coming down at all, really.

RISK wanders back into the kitchen, turns the TV off, consumes a cashew and a filbert, returns to the landing just as the old man appears around the bend.

"Hey, Grandpa."

Tristan reaches the bottom and lays a hand on RISK's shoulder. "So. What the hell have you done to your old lady?"

RISK shrugs. "I was drinking."

Tristan lifts an index finger. "Good idea." He points toward the living room bar, and RISK backs out of his way. Tristan makes a slow beeline for it, and pours them each a scotch. "Have we got some nuts or something?"

"Sure." RISK darts to the kitchen, dumps the contents of the tin into a wooden serving bowl shaped like a fish, and reunites with his grandfather on the living room couch.

Tristan reaches for the bowl and fills his palm. "Now, really. Why has your mother deposited you here?"

"Where's Grandma?"

Tristan gestures with a fist full of nuts. "Off teaching or something. I don't recall. What day is it?"

"Saturday, Gramps. I don't think there's any class." He reaches for a yellow legal pad lying on the coffee table, pulls a red Sharpie from his pocket, and absentmindedly begins to trace the outline of a piece.

"Quite right." Tristan peers at the leather-banded watch slung loosely around his wrist. "I imagine she'll return soon. We've got to have some dinner, for Christ's sake." He crosses his legs, jiggles his ice. "Where were you drinking?"

RISK adds some old-school 3-D effects to his outline. "At a bar mitzvah I was DJing."

"You mean to tell me you were boozing it up in temple?" From the expression on the old man's face, RISK can't tell if his grandfather finds the notion scandalous or funny.

"Yeah, but not *in* temple. They had a party for the kid afterward, with a bar. It's not like I was swigging from a brown bag during the service."

"I see. How much would you say the affair cost the parents of this young schmuck?"

"Plenty. Renting the space from the synagogue's a few thou in itself. Then you've got food, music, party favors. Each kid got a hollow ceramic sneaker with his name stenciled on it—I guess it was supposed to be like a pencil holder or something. They were filled with bags of green M&M's, the bar mitzvah kid's favorite candy. Oh, and there was a caricature artist, too, drawing pictures of the guests."

Tristan shook his head. "It's the end of the goddamn Jews. You know what I got for my bar mitzvah?"

"A tongue sandwich with mustard and a gold pen. Which you bet in a craps game against Sammy Fischer."

"Correct."

"What ever happened to him anyway?"

"Fischer? Who the hell cares?"

RISK finishes his drink and points toward the staircase with his chin. "How's it going up there?" he ventures.

Tristan's eyes narrow. "What is this, an interview? Terribly. I don't have the stamina for this shit anymore."

"You've been saying that for as long as I can remember. But every time I come over, you're in your study."

"And what have I published in that time? One shitty book, the year you were born."

"I liked *The Organist*."

"You're not old enough to understand how bad it is. I tried to be a man of the times, go with the flow for once instead of against it, so I wrote a sex novel. It wasn't me, sonny. I've never cheated in my life.

Probably the only writer alive who can say so. That novel was my infidelity—I cheated on myself. The critics were right that time; I've thrown better novels in the trash can. But I was desperate to come in out of the wilderness and publish something."

It is far more than his grandfather usually volunteers. "Tell me about your process," RISK says, emboldened. "I mean, do you start with a plot and—"

Tristan grimaces. "For God's sake. Talking about it will do me in for sure."

RISK stares at the carpet, prepared to endure the thirty seconds of awkward silence that will pass before his grandfather conjures a topic of his own. After ten, though, he decides to push. It's his job in the family, has been since RISK was a toddler. Nobody had ever dared disturb Tristan before he came along; that's the way his mother tells it anyway. At three, he wriggled free of her admonishments—or had she set him loose?—and barged into his grandfather's study. Climbed onto Tristan's lap, to the novelist's consternation and, after a moment's consideration, his delight.

"C'mon, Grandpa. Tell me something. Anything. I'm not gonna learn jackshit from the failed novelists teaching English at my school."

The old man snorts. "What makes you think you want to write?"

"I'm good at it."

"That's not a reason."

"It beats working?"

"If that's what you think, forget it."

RISK caps the Sharpie, taps it against his jawbone. "I want to make sense of this fucked-up world."

Tristan takes both glasses to the bar, pours refills. "I suppose that'll do. Until you come up with something better." He hands RISK a second scotch, larger than the first, and returns to his seat. "Imagine you're taking a dump. I'm willing to bet that every single time you wipe your ass, you do it the exact same way. Maybe you ball up the paper against your thigh, or fold it over your hand. It doesn't matter. The point is, you've probably never bothered to notice how you do it, this thing you've done thousands upon thousands of times."

"A writer notices."

"No. A writer finds somebody else to wipe his ass, so he can concentrate on writing." Tristan sips his scotch. "That's a joke. Yes, a writer notices." He runs a palm over his soft white hair. "I could really do with a haircut. It's either that or buy a violin."

He shifts to look at the pad in his grandson's lap. "What are you doing there?" RISK holds it up for him, not sure he likes where this might go.

"What does it say?"

"RISK. My alias."

Tristan squints. "I don't see it."

RISK traces each letter for him. "It's supposed to be hard to read. Another graff—" He stops himself, not wanting to utter the word. "Another writer would be able to read it."

"*Writer*, you say?"

"The guys who do this stuff, they call themselves writers. Because the medium is words."

"I see. The subways in the city used to be covered with this sort of thing, you know."

RISK can't help but smile. "Yeah, I know. Guys figured out that if they wrote their names on trains, a million people a day would see it. That's the allure—fame."

"Writing and fame. There's a match made in hell. You actually do this sort of thing, or do you confine yourself to paper?"

"No," says RISK, feeling his face flush. The burn of the liquor draws away the heat. "I mean, yeah, I actually do it. I'm not bad."

"It can't be legal, of course."

"Well, getting away with it is half the fun. And there are rules. Private property's off-limits, sort of."

"Deface the public and respect the private, is that it? Reverse communism?"

"I never thought of it like that. Most guys, their philosophy is basically that the system fucks them over, so they're gonna strike back, claim something. Beautify the city, or destroy it. Those two words are almost interchangeable when it comes to writers."

"Creative destruction. More reverse communism." Tristan peers down his nose, considers the ice melting in his glass. "Another drink?"

"Come with me," RISK says. "There's a freight yard ten minutes from here. You can see what it's all about."

The old man eyes him for a moment. "I'd need a new name, wouldn't I? I couldn't just write Tristan Brodsky, or they'd come straight over and arrest me."

RISK nods. "Plus, it's too long. Three to five letters is ideal." He can't tell if his grandfather is just humoring him, fucking around. But RISK is already wondering where he can score some cans, and whether Tristan is ready for the next hard truth of the graff game: that only toys buy paint, and the accepted method of acquisition is racking.

"How about BRONX? That sounds suitably tough, doesn't it?"

"That's so perfect, I can't believe nobody's used it yet. Especially since the Bronx is where hip-hop was born." RISK winces, realizing his mistake. *What's hip-hop?* He doesn't want to derail the momentum by trying to explain. It never takes him less than twenty minutes to get through the speech, finish linking Afrika Bambaataa's breakbeats to Robert Moses's Cross-Bronx Expressway, graff and b-boying to school budget cuts. Friends of his parents and grandparents have forced RISK into the role of cultural translator often enough that he has the recital down. It's his duty to distinguish *rap* from *hip-hop*, describe the iceberg submerged beneath the visible tip of MC Hammer and the Fresh Prince, because RISK is safe to ask. Not to mention available. They'll never get the chance or the balls to query a black kid.

But Tristan lets it pass; he either knows what hip-hop is or doesn't care. "I imagine we'll need spray paint. There should be some in the toolshed."

RISK bounds outside. The toolshed is really a tool chest, rotting into the soil of the side yard. He opens the hatch, and there, huddled next to bags of potting soil and Miracle-Gro and rusty hand tools, are four cans of Red Devil spray paint. Zone would shit if he saw them: Red Devil has been out of production for years. Writers fiend for it, trade five Krylons for one can. It's some of the highest-quality paint ever made, and the colors are off the hook. RISK picks the cans up one by one, shakes them to gauge the contents. White: full. Emerald Green: half full. Flat Black: almost empty. RISK picks up the final can, shakes it, and pumps his fist in triumph. A full can of Bermuda Blue, the rarest, hottest Red Devil of all. A shame to waste it on throw-ups, but what the hell.

Fifteen minutes later, the cans are in a knapsack, thumping against the small of RISK's back as he and his grandfather stalk toward the freight yard through the weak light of the waning afternoon. On the foyer table lies a note for Amalia: *Out vandalizing trains. Back soon. Love, BRONX and RISK (T. Brodsky & T. Freedman). P.S. Don't tell Linda.*

Out on the street, away from cocktails and couches and the foothills of unpublished pages stacked around his desk, the old man doesn't seem so old. He's only sixty-eight, after all. A kid from the Bronx; RISK can see it now, as never before: his grandfather juking and weaving through the crowded city streets, looking for trouble or, at the very least, not always knowing how to avoid it. Tristan slaps 80 percent of all questions concerning his youth out of the air, but RISK's great-uncle Benjamin is quick to tout his older brother as the most feared stickball slugger on the block, and good enough with his hands that Ben, five and a half feet tall on his best day, never had to worry about bullies. Put all that together and you've got an athlete and a roughneck who whizzed through college by eighteen, plus knew his way around the jazz spots back when that meant something. Hell, young Tristan Brodsky was a fucking ghetto superstar.

"These trains travel from coast to coast, carrying cargo," RISK explains as the neighborhood turns industrial, "and they don't clean 'em unless you paint over the serial numbers. Now that the subway era's over, a lot of writers have been turning to freights. It's not the same, but at least they move."

BRONX is hungry for graffiti lore; it seems to have captured his literary imagination. RISK can tell by the intensity with which his grandfather listens. He's seen the old man in this mode before, watched BRONX swallow stories whole at parties and ask precise questions designed to draw out the kind of minute details that will keep the anecdote alive as he transplants it to the page.

RISK regales him proudly, flashing his expertise with tales of BLADE and COMET and their five thousand whole cars. Tells horror stories about head-busting Vandal Squad infamosos like Curly and Ferrari from Queens, Rotor and Wasserman from Brooklyn—cops with the same lust for fame as any writer. He profiles icons: the one-armed KASE 2 and the magnanimous superstar LEE. Discusses the innovations of pioneers like PISTOL and RIFF 170, style masters like DONDI and SEEN. Touches on the esoteric theories of aerosol philosopher RAMMELLZEE, whose Iconoclastic Panzerism holds that letters derive their power from the angles of their intersecting parts, so *K* annihilates C and *X* trumps *Z*.

The afternoon is fading into dusk, a prime time to be invisible but still have light by which to paint. They circle the fenced-off perimeter of the yard, gazing through the ten-foot chain-link fence at rows of rust-colored trains slumbering nose-to-ass. RISK has pieced here once or twice a month for the past year. Whenever somebody can get a car, this is the spot of choice.

BRONX's glance floats to the rolls of razor wire atop the barricade. "You don't expect me to climb that, do you?"

RISK finds what he's looking for: a four-foot flap some writer surgeoned open with bolt cutters years ago. He pulls it back, beckons his grandfather inside.

They half-jog toward the first row of trains, RISK glancing over at BRONX every two seconds to make sure he's all right with the pace until the old man grunts, "I'm fine." They high-step the junction between two boxcars, the left one already covered in ugly silver Krylon throw-ups, probably the work of some kid from West Clusterfuck, New Mexico, whose backyard opens onto train tracks. That's the problem with freights: too much access and not enough accountability. Toys use them as practice walls, and nobody can find the culprits to backhand some sense into them.

There are only a few feet of space between the rows of trains. RISK and BRONX are well hidden, but at the expense of being able to see well themselves. No matter; RISK has painted in pitch-black before. He shakes the can of white sideways, leans over to BRONX, and continues the tutorial in a whisper. "Imagine painting a forty-foot, fifteen-color mural under these conditions—only it's darker, the trains are closer together, you're underground, and cops might raid you anytime."

He steps up to the train, raises the can above his head, then freezes at the sound of boots crunching over gravel. RISK flattens against the train, looks to his left. Three figures are approaching. His instinct is to grab his grandfather and break out, but yard security doesn't roll that thick. RISK has been chased here only once in twenty-something missions, and it was by a single patrolman, whose darting flashlight beam gave him away before he got within a hundred feet. These must be other writers.

"Get down," RISK hisses. "Hide." Out of the corner of his eye, he sees BRONX comply, scuttle between two train cars and disappear from sight.

Writers are like Siamese fighting fish; whenever two squads meet in an enclosed space, things could get ugly. That's why crews formed to begin with: not out of camaraderie, but for protection, because dudes running alone got jumped and robbed, or extorted for spray-can tributes. Not that this is the Washington Heights Ghost Yard circa 1979. The vast majority of cats out here in Connecticut are pleased to make your acquaintance. It's just freights; there's room enough for everybody. You usually end up trading stories and phone numbers, not mouth shots—although the very provincialism of the scene makes some dudes feel the need to start shit, just to prove that they're true to the spirit of the thing. The most enduring stories in graffiti are about fights, after all, not art.

The trio stops short of the light slashing in between the cars. Two skinny kids on the flanks, RISK's age or younger, each holding a shopping bag bulging with paint. One sports a messed-up Afro and a long-sleeved black T-shirt, down almost to his knees. The other wears a hoodie, his free hand sheathed elbow-deep in the sweatshirt's front pocket. The guy in the middle is bigger, thicker, older. He carries nothing. Two apprentices, one master.

"Hey," says RISK, standing in full view now. "Nice day to paint, huh?"

The master walks up to him and folds his arms over his chest.

"What chu write?" he demands. The standard question: name, rank, and serial number rolled into one. It can be asked a lot of ways, most of them more pleasant than this.

"RISK ONE. How 'bout you?"

"I never heard of you. Look like a cop to me." He turns to his cohorts. "You ever heard of RISK ONE?" His tone makes the desired answer clear.

Instead of delivering it, the kid with the Afro scratches his scalp. "You was in *IGT* once, right?"

"Yeah," RISK says hopefully. Being known is the better part of being respected. *IGT* is *International Graffiti Times*, aerosol grandfather PHASE 2's sporadically published newsletter, and getting a flick in there is the crowning achievement of RISK's career to date. Of course, smacking up a known writer carries infinitely more cachet than stomping out some toy, so it's also possible that this kid's photographic memory has just fucked RISK right in the ass.

The main dude turns back to him; he seems to have decided that RISK is worth impressing at least. "CLOUD 9, RTW," he reveals, proclaiming his name and his crew's as if the words part seas and shatter boulders. They come close. Rolling Thunder Writers is one of the most feared collectives of the eighties. They ran the Coney Island Yard, the biggest in the city, handed out beat-downs like raffle tickets. CLOUD 9 is a lesser light, not in the class of RTW all-stars like MIN, BOE, RICH, and SAGO. But he got up. Straight letters, mostly—not a master of style, but a workhorse with a nice clean hand, the kind of guy whose pieces you'd see in magazines by virtue of their sharing a car with burners by his boys. Had a famous fight with KYTE 202 from Psycho Artists at the Hall of Fame. Knocked him the fuck out.

"Oh, word?" RISK tries to sound impressed but casual, keep the fear out of his voice.

"Word. And who the fuck is that?"

RISK turns to find Tristan walking toward him, and his stomach drops.

He gives the old man a baleful stare. "My grandfather."

"Fuck he doing here?"

RISK cracks his knuckles. "He's about to get up. First time ever."

"You're shitting me."

"Nah, for real."

"What chu write, Grandpa?" CLOUD 9 shouts, as if he suspects the old man might be deaf.

"BRONX," says Tristan, just as loud. It's the same authority-freighted voice that might boom forth from behind his study door, telling a visitor that he is too busy to socialize. But it sounds more vital out here, in the open air of the dark train yard—sounds, perhaps, the way it did fifty years ago, on some steaming city block.

"You from there?" calls the Afroed kid, incredulous. His fellow apprentice shoots him a screw face.

"Born and raised."

CLOUD 9 shifts his stance. The gravel rasps beneath him. "How old are you?"

"I'm sixty-eight. And you?"

CLOUD 9 cracks a smile, drops his arms and lets them dangle by his sides. RISK nearly pisses himself with relief. "I'm twenty-five."

Tristan walks up to him. "Well, that's nothing. I was in Baghdad when you were in your dad's bag, kiddo."

CLOUD 9 throws back his head and laughs. "Shit. Y'all motherfuckers crazy," he declares, and swings a splayed hand toward RISK, who startles, then recovers in time to extend his own. Their palms meet with a satisfying clap. CLOUD nods at the old man. "Go ahead, BRONX, do your thing. You 'bout to make the record books. Oldest writer in the history of this shit. Hope you appreciate I'm here to bear witness."

Tristan takes a can from the knapsack. "Only thing I've ever painted is a lawn chair," he apologizes, squaring off before the train.

"That's okay, BRONX. All gotta start somewhere. My first piece was wack as hell."

Tristan depresses the nozzle, and an inch-thick caterpillar of color wiggles up the train.

"Paint top to bottom," CLOUD instructs. "Control the drips better that way." He bends at the waist, peers forward. "Whoa. Bermuda Blue?"

"Yeah, man. I found it in his toolshed."

"Damn."

Tristan steps back to examine his handiwork. A wobbly bubble-letter *B* floats before him, bleeding Bermuda Blue. It looks like a relic from 1970: the dawn of history, when guys first switched from homemade purple-ink markers to spray cans refitted with oven-cleaner nozzles. The old man shakes the can, then sets to work on his *R*.

"You live out here now?" RISK asks CLOUD as they watch.

"Nah, still reppin' BK. My nephews. I'm showin' 'em the ropes." He gestures behind him. "All right, you pussies are off the hook. Come introduce yourselves. Shit."

The kids hustle to his side, offer RISK pounds, mumble their names. MEGA and SCRIPT. Thirteenish, upon closer inspection. Their handshakes are loose, no muscle behind them yet. No bluster, even. "Okay, now get to work," CLOUD commands, and they scurry down the line.

CLOUD shoves his hands into his pockets. "Lucky thing you brought the old man out tonight. I mean, you cool. It's all love. But see, I wouldn't have known that." He gazes past RISK at SCRIPT and MEGA, both consulting sketchbooks as they paint their outlines on the next car over. "These kids, they're fuckin' art students. They read the mags, think shit is sweet. I'm tryna make 'em understand that if they wanna write, they gotta pay some dues. Be ready to throw hands. Maybe catch a few bad ones, like I did coming up." He laughs. "I brought these kids out here straight *looking* for a fight. Not giving a fuck whether they won or lost. Just so they'd realize graffiti ain't no weekend sport."

RISK goes quiet, considering this. "Sorry I couldn't help you out."

"Shit." CLOUD laughs. "BRONX looks like he might still be able to whup some ass. Bronx Jews were nothin' nice back in his day, huh?"

RISK stares at his grandfather's back, lulled by the slow, arthritic arcs of his right arm, the soothing *pssht* of the paint. "How do you know he's Jewish?"

"Shit." It seems to be CLOUD's all-purpose way of opening a sentence. "How do you know I'm black?"

BRONX has finished his outline. It looks like something a third grader might carve into a desk. He turns, walks over. "So now I fill it in?" he asks, sounding embarrassed to be proud. His hands are caked with paint. They look like Smurf gloves.

RISK nods. "I'd go with the white. And don't worry about fucking up the outline. You're gonna go over it again anyway."

BRONX hands the Bermuda Blue to his grandson, picks up the white, and trudges back to the train. He fills in the *B*, then takes a break to check out MEGA and SCRIPT's car, which is coming alive with color as they apply fills, cuts, and blends to their intricate outlines.

"Amazing," RISK hears his grandfather exclaim. "How old did you kids say you are?"

RISK shakes the Bermuda Blue, then passes it to CLOUD. "For you," he says, thinking that this gesture of friendship could just as easily have been one of submission.

"Thanks."

"Do something dope with it."

"No doubt." CLOUD looks at the train. "I can't believe you're not taking flicks."

In a world of chemical buffing agents, vandal squads, and rival writers playing cross-out, cameras are a writer's best friend, photographs the difference between immortality and empty boasts.

"Aw, fuck. You didn't bring one, did you?"

"Shit, I'm a professional." CLOUD reaches down and pulls a compact automatic from the cargo pocket of his camouflage pants. "Yo, BRONX," he calls. The writer turns. "Let me get a shot of you next to your piece."

BRONX looks indignant. "Well, I've got to finish it first. That's like asking to read a first draft. Take one of my grandson and me instead."

CLOUD lifts the camera to his eye. "Say 'Gorgonzola.' " RISK throws his arm around the old man's shoulders as the flash goes off.

BRONX squeezes his grandson's wrist. "Thank you, Tris."

"Thank you. Now get back over there and finish your fill."

An hour later, Amalia Farber will pace her foyer, Tristan's note in one hand and a cordless telephone in the other, wondering whether she should call her daughter. When she does, the phone will ring and ring. Linda will already be in her minivan, en route to her parents' house to relieve them of the burden of their grandson, ashamed of her own selfishness in dumping him there. As if her mother needs more crap to deal with.

When Linda arrives, BRONX and RISK will be sitting in a nearby steak house talking graffiti history with CLOUD 9, SCRIPT, and MEGA, the old man having insisted on treating all of them to dinner. The Brodsky men will come home several hours later, to be confronted in the foyer by RISK's mother and grandmother, BRONX's wife and daughter. The women will be holding white mugs of hot peppermint tea, their concern dissolving into anger as the front door opens. The two writers will pocket their paint-crusted hands and insist that they've merely been out to eat, that the note they left behind was nothing but a joke. The empty spray cans rattling in RISK's backpack will put the lie to that.

CHAPTER

FOUR

Soon, Tristan thinks, staring out the taxi window as the Bronx recedes behind him, the neighborhood would have been right. It might have taken as little as another month or as much as another year, but before long, Tristan Brodsky, fabled scion of Maimonides, dashed hope of the Jews, would truly have lost his mind. Already, just twenty-one, he has been considered a failure for three years. A crack-up. "That Brodsky boy, he refuses to take a job," the matrons whisper in the fetid stairwells, when they aren't fretting over the rumor that every Jew in the German-occupied world is being made to wear a Star of David, or cursing Lindbergh and Coughlin for speechifying that their people are leading America toward war. At the greengrocer's, they shake their bulbous heads. "A college graduate, and for three years he's done nothing, day and night, but sit in his room. Watching the paint peel! A regular meshuggener!"

A hush falls over the craps game, even, when Tristan strides toward it—something he's seldom done of late and never will again, now—as if the fellows expect Tristan to gibber like an ape, or throttle them. Instead, he takes his turn and takes their money and takes his leave, deposits the bills on the kitchen table for his mother to find and returns to his room. He has hated the room more each day, but at the same time he has noticed it less; he looks either at the page before him in the typewriter or else out at the street. When the wash hanging across the block is hauled back in, it is lunchtime. He eats the sandwich waiting for him in the icebox, guzzles a glass of tap water, goes back to work. His neighbors black out their windows, obliterating themselves out of dunderheaded fear that German warplanes will materialize above the Bronx. Tristan blacks out the world, replaces it with what's inside his head.

Being labeled an eccentric has its perks. Not even his family bothers him with questions anymore except for Benjamin, a college man himself now and still loyal to his brother. He is the only person with whom Tristan speaks of his writing, and only because Benjamin has the good sense merely to listen; he limits his responses to quotations, like the old men arguing the Talmud. He remembers everything Tristan has told him about the novel in the past, and thus he can remind his brother of old insights, things Tristan himself may have forgotten.

It was Benjamin who watched him drink and listened to his perplexity crest into rage two years ago when the first reply from a publisher came in the mail—a man to whom Pendergast had spoken on Tristan's behalf:

21 September 1939

Dear Mr. Brodsky,

There is no doubt that you possess gifts as a writer. But as we have recently published Mordecai Kaplan's superb Judaism as a Civilization, I regret to inform that we have decided to pass on your novel. Best of luck.

Norman Jameson
Frontier Press

That was the day the neighborhood chatter intensified. Enough people saw and heard Tristan on his treks to and from the liquor store, finishing a bottle on his way there and beginning another on his way home, to elevate the fallen prodigy to the status of juiciest morsel on the winding shtetl grapevine.

There are other publishers, Benjamin counseled, accepting the bottle when Tristan passed it, rarely drinking from it but holding on until his brother beckoned for the booze again.

Sure, Tristan replied, *but none of them is any different*. He looked out at the street, imagined hurling his typewriter from the window and watching it explode against the pavement, vowels and consonants embedding themselves in the flesh of gossiping passersby like bits of shrapnel.

Let them talk now, he thinks. Let them stir their words into their bland, greasy soups and slurp them down by the bowlful. Tristan has sold not one but two novels today—both written in that gerbil cage of a room, over the sounds of kvetching from all sides, in the sweltering heat of the Bronx summer and the hand-numbing winter cold—and he does not intend to be seen in these parts again. He could linger to see his success transform his mother's demonstrative disapproval and his father's halting diplomacy into pride, but Tristan has no desire to do so. Their contribution has been to leave him alone—out of deference and befuddlement, never faith. He will repay them in kind.

Everything he owns is in this taxi: the suit he wore down to Times Square this morning to meet with his new editor and publisher, the rest of his clothes, heaped into the trunk by the armful, still on their hangers, a box of books mostly borrowed from the New York Public Library, and his typewriter. Plus enough money—on loan from Pendergast, whom he visited after signing the deal, with the purpose of securing an advance against his forthcoming advance—to install himself in a For Rent apartment he passed on his way from the subway to Peter's writing studio.

"That was fast," the building's superintendent says, emerging from a basement bulkhead a few minutes after Tristan pays the taxi fare and rings his bell. He glances at the small mound of belongings by the young man's feet. "What line of work you say you're in?"

Tristan takes a deep, exhilarating breath. "I'm an author."

"No kidding. Ever do a Western?"

"Suppose I'd have to get out west first."

The super waves a grubby hand. "Nothing out there you can't imagine. Just throw in a coupla gunfights, bandito or two. Some hard-drinkin' lawmen. A pretty dame." He laughs. "Hell, I could probably write one myself. Beats shoveling coal into the furnace. Here, let me help you with your things."

Three flights up, the super unlocks the door. "There's no kitchen, you know," he says as he leads Tristan inside. "That's why it's advertised so cheap."

There is nothing in the place save a naked mattress lying on a boxspring, a telephone parked on a desk, and one chair. The emptiness cues in Tristan a great flush of happiness. Half the objects in the universe are crammed into his parents' home: bolts of fabric and mounds of cutlery and stacks of magazines, all so permanent, his mother cleans by dusting them.

He saunters around the two large, airy rooms. Light slopes in through a floor-to-ceiling window in the front, and the shadow of the fire escape pulses darker and fainter against the floor as clouds move across the sun.

Two hours later, Tristan is in his suit and out the door, feeling as sharp of wits and dress as ever he has. The shul grants manhood at thirteen, the street upon the authentic or well-fabricated loss of virginity. Those milestones lie well behind him, thanks to a long-forgotten haftarah portion and the feminine wiles of Leah Krasner, but only now is Tristan certain that he is no longer a boy, and that he hasn't been for years.

He stands at the windswept corner of Seventy-first and Madison, reaches into his pocket and closes his fist around the gold pen he received at his bar mitzvah—a durable instrument, its elegance uncompromised by either the years of Hebrew school he had to suffer through to get it or the fact that everyone else got one, too. He'd bet the pen in a craps game with Sammy Fischer an hour after the ceremony, won, and made Fischer beg for a week before allowing him to buy his own pen back.

"You look like the cat who swallowed the canary, kid." Tristan turns, to find a grinning Loren Leonard, hand jutting at a right angle to his body. Tristan shakes it, smiling into the editor's hypnotic, flecked-gray eyes. Their precise shade is echoed in his suit and hat, and it is one of many to be found in the spectrum of the editor's thick mustache. Loren is a creature of deceptive age. Tristan guessed that he was fortyish and prematurely bald, but Pendergast corrected him by twenty years, adding that during the considerable span of their acquaintance, Loren had hardly aged a day.

"I feel like him," Tristan says as they walk east, toward the party.

"Well, you sure as shit should." The editor is a small man, spry and keen, possessed of a deeply embedded dignity. Tristan has not yet been able to determine whether his constant vulgarity has been calibrated to counterweight that dignity or emphasize its fixity. To be colorful is a common appetite among these Mayflower types. They are so accustomed to fitting in that now they seek to stand out, and thus they strive for a bit of coarseness, act the way they guess the lower classes might. The lower classes, meanwhile, are busy trying to behave as if they'd shared a stateroom with these schlemiels on the way over from merry old England.

"Now listen," Loren goes on, "I want you to think of tonight as part of your job. At this moment, you're a writer, and a hell of a fucking talent. But we've got to make you into an *author*. Get you schmoozing, know what I mean?" Tristan nods, wondering whether Loren only trots out the Yiddish when he's speaking to a Son of Zion.

They cross onto Fifth Ave., walk south beneath awnings that cover the entire breadth of the sidewalk. Jacob once had a line on a doorman job down here. His accent ruined his prospects.

"A lot of my authors, they've got their heads up their asses about this shit. They think the artiste is just supposed to sit in his study, sniffing the mildew wafting from his leather-bound editions of Milton and Shelley and dipping the pen in the fucking inkwell. If that was how it worked, I'd be a crap-happy bastard, Tristan. I'd be at home poring over Shelley right now myself. But publishing is a business like any other, and if you want to get a leg up, you have to learn to play the goddamn game."

"I'm all ears," says Tristan, thinking that these writers unwilling to engage the literary world must be incredible pricks, or wealthy enough not to care, or else they've figured out a way to write that's far healthier and less consuming than his. He imagines them puffing on their pipes as the words fill the pages, tousling the hair of the kids underfoot as they pour themselves a late-afternoon brandy, nestling against the bed-warm bodies of their wives and sighing in contentment as they drift easily to sleep.

"Good man. Now, first things first: can you hold your liquor?"

"I can hold it in my hand."

Loren nods. "Right. Do that, then. Midget sips. Build the tolerance.

Nothing worse than a soused writer. Second: when you go to a party with me, assume that I am singing your praises to everyone who matters. You don't strike me as a braggart, but I'll tell you anyway: don't walk in the fucking place and start yammering about yourself. Wait for me to work the room. Pretend not to notice if people glance over at you. When they sidle up and start asking questions, act surprised but be prepared to charm the piss out of them.

"You have to understand, these people have the highest respect for literature, and high enough opinions of themselves that they expect to be presented with writers on a regular basis. Nothing makes a man who's earned his fortune in, say, coal feel grander than chewing the fat with an honest-to-shit writer. These fellows think like investors—they want to get in on the ground floor. They love to feel that they're playing some role in your success. And they are. They'll buy your book the day it hits the shelves, then call me up begging to throw a publication party."

"They actually read, then?"

"Some of them. The women more so than the men. They have more time for it." Loren stops before a corner high rise, and Tristan throws his head back and stares up at it—rather pointlessly, he thinks, and stops. "The host and hostess are Maurice and Natalie Farber. He's in textiles, import-export, real estate. That sort of thing. Also philanthropy. She's very active in it, too. Exceedingly smart lady."

"They're Jewish."

"Yes, of course. You're not anti-Semitic, are you?"

"I—"

"Look. The publishers don't realize it yet, but these high-society Jews are the new tastemakers. And they're going to love you, Tristan, because you're telling them what's going on back in the old neighborhood. You know why *Angel* is beautiful? Because it's dick-in-the-dirt honest. These people don't know it yet, but they want that."

As the arrow above the elevator door sweeps from L to PH, Tristan wonders if they do—these people, or anybody else. *The Angel of the Shtetl* is populated with dressmakers, cockroaches, petty thugs, butchers, crapshooters. Talmudic scholars whose immigrant families are starving because learning is the greatest thing in life and they refuse to sideline the pursuit of knowledge and find work. Tristan has written of the shapeless dresses and mild charms of their homely, aspiring daughters and the pinched mouths of their bitter wives, about the way their timid sons push their spectacles up the bridges of their sweaty noses and doggedly pursue elusive New World manhood. Narrating the tale, and meddling ineffectively in the lives of its characters, is a haggard, pork chop–obsessed angel named Lew, the least-favored emissary of an overworked, bureaucratic God saddled with unmanageable debt and alternately furious and resigned about having chosen the Jews, of all the world's people, to be His.

What does writing such a book make Tristan? *An author* seems suddenly a naïve answer, an evasion, but he cannot allow the mantle of Jewish Writer to be draped over his shoulders. Whether it is brave or cowardly or impossible to refuse to let heritage and ideology define and obscure him like a Halloween mask while the Jews of Europe are being herded into ghettos, stripped of rights, Tristan does not know. But he can't let his life be one long run through the gauntlet of the City College cafeteria, lined on all sides with competing factions slamming their fists against tabletops and shouting for allegiance. The world is the Bronx, and the Bronx is the world. They can't banish him back to his parents' apartment for insisting he speaks for no one, claiming the right to tell the stories that compel him and to be compelled by anything at all. Can they?

The lift's doors do not open onto a hallway, unlike those of every other Tristan has ever ridden. Instead, they slide away to reveal the Farbers' living room—an enormous hexagon, cathedral-ceilinged, full of rising smoke and voices. Everyone has turned, mid-conversation, to witness the latest arrivals, and Tristan is pleased to see more than a few faces register recognition at the sight of his editor. The young writer falls into step behind him, smiling in a general kind of way as he moves through the crowded room toward the statuesque dark-haired woman speaking Loren's name.

In one gloved hand, she holds a highball glass. In the other, a cigarette smolders at the end of a long holder. She bends toward Loren at the waist, presenting her cheek and, perhaps advertently, cleavage Tristan suspects he will reconsider later.

"Inconceivably delighted to see you, Mr. Leonard." She cuts her eyes, looks left and right, and drops her voice. "Wall-to-wall bores here tonight, Loren." She leans past him, flashes her eyes at Tristan. "And good evening to you, Mr. Brodsky." She consolidates her accessories in her left hand and extends her right. "Natalie Farber. Very charmed to meet you, and mazel tov." Her handshake is firmer, more authoritative, than that of any woman he has ever met. "I look forward to reading your book—books, I suppose I should say."

Tristan affects a slight bow. "Thank you." The noise of the room swells, and he raises his voice. "You have a lovely home."

Natalie glances toward the elevator, then back at Tristan. "Much lovelier without so many businessmen in it."

Tristan opens his mouth, decides discretion should be his watchword, and closes it. Then he changes his mind.

"But isn't this your party, Mrs. Farber? And isn't your husband a businessman?" He feels Loren's eyes boring into the side of his head, imagines the editor making a quick stop back at the office to set his book contract on fire.

Natalie laughs; Tristan expels a breath he didn't know he was holding. "Yes on both counts. How do you think I know?" She draws on her cigarette. "One at a time is acceptable, but en masse they tend to drag a soiree down. Obligations, Mr. Brodsky, obligations. You're not related to the attorney Brodsky, are you?"

"No, ma'am, I'm afraid not."

"Good for you. Most tiresome man in New York State." Her eyes flick over to the elevator once again. "I'll spare you the tedium of explaining what your novels are about, as I must now welcome to my home the second most tiresome man in New York State. However." And with that she sails away, a proud boat cutting through a jittery ocean. Tristan stares after her, wondering whether the various elements of Natalie's hostessing repertoire—the mock boredom, the cutting wit, the nonstop motion, the odd farewell—are standard to these circles, or if she's as strange and intriguing a creature as he'd like to think.

Loren claps his hands. "Drinks. Scotch, I presume? All us literary cunts drink scotch, don't we?" And he, too, walks off, making it a mere five feet before he stops to pump the hand of a portly fellow cupping a napkin full of hors d'oeuvres to his vest. The bar is on the far side of the room, a long, low table manned by two servers dressed in white. At his current rate of progress, it will take Loren twenty minutes to make it there and back.

Tristan is relieved to be on his own for a spell, content to wander and overhear, pluck toothpicked delicacies from the silver trays of passing waiters and taxonomize this much-mythologized and seldom-seen species of Jew. This room is full of the men in whom the Bronx glories—and whom the Bronx monitors from afar, waiting to curse them with that awed and bitter-tongued refrain: *he acts like he isn't even Jewish.*

Of course, not everyone here *is* Jewish, and this free mingling, this blurring of distinctions, is worth considering. Do tonight's Gentiles simply enjoy the succulence of Natalie Farber's spread, or do they note that nothing being served contains a drop of dairy? If so, do they find the fact extraordinary, mundane, charming, or absurd? Tomorrow night, when half these people turn up at a party down the block thrown by some Episcopal business associate of Mr. Farber, will the goyim watch to see whether their Semitic friends consent to sample a shrimp cocktail, or an oyster wrapped in bacon? Will they widen their eyes as the trays of verboten appetizers are presented to the Chosen People, thinking *take it, take it, act like you aren't even Jewish?*

"I haven't seen you before," says a voice at Tristan's side. He turns and looks into the placid face of an exceptionally pretty girl, about fifteen.

She sips from a glass of wine. "Do you speak French?"

"I'm afraid not," he says, attempting a Lester-Young-by-way-of-Pendergast smile, detached and knowing and flirtatious all at once. "Is that requisite around here?"

"I was going to tell you a joke, but it's only funny if you speak French."

"I could laugh anyway."

"It's very kind of you to offer." Her eyebrows are arched and thin, and her eyes, a mottled hazel like his brother's, radiate an intelligence all the more daunting for its lack of attitude. Her brains are not something that has caused this girl pain, not something she's ever had to hide or defend. Or so it appears. "Do you play chess?"

"Never learned that, either," Tristan says, beginning to feel his dander rise. "Do you play craps?"

Her smile is broad and closed. Something in her eyes says she knows he is fucking with her, and likes it. "Is it a card game?"

"I'll take that as a no. How about stickball?"

"I've seen it played."

"Really. I didn't know it had taken hold in this neighborhood."

"No, not here. I do leave the Upper East Side now and then."

"Whatever for?" asks Tristan, pocketing his hands.

"Stimulation. And may I ask your name?"

"I'm sorry. Tristan Brodsky."

She scrutinizes him. "The lawyer? I thought you'd be much older."

"No, that's a different Brodsky. I'm a writer."

The girl's face comes alive, and Tristan realizes how little attention she's been paying to the conversation until now. "You don't say. So am I. I knew you looked interesting. What sort of things do you write?"

"Novels." He gives his hand. "And may I ask yours?"

"I'm sorry, I assumed you knew. Amalia Farber."

"You have your mother's handshake, Miss Farber." He seizes upon the momentary diversion of a passing waiter to look her up and down and thinks *her tits, too*.

"How many books have you had, Mr. Brodsky?"

"I've just sold my first two. What about yourself?"

"I'm a poet. But I've just begun. No books yet."

Tristan smiles. Of course this girl assumes she'll publish books. Her parents, or her nannies, have no doubt raised her to believe she will be anything she wants. Hell, she could be nothing, and what would it matter?

"I'd love to hear something. Can you recite your work?"

"I can, but I won't. It's not a parlor trick. If you'll leave me your address, perhaps I'll mail you one. I'd like to have a real professional's opinion. The teachers at school are occupied with building our confidence; they claim that everything I write is marvelous."

"You don't believe them?"

Amalia eyes him over the top of her glass. "Of course not. How could I be any good after only a year?"

"Some people are naturals."

"Did you write anything decent in your first year?"

"Sometimes I think it's all been downhill since. I'm not saying I'd want to see any of it published. But I was full of energy then, convinced that everything I wrote was utterly original. That fades as you go on, unfortunately, to be replaced by a more—" Tristan stops, shakes his head. "I'm sorry. I sound like a pompous ass, don't I? I haven't quite figured out yet how an author is supposed to talk."

"I thought you were doing fine. The phrase 'pompous ass' hadn't crossed my mind."

"You're very generous."

Amalia cocks her head to one side. She seems to be deciding what to make of him. Tristan wonders if she does this at every party: find the one person who doesn't belong and monopolize him. He watches her watch him, trying to pinpoint what it is about this girl that makes her so attractive. It has less to do with looks or charm than with the absence of the striving desperation that sits like a weight in most people he knows, tethering them to the ground. It gives her a lightness, a purity, which he wants both to bask in and destroy.

"You look like you work too hard," she says at last. "Authors are supposed to have an air of leisure about them, don't you think?"

"Interesting that you should say so. Where I come from, writing is hardly considered work at all."

"Oh, I think it's very hard work. Without question, the hardest I've ever done."

"But not as hard, say, as pushing a cart down the street for twelve hours a day. Or loading cargo onto ocean liners."

"Have you done such things?"

"No," Tristan admits. "I've only written. But if I fail, it's what I'm bound for. How about you, Miss Farber? What are you bound for, if poetry doesn't work out?"

"I'll have to give it some thought," she says, and turns slightly away. They stare into the ever-growing crowd. Tristan curses himself and wills her to resuscitate the conversation, chagrined that he is looking to this girl to take the lead.

"I'll be happy if I'm a true poet by sixty" is what she comes up with. Her voice is petulant, as if Amalia expects to be mocked.

"Sixty? You'd be content with mediocrity for the next forty-five years?"

"The next forty-two and a half, thank you. By sixty, I'd like to think I'll have something to say. I will have lived." Her forehead crinkles. "Do I really look fifteen?"

Tristan rubs a glint of perspiration from the side of his nose. "Let me ask you something. Do you consider yourself a Jewish poet, or just a poet?"

"I'd never think to identify myself that way. I can't see what bearing it has."

"But it must have some, no? It's the single factor in millions of people's destinies."

Amalia shrugs. "It does for you, I take it."

"I don't know. Forces greater than myself want me to be Jewish. And I mean my publisher, not the man upstairs—He couldn't care less what I do. It's funny; I realized recently that virtually all the Hebrew I once knew is gone. It's as if for every word of English I've written, a word of Hebrew has disappeared."

"Oh, I'm sure it's still in there. Come, let's have a quick Shema."

"Even if I could recite it, I'd have no idea what it meant."

"Does it matter? The sound is beautiful, whether you know or not."

"From a cantor, maybe. From me, it would be an auditory pogrom."

Loren reappears at Tristan's side, a glass of scotch and melting ice in either hand. "Hello, Amalia dear," he says. "You're looking splendid tonight. If you'll permit me, I must borrow Mr. Brodsky for a moment. Some gentlemen across the room are just dying to meet him."

Tristan takes his drink from Loren and lifts it to Amalia.

"The life of an author beckons," she says, raising her wineglass an inch.

"Send me a poem."

"I will," she promises, and slips into the crowd.

Almost a year passes before Tristan extracts a slim envelope with no return address from his mailbox and stuffs it in his jacket's breast pocket, running late, as usual, to make it to the uptown train. The world is different now. He is a published author and the country is at war, and what it means to be a Jew has changed again.

They are a side issue in this conflict; what is real to them seems unreal to the rest of the world, and so there the Jews huddle, in colonies along the eastern seaboard of the United States, a paranoid race of the past, trading rumors about their own annihilation, a new one every week. At the second battle for Kharkov, the latest horror story goes, the Nazis sacrificed a tactical advantage—actually *decided to lose*—in order to round up Jews. No one took notice when the reports of absurd laws and cresting violence first began to trickle into the United States; no one listened when the deportations started. Now only a deafening silence booms from the European Jewry, Rachael's and Jacob's families included, and still "the Jewish problem" is of little concern to Roosevelt. In the global theater of war, it is a stray cough from the balcony.

Sometimes Tristan can hardly focus on the paper in the typewriter before him. Yesterday, after eating his usual blue-plate lunch at Pluto's Diner, he lingered for an extra half hour, eavesdropping on a hushed conversation between two old Jews, both grimly satisfied to have incontrovertible proof of what they'd always known: that the world's hatred of their race continues unabated. An hour later, standing in the subway's rush-hour crush, Tristan found himself six inches from a young uniformed draftee, watching the boy's eyes, imagining them glitter with mortal terror and blaze with the cold, naïve desire to kill. That night, stretched out in bed with the *New York Times*, Tristan came across the suicide note of a Polish Jew exiled in London, hidden away in the back pages: *It was not my fate to die with my comrades, but I belong to them, and in their mass graves. By my death, I hope to express my strongest protest against the inaction with which the world is looking on and permitting the extermination of my people.* He read it twice through, closed his eyes, and tried to understand why a man worried about the obliteration of his race would kill himself. He wondered whether living or dying required more of this man's courage, then turned the page and worked his eyes over the sports column, retaining nothing. He dropped the paper by the bedside, atop an issue of *The New Republic*, which seemed to suggest that the editors were equally horrified by Hitler and by the revelation of Ezra Pound's anti-Semitism.

The war rages in headlines and in minds, in the window-box victory gardens hanging from every apartment building and the hulking warships being hewn into existence down at the Brooklyn Navy Yard. It is in evidence all around Tristan, right down to the cuffs of his pants—the extra inch of fabric marks the trousers as prewar, manufactured before the military declared a textile shortage. And yet he still has books to write, an imagination through which to filter the world. Tristan doesn't know whether to feel guilty about his daily escapes from reality, or to pity those who have found no such respite. But he is resolute in the desire to hold on to the same sense of complexity that he had before the bombing of Pearl Harbor, and thus he does not stand among the proud, the vocal, or the desperate.

Neither does he stand in the long procession of young men snaking from the draft board's office and down Broadway—the recruitment line has replaced the breadline, he thinks whenever he passes—nor tremble with dread as he inserts his key into his mailbox lock and turns. No draft notice lies inside, and not because Tristan has been deemed unfit to serve, or judged so frail that his name was reshuffled to the back of the list. He does not stand among the gimps, the asthmatics, the high of blood pressure shunted by their country even in its hour of need.

Instead, Tristan stands behind a podium in a large, dingy classroom at City College for three hours a day, five days a week, shepherding freshmen through the greatest hits of Western literature. When the draft began, he did as he was told: typed up an application and a résumé and mailed them to the recently appointed chairman of English and Comparative Literature, Peter Pendergast, who promptly offered Tristan a job. Teachers, Peter explained during what passed for an interview, would be among the last men called, like farmers and automotive workers.

Every day, as he rides the subway up to school, Tristan thinks of Achilles. Not the fierce warrior stalking the killing fields of Troy, nor the mercurial demigod sulking in his tent, but Achilles on the day Diomedes and Odysseus came to fetch him to battle and found the hero-to-be hidden among maidens, disguised in a dress. Tristan might as well be wearing an evening gown himself, because he will sooner develop a pair of knockers than an ability to teach.

And yet Professor Brodsky's classes are as full as the school registrar permits. His students are boys like he was, commuters from the Bronx and the Lower East Side, and all of them, it seems, have read *The Angel of the Shtetl*. After class, they want to talk to him about it—tell him that they cried when they got to the end, or that their fathers threw the book across the room in anger, then walked over and picked it up and resumed reading. Tristan never tires of hearing it. He hopes they cannot tell how much he enjoys being read, received, loved or despised or both. Half his students want to be writers themselves, and half of those only since reading Tristan's novel.

Every week, he promises himself he will be more professional, more professorial, that he will sit down, compose his thoughts, structure a proper lecture. Fat chance. The new novel is progressing with infuriating torpor as it is; if he actually prepared for class, he'd be sunk. Tristan is learning that his mind does not switch gears without a fight. It sputters every morning, wanders, freezes. The anticipation of having to stop writing and teach hinders him from getting started, and once he's ground past that, the workday's nearly gone. The subway ride to City College would be an ideal time to map out his impending class, but Tristan tends to spend it clamping his molars together and pondering his tendency to resent everything for which he should be grateful.

Today is the third time Pendergast has sat in on Tristan's classes, acting not as his boss but as his friend. He seems to find his former student's incompetence amusing, or perhaps reassuring, and he very much enjoys the opportunity to dispense advice.

"I've never seen a teacher free-associate so obviously," he tells Tristan at Mama's Coffeeshop, across the street from campus. Pendergast tamps some tobacco into the pipe he's taken to smoking, then pats himself down, feeling for a matchbook. "Not that you aren't interesting. But come on, man. A chimpanzee could tell you're not prepared."

"Yes," says Tristan, hunched low to his coffee cup, "and who knows? Maybe one day I'll even have a student who notices."

Pendergast gets his pipe lit and leans back, waving it in the air like he's Mark Twain. "I'll tell you again."

"I know, I know, it's a performance. I'm an actor. I could give this speech myself by now. Look, Peter, if I'm so hopeless, just can me. No hard feelings. Hell, I'd thank you. Do you know I stared at a wrong sentence for half an hour this morning before I could muster up the brainpower to fix the goddamn thing?"

"You know I'm not going to fire you. Why do you even say it?" Pendergast affects a slight hurt, aims a smoke ring at the ceiling. "Christ, Brodsky. You're not even twenty-four and you've got your second novel in the pipeline. Why put such pressure on yourself? What's the point?"

Tristan toys with the book of matches, lights one, lets it burn down, shakes it out. "The point is to write."

"How noble."

"Oh, fuck you, Peter." He lights another match and waves away a puff of acrid smoke. "Finish your lecture. The coffee's getting cold."

Pendergast grins around the stem of his pipe. "All I'm trying to say, schmuck—that's Yiddish, by the way, I'll tell you what it means later—is that at some point, you may not be running a fan club anymore. I had one, too, when I was the young hotshot novelist around here. It's great fun, but it doesn't last. Someday you may have to teach students who don't know you from Adam's house cat. Might as well learn how to go about it, don't you think?"

"Someday this war will be over, and my teaching career with it." The rest of what Tristan thinks, he refrains from saying: *you were never the young hotshot novelist around here*. Pendergast's first book was a moderate commercial success and a critical belly flop, and he's produced only two in the ten years since, garnering respectable sales and the general indifference of reviewers. Tristan tries to avoid talking craft with his old teacher, but the day is fast approaching when Peter will hand over his new manuscript to be critiqued. Just the thought of putting his own novel on hold to wade through Pendergast's earnest drama of high-society mores and immores, with its bloated word count and its Magical Colored Folk, is maddening. And then there's the question of what in the hell Tristan will say to the man whose machinations have prevented him from being fitted with a rifle and shipped overseas to kill and die. *Your punctuation is absolutely flawless, Peter.*

It is not until the meeting is over and Tristan is back on the subway that he remembers to remove his mail from his pocket. The paper stock of the cream-colored envelope is heavy, his name and address neatly typed. He checks the back again. Still blank. Six months ago, Tristan would not have noted any of this before ripping the letter open, but he is wary these days. He's received a few disturbing letters from readers, some forwarded by his publisher and others sent directly to his address.

He opens the letter anyway, and inside finds a single page, as heavy as the envelope, with fourteen lines typed in its center. A sonnet, unsigned. Tristan looks up from the page and smiles. The Farbers' daughter. He prepares himself to read the nineteen-year-old's poem; if it's as precious as her letter's guise of anonymity, it will give him a perfect opportunity to get in some practice for responding gently to Pendergast's book.

He hasn't seen Amalia since the night they met, but her parents have been among his greatest supporters. Natalie Farber rented two hundred sets of metal and silk wings and threw him an *Angel of the Shtetl* party the day the novel reached stores: turned her apartment into Heaven, replete with a harpsichordist and big cotton clouds suspended from the ceiling and a white-bearded God on a gilded throne. She served champagne and angel food cake to half of Manhattan for his sake.

The whole evening was so surreal that Tristan was forced to make sense of it by getting stupendously drunk, which turned out to be an entirely acceptable, even proper, thing for a novelist to do at his book party. Somehow, as he careened around Heaven, heaping praise on Natalie and Maurice whenever he crossed their paths, Tristan managed to sign three hundred books. He woke up the next morning to a phone call from Loren, informing him that he had made the society page. Tristan lurched to a newsstand for a copy, and sure enough, there he was, grinning at the camera with an arm around his hostess, looking like an imbecile in his feathery wings—a decidedly New Testament imbecile. The Bronx thought who-knew-what. The book took off. The author spent half an hour goggling at the photograph, stuporously gratified, his pounding hangover burned away by an ecstatic, surging sense of possibility, a wild feeling of staring directly at the godhead of success. Then the hangover rallied, and Tristan staggered back to bed.

He'd asked after Amalia before he'd gotten sauced, or perhaps after, and learned that she would be attending Vassar in the fall; Natalie promised to let her know he'd asked. Tristan examines the postmark, and sure enough: Poughkeepsie. He wonders for a moment what it's like to attend an honest-to-goodness college, with a real campus and professors who aren't just biding their time until the Allies cream the Japs and knock off Hitler, then realizes he's only stalling and turns his attention to the words, crossing his fingers in the hope that Amalia's creation is passable.

Two lines in, he uncrosses them. The best writers, to Tristan's mind, make him feel stupid and oafish by doing what he cannot. And with these fourteen lines, Amalia Farber has made a bid to join the list. Her poem is as smooth and well formed as an egg, as fragile and as full of life. Her brevity cows Tristan most; his greatest fear is to leave anything out. Amalia trusts the power of the single brushstroke. Her poem glows with a quiet belief in the reader, and yet there is a hard kernel nestled at the sonnet's center.

The girl is me, it begins, and describes a terrified six-year-old, her grainy face spliced into a newsreel played before a motion picture: a Polish child standing huddled against her family, eyes on the crisp legs of the battalion marching past.

The newsreel image switches and *The man is me*: a squint-eyed, square-jawed blond soldier whose military affiliation the author never reveals. In the course of the poem, Amalia imagines herself as innocent and vicious, as a Nazi and a Jew and an American, inhabits each face in the newsreel swiftly and completely, until the screen goes blank and the poet sits alone and exhausted in the blackened theater, her empathy draining away. And then, as the movie begins, the poem ends: *I am Betty Grable*.

Tristan reads it through a second time, folds it, slides it back into his jacket. He begins composing the first lines of a reply, then breaks off, unfolds the poem, and reads it again. The first stanza is burned into his memory by the time Tristan steps off the train. He recites it to himself as he walks up the stairs and down the street and through the front door of his building, chopping the lines into syllables and examining the stresses and the sounds, the rhythm.

Amalia, he writes as soon as he reaches his desk. *I am in love with your poem*. The line sits there, atop his typewriter, and Tristan stares at it for several minutes, growing lonely. He doesn't want to offer rhapsody, or writerly observations. He wants to sit down with this girl, tell her that he, too, is Betty Grable, and talk to her for hours.

The community of wordsmiths into which Tristan always imagined being ushered has not materialized; no one slipped him the key to a private club upon the publication of his book. He knows where the cliques meet now, but he doesn't want to vie with the young book reviewer Saul Bellow for king of the Hillel, or sit awkwardly at the knees of Langston Hughes. The New York Intellectuals, as they somewhat ridiculously call themselves, Trilling and Kazin and the rest of the Tribesmen, have been nothing but cordial, but Tristan has skirted their entreaties. He is younger than all but the youngest of that crowd by ten or fifteen years, and far worse educated, and he imagines they would treat him like a child, or grill him on politics if the conversation went on long enough, and be disgusted by his lack of certitude. It is a different kind of intimacy Tristan craves.

I want to read more, he types, *and I would be honored to take you out whenever you are free, in celebration of your sixtieth birthday. Best regards, Tristan Brodsky.*

Two weeks later, a reply:

Tristan,

I thank you for your kind words. Here is another recent attempt at a poem. I beg you to be less merciful this time. You have done wonders for my ego, but what I really want is to be ripped apart. Please do not hesitate to reciprocate by sending anything on which you might desire an (amateur) opinion.

I finally picked up The Angel of the Shtetl last week, as I've been meaning to for months. I haven't had a spare moment since. I'm halfway through and enjoying it immensely, but I'll wait to say anything more until I'm done.

As for your invitation, I must regretfully decline, on the grounds that in poetic terms I am perhaps just turning twenty-five. Which, I might add, makes me far too young for a man of forty-one such as yourself. I am also, as previously noted, completely occupied in classwork and your novel. When I do finish it, however, I would very much like to meet for a drink. Might you find your way up to Vassar, or will it have to wait until my spring recess?

Best Wishes,

A.F.

Tristan does his best to find fault with the poem enclosed. It is longer and riskier than the first, and far less polished. Still, it glows. He handwrites long annotations of both pieces, desperate to praise all that is worthy and to criticize lucidly the lack of clarity he finds in certain images, the dubious usage of one or two words. It takes him three drafts. He needs to prove to both of them that he can handle poetry, that he is not the brutish, boorish Great Novelist type who falters when forced to deal with the world writ small. He says so in the letter, excises the admission from the second version, restores it in the third, reads it over and sees how silly it sounds and decides to keep it anyway. He will be as open as he can with her, honor Amalia's work by making himself as vulnerable as the girl in the sonnet.

Tristan ends with an offer to make it up to Vassar whenever Amalia has a free evening and the inclination to go out, then mails the letter together with the first chapter of his work in progress, which he's shown no one. He has to force himself to slide the carbon into the envelope, the envelope into the mailbox; it is against everything he knows to share any piece of a novel until the final period is typed, the draft complete. He wonders if she will appreciate these shows of trust.

A month passes, and the chapter comes back hemorrhaging red ink, slashed to ribbons. Tristan's brow wrinkles in consternation—indignation, even—but when he lies down on his bed and looks the pages over, he learns that Amalia brings the same rigor to reading as to writing. By the time he finishes absorbing her comments, Tristan is embarrassed for sending such embryonic material. He breaks another of his rules and doubles back to revise the chapter, instead of forging on toward the end of the draft.

Letters and poems, chapters and promises of drinks fly furiously between Poughkeepsie and the Upper West Side. Amalia sees sides of his characters that Tristan himself cannot. She treats them with a friend's sympathy, and when Amalia and Tristan discuss one of his people, they are like two friends conferring over the problems of a third, or a couple discussing their child. When his people disappoint her, Amalia forgives them and turns instead on Tristan. *This is baloney*, she is unafraid to scrawl in his margins, no less than *This is beautiful*. The passages Amalia brutalizes tend to be the ones in which Tristan himself has the least confidence, the ones he's bullshitted his way through and hoped were good enough to just squeak by. *This is not the way a woman thinks*, the red ink blares, *this is the way you male writers conspire to pretend women think. Can you see your mother thinking this? Can you see* ME?

A few times, Tristan catches himself composing a sentence just for her, wanting Amalia to write *MUCH better!* in the margin on the next pass. He finds evidence of the same impulse in her. The poems she sends grow in their narrative awareness, their patience in allowing characters to be more than one thing, their willingness to let ideas roll over and bare their ugly underbellies. They branch away from what Tristan regards—disclaiming his authority to say so all the while, only to find that Amalia agrees with him—as the weaknesses of poetry. His aesthetic and hers are like two dancers in a ballet, flitting in and out of each other's orbits until the entire stage becomes a shared galaxy of space and they are dancing both alone and together.

The two-step of their own relationship, Tristan and Amalia don't discuss. He leaves the question of what they mean to each other unarticulated as the letters grow in depth and frequency, as reading and writing Amalia become the things Tristan relishes most. She does the same. Whether he is following her lead or she his, Tristan does not know, and fears to discover. Some things must not be said inside the house of words they are building around themselves. Words tell stories on pages, but a thousand other things tell stories in real life, and to overuse words, employ them to describe all that exists between people, that is weak and could be dangerous. Where this suspicion comes from, Tristan is not sure, but he feels it. If people explained themselves the way writers explain characters in books, the world would be far more insufferable than it is already.

It is frustrating, to know Amalia only through letters, and yet delicious. To savor and reexamine not his own words, for a change, because they've been surrendered into the hands of the U.S. postal service, but someone else's. To write not for the world, not for posterity, but for a single human being. To forgo the pretext of plot and character and describe for her the panic that sometimes overtakes him at cocktail parties, when Tristan finds himself telling an old anecdote to a new audience, chances to glance over at Pendergast, who's heard the tale at least seven times, and finds him preparing to feign a hearty chuckle. It keeps him sane, being able to confess that it's all he can do not to drop his highball glass and bolt for the door before he is smothered by the feeling that he and Peter and everyone else in the room are colleagues in a conspiracy of fakeness. Whether Amalia responds directly to the story doesn't even matter. Something in her next letter will rhyme with it, bounce against it, provide a perspective or an analog.

Soon, the second anniversary of their one meeting is only months away. Amalia mentions this fact in a letter—with a peevishness so subtle, it's like a whisper behind the words—and Tristan rubs his eyes and dredges his mind, straining to recall her face. An image starts to come together, and he wonders what has changed: whether Amalia has grown her dark hair down past her slim shoulders or cut it short, as fashion would dictate, and bared a graceful slope of neck. He tries to hold the image, freeze it. A wave of shame slams into him instead, at his failure to get on a goddamn train and go see her.

Something else is always demanding his attention, sure, but who is he kidding? Tristan hasn't visited because he's afraid of rending the elegant fabric of their communication with his careless body. It's all too easy to picture both his own expectations and Amalia's deflating over the course of an evening together, all too awful to imagine how everything could be lost when word gives way to flesh.

Tristan smells the letter in his hand, as he always does. Amalia has never perfumed an envelope, and he can't believe she would, but it's a habit anyway. In his mind, she smells like ink and stationery. People have gotten married in less time than this, and without knowing half as much about each other as he and Amalia do.

Or do they? Funny, that he's so quick to think so. Tristan has not written to her of his romantic entanglements—which are so brief as to be barely worth mentioning, he hastens to note to himself, and which could hardly say less about him. He begs his way out of fix-ups with the daughters of Jewish society types on a regular basis, citing nonexistent deadline pressure and a paucity of time. He's screwed only two girls in the past year. One was a mediocre-looking Upper East Sider who let him know before the appetizers reached the table that she was game; this did not turn out to mean that she was any fun, in bed or out. Things between them tapered off inside of three weeks. Neither one pretended to care.

The second liaison was with a fan, Italian—she came to a reading he gave at the New York Public Library, then took him back to her place, stripped both of them naked, and told him to do anything he wanted. Three exhausting nights later, when Tristan told her that he'd need to spend the following evening alone, tackle a bit of work, she heaved a metal candleholder at her own bedroom mirror, shattered it, ejected him from her apartment. His phone was ringing by the time he got home; she begged him to come back. He declined and she called again and again, at ten-minute intervals, alternately passionate, tearful, and toxic, until he pulled the phone out of the wall. By the end of the week, Tristan had a new phone number and an enhanced appreciation for the sanity of the general population.

If Amalia has suitors, and she must, she keeps it to herself. She's written that she longs for closer, more exciting friends, girls who'd drag her away from her studies and her typewriter and take her on adventures, but she's tight-lipped about her actual social life. The truth of the matter is that Tristan and his pen pal know a great deal about the way the other thinks, and creates, and perhaps feels, but little about how the other lives.

Vassar's spring break draws near, and Tristan suggests that if Amalia can forgive him for his failure to appear in her neck of the woods, perhaps they can meet in the city. But the Farbers are slated to spend the week in Bermuda, so no dice—although the full story might be that a stroll down the street does not constitute sufficient effort on his part: Poughkeepsie he promised and Poughkeepsie she wants it to be. Amalia sends a postcard instead, as well as a mildly bloodied chapter, which, when Tristan slides it from the mailer, sprinkles his bed with fine white sand.

He resolves to haul himself to Vassar before the conclusion of the school year, but the end-of-semester crunch is on before he knows it, and Tristan is stuck in the city. He writes Amalia his three longest letters yet; they go unanswered for three weeks. Such a lag is an eternity. Every day he finds his mailbox empty, it takes Tristan longer to keep his disappointment from metastasizing into anguish.

Not until the day Professor Brodsky returns from his last class, briefcase stuffed with enough exams and term papers to ensure that the coming days of his life will be a slow slog through a field of shit, does he find the letter he's been waiting for waiting for him. And it is locally postmarked. He imagines Amalia writing it on the train back from school, curled over a notebook, the contents of her dormitory room stowed in the bin above her head. Tristan picks up his phone and rings the operator. His hands shake as he waits to be connected.

CHAPTER

FIVE

Her first month in America, Nina is not allowed to take a single picture. "Just watch," says Marcus. "Get your bearings. You'll be working soon enough." A thousand times, her hands dart to her rib cage, wanting to lift a camera that's not there. Nina doesn't complain, although it feels like an insult. Would a new trumpet player be forbidden to touch his horn? Marcus tells her she's being trained to pay attention, that she's got to understand what's going on before she can know how to shoot it. Photography is more than composition, it's communication. Why be so quick to talk before you listen?

Nina does her best to be chastened, and to trust him, but her camera is the only thing she has to justify her presence. Without it, she feels as if she's being winked about—as if the band suspects *apprentice* to be a code word for something else. Marcus doesn't seem overly concerned with correcting such impressions. If anything, he encourages them. He stands proprietarily close to Nina when others are around, speaks in confidential tones when none are necessary, touches her forearm or the small of her back. Never when they are alone. Then, Marcus is all business. Nina bides her time, waiting for things to work themselves out.

Everything's too new: the rules, the country, the people. The variety alone is dizzying—thirty TV channels in every hotel room, vegetables she's eaten only out of cans, tasteless and mushy, laid out in long, fragrant rows in every supermarket. The cats laugh at her when the bus pulls off the highway to stock up on snacks; they dump pretzels, chips, trail mixes on the conveyor belt—itself a marvel, like a miniature version of the moving walkways at the airports, America a land of automated movement for humans and food alike—and Nina brings up the rear, clutching heads of broccoli and bags of miniature carrots to her chest.

Day by day, she's decoding the illogic of English as a spoken language. After a week, she determines that the proper way to respond to "How's it going?" or "How you feeling?" or "What's up?" is not by accounting for your emotional or physical state, or your current activity, but by repeating the inquiry. Americans smile without provocation or sincerity; Nina trains herself not to be freaked out by all the flashing teeth, internalizes the fact that the default demeanor that passes for serious back home comes off as dour in this land of fluorescent produce.

The malaprops are unavoidable, though. A mound of jackets in the corner of an ill-equipped Pittsburgh dressing room prompts her to assert that what they need are some hookers; Nina has to stand and smile patiently for a full five minutes before the laughter dies down enough for Devon to explain the difference between the things you hang your coat on and the word she just said.

Thank God for Devon. Sometimes days pass without the two of them sharing more than a few moments, and Nina has to take her instruction amid the hustle-bustle, in the form of offhand comments, minuscule gestures, a whole lot of eavesdropping. But at least once a week, the two of them stay up late together on the bus, and Nina is privy to one of the trombonist's long, low ruminations on America, his voice as soothing as the hum of the big engine.

"Listen, Pigfoot," he tells her, "the first thing you gotta understand is this: the legacy of black folks in America is so profound that it functions as a metaphor for all humanity." Devon reclines in his plush captain's chair, stares out the window as the highway chugs by. Nina curls into the seat beside him, hugging her knees to her chest. "That's why all kinds of people love this music. It's like the great man said: every American is part black."

Nina has no idea who the great man is, but she believes him great. Of course, all she knows of America are its clubs and restaurants and airports, and every nook and cranny of the custom-fitted thirty-five-foot vehicle in which the octet rides whenever the distance between gigs spans fewer than a thousand miles. "The men who built the music traveled this way," Devon explains, "and the chemistry of those bands owed plenty to the tour bus. Besides which, I hate flying—and not just because Ellington did, the way Sparkplug likes to claim."

When Nina professes to have developed only a vague impression of the country thus far, and blames her diet of hotels and concert halls, Devon wags a finger. "You gotta pay attention, 'Foot. You can find some of a place's character even in a hotel or a concert hall. A club in Portland and a club in New Orleans are like noon and midnight, know what I mean?"

Nina resolves to. Something else to mull over, another concept to try to understand. Occasionally, it all hits her at once: how much she has to learn and how much of it these men were practically born knowing, how hard it is and will remain. And even if she learns it all—if that is even possible—she'll still be an outsider. Not black and not a man and not a musician, her one ability the trick of showing them who they are, reflecting their images back at them. How lonely it is, here on this dark bus, when you are small and female and unable to sleep, surrounded by the sounds and tremors of big, slumbering, indifferent men.

Nina drifts off herself, and awakens when the bus jerks to a halt. She lifts her head, expecting to see a swarm of bellboys, but outside the window is only the grassy shoulder of the highway.

"We break down?" she asks groggily, thumbing the sleep out of her eyes.

"Naw," says Torrence, one of the horn players, as he passes. "Recreational stop." Nina follows him off the bus, into the sharp early-morning air, and finds the octet, plus Marcus and Greg, the bus driver, ambling over a small incline.

On the other side, just barely shielded from the highway, sits a lonely cement basketball court, complete with rusting poles and chain-link nets and faded yellow paint. What it's doing here, in the dead center of nowhere, is anybody's guess, but Devon keeps an eye peeled for such things.

He's on the court already, ball in hand, facing off against the drummer, Rasheed, the tallest and youngest member of the band.

"You know"—Devon feigns left, gets his man to lunge, then crossover-dribbles behind his back—"the only thing sadder than your inside game is your outside game, 'Sheed. You a goddamn waste of height, bruh. I was tall as you, I'd be in the NBA instead of out here bullshitting with you no-music-playin' motherfuckers." He turns his head and sees her. "Uh-oh, look who made it off the bus. They got basketball behind the Iron Curtain, Pigfoot?"

He whips her a no-look pass. Nina catches it.

"Of course. I played in gym class." She steps onto the court, takes a few dribbles, and tosses the ball at the basket—a push shot, from the chest; even Nina can tell her form is terrible. It clangs against the backboard hard enough to shake the pole, and falls into the hoop. The chain net caresses the ball, and it drops into Pipe Man's hand. He fires a two-handed pass back at her, and she shoots again. Another two points for the girl from Prague.

"You gonna break that backboard, Pigfoot. Damn. Shoot like—"

"A girl?" Nina shows her palms to Pipe Man, and he scoop-tosses her the ball.

Devon smirks. "I was gonna say 'photographer.' All right, me and No Game here are captains. Call it in the air, 'Sheed." The coin flashes in the sun, falls into Devon's palm.

"Tails."

"Tails it is."

Rasheed points. "Pipe Man."

Devon appraises the field. "Torrence." The reed-thin reed player jogs to his side.

"Greg."

"Teo."

"Antonio 'Human Highlight Film' Graves."

"Hackmaster General over here," Devon says, pointing to Conrad, the bassist.

At last, only Nina and Marcus stand unchosen. It is Devon's pick.

"Youth or experience?" he muses. "A proven waste of court space, or the chuck-happy Creole rookie?" He deliberates a moment. "Come on, Pigfoot. You can sub in, Plug."

Nina bends to tie her sneakers. When she looks up, Marcus is hunched over her. "They're going to think you're a dyke," he whispers fiercely.

Nina stands and looks him in the eye. "Good."

Marcus shakes his head and stalks back to the bus, not to be heard from again that morning. Six hours later, when the octet pulls into Detroit, he tells Nina she can use her camera.

Looking back, she cannot identify the moments when things changed. Strange, since that is what she does, what she believes: that no matter how fast or slowly life unfurls, the crucial instants can be pinpointed and captured. Perhaps it's a failure of memory, then, or perspective, or perhaps there are exceptions, processes that defy perception. Maybe the only way to document the eighteenth and nineteenth years of Nina's life would be with some kind of time-lapse photography. Set cameras to go off every five days, analyze the stills, and you might be able to see her and Marcus's shoots together evolve from clumsy tutorials—the teacher impatient, the student awkward and indignant, the space always a bit too small—into duets of shared sensibility, the two of them reading each other's minds and bodies and emerging with the images to prove it.

Perhaps with proper data, you could isolate the instant when their comfort with each other began, take a wax pencil and circle the day Nina and Marcus became capable of sitting shoulder-to-shoulder without speaking at all. Or the night they started arguing with the kind of fearless vehemence that only families and lovers usually dare employ—a ferocity born of the certainty that no matter how foul the invective, they will still be bound to each other come daylight.

Could it be that there's simply a quota? That intimacy comes automatically once you've logged five thousand hours with someone, or fifteen thousand miles? Once you've seen someone puke ten times—thus learning that Thai cuisine and Oklahoma City are a bad combination—or clicked off twenty-five thousand exposures? Once you've shared enough darkrooms, met enough deadlines, seen your names printed together in enough brochures and catalogs?

It doesn't matter. That closeness, that love, is natural, what the road, the gig, the life are all about. The real question is how it went from that to what it is now, in the fall of 1990, six weeks shy of her twentieth birthday. Nina has barely eaten in days. The stress is ravaging, finally too much, and so here she is walking to Devon's berth at the back of the bus two hours before dawn and leaning down to wake him with a whisper and a nudge.

"Bruh."

One of Devon's many talents is the ability to be sound asleep one instant, totally alert the next: a by-product of his tendency to keep late nights and use the morning's first phone call as an alarm clock.

His eyes pop open. "Yo."

"I gotta talk to you."

He doesn't say another word, just wraps the blanket around his shoulders like a shawl and follows her up front. It delights Nina to know that she can yank the Prince of Jazz from his bed and he will ask no questions, simply accept that she needs him. Just as he has awakened her countless times, sent Nina on myriad late-night and early-morning errands without so much as a pleasantry by way of coaxing.

Devon seldom even bothers to tell Nina her schedule, just assumes she can walk out the door at any time on half an hour's notice to shoot one of his elementary school visits or accompany him to a TV taping so he has someone to talk to in the car. Taking photographs is only half of what Nina, as the juniormost member of Devon's entourage, is expected to do. She's been a messenger, a secretary, even a liaison between Devon and a few of the more demanding women in his vast collection.

He slides onto a built-in bench, pulls the blanket over his head, and hunches forward, elbows on the table.

"I can't take his shit anymore," Nina whispers. "Look at this." She points to her forehead. "I'm breaking out."

"You call that breaking out? Shoulda seen me at your age." He rubs his eyes with the heels of both hands. "Look, sis. I told you before, you gotta deal with it yourself. Tell him, 'Negro, leave me the fuck alone.' "

"You think I haven't tried? He doesn't listen to me, Devon." She looks over her shoulder at the shadowed bunk where Marcus is presumably sleeping. "He listens to you."

"So make him listen. If you can't get people to listen to you in life, sis, that's a major problem. Cuz it won't be the last time a motherfucker wants some toonyan."

"He doesn't just want some toonyan, bruh." It is one of a hundred synonyms Nina has picked up, and learned to toss around as casually as any one of them. "Pipe Man just wants some toonyan. That I can deal with. Marcus wants to leave his wife for me."

Devon cracks a smile. "I've known Cherokee Slim since I was born, Pigfoot. Trust me. That brother just wants some toonyan."

Fuck you, thinks Nina, surprised at how much the assertion offends her. "Just talk to him."

Devon shakes his head. "If he was popping shit in public, I could step in. But he's not."

The bandleader is right about that much. As soon as Marcus got it in his head that the two of them should be together, the displays of intimacy stopped. Now he waits until they are alone, then tells Nina how beautiful she is, how deeply he admires her talent, how much he loves her, how badly he wants her. What an amazing team they make, and how they could travel the world together, lovers and partners, shooting project after project, book after book, from Mozambique to Japan.

He doesn't do it every day, or even every week. As unsettling as anything is the way Marcus's entreaties rise out of nowhere, return as fervent and flowery as ever just when Nina thinks she's made herself clear and the two of them have fallen back into a shit-talking, fraternal rhythm. She'll find him staring at her, feel her face grow hot, force herself to turn and ask, "What?" because Marcus will go on staring like that until she gives him an opening, and the sooner it begins, the sooner it'll be done.

The next day, as Nina is sitting on her hotel bed, going over contact sheets with a magnifying glass, she senses him looking up from his own paper, feels his eyes set on her. Nina looks like crap; she's wearing a bulky pair of Devon's sweatpants and a billowing bright blue T-shirt from some festival they've played. Smudged glasses, coffee breath, a pen lodged in her hair to hold it in a bun.

"What?" She sounds as irritated as she knows how.

Marcus affects a wounded, romantic murmur. "You *know* what, Nina. I can't do this anymore. It's killing me."

She continues to work, hoping to look impervious and bored. "You're married, Marcus." A beat, and Nina turns her head and looks over her glasses like a schoolmarm. "You've been married longer than I've been alive."

"I'll end it. Give me the word, I'll end it right now." He snatches the phone off the desk and holds it in the air.

"Put it down, Marcus."

"I know you love me."

"Not like that, bruh."

"You're not attracted to me?"

"Of course I am." It has taken months' worth of these confrontations for Nina to admit it, for fear of encouraging him. But lately, her strategy has changed. Now she thinks that if she gives him this much, he will realize that attraction is irrelevant, that it poses no challenge to Nina's will and thus the whole thing is a dead end.

"You're a very handsome man. That's not the point. You're married, we work together, and I'm way, way too young for your old ass. It's not going to happen, okay? Just stop. You don't know what you're doing to me with this shit."

"You know what you're doing to *me*?" he retorts, sulking. Every time, Marcus manages to act freshly heartbroken. His frustration grows darker, uglier by shades, as if he's working up the venom to change tack. Already, there's a hint of menace to him, like some evil, brooding prince thrown over for a virtuous stable boy early in a bad movie.

"I can't do this anymore," he mumbles after a moment.

"You said that already," Nina snaps. "Is it a threat now, or what?"

She's playing with fire; Marcus has more control over her fate than anyone, even Devon. If he won't work with her, Nina's out of a job. She's his assistant, and it's not like Devon's going to fire the venerable Uncle Sparkplug and replace him with a nineteen-year-old Czech girl, even if he thinks she's twenty.

Nina doesn't even have her own darkroom, just keys to Marcus's. That's where she crashes when they have a few weeks off: on a cot amid the gear and files and boxed-up ephemera filling his Brooklyn studio. Which is just as well, since all Nina does in New York anyway, during her alleged free time, is print. She can't even cash a goddamn check; Devon writes Marcus one each month from a discretionary fund, and Marcus gives Nina cash. Or, just as often, buys her what she needs, like a fucking pimp.

"Why would I threaten you?" he replies, offended but not answering. "I'm just saying, Nina, the way I feel, I don't know if I can be around you if you don't feel the same. It's too painful for me."

"So what, Marcus?" she demands, growing frantic. "If I don't sleep with you, I lose my job? If that's what you're trying to say, at least have the balls to say it." She crosses the room and stands by the door, unsure whether she's about to kick him out or leave herself.

"That's not what I'm trying to say at all." He's still sitting in his chair, pencil in hand, looking stricken—shocked and ashamed that she can think such things of him. And then Marcus's face softens, and he regards her with vast, calm sympathy, as if realizing how tenuous and scary her world is. He seems desperate to comfort her, to shield Nina from the ugliness of her own thoughts, and sad that she is so confused as to see treachery where there is nothing but devotion.

"Come here." He says it as if she's seven years old and his only desire in the world is to turn on her bedroom lights, show Nina that the monster is really just a pile of laundry sitting on a chair. "I'd never do that. Listen."

She takes a deep breath and exhales, the panic dissipating. This is not going to be the final showdown Nina's been dreading. But she still isn't going for his I'm-so-misunderstood routine. The only thing Marcus regrets is having his hand forced.

"I've got to go," she says, cold but not as cold as she could be. "I'll see you at the club."

A minute later, she stands before Devon's suite, staring at the DO NOT DISTURB sign dangling from the door handle. It means one of two things: either he's composing or he's fucking. It's noon, and the remains of a room-service breakfast for one sit on a tray against the wall, but Nina will not knock and risk being wrong. The sound of Devon yelling "not now" from the bed, the sight of his flushed face between the door and jamb, even the thought of him in there is too much to bear.

Nina turns and walks back the way she came, reflecting that as long as she is with the band, her chances of meeting anyone herself are nil. Marcus would cock-block in a second, and if he wasn't available, Devon would do the same. Any of the guys would, really; the ones who don't act like older brothers act like older brothers' friends. Protective or proprietary, a secret brotherhood charged with protecting the sacred treasure of Nina's virginity—not that anybody knows she's a virgin, thank God. That would be the living end.

The problem is bigger than road life and the octet. Bigger, even, than Marcus Flanagan and his bullshit. Nina knows nothing about flirting except what she's picked up by watching Devon—and his vocabulary of cool, just-short-of-condescending banter and sly, sexually charged presumption is guaranteed to translate poorly.

Nina has assimilated just as much of Devon's language, his dogma, as anybody in the band: become the latest member of the growing jazz-world population to emerge from the trombonist's tutelage sounding like baby Devons, mixing and matching words like *soulfulness* and *nobility*, *greatness* and *sophistication* and *conception*, mouthing opinions they haven't studied hard enough to comprehend fully, much less disseminate.

For Nina, though, such mimicry lends a much-needed authority. She's built a persona that discourages advances and commands respect, but in so doing, she's desexed herself. You'd have to spend the kind of time with her that Marcus does to realize just how beautiful Nina is—see past the insipid, unflattering clothing and the broad, mannish body language she's developed as a way of taking up sufficient space among the kind of dudes who eat until the food is gone and spread their legs wide on crowded subway cars.

With Devon not to be disturbed and Marcus probably still waiting in her room, Nina has nowhere to go. She decides to write her mother. It's been six months since Nina last sent a letter, and her country has changed completely. She watched it happen like a foreigner, spent the last two weeks of November perched before television sets in a string of hotels, watching the Velvet Revolution the way the octet watches the final minutes of a football game. The total transformation of Czechoslovakia unfolded in a stupefying flurry. November 16: the student protests; November 17: the riot on Národní Street; November 18: the student strike; November 19: Havel, the Civic Forum. By year's end, Marxism had been stricken from the Constitution. The People's Militia had been disarmed, its every action since 1948 declared illegal.

The files of the secret police smoldered; the barbed wire that had once lined the Austrian border was a jumble of scrap metal. Censorship was finished. Now, the president's a playwright.

Nina's exhilaration has been cut by an awareness of just how much maneuvering, how many thousands of secret meetings, must have laid the groundwork for this bloodless coup—all of it unbeknownst to her for the entire seventeen years she plodded through the Socialist Homeland. The knowledge multiplies the thousands of miles separating her from Prague. She's not a part of that, either. She wishes she could have photographed it, but it wouldn't have been worth waiting for, even if Nina had known what was coming. She wouldn't swap her liberation for Czechoslovakia's, this freedom for that one.

Letters from Rayna pour into Devon's office, where his secretaries add them to the bulky packages awaiting the band at the front desk of every new hotel. Her neat script fills pages and pages of the rough gray paper Nina grew up writing on—who knows, even now some international corporation is probably shipping tons of eleven-by-fourteen blue-ruled American-made legal pads over there, and this low-quality stuff will be forgotten.

What seems to excite Rayna most is not the parliamentary elections or the nascent availability of books long suppressed, not the possibility of visiting her daughter or the fact that Nina can now return to the city of her birth without risking imprisonment. Instead, to Nina's consternation, the thing her mother goes on and on about is the new religious freedom. *I can be as Jewish as I want*, she writes ecstatically, in a hand grown slightly bigger, swollen with elation. President Havel's trip to Israel, accompanied by a planeload of Czech Jews, is recounted in great detail. Rayna describes planned museums celebrating the life of Kafka and commemorating the Jews killed at Theresienstadt as if she herself is slated to curate. Jewish study groups are forming, and Rayna plans to join one. *Not because I intend to become observant*, she writes, as if anticipating the face Nina will make. *Because I can.*

Nina grabs a pad of stationery off a table in the lobby, retreats to a corner of the empty hotel restaurant, and orders a fresh-squeezed orange juice and a croissant, paying with Marcus's name and room number. *Dear Mom*, she scrawls, then finds herself staring into space, confronted with the same problem that has aborted every attempt at writing back. It is ludicrous, shameful, but a part of Nina resents the revolution for scouring away her past, rendering her trials irrelevant. The ogre that stole away her father, poisoned her mother, locked Nina away in a dark tower, scattered her family like bread crumbs: the motherfucker's body lies dust-covered in the town square, brought down by a band of villagers wielding torches. The dead student who started the upheaval isn't even dead—in fact, he's rumored to be a KGB agent. This is what they cowered before, hid from, whispered about?

Nina pushes the pad away. It's not her mother she wants to talk to anyway. It's her dad. Miklos is the first man she ever knew, and now that she's surrounded by men—smothering beneath them, it seems sometimes, like a fumbled football at the bottom of a pileup—Nina sees her father more clearly. She remembers a gentleness she hasn't felt since, and to think of it now, at a time like this, is to invite tears.

Marcus almost understands. His whole wounded-loverman seduction routine is intended to seem gentle. But Marcus's slow-and-careful is not the slow-and-careful of somebody picking up a wounded baby bird. It's the slow-and-careful of a hunter stalking prey. He wears it like a tactic, a tuxedo he can't wait to shed; his eyes say that the caveman club would be far easier. Perhaps the only man in the world who can be gentle to a girl is that girl's father. Nina's always known what she needed. And even though he's gone, she cannot imagine Miklos any other way, were she to present her bedraggled self on his doorstep. Provided he has one.

Nina's gnawed the cheap Bic pen to bits. It's full of drool. Fuck this. She drops it on the pad, disgusted, tucks her head to her chest, and advances on the door to her room. Throws it open, hard. It hits the rubber doorstop and shudders.

Sure enough, Marcus is sitting right where he was, as if the whole exchange has left him too distraught to move. Except that the TV clicker is in his hand, so really he's been watching the Lakers play the Suns.

"Please get out," Nina says flatly, and to her surprise, Marcus stands and begins gathering his things. She seats herself on the bed, back to him, takes the phone from the nightstand, and holds it in her lap. It's old and clunky, as heavy as a newborn baby. The door shuts behind

Marcus; Nina's kingdom is reclaimed. She is Penelope and Odysseus rolled into one.

The operator picks up on the second ring. "What city and state," he asks.

"San Francisco, California."

"What name?"

"Hricek. Miklos Hricek."

"Can you spell the last name, please?"

"Sure. H-R-I-C-E-K."

There is no such listing. The operator offers her a Vassili Hricek on Jersey Street and a Hricek Hardware in someplace called Castro Valley. Nina thanks him, hangs up, redials.

"What city and state, please?"

"Los Angeles, California."

There are two Hriceks in greater Los Angeles, both female.

There are no Hriceks at all in San Diego.

The trail's gone cold. She could dial 411 and browse phone books forever. The clicker woos her from across the room, where Marcus set it down. Why not slide beneath the fresh, clean hotel sheets with it, anesthetize herself with some dumb movie, then pass out? Nina gives in, snatches it, pulls back the covers.

The television is a dim convex mirror; she can see herself reflected there as she points the remote. There's something cold and executionerlike in the gesture, as if pushing the power button will kill the girl inside the frame.

She drops her arm, looks at the phone. Why is everything in her life a machine? It makes Nina feel like an invalid, all this metal and plastic and rubber and glass, all these gleaming, essential, unfathomable devices. Her best friend is a camera, and damned if she knows how it works, or how to fix it if it breaks. Nina picks up the receiver and listens to the dial tone. It's soothing, the sound of possibility—until that hostile off-the-hook beep takes over, a reminder that opportunities must be grabbed up quickly.

A thought strikes her, and Nina presses the redial button.

"The University of California, please."

"Which campus?"

Nina requests the main number, if there is such a thing. She is connected, no surprise, to a machine. "If you would like Admissions, please press one. Financial Services, please press two. . . ." Nina presses eight: Human Resources. She enters the first three letters of her father's name on the telephone keypad, then listens to a litany of men and women whose surnames correspond to 474.

And there he is. Miklos Hricek, nestled fifty-plus names into the interminable list. Nina is so surprised, she fails to catch his phone number, has to call back and listen through the whole sequence again. And then it's over, and she holds a ten-digit map in her quivering hand. Nina memorizes it but does not call.

It gives her strength, just knowing that she could. When the parabola curve of Marcus's ardor begins to crest, as it does every six or eight weeks, Nina recites Miklos's phone number to herself, a reminder that she has options. She can leave anytime—her father is a professor of philosophy at the University of California. She can see him now more clearly than ever, fat and magisterial behind a thick oak desk in a dark, messy office full of books. A pronounced accent to his sonorous English, a beard gone mostly gray. A faint sadness cloaks him; he seems stooped beneath some invisible weight. Students and colleagues ponder it, but they aren't close enough to ask. Miklos keeps to himself now, doesn't preside over dinner parties anymore, is well liked but thought aloof. It is chalked up to his homeland, his intellect. At most, one or two close friends know the truth. A photo of his wife and daughter stands amid the clutter on the desk, but Miklos has learned how not to look at it. Still, on every walk through campus he peers at the female undergraduates from beneath the brim of his fedora, and wonders what his little girl looks like today.

Now and then, Nina calls the University of California's information number, just to make sure Miklos is still listed. But nothing more. Life on the road improves with time; she turns twenty in New Orleans, and Devon throws her what he thinks is a twenty-first birthday party at his parents' house. His mother, Sondra, cooks for the whole band, bakes Nina a sweet potato pie in lieu of a cake.

There is champagne. Marcus and Devon make lovely, warmhearted toasts. So, too, surprisingly, do Torrence and Pipe Man. The whole band, it seems, is fonder of the young photographer than she knows. Nina gets to hear stories about herself—actual committed-to-memory, fully embroidered tales that take on new and uproarious dimensions in the retelling. She drinks enough to get tipsy, and for the first time feels like a full-fledged member of the band, the family. Devon's mother and father take to her like long-lost grandparents from the moment their son brings her through the door.

"Mom, Dad, this is Nina Hricek. We call her 'Pigfoot.' "

Jenkins, it seems, has run its course. Nina's earned her surname back.

"Found her in Prague, but she's Creole three generations back."

Nina likes that immensely—especially after she learns that Sondra, too, is half Creole. To Devon's delight, she begins deploying the line herself when people ask, which is all the time. Nina's ambiguous features and green eyes and honey skin, her hard-won attitude and the slightly foreign, slightly southern jazz lilt of her voice make an ethnologist of everyone she meets. Soon, it's become a standard riff in both their repertoires.

Halfway between her twentieth birthday and her twenty-first, Marcus backs off. Not entirely, but mostly. It's as if he's decided his window of opportunity has closed. Very astute of him, because after Nina's party, something shifts and settles. She's at home now, finally certain that if she fell backward, she'd be caught. The realization frees her to look up, look around, appraise her life, and all in all it's pretty fucking excellent, and nowhere near as lonely as it once was. She's visited every jazz town in North America at least five or six times now, traveled the circuit enough to have people she looks forward to seeing all over the place.

In St. Louis, Raleigh, and Columbus, Nina feels a huge fondness for the cadres of elderly musicians hunkered down at the back tables of the clubs where the octet plays; they pat her hand with avuncular affection, call Nina "dear" and "sweetheart" and tell her stories about Bean and Papa Joe and Lester Young. In Miami, a rich art collector and his wife invite the band over for sumptuous lunches whenever they pass through; Marcus told Nina the first time to bring her portfolio, and since then the couple has bought six prints from her. In Boston, two senior members of Harvard's African-American Studies Department always make the scene, along with their spouses. Some of Nina's most memorable conversations have been with them, in the lobby of the Charles Hotel, downstairs from Regattabar.

A few of Nina's friends are even hers alone. A young woman in Austin, Texas, an aspiring photographer, looks up to her like a big sister; she'll drive halfway across the gargantuan state just to meet Nina for dinner. When the band is off the road and she is able to escape the darkroom, Nina can take in a movie with Grace, Devon's newest secretary and a casual girlfriend, or simply savor the experience of strolling through a museum alone. She's even gone jogging with Torrence a few times in Prospect Park.

But Nina's acculturation does nothing to remand her father's phone number to the far recesses of her mind. Rather, the more secure she feels, the more soberly she contemplates making the call. No longer would meeting him be freighted with the dread of expectation; Miklos doesn't have to represent the means of escape, because Nina needs no rescue. And the image of him gazing across his desk at a confident, accomplished young artist is far more attractive than the image of Miklos receiving a refugee desperate for asylum. Especially since there is no way of knowing whether he would grant it.

This is the crux of the problem: she has no idea who Miklos Hricek is anymore—or who he ever was. Informant? Victim? Deserter? Betrayer? Betrayed? Until she finds out, there is a part of herself Nina can never know. Still, she's glad she has waited. Come strong or don't come at all, as Devon would say. She's built a life without her father twice, and if Miklos wants back in, he'll have to prove that he deserves it.

His area code, 530, is northern California. The closest the octet will ever be is at Yoshi's in Oakland; they arrive there two days before Nina's twenty-first birthday, for the last week of a monthlong West Coast swing. And so on Nina's final night as an underage drinker, she returns to her hotel room after the show, drops her Styrofoam take-out box of salmon teriyaki on the bed, and lifts the phone, nervous even though there's no way Miklos would be in the office at this hour. She's calling for clues. Something on his answering machine is bound to tell her where to find him.

The phone rings eight times, and then Nina hears a mechanical click, and the sound of empty air, as if whoever recorded the message was bumbling his way through unfamiliar technology. Another moment passes, and then "This is Miklos Hricek at Kroninberg Library. Please leave me a message." A muffled fumbling noise. A beep.

Even at such distance, and with such dispassion, his voice brings her to tears. It bends the line of Nina's life into a circle—posits the uplifting, terrifying notion that the past can be reckoned with instead of merely fled.

She heaves a shuddering sigh and swipes a wrist across her nose. To find herself crying is a worrisome surprise, but maybe she can get it all out now. Nina squeezes her eyes shut, then blinks rapidly, trying to stimulate the ducts. It reminds her of the way she used to shove sadness down her throat those first few years after he left, when she considered it her duty to mourn his absence. A few forced tears used to lead to gallons of real ones. But not anymore. So fuck it.

Nina walks to the bathroom, splashes a handful of cold water on her face, and heads downstairs to find the concierge. She asks the tall, round-faced young man what university houses the Kroninberg Library, and he bends over some obscure book full of maps, flips a few laminated pages, and tells her UC Davis. He says it as if hoping that by answering quickly and correctly he'll advance to a more difficult round of questions. Nina obliges, asking where Davis is and how to get there.

At least an hour and a half to the northeast, he tells her. She'll need a car. Shall he arrange for her to rent one?

Shit. Nina is licenseless; just one of the many ways in which true independence still eludes her. She thanks the concierge, then jogs across the street to Yoshi's.

When she left, Devon was just sitting down to sake and tempura with the club's owner. Nina finds them on folding metal chairs in the dressing room, fluorescent ceiling bulbs splashing brightness against the banana yellow walls. Why every jazz club decorator seems to feel that the starkest, most unflattering lighting imaginable is a backstage necessity on par with a minifridge ranks high on the list of questions Nina would like answered someday, but now is not the time.

Devon looks up when she enters, and raises a tiny ceramic cup in greeting. A pair of chopsticks is scissored in his other hand.

"Hey, girl," he says, chewing. "You want some sake?" The owner rises a few inches off his seat, gives Nina a minute bow, then picks up the thin decanter and pours her a trickle.

"Thanks." Nina curls the cup to her chest. "Sorry to interrupt."

Devon lifts a piece of battered broccoli. "It's cool. What's up?"

"I need tomorrow off, bruh. Me and Sparkplug both."

"We got a master class at Berkeley, Pigfoot. You know that." He pauses, lowers the morsel until it hovers just above his plate. "You and Marcus both?"

"Yeah."

Devon shakes his head. "I need one of you, for sure. Told Berkeley they'd get some images. Flip a coin or something."

"Please, bruh. Have I ever asked you for a day before?"

"No, you haven't, because you know how things work in my band. Why do you and Sparkplug—" Devon stops short. "Tomorrow's your birthday, huh? Damn, sis, almost forgot. Tell you what. We'll celebrate after the gig, all right?"

"Devon, I need the day. For both of us."

He smirks. "Don't tell me you finally decided to give Old Man River some toonyan?"

Nina had hoped to get out of this conversation without telling him what's going on, but he isn't giving her much choice. She's never mentioned her father to any of them, and it feels too late to bring him up now—like an insult to their friendship, that she's kept something so important hidden for so long.

Nina takes a deep breath. "I need Marcus to drive me to UC Davis to see my father."

Devon stares at her for a long time, and Nina steels herself, wondering how succinctly she can fill him in, should he ask.

"Your father."

"He's a professor there."

Devon leans his chopsticks against the lip of the plate, clasps his hands over his folded leg, and resumes staring. Nina waits it out.

"I didn't know that," the trombonist says at last.

"Neither did I."

"You could've asked me. I would have driven you."

"You've got a master class."

"I would've canceled it."

Nina smiles. It's pure Devon, this blend of care and competition.

The bandleader pours himself another drink. "Just be back in time to hit. And bring your daddy. I'd like to meet the man who brought Pigfoot Hricek into the world."

"We'll see." She steps forward, plants a kiss on Devon's cheek, then turns to leave.

"Hey, sis."

Nina halts. "Yeah?"

"You're sure you wanna take Sparkplug? I mean . . . If you can wait, I'll go with you on Friday."

Friday is three days away. And Nina knows from playing college gigs that university weekends begin on Thursday night. She could miss Miklos entirely.

"Thanks, bruh. But I don't think I can."

She walks straight to Marcus's room and lifts her fist to the door, then reconsiders, retreats down the hall to her own room, and calls him instead.

He answers on the first ring. "Flanagan." Nina hears the TV in the background, and pictures him lying on his back in bed, wearing his Bill Cosby old-man pajamas.

"Hey, I need a favor."

"Sure."

"Drive up to Davis with me tomorrow. I already got us out of shooting the Berkeley thing."

"What's in Davis, besides a whole lot of nothing?"

"I'll tell you tomorrow. Meet me at the concierge's desk at nine, okay? He'll get us a car."

"Make it ten."

"Fine, ten. Good night. And thanks."

"What time is it right now?"

Nina glances at the clock on her nightstand, certain that Marcus's room is equipped with an identical one. "Half past twelve."

"In that case, happy birthday."

"I always wondered what your mother said to you that night," says Marcus, running his free hand down the bristles of his beard as he pilots the rented Chevy up the sunbaked freeway at seventy-five miles an hour, with the air conditioner on full blast.

Nina stares into her lap. Marcus steals a glance over the shoulder of his driving arm. "Relax. I guarantee you he's gonna be blown away by what a beautiful, amazing young woman his little girl turned into."

For once, Marcus's flattery is without ambition. "I'm glad you're with me," Nina tells him.

"Honored to be here." He settles demonstratively into his seat and turns his attention to the road, leaving Nina by herself. The strength of their partnership fills the car, and props her up; she finds herself marveling at it instead of thinking about her father. Marcus has positioned himself with great delicacy: distant enough to be unobtrusive, but grim and focused as a bodyguard.

They travel the rest of the way in silence, and arrive at UC Davis just before noon. Marcus parks at a two-hour meter, drops some coins into the slot. The hand leaps halfway up the dial.

He hangs his thumbs from his pockets. "You got any change?"

"No. But an hour might be plenty." Nina squints at him through her shades, then raises the flat of her hand to her brow. The whole climate's different here, seventy miles inland, dry and stagnant and oppressive.

Marcus leans against the driver's door. "Want me to come?"

"I don't know. Maybe I should see him by myself. No—yeah. I do want you to come. I guess." She walks over and links her arm through his, as if it's he who needs encouraging. "Come on. Let's just go."

A campus map directs them to a modern five-story building just off the main quad. Engraved on a low bronze plaque, just left of the entranceway, is THE ALFRED KRONINBERG LIBRARY OF PHILOSOPHY. CORNERSTONE LAID MAY 12, 1951.

"Guess we found it," Nina says fake-breezily. She waits a moment, as if hoping a boulder might drop from the sky and block the door. When none does, she squares her shoulders, adjusts her skirt, and walks into the cool, dark lobby. Marcus follows, a pace behind, and trails Nina to a directory mounted beside the elevator, a black plastic board with movable white letters like an old-fashioned theater's marquee. The department of philosophy is on the top level, above the two-floor library. Nina jabs the elevator button, clasps her hands behind her back, then tires of waiting and rings for the lift again. She glances back at Marcus, half-expecting him to say something about patience, but he is quiet.

Hello, Father. That will be her line, Nina decides as they glide upward. She'll say it from the threshold of his office, and she won't move. He'll have to come toward her, carry his disbelief across the room. Perhaps other students will be waiting in the hall to see him. Maybe another professor, even, will be sitting in Miklos's office, chatting with him, when Nina appears.

The elevator opens. Twenty-five feet to the left, linoleum gives way to carpet and the hallway terminates in a circular suite of faculty offices, set behind dark wooden doors. Twenty-five feet to the right is the glass-walled departmental office. Nina can see a wall of mailboxes, some copy machines, a few secretarial types milling about.

She turns left, and by the time the carpet muffles the clunk of her footsteps, the pounding of her heart is just as loud—so strong, she feels the pulsing in her throat. A name is stenciled on each door. Grey, Wilkerson, Glenz . . . Nina turns away from them and nearly bumps into Marcus.

"What the fuck?" she demands, throwing an arm at the names. "He's not here. There's no Hricek." Hysteria churns in her stomach. "What the fuck?"

Marcus pats the air in front of her. "It's okay. He's probably just on a different floor. Let's ask." He points down the hall. Nina nods, stalks off. Pushes open the door, pastes a smile on her face, and bends over the chest-high cubicle of the first secretary she sees.

"Excuse me."

The woman looks up over a pair of rainbow-framed reading glasses. "Yes?" She sounds about a pack short of a tracheotomy.

"I'm looking for Professor Hricek. Could you tell me where his office is, please?"

The secretary squints at her. "Professor who?"

"Hricek. Miklos Hricek."

The woman interlocks her knob-knuckled talons, rests them on the desk, and leans forward. "Miklos Hricek works in the library, dear. The circulation desk. Third floor."

Nina backs out the door, too stunned to answer. Miklos Hricek *works in the library*?

Marcus is waiting by the elevator. "Well?"

"He's not a professor," she hears herself say in a monotone. "He works in the library."

"Great!" Marcus presses the button. "Which floor?"

Nina whirls toward him, furious. "What do you mean, 'great'? He's supposed to be a professor, not some fucking librarian. He had an office in Prague as big as this whole floor!"

"Who cares what he does? He's your father, and you found him. That's the important thing. Right?"

Nina crosses her arms over her chest.

"Shit, Pigfoot. My daddy mopped floors in a nursing home. You think I'm not proud of him?"

The elevator dings and opens. Nina stays right where she is. "You know how many cats who were professors and architects and doctors back in their home countries come here and end up driving cabs?" The doors begin to close, and Marcus blocks them with his foot. "Come on. Go see your old man."

She shuts her eyes. "Just give me a minute, okay?"

"Sure." Marcus gives the hands-off sign, spins on his heel, walks across the hall to the water fountain. A moment later, Nina hears his footsteps coming closer, and looks up in time to see Marcus thrust a piece of paper at her, its bottom third fringed into tear-off slips.

Philosophy Tutor Available, it reads in large hand-drawn block letters. *Undergrad and graduate levels. All topics. Thirty years teaching experience, published author, Ph.D.* On the slips are Miklos's name and what must be his home phone number.

Nina stares at the flyer for a long time, as if she expects this advertisement to account for nine missing years all by its lonesome. She hits the elevator button, then changes her mind and barrels down the stairs.

Nina busts in like a gunfighter entering a saloon, and scans the room. This library has none of the majesty of the one in which she logged so many hours as a girl. It's got more in common with the one at the prep school in Pasadena where she and Devon spent an afternoon last week, teaching the kids about jazz. Students hunch over blond-wood tables, half of them half-asleep. Backpacks dot the ground like gumdrops. Ancient green-screened computers hum; metal carts of books sit marooned in aisles. A white-haired woman in a ratty cardigan pushes a sliding ladder across a wall, about to reshelve the thick tome in her hand.

For the second time in five minutes, Nina approaches a total stranger and asks the whereabouts of her father. "He's in the break room," the boy behind the main desk tells her, pointing behind him at a closed door labeled STAFF.

"May I?" Nina passes before he can answer, curls her hand around the cool brass knob. She takes a moment to collect herself, turns it a fraction of an inch, and stops. Voices murmur on the other side. One male, one female. And they are speaking Czech. Nina yawns to clear her ears, then listens harder. She makes out a few disjointed words—*almost*, *weekend*, *movie*, *napkin*—and throws open the door.

A man and a woman sit opposite each other at a small table in a bare Formica-countered room that smells of stale coffee, both of them biting deeply into what look like peanut butter and jelly sandwiches on whole-wheat bread. A Ziploc bag containing two more lies between them. They look up, startled.

The man swallows, then dabs at his mouth with a paper towel and turns in his seat. It is Miklos all right. He's thinner than she's ever seen him, about ten pounds up from gaunt. A plaid flannel shirt that might once have stretched snugly over his belly hangs baggy instead. A network of thin wrinkles surrounds his caved-in eyes, like minor streets on a road map, and his hair and beard are a dull gunmetal gray, with not a glint of silver. His bifocals are off a drugstore rack.

"Can I help you?" he inquires. The woman takes another bite.

"Hello, Dad," Nina says in Czech.

He blinks at her, then stands up so fast, his plastic chair falls over backward, clatters against the floor.

"Nina? It's really you? My God!" He laughs the laugh Nina remembers: a big round sound like shouting into an empty barrel, undiminished by the loss of untold pounds.

Before she knows what's happening, Nina finds herself wrapped in a long, airtight embrace, breasts pressed flat against his chest, face buried in the shoulder of his shirt. He smells first of cigarettes, second of sandalwood, and third of old sweat. Slowly, she brings her arms up to his shoulders and hugs back.

"I can't believe it!" He rocks her from side to side, then steps away and clasps Nina's forearms with his hands. The same hands I remember, Nina thinks, looking down at them. She realizes she's seeking out the unchanged in her father, dwelling on what weight and time have not transformed.

He looks her over, then twists at the waist without letting go. "My daughter," he proclaims to the woman, who is standing now, shaking out the pleats of her long skirt and smoothing down her bunned-up hair. "She is beautiful!"

Miklos turns back to Nina and grins, revealing a row of yellowed teeth. She does not return it, fixing him instead with a hard, expectant look she slapped together while his back was turned.

Miklos sees it, and his exuberance drops away. He picks up Nina's hand, holds it in both his own. "Every day I've wondered where you were, how you were doing." He stares at her with wide bloodshot eyes, as if imploring her to search them and confirm his sincerity.

Nina switches to English. "Then why haven't you called, or written?"

Miklos hangs his head, nods, sighs so hard that his shoulders rise to his ears, then slump almost to his rib cage. It's a ridiculously oversized gesture, and yet one that seems to acknowledge its own failure to convey all it seeks to.

"For a long time," he says, shifting to English, too, and his accent is stronger than Nina remembers, far stronger than it should be, "I simply could not. It was too much of a risk. And then, by the time it wasn't . . ."

Miklos looks up at her, his face so slack with shame that for a moment she actually fears for him, worries with an abrupt, intuitive concern that getting through the next few moments may be more than her father can bear. "Then, Nina, I had nothing to say."

He looks around, as if this break room is the physical manifestation of his fate in America. "I had failed. Our plans had come apart, and I had trapped myself here, with nothing." Miklos tries to laugh, but he cannot. "A college kid's job, shelving books. You and your mother were better off without me."

"We just wanted to talk to you. We just wanted to know you were okay."

"I was not okay, I'm afraid. I became very depressed. And in my depression, I began to drink. Only when I met Rayna—" He beckons to her, and the woman steps forward and stands at Miklos's side. "Her name is Rayna, too," he says apologetically.

The woman extends her hand to Nina and says in Czech, "I have heard all about you." Nina takes her hand and shakes, stuporously, barely looking at her, waiting for Miklos to go on.

"Only when I met Rayna did I see what I was doing to myself," he resumes after overseeing the handshake. "She got me in a program. I'm sober three years now." Miklos looks at the floor as he says it. If he's proud, he doesn't want to appear that way.

"How is your mother?" he asks after a moment, with an awkward formality. "She is here with you, perhaps?" Nina watches Miklos's face brighten and then darken as he gives further thought to what he will be in for if she is.

"No. Mom is still in Prague. She'd kill me if she knew I'd come here." She pauses, then decides that he deserves it. "You ruined her life. You know that."

Her father touches his beard, glances skittishly at the new Rayna.

"She is a strong woman." His eyes shuttle from Nina to his sandwich to his shoes, aimless, like a fly alighting on whatever seems to offer harbor. "I'm sure she is all right. Her father—your Deda—he is still alive?"

"He died six years ago. She's not all right. She's fucked-up. How do you even have the balls to say that? How the hell would you know?"

Tears sit in the corners of her father's eyes. He blinks through them. "What I have done is unforgivable. I know that."

"Nothing is unforgivable," Rayna chimes in. "God forgives all."

"Shut up," says Nina. "Who asked you?"

Rayna crosses her arms, retreats into herself.

"I never meant to hurt you," Miklos declares. "None of this is how I meant for things to be."

Nina nods. She wants to be fair. The power she has over him is too much; it's become something she's afraid to wield.

"Please, Nina. I've missed you so much. Tell me about yourself. What you've been doing."

"Since I was twelve?"

Miklos can't seem to figure out how to respond. "Yes," he says, opting for a kind of hungry grandiosity. "Yes. Tell me everything."

"Well, let's see. Mom pretty much went crazy after you left, what with supporting the two of us and worrying about you, and agents trying to swindle her out of the house. I took care of myself, basically. Um . . . started taking pictures for *Lidové Noviny*, met Devon Marbury when I was seventeen and came to New York with him. Been working as his assistant photographer ever since, and traveling with his band. I'm twenty-one now, in case you've lost count."

"Of course." Her father taps his watchless wrist. "Today."

"Right," she says softly.

"Is it a happy birthday, Nina? Are you sorry you found me?"

The question is an arrow shot from Nina's childhood, whizzing through time and finding its mark. She remembers her father's habit of presenting her with moral dilemmas, of randomly requesting emotional self-evaluations. *Would it be right to steal a loaf of bread if you were starving, Nina? Do you feel happy today? Happier or less happy than yesterday? How do you know?* He never made her feel that there was any motive behind the questions, or any judgment of the answers. Nina enjoyed responding because it seemed like grown-up talk, reminded her of the way Miklos was in his classroom. How strange that she'd forgotten all about it until now.

"No, Dad," she hears herself reply. "I'm not sorry."

"You don't hate me, then? Like your mother?"

The weasel. It's a force play, a gambit out of Marcus Flanagan's old bag of tricks. If Miklos is brave and wretched enough to ask, she is supposed to be gallant enough to lay aside the minority share of her feelings and reassure him.

"Yes and no. I don't think you understand what you've done to me."

Rayna steps forward, tries again. "Your father is a good man." She reaches for Miklos's hand and interlocks her fingers with his. "He thinks about you all the time. God has brought you together again, after all these years, so you can both make a fresh start."

"I brought us together," Nina snaps.

"Well then, why did you?" Rayna retorts, and the three of them stand silently for a moment before Miklos speaks.

"Nina," he says, "we have much to discuss, you and I. Far more than we can hope to in the few minutes we have now. Please, let me take you to dinner tonight. To celebrate your birthday. If you will still be in town." He clears his throat. "I am still your father, and I love you very much."

Nina looks at her father and sees a man with nothing left to offer her. He's hollow, he and his excuses both. She feels tears forming, and catches herself before any can rise. "I love you, too. And I'm sorry that I can't have dinner with you. This is the only time I could get away."

"Take my phone number, Nina. You'll call me, and we'll talk."

She pulls the crumpled flyer from her purse. "Already got it."

"Ah. Yes."

"I should go."

They each step forward. Another tight hug. Nina backs out of it. Miklos lets go reluctantly.

She pauses at the door. "I have your camera. I still use it. It still works."

"I hope soon I will have a chance to see your work."

"I'll send you something. Good-bye, Dad."

"Good-bye, Nina."

She nods at Rayna, who nods back.

Marcus is waiting just outside the library. By the time Nina finds him, tears are streaming down her face. She walks into his arms and Marcus holds her, rocks her, strokes her hair with a hand almost the same hue as her own. She doesn't want to let go, and so they make their way back to the car in a kind of mobile hug, with Nina's head tucked just below his chin, her arms wrapping his middle. His smell is dark and safe.

"You must be hungry," Marcus says, and Nina jolts awake. Last she remembers, she was staring out the car window, replaying the meeting in her mind, trying to work her way through it and getting impossibly forestalled in the image of Miklos with his face buried in that idiotic peanut butter and jelly sandwich.

"No. At least I don't think I am. Where are we?"

"Almost home." Meaning the hotel, she thinks. "You eaten anything today, Nina?"

She shakes her head, and for some reason remembers how she used to shake it as a little girl: chin to shoulder, like a model in a shampoo commercial, at a speed that made her hair sweep gently across her cheeks. She undoes her ponytail and tries it now, losing herself in the experiment and then in the forgotten feeling.

She slips out of her shoes and hugs her knees to her chest. The action makes her skirt ride up and bare her thighs, but Nina tells herself she doesn't notice. "I don't wanna eat," she pouts, dropping her forehead to her knees and watching Marcus out of the corner of her eye.

He plays along. "You've got to eat."

Nina speaks into her legs. "I'm not hungry," she says, and a bit more of her childhood returns. How high the stakes were in arguments like this one, when your sole power in the world was that of gatekeeper to your own body. And even that contested.

"We'll see," Marcus tells her with a smile, and they speak no more. Nina tries to think young, wonder-filled thoughts, but nothing comes. Ten minutes later, the car shoulders into the parking lot. Nina stays put, waits for Marcus to come around, open her door, offer his arm. She's not sure anymore what part she's playing, whether this is the act of a child too sleepy to walk unassisted from the car to the front door, or that of a diva awaiting escort from her limousine.

"Now I'm hungry," she tells Marcus as the hotel elevator closes.

"We'll get some room service. Okay?"

Nina nods and clasps her hands in front of her, her arm still linked with his. "Okay," she whispers. And then, louder: "I want mashed potatoes. Lumpy. And lots of gravy."

"We'll get you some."

"And macaroni and cheese."

"Of course."

"But only if they have Trappey's hot sauce." The door opens.

"I'll run out and get some myself if they don't."

"Red Devil would be okay, too. And some wine. Some good wine." Nina slides her key into the lock.

"I hear that."

She flops facedown onto the bed and props a pillow underneath her chin. Marcus orders comfort food for two, and a cabernet the waiter on the other end of the phone claims is the region's best. Nina stares down at the bland tan carpet. The feeling of Marcus trying to cobble together some kind of comforting, philosophical assertion is as palpable as the sensation of blood rushing to her arms.

"You know, we're all just human—"

"Please. Don't."

She rolls onto her back, kicks off her shoes and lets them sail over her head and thud onto the floor.

"Here." Marcus has liberated a six-dollar chocolate bar from the minifridge. "Have an appetizer."

Nina places the square beneath her tongue to melt, extends a palm for more. Marcus breaks off another chunk. By the time the bellboy knocks, he's fed her the whole thing.

They pull two chairs up to the table on wheels, pluck the metal covers from the plates, and pour the wine. Nina drinks hers in two gulps, hardly tasting it. Marcus gives her a refill. There's the slightest hint of remonstration somewhere in the angle of his eyebrows, and so rather than lift the glass again, Nina unrolls her silverware from the cloth napkin and swoops down on the mashed potato mountain with a spoon. The Trappey's bottle is new. Marcus breaks the plastic seal and douses his portion of mac and cheese in the vinegary orange concoction.

The urge to speak with a mouth full of potatoes is too great for Nina to resist. "I feel," she warbles, smacking her chops, "like a little kid." She pauses, realizes this is a lie, and reaches for the wine. "A little kid would never say that, huh?"

Marcus smiles, noncommittal but supportive, the way a therapist might. He shifts his weight, hitches his pants at the knee, and crosses his legs in that mannered, Michael Corleone way he has. A full second beforehand, she could tell he was about to do it. Before Marcus himself, probably. Such precognition is the greatest intimacy Nina knows.

"Fuck feeling like a kid. That's how he's made me feel all these years. I'm over it. I wanna feel like an adult."

She stares at Marcus hard, tipsy, emboldened by her own words, half-jellified by the serial rush and retreat of adrenaline through her system all day. Make love to me, Marcus, she thinks, daring him to read her mind. Her heart is thudding just as hard now as it was this morning when she turned that corner and came face-to-face with what she thought would be her father's office; the same brew of power and fear suffuses her.

But she's learned something today: better to focus on the power. That's what being wanted is. The thought is anathema to the entire construction of her sexual self, and thus it takes on the sheen of revelation. Marcus's desire means that Nina is in charge.

It's just like the music. His love or lust or whatever—who gives a shit which it is right now—is the drumbeat, the foundation of the song. Marcus is locked into his rhythm. Nina is the bass. She can play behind the beat, drag everything down to a standstill, or she can push the tempo. There are thrills to be had here, thrills and cruelties and God knows what, and all she has to do is say fuck fear and take command. What is there to be afraid of anyway? She's sick of running from what everyone else is pursuing, from what being a goddamn independent grown-ass human being is all about.

This is the world to which Nina alone, of everyone she knows, is denied entry. Not jazz, not America, not blackness. Constructs, all of them. What separates Nina is sex, and fantasy—virginity and the stupid, secret, make-believe realm in which her father is a UC professor of philosophy sitting in a plush corner office. As one ends, so must the others. They are embarrassments, not treasures.

"Marcus. I want to get laid. Make love to me."

From the look on his face, you'd think Nina had asked him to donate a kidney. Marcus brings his napkin to his lips. The gesture buys him only a moment, but it is enough time for Nina to begin to loathe herself, and to start to understand what it means to be the pursuer.

"I think maybe you ought to get some rest," he says.

"After." Nina rises; this is not a conversation to hold over dirty plates. She arrays herself before him, takes a deep, courage-summoning breath she hopes is invisible, crosses her arms in front of her, and grasps the bottom of her shirt. In one slow, continuous motion, she pulls it up over her head. The bruise-colored garment slinks to the floor, and Nina is standing in her bra.

"I want to lose my virginity to you." She slips one strap down off her shoulder as she says it, then reaches slowly for the other. She wonders if he's hard, and glances deliberately down at his crotch. Yes.

Nina runs her fingers along the blade of her shoulder—shuddery with nerves, but not so much so that she isn't savoring this moment. It is nothing short of life-affirming to give in to sexiness, to occupy these tropes she's always shied away from, to know that she, Nina Pigfoot Jenkins-Hricek, is the woman in this room, the woman showing herself to this handsome man, watching him watch her. The woman sliding off her bra and feeling the caress of the warm air, charged with lust. The woman approaching him now, bold, unmindful of consequence.

He starts to stand, to meet her, but she straddles his lap before he can, thrusts her breasts into his face. She wants him to kiss them before he kisses her; it will render turning back impossible somehow. He takes one in his mouth, traces a circle around her nipple with his tongue, and Nina sucks in a sharp shock of breath, already learning things about herself, her body's cravings. She cups his face, lifts it to hers, and kisses him as hard as she knows how, wrapping one arm around his neck and reaching to fumble at his belt buckle with the other.

Marcus chases down her hand, traps her fingers with his own, pulls back and looks her in the eyes. "Let's do this right," he whispers. "There's no rush. Right?" Nina nods, flushed. He touches her lightly on the back of the neck, bends forward, shuts his eyes. The kiss is elegant and slow this time, under Marcus's stewardship, barely related to the lip-mashing, tongue-down-the-throat fervor that was Nina's attempt at communicating passion. She resolves to let herself be taught.

Forty minutes later, the lesson has ended, and Nina lies beneath cool, fresh white hotel sheets, pressed tightly to Marcus, head resting on his chest, mind racing. Even without a point of reference, Nina cannot help thinking that he is a wonderful lover: gentle in all the right ways and moments, worshipful and tender and yet burning. She runs her hand over the damp curlicues plaiting Marcus's chest, unable to believe how close she feels to him—her best friend, mentor, and lover—and how unexpectedly . . . *spiritual* an experience can be that's literally the opposite, the quintessence of physicality and instinct and biological imperative. Among the many things she feels right now, most of them warm and languid and expansive—plus a few, such as the fact that Marcus is as married as he's ever been, or the fact that the moment he stopped acting like a suitor and started acting like a father is the moment she chose to make love to him, that are too fraught to venture anywhere near—is a stunning, abject foolishness for not understanding all this years ago. Marcus tried to tell her, show her, lift the two of them to the next level, and she rejected it, and him, time and again. There's more to it, obviously; this analysis might not stand up to sober reasoning, but at the moment it feels very real. It feels as if she's found what she's been looking for.

That night, when the second set begins, Nina slips out of Yoshi's and buys a phone card at the liquor store up the block. She's dressed for work, for a room insulated by the warmth of two hundred bodies, and she has to walk with her arms crossed over her chest to keep from shivering as she scours the empty blocks for a pay phone. The conversation she's about to have will be difficult enough without a backdrop of coitally twisted bedclothes.

Nina punches a long succession of metallic buttons, then checks her watch and adds nine hours. It is 7:30 the next morning in Prague. Her mother will be making breakfast before dashing off to class. Good. Rayna will have work to distract her from thinking about Miklos. As always.

Three rings, and then "Hello?" A man's voice, deep and pleasant. Shit. Half her phone card wasted on a wrong number.

"I'm sorry, I must have misdialed. I'm looking for Rayna Hricek."

"Who may I tell her is calling, please?"

Really, this is fantastic: a man in Rayna's house at 7:30 in the morning, comfortable enough to answer her phone. Every time Nina calls her mother—and she's only marginally better about calling than writing—she winds up delivering a pep talk, telling Rayna to get out there and meet someone. Sometimes, Nina manages to do it jokingly, as when Rayna reports on the legions of young American ex-pats now swarming over the city, opening bagel shops and sports bars and deciding with a communal mind that they will descend upon a particular café and render it uninhabitable by locals, and Nina responds that her mother should snatch up a cute one and school him in the arts of European living. Other times, it is in earnest, Rayna sounding close to tears and Nina trying to balance sympathy with relentlessness, build Rayna's confidence and at the same time take advantage of her mother's pliability to give a direct order: *Next time a man asks you to dinner, Mother, just say yes!*

Nonetheless, hostility is Nina's gut reaction to this voice. "Her daughter. Who is *this*?"

"Nina! It's me, Vasek. Good to hear your voice, child!"

"Vasek?" she says like a half-wit, unable to process the notion that her father's friend, her former boss and booster, is on the other end of the line. "How— What are you doing there? Is everything all right?"

The silence stretches past the two seconds it takes her words to travel five thousand miles, and answers Nina's question. She can see him standing in her mother's bedroom with one hand on his hip, puzzling together a reply, a towel wrapped around his waist and his stout belly falling over it.

"Your mother and I have . . . found each other. Perhaps I'd better give the phone to her. One second. A big hug, Nina."

"Big hug," she hears herself repeat. Then Rayna is on the line.

"Nina! Happy birthday, sweetheart. I would have called, but I didn't know where to reach you. We drank a toast to you last night, Vasek and I."

"You and Vasek, huh? That's . . . that's great, Mom. Quite a surprise."

"Isn't it? I can't believe it myself," Rayna says with an uncharacteristic little giggle that crackles over the line. Nina smiles.

"I did just what you told me to," her mother goes on. "I said yes to the first man who asked me out to dinner." In the background, Nina hears a laugh. "And it was Vasek. I only had to sit in his café every day for a week before it occurred to him.

"I've always thought him very handsome, you know," Rayna says, and Nina realizes she is a tertiary member of this conversation, that Rayna is looking at her lover as she speaks into the phone. "Even when he was aiding and abetting in your delinquency." Behind Rayna's voice, another laugh.

"This must be brand-new. You didn't say anything in your last letter."

"It had barely started when I wrote it. Perhaps a week before. So no, I thought I'd better keep it under my hat. In case he jilted me for some silly young thing. But Nina, I am very happy. He's going to move in."

"That's wonderful, Mom."

"I'm glad you approve. I wasn't sure you would. I don't know why. And how about you? Are you having a happy birthday? Tell Devon I love his new album, by the way. Thank him for sending it."

"Listen, Mom, I have to tell you something. It's about Dad."

"Hold on." Her mother asks Vasek to put on water for coffee, slice some bread and cheese. When Rayna returns to the phone, her voice is muted, dark.

"You've seen him."

"Yes."

"I knew you wouldn't listen to me. So? No, forget it, I don't want to know." A pause. "Is he all right? What in God's name is he doing?"

"He's okay. He's a librarian. Super-skinny. I couldn't really stand to be around him, to be honest. I couldn't stand how sad he is. Nothing has really worked out for him, Mom. But he's . . . okay."

She stops, unsure whether to mention Miklos's girlfriend. Nina is inclined against it, but the portrait of her father's life will be too bleak without her. "He's met someone. A Czech woman. She seems to look after him. He was drinking, and she made him stop."

"I see."

Nina waits, but her mother offers nothing more.

"I'm sorry, Mom."

"It was never fair of me to make you promise. I just wanted to protect you, Nina. And now he's hurt you again."

"Not really. I was glad to see him. It's better than not knowing. And Mom, he didn't inform on us. There's no way."

"Of course he didn't. I know that. Of course."

"Good."

"I realize you didn't have to tell me that you saw him. Thank you."

"You're handling it better than I expected."

"Well, it's been years and years. At some point, we have to move on, right?"

"Sure."

"He's not coming back here, is he? He could, I suppose. There's no more danger. Not *here*, I mean, but to Prague. If he's doing so badly, perhaps he should come home. A *librarian*, you say? He must be miserable. Here, he could at least teach, if he's still able."

"I don't know. I doubt it."

"Not that I ever want to see him again. He's still a bastard, even if he's miserable."

"I'm almost out of time, Mom. I'm calling from work."

"When will you come and visit, Nina? Soon? The museum is opening in May."

"I don't know, Mom. If I can."

"Happy birthday, dear. I'm sending kisses."

"Thanks. I love you. Bye."

"I love you, too. Be safe. Good-bye."

Nina hangs up, recrosses her arms, and walks back toward the club. Well, good, she thinks. We're all moving on.

CHAPTER SIX

Amalia leans over her daughter's crib, slides her arms beneath the sleeping child, and starts to lift her, then changes her mind. Better to let Linda nap until the sounds of typing across the hall abate and the trip is officially under way. She's bound to wake up the moment they start the car, and at this time of day that means uninterrupted caterwauling for the whole three-hour trip from New Haven to Cambridge—especially since Amalia can't breast-feed her and drive at the same time, and Tristan, after six years in Connecticut and eight months as a father, can't yet handle a car or comfort a baby.

The calming regularity of a noontime nap is the only tenet of her mother's child-rearing philosophy to which Amalia has adhered. Linda will be raised by her parents, not a procession of nannies hired because their native tongues correspond to the latest culinary trends. Maternal caprice and passing fancy will not determine the course of her education. Unlike Amalia, she will never awaken and find her entire schedule remade: tennis swapped for horseback riding, German supplanted by French, piano lessons replaced by a pair of long-eared rabbits intended to teach her responsibility.

Tristan's study door clicks open, and Amalia straightens and turns, one shushing finger to her lips to remind him of the obvious. He nods, crosses the hall in four long strides, peers down his nose into the crib with the air of a patrolling watchman confirming that all's well. A moment passes, and Tristan extends a hand—haltingly, as if his daughter is an unknown dog equally likely to sniff and wag or growl and lunge. He strokes the baby's cheek with a finger.

"Kiss her," Amalia whispers, smiling.

Tristan replies with a look that yanks her back ten years, to 1943 and their first months of marriage, when they were still sharing his two-room New York apartment and Tristan was hoarding royalty checks until he felt he had enough money to match her contribution to the purchase of a house, this house: one big enough for both of them to write in. His desk was in the bedroom then, and this is the look Tristan used to turn and give her when she told him, *Honey, come to bed.* It is simultaneously apologetic and indignant—a forlorn plea for her to understand that he cannot comply although he knows he should, cut with resentment toward her for asking and toward himself for being who he is. It is a mute, searching, almost canine look, lengthy enough for Amalia to realize anew that challenges only strengthen her husband's rigidity. It was built on them. He knows it, and he's asking her not to make things worse.

The look dissolves, so fast Amalia wonders if she imagined it this time. Tristan bends forward and kisses his daughter just below the ear. Sometimes he came to bed, too. Even when he didn't, it upset him more than it did Amalia; she'd wind up reassuring him that it was all right, that she understood. For longer than it would have taken them to make love in the first place, sometimes. It's funny now, almost.

"We should go," she whispers. "Can you take the suitcase? It's by the bed."

"You packed for me, too?"

"Of course. Here." She hands over the diaper bag, lifts Linda onto her shoulder. "I'm hoping she'll keep sleeping."

Miraculously, Linda does. Sporadic, introverted gurgles rise from the backseat as they cut across the maple-shaded neighborhood, but in ten minutes' time, the baby is dozing soundly and the car is quiet.

"You had a good morning, didn't you?" Amalia says, reaching into her purse for a cigarette. The whole atmosphere of the house changes when they're both writing and writing well—and particularly when one of them is coming out of a bad spell, or beginning a project. Then, it's practically electric.

Tristan looks up from the jagged sheaves of paper strewn over his lap, tilted against his chest. He gets carsick when he reads, but he reads anyway.

"The classroom scene is no longer kicking my ass. I finally got the voice down. I'm taking it from the teacher's perspective."

"Didn't I suggest that two nights ago at dinner? And you shook your head at me and said, 'No, no, that's impossible'?"

Tristan lays his hand on her thigh. He rubs back and forth, gives her a squeeze, withdraws. "Thank you. I may even be kicking its ass now."

"So much violence going on in that study of yours. It's a wonder it's not louder."

He stares at a smattering of dairy cows, scattered idly over a meadow, with a city kid's interest. "What's violent is these talks. You'll see what I mean. Even Christ was crucified only once."

"To name another controversial Jew. So why do them?"

He shrugs. "They want me to come. They pay me. How can I refuse?"

"Just say no. We don't need the money." Amalia scrutinizes the road, memorizes the next hundred yards, then chances a quick glance at her husband, hoping her declaration has not soured him. Tristan doesn't like to be reminded of his security. "You're funny. You won't take a day off to relax, but you'll miss two to drive to another state and have the same fight you've been having for two years. What do you think will happen if you say no?"

"They'll stop calling."

"I doubt it. But what if they did?"

"I don't know. How would it look if I refused to account for myself?"

"Busy. Above the fray."

"I'd feel like a coward."

"Life is not a battle, sweetheart. Not unless you make it one. It's an adventure."

"Tell that to Darwin."

Amalia lifts herself off the seat for a better angle and flicks her eyes at Linda in the rearview mirror. She's beginning to stir. "You've already passed your genes down. Darwin's done with you. Now stop being such a curmudgeon. You're lecturing at Harvard, Tristan. I've published books, too. Nobody's asked me to lecture at Harvard. Where's the joy?"

"It's just Peter showing off. Probably bucking for tenure already."

"Tristan."

"Hmm?"

"Where's the joy?"

Linda screams.

The lecture hall is cool and dark, like the inside of a cave. Eighty Harvard men and thirty Radcliffe women half-fill the room. "Good turnout for a Tuesday night," Pendergast assures Tristan. The two of them stand onstage, indulging in various preshow conceits: that the audience does not exist, that their own outsized glad-handing, the thrown-back laughing heads and backslapping, are not demonstrative but pseudoprivate, glimpses at the thrilling lives of whatever the hell they are supposed to be.

Tristan's eyes fall to the empty front-row seats, cushioned and burgundy and probably more comfortable than the hard wooden one sitting onstage before a battered table supporting a microphone, a pitcher of water, a glass bearing the school insignia. He's supposed to sit there during Peter's introduction, then cross the stage and give his talk from behind a small and equally shopworn podium. The gig is scheduled to begin now, at 7:00, but Pendergast insists that they hold off. Of the thirty-five undergraduates enrolled in his two seminars, he counts only twenty-three present, and refuses to believe the rest of them are not sprinting heroically through Harvard Yard right now, mortified at the myriad personal crises that have delayed them.

At 7:15, with twenty-five Pendergastians accounted for, Peter kicks things off. Tristan zones out, absents himself in mind and spirit not just from Peter's opening remarks but also from his own twenty-minute reading. He'd planned to debut a section from his book-in-progress, as a means of engaging himself and culling some reactions, seeing if real people—well, Harvard kids—would laugh in the places they're supposed to. Somewhere en route, he chickened out, decided the new stuff wasn't ready and also that as long as he was in for another evening of defending and explaining *Manacles*—his most recent novel, the saga of a Jewish slave ship's voyage to America, published in 1951 to a cacophonous, knee-jerk chorus of antipathy and disbelief—then he might as well give them a piece of it.

He reads the same chapter as always: a passage in which the ship's captain realizes that sharks are following the boat, gorging themselves on the bodies the crew tosses overboard when the slaves-to-be, three hundred Africans shackled leg-to-leg in a hold intended to transport rum and molasses, die of starvation or dysentery. The words travel a well-trod path from page to brain to mouth, the usual memorized half sentences granting Tristan the usual chances to look up from the page, into the crowd. It's all preamble. The moment he closes the book and asks if there are any questions is when the gig begins.

In the foremost occupied row, an arm shoots up. Tristan pretends not to see it. If he's learned anything, it's that the first raised hand is always attached to a troublemaker or a crackpot, somebody eager to monopolize the spotlight with a caustic question or a lengthy rant containing no question at all. That goes double if the interlocutor is sitting in the extreme front or the far back. The arm sways and Tristan bides his time, locking his elbows and leaning on the lectern as if he'd like to push the thing into the ground. Just as his gambit begins to teeter on the brink of farce, another hand breaches the air.

Tristan recovers his eyesight. "Yes?"

A young man stands. In his hand, he holds a sheet of paper rolled into a telescope. He taps it against his thigh, looks to his left and right, then squares his shoulders to the stage.

"Mr. Brodsky, are you now or have you ever been a member of the Communist party?"

The audience titters. The joker bows and takes his seat. Tristan glances over at Pendergast, who's sitting in the wings on a folding metal chair. Peter waves a finger back and forth beneath his chin and mouths the words *Not one of mine*.

Tristan pretends to mull the question over. "Hmm. That's an interesting proposition, Senator. Will there be booze at this party?" He listens closely to the laugh that follows, hoping it is louder than the joker's. It is. Round one, Brodsky. Before the sound dies down, two more hands go up—the front-row kid again, and then a woman farther back, with glasses and dark hair. Tristan lifts his chin toward her. "Yes. In the middle."

This one doesn't stand. Instead, she slouches in her chair, one knee wedged against the back of the seat in front of her, and reads from a small notepad balanced on her thigh. Written questions always annoy Tristan. Too full of flourish, portent. He sips his water, rocks back on his heels.

"Mr. Brodsky, in an essay published in the *Partisan Review,* Lionel Abel contests that modernist culture and radical politics can no longer be presumed central. The critic Harold Rosenberg responds that the historical crisis that spawned modernism is so constant that, and I quote, 'there is no place for art to go but forward.' My question, Mr. Brodsky, is this: what might come after modernist culture and radical politics, given both the subversion Mr. Abel suggests and the impact that the existentialism of Camus and Sartre is beginning to make?"

Tristan clears his throat, feels his face hardening, tries to smile. "I couldn't possibly care less. I'm sorry. I'm sure it's a fascinating question, and it certainly sounds smart, but I can't make heads or tails of it. I like that bit about art moving forward, or whatever you said. And I think *The Stranger* is a fine novel—made me want to run right out and kill myself, which is a real mark of excellence. I can also add that Harry Rosenberg, if you're able to distract him from the topic of modern art, has some marvelous stories about getting drunk with Joe DiMaggio."

He senses a barometric shift, and pauses. There's something unnerving in the tonal quality of the room's silence, its sudden airlessness. Are they disgusted, shocked? Is it pity playing on their faces, his own obsolescence looming in the mirrors of their eyes? Is he giving them a fight, when it was an adventure they came for?

"Where's the joy?" he hears himself ask. "If literature is just a ring for ideologies to box in, why bother? Why not nail broadsheets to walls, or vandalize buildings with slogans? I don't write because I believe in something; I write because I believe in writing. Novels are not illustrations of ideas. At least, mine aren't. They're novels because they can't be any shorter. Does that make sense?"

The dark-haired girl raises her hand again. "I have a follow-up question, Mr. Brodsky."

"Since I so eloquently answered your first."

The briefest flicker of a smile as she bends over her notepad, flips a page. "Irving Howe, reviewing *Manacles* in *The Nation*, wrote that 'it is nearly inconceivable that in the immediate aftermath of the greatest tragedy in Jewish memory, a writer as gifted as Tristan Brodsky could strike a note so utterly wrong, so aggressively out of step with what the morality of these times demands.' "

She looks up, pushing her glasses against the bridge of her nose.

"Right," says Tristan. "I remember."

"Would you care to comment on the review?"

Tristan sighs. "It hurt me deeply. But if Irving Howe—whose parents named him Irving Horenstein, incidentally, and who taught me the breaststroke at the City College pool in 1938, so I could pass the swim test and graduate on time—if Irving finds *Manacles* inconceivable, that's Irving's problem. He wasn't very kind to Ralph Ellison's book, either, so at least I'm in good company."

"How could you do it?" It's the front-row kid—standing, shouting, arms raised to his shoulders. His accent is unmistakable. The Bronx is in the house. Out of the corner of his eye, Tristan sees Pendergast stand up, ready for action.

"What gives you the right, Mr. Brodsky? Do you hate yourself so much? Do you—"

"Stop right there." Tristan gives his interrogator a straight arm, an open palm, feels his own heart rate spike and his adrenal glands kick into action. Finally, some outright antagonism. The borough of his birth delivers.

"Let's stick with that," Tristan says, and the boy drops his hands to his hips. "I'll answer that. The answer is no, I don't hate myself. No more than I did when I wrote my first two novels anyway, the ones the Jewish reviewers fell all over themselves praising. And let me tell you something. Those books were full to the hilt with stereotypes, New York Jews acting just the way America expects.

"Now I've abandoned the clichés, and the Jews have abandoned me. They want to recognize themselves, not face the truth. *Manacles* is not some fantasy I generated out of loathing. Jews were involved in the slave racket just like the rest of Europe—but I'm a pariah for writing about it? Bullshit. Excuse my French. This isn't the time? Says who? My father was the only one of his six brothers to leave Poland. His whole family is gone. My mother's, too—aunts, uncles, cousins, everybody slaughtered. But I'm a traitor when I suggest that Jews are not always the prey? That they, too, have been slave masters and killers?

"Am I wrong? Nobody said I was wrong. Just that I'm self-hating—an adjective that rolls so easily into *Jew* that it seems built to modify it. But how can we understand evil if we can't recognize it in ourselves? Why do the Jews applaud me when I'm exploiting and exposing their weaknesses—when my fiction is nothing more than a crude account of the experiences of a kid from the shtetl—then turn around and stone me when I train an eye on history's greatest cruelty?

"Can the Jews only recognize themselves in caricature? Why are we so comfortable reduced to vaudeville? You know who was filling up those theaters for the first quarter of this century, laughing their asses off at the scheming Jewish miser, the hook-nosed buffoon with the face full of putty and the too-small cap and the absurd Yiddish accent? Who do you think bought the sheet music to 'Yonkle The Cow-Boy Jew' and 'When Mose With His Nose Leads The Band,' and had family sing-alongs around the piano? Jews! Who else? The same people who wrote the jokes and played the parts. Jews laughing at Jews, so they could feel less like Jews! They should thank me—I made them feel like Nazis!"

An hour later, Tristan pulls the car door shut, rolls his neck until it cracks, and palms his forehead. "Fuck."

Amalia starts the engine. "It can't always be like that."

"Yes. Yes it can."

She consults the slip of paper on which Peter's wife, Judy, has drawn a map to the restaurant, then shifts into drive. "Admit it—part of you loves standing up there, battling it out. I get an ulcer just watching, but you, you're like a—"

Amalia glances over, and to her surprise finds her husband's head thrown back, his jaw trembling.

"Honey! What is it?"

Tristan takes a deep breath, and when he exhales, it is slow, controlled. He pinches the bridge of his nose, leans toward her until his head rests awkwardly against her shoulder. "I'm just tired. I mean, what can I say, Amalia? I wasn't at the death camps. I don't even know anyone who died—not personally. I'm sure I'll never write about it. It's as abstract and incomprehensible to me as it is to any American."

"I very much doubt that."

Tristan pulls himself upright. "Well, it's no less abstract and incomprehensible to me than the Middle Passage. They'll never forgive me for that. And you know what? I don't *want* to make sense of it."

They sit quietly for a moment as Amalia pulls out onto Massachusetts Ave.

"I saw you talking to that boy who yelled at you. What did he say?"

Tristan snorts. "Asked me to sign his book."

"He didn't. *Manacles?*"

"God no. *Angel.*"

"And what did you say?"

"I said, 'Sure, kid, who do I make it out to?' And then I wrote, 'Dear Joshua, learn some fucking manners.' "

"You did not."

They make a few quick turns, and then Amalia parks outside a large brick building, the words *Abruzzi Brothers Family Style Italian* stenciled on the window. "I met a fan," she says. "A Radcliffe woman."

"At least I had one."

"No, Tristan, a fan of mine. She said she'd come hoping I'd be there. She was very sweet. Asked if I'd ever considered teaching."

"You'd be great. I've told you that."

"Maybe when Linda starts school I'll look for something." She opens the back door, unstraps the baby.

Tristan takes Amalia's hand as they walk toward the restaurant, up a slate path lined with parched, shriveling geraniums in pots.

"Usually, someone asks me what it's like to be married to another writer," he tells her. "Whether we're competitive, whether we read each other's drafts, whether we talk about anything but writing."

"And what do you say?"

He wraps an arm around her waist. "That I'm a lucky bastard, and my wife is brilliant. And extremely patient."

"And taught you to say 'Where's the joy?' to people."

Tristan smirks. "Yes."

"Even if you don't know what it means, because all you do is work."

"Yes."

She shifts Linda to her other arm and elbows him in the ribs. Tristan plays stoic, attempts a thousand-yard stare but gets only as far as the Abruzzi Brothers' door, five feet away. He holds it open for his wife and child, follows them inside.

The next morning, Tristan and Amalia entrust their daughter to the care of Peter and Judy's baby-sitter, a grandmotherly type whose easy, take-charge manner with Linda makes Amalia feel superfluous and amateur. The two couples clamber aboard the Pendergasts' station wagon and drive to their country club to play golf. Amalia grew up with the game; she taught it to Tristan after the move to Connecticut, overcoming his objections to learning a leisure-class pastime by promising him he'd excel at it—reasoning that anyone who can lay a broom handle to a pink rubber orb whipped at him from forty feet away can surely hit a helpless white ball off a tee.

The day is warm and breezy, and Amalia breathes in the scent of her own sun-warmed skin, admires the rolling green landscape, does what she can to ignore the lingering aftertastes of last night's garlic-drenched shrimp scampi and today's early-morning conversation with her husband. Strips of sunlight started slanting through the blinds of the Pendergasts' chaste little doily-filled guest room at dawn, waking them far in advance of Linda's warbles, the waft of Judy's weak coffee, the off-to-school prattle of Caroline, Marjorie, and Pete Junior. Tristan and Amalia lay in their matching twin beds, whispering across the shared night table, and he rubbed the hangover out of his eyes and asked her if he was a hypocrite for continuing to accept Peter's patronage.

If there is anything her husband hates, it is having his ambitions pitted against his conscience. Amalia told him not to worry, that his opinion of Pendergast's writing was immaterial. Now—as Peter struts across the manicured lawns of his natural habitat, bragging that he is "ruffling the feathers of these blue-blooded Harvard bastards" by championing Negro and Jewish men of letters and proclaiming gleefully that the Boston Brahmins are shitting themselves to find one of their own shouldering open the doors of access—Amalia can see she failed to fully understand the question. By virtue of marrying her, Tristan is as wealthy as Peter, and by his own merits he's already surpassed the older man as a writer. But there are rich Jews and then there are Brahmins, and as Amalia considers the graying, handsome patrician who is her husband's benefactor, she begins to wonder if Peter's goal in fighting for the social upliftment of a Jew like Tristan is to reinforce the differences between them.

By the time the Brodskys and the Pendergasts tee up at the fifth hole, another foursome is already putting on the fourth. Peter and Judy take their swings, and as Tristan is sliding his driver from his bag, the other group pulls even.

Three of them are silver-haired, the fourth younger and leaner, with the glint-eyed look of an ambitious son-in-law. Hanging from each of them, slung across the shoulders like a golf sweater, is an aura of fantastic privilege. Even before she hears their last names, Amalia knows she's face-to-face with Brahmins among Brahmins, men whose forebears leapt off the Pilgrim ships and into the frigid knee-deep Atlantic, charged onto the New World's salt-caked shore and claimed the continent. These are the men who own the companies that publish books, the men who decide whether newspapers will deign to review them and if colleges will hire the kinds of teachers inclined to assign them to their students.

Pendergast makes introductions all around. Amalia listens for a bit of defiance in his pronunciation of the name Brodsky, a bit of pride. She looks for a twinge of surprise, ineptly concealed, darting across the faces of the men who shake Tristan's hand. But men like these are not so obvious. Or perhaps they don't give a shit, don't take such things into consideration any more than the Captains of Industry with whom she spent half her adolescence bantering in her parents' living room.

These men, like those, are impeccably friendly, standing here with their hands pocketed and their spiked shoes gripping the soft manicured earth. They inquire as to Tristan's line of work—not hers, naturally; she's used to that—but in the most perfunctory manner, as if to say, *Yes, yes, of course you must be very good at whatever you do, but what does it matter, really? After all, here we are on a Wednesday morning, golfing!* It's refreshing and familiar, this disregard of professions, makes Amalia simultaneously aware of how seldom work was mentioned in her parents' circles and how ceaselessly she and Tristan and their friends go on about it.

She looks over at her husband. He doesn't get it; he's waiting for a follow-up question that will not come: *What do you write? Anything I might have read?* It's been a long time since he's met people who are not impressed with him, or at least angry.

Soon the chitchat lulls and it is Tristan's turn to drive the ball. He walks three paces to his tee.

"Looks like a real golfer," the silver-haired gent closest to Amalia says. She's just near enough to smell his aftershave. It's subtle and spicy, clean, a perfect scent for a man his age. She wonders who bought it for him, his wife or his daughter. Tristan, in the entire time she's known him, has never worn aftershave, cologne. She resolves to get him some, and just as quickly acknowledges that he would never use it.

"Show us how it's done, old man," the Brahmin calls, and winks at Amalia. She winks back.

Tristan smiles over his shoulder, balances himself, and swings. He misses the ball completely, uprooting a clod of perfect grass and spraying luscious nutrient-rich dirt into the wind. He hauls off again and sends the gleaming, dimpled thing bouncing along the fairway. It comes to rest seventy-something yards away, far short even of Judy's shot.

Tristan flips his club in the air, catches the neck in his fist, and turns to walk back toward them, face red with exasperation. *Get me out of here*, his eyes seem to say. *Get me out of here. I don't belong.*

Amalia knows she must do something, cover for him somehow. Before she can think, her comfort and discomfort have collaborated on a response.

"My husband is usually an excellent driver," she hears herself say. "You gentlemen must intimidate him."

They chuckle. The young one says something about golf being a hell of a frustrating game. Tristan cracks a fake smile, grinds his teeth as he jams the driver back into the bag. Amalia walks over, wraps her arms around his waist, gives a jokey little tug, and looks up into his eyes. He stares down at her with a coldness so cutting and so private that Amalia feels her whole body go numb.

She stumbles through the rest of the morning, looking for an opportunity to apologize. He grants none, speaks to her only as much as necessary to maintain appearances. She tries to catch his eye, but when she finally does, Tristan gives her a look of such rage that she drops her gaze, cowed.

His game rebounds on the next hole, as soon as the Brahmins are out of sight. Amalia's falls apart so completely that she has to invent a stomachache to account for herself. The Pendergasts fuss over her, ask if she'd like some water, some shade, and their concern only makes Amalia feel her husband's anger more acutely. By the time they're back in Peter's car, the ailment is no longer a fabrication. Dread blooms in her like some dark flower as Amalia stuffs their things into the suitcase, strips the sheets from the beds in which they slept, breast-feeds her daughter.

"I'm sorry," she says the second they're alone, tires crunching over the gravel of the Pendergasts' circular drive and quieting as they hit fresh asphalt. "It was a dumb thing to say. I didn't mean to embarrass you."

He says nothing.

"Talk to me, Tristan."

He folds his arms.

"Come on. It's that bad?"

He grunts. Caveman for yes, Amalia supposes.

"Why? At least tell me why."

He purses his lips, and at first she thinks he's figuring out how to explain. But one minute becomes two, five, ten, and Amalia settles into

Tristan's refusal, her own guilt. I have driven him to silence, she thinks. An hour passes. Linda cries, and Amalia pulls off the road and nurses her in the parking lot of a diner.

"I need a cup of coffee," she tells Tristan. He follows her inside, slides into the booth across from her. She sits and sips, hands tight around the warm white cup, and watches her husband consume a wedge of cherry pie in four huge forkfuls.

Amalia speeds for the last eighty miles, ratchets the engine into a frenzy it has never seen: worth the risk if it gets her out of this car ten minutes sooner. Even getting pulled over doesn't sound so bad. At least the cop would talk to her, explain what she'd done wrong.

They make it home by dark, and Tristan walks straight to his office. Amalia bathes the baby, puts her down for the night, and curls up in bed, exhausted. She goes to sleep alone, and stirs at three in the morning, when Tristan slips beneath the covers. He doesn't press his body against hers, doesn't touch her at all, but Amalia takes his presence as a sign that the argument is over. *Argument*. It's the wrong word, but she can't think of the right one. She falls back asleep, and when she wakes up to feed Linda, her husband is gone. She wanders the upstairs in her bathrobe, cradling her daughter to her tit, pushes open the door of the guest room with her bare foot and finds Tristan sprawled out on the unmade bed, swaddled in a quilt her mother gave them.

He avoids her all the next day, and that night, and by Friday, Amalia is a wreck, dull pain behind her eyes, too drained to do what she wants to, which is scream at him, tell him to knock it off and act like an adult. He wouldn't even hear her. Tristan's anger is glacier-solid, and he's trapped inside.

No, that's not right; she's the one trapped. When the telephone rings, she hears him laugh and exclaim into it, talk loud and long. Tristan is typing away as usual up there. He's not dwelling on what happened, incapacitated by the betrayal committed against him. He's punishing her. On Saturday, she calls her baby-sitter, a college girl whose twice-weekly visits guarantee she gets some writing time, and gives her the week off. Amalia can't even think straight, much less work.

The next morning, a wave of revulsion hits her when she gives

Linda her breast, and Amalia has to avert her eyes. It's as if her daughter is sucking the life out of her, here in the featureless blank-walled nursery, the chill gray dawn, and all Amalia wants to do is run—hand her daughter to someone, anyone, drag herself to her feet and sprint out to her car and drive into some ancient, simmering forest where no one will ever find her. Carve her poems into tree trunks with a sharp rock. Buy a mammoth house on four acres of land and invite every female poet and painter and sculptor and dancer around to come and live and thrive.

But she cannot run. Look at her body, at the grotesque proportions to which it has swollen in order to strip her of options. She cups one heavy, hard breast, weighs it in her hand. She is full of food, and who is feeding her?

Amalia yanks the nipple from her daughter's mouth and lays Linda, squirming, across her knees. She bends low over her own breast and forces the stiff, spit-slick nipple between her lips.

Amalia's cheeks go concave and she suckles, terrified that she will look up and see Tristan's backlit silhouette at the threshold, though he has never awakened to keep her company before. The milk is thin, sweet, nauseating. Amalia shuts her eyes, and for a tiny moment, the space of one breath, self-disgust and guilt lift away and she feels a drowsy kind of comfort, as if she is both mother and child. Then Linda wails, and the nipple slips from Amalia's mouth and her own wrongness stares her in the face.

That afternoon, while the baby naps and Tristan is away somewhere, Amalia cloisters herself in her study and her pain finds form, becomes a poem. The sun has set by the time she rips the sheet from the typewriter. It is the best thing she's written in months. She holds the poem in trembling hands, reads it again, and then Amalia opens the deepest drawer of her desk and drops the page inside. It settles at the bottom and she stares down at it, feeling as if she has just zipped a kitten in a duffel bag and thrown it in a lake.

But no—she's shot a lion, a man-eater. The poem maps a terrain too intimate, too ugly. Regardless of what he's done to her, Amalia will not hurt and embarrass her husband by displaying her wounds to the world, even the minuscule, faithful world of her readers. A premonition hits her: this drawer filled with poems, a mass grave. She reaches down to rescue the paper—what good is a poet who is afraid to share her pain?—then stops herself, straightens, closes the drawer.

Two days later, Tristan saunters into the kitchen as Amalia is heating a jar of strained peas for Linda's lunch, the era of solids foods now under way.

He sits down at the table, crosses his legs, and tickles the child beneath her chin until she giggles.

"I've had a call from my brother."

Amalia turns, fearing the worst. Benjamin has cancer; his wife, Dora, has learned she can't bear children; Jacob or Rachael is dead. "Yes?" she gets out, swallowing hard.

"He told me a rather good joke." Tristan launches into it.

Amalia dries her hands on a towel, leans against the stove, and listens. When the punch line comes, she emits peals of laughter, absurd volumes of the stuff, then asks what else Ben said, how Dora's doing. And just like that, they're having a conversation, discussing a trip to Brooklyn to see Ben and Dora, and Amalia is so relieved that she accepts it, this casual resumption of normality. She does not ask Tristan what she's done to deserve his forgiveness, or what he's been thinking about up there in his annexed guest room every night, or point out that not only has he ignored her for a week but he has barely interacted with his daughter, either. She does not tell him that he's dragged her through hell and it needs fixing, real fixing, not a joke about two Jewish beggars in Vatican City.

Now it's too late. Tristan is on his way back upstairs, cupping a handful of mixed nuts for the journey, and she's agreed that they'll hire a sitter, go out to dinner, eat somewhere nice. Perhaps that's his apology? Is this the next step, to convince herself, stretch what she has until it looks like what she needs? Already, Amalia knows she won't rend the peace at dinner, either—insist over her wineglass that they talk the whole thing through, or make him swear never to treat her this way again.

That night in bed, Amalia will lie on her side, Tristan's palm heavy on her thigh and his breath slow in her ear, and wonder, What have I let him get away with? She will squint in the darkness, trying to recognize herself, then give it up, close her eyes, and get her first decent night's sleep in a week.

CHAPTER SEVEN

Check the appropriate box. How easy they make it sound. Nina has been staring at the page for twenty minutes now, hunched over a desk in a hotel in Saratoga, playing sick while the band performs and Marcus shoots alone. It is 1997; Nina is twenty-six and desperate, and college is the most plausible escape she can conceive. She's learned something about herself in the last year: she's not as strong as she once thought. Or, more accurately, she's not as strong as Marcus. If she were, they wouldn't still be sleeping together.

Nina tries to end it as often as Marcus once tried to get it going, and just as weakly. The standard scenario, most recently played out a month ago in Portland, goes like this: the postshow hang in Pipe Man's room breaks up around two in the morning, and Marcus tiptoes down the hall to hers like a smug bandit, probably humming the *Pink Panther* theme song to himself. He knocks, and Nina, already asleep, hauls herself out of bed, cracks the portal, squints at him.

"I don't want to do this anymore," she says, leaning into the door as if afraid he'll try to push his way inside. She ought to have the sentence printed on a goddamn T-shirt.

Marcus sighs, infinitely patient and impatient. "Nina . . ." is all he says. She relents and admits him, as if her name is a password, telling herself that it's better to argue in private. They are still a secret, after all, if only a pretend one.

She shuts the door, already feeling like a hypocrite because she's mouthed her shallow protests so many times before. Occasionally, they've led to her sleeping alone, for a night or two. A whole tour, once.

"I need to move on with my life," she tells him.

Marcus has mastered the craft of pretending to be as emotionally bound to Nina as she is to him, and so he says, "You're all I know, baby."

Marcus is fifty-six and married, but what he means, and what she hears, is *I'm all you know, baby*. Which is correct.

"I don't know what I'd do without you," he goes on, forcing Nina to consider just how terrifying the prospect of navigating the world alone has become. "We know each other so well. . . ."

If she hasn't folded by now, Marcus's sudden hug will do it. She'll feel herself enveloped by a comforting frankincense-tinged masculinity, and her breathing will slow as if she has been drugged. The child-like intensity of Marcus's embrace will be a final illustration of her feelings, a last reminder of her weakness.

Marcus understands the kind of care she craves too well, and he metes it out cunningly. Nina's on a subsistence diet, and even worse, she's used to it. Trained. She knows to slip out of the room when Marcus's wife calls, lest Nina hear something she can't handle, like Marcus telling Carol that he loves her.

Nina's threats have become tactical. She throws tantrums to cue Marcus's five-days-of-sweetness routine, and they pretend they've turned some corner and the sun is shining and everything is real and honest and out in the open. Gradually, it fades, and Nina resumes cataloging her discontents, building up strength, scorning her own pathetic, forlorn, damn-near-unrecognizable self. Her first relationship has not just shredded her identity, it has confirmed her worst fear. Make yourself vulnerable, and you are fucked.

Thus, come September, Nina will retire from road life and reinvent herself as a college student. Applications to Columbia, NYU, Hunter, and the City College of New York are spread before her, and four copies of a recommendation from Devon are already en route to the admissions offices. After enormous wrangling, by Rayna and Devon's homeboy at the State Department, the Czech government has supplied the documents she needs to apply for a student visa; with an admissions letter, she'll finally be able to make herself legal. Her high school grades have been forwarded from Prague, and Nina has made up for the missing year of course work by acing the GED exam after a month of intense study, the octet quizzing her on chemistry formulas and historical dates as the bus carries them from coast to coast.

The page in front of her, though, Nina has put off until now. She presses her fingertips tight to the pen and checks off the box next to the words *African/African-American/Creole*. Her hand darts down the sheet, and she makes another mark, this one indicating her desire to be considered for something Hunter College calls the Howard H. Dawes Scholarship for Black Achievement in Photography.

There, done. And she feels mostly fine about it. After all, Nina has spent the last nine years living on a bus with a bunch of brothers who consider her a sister. Devon Marbury, who should know if anybody does, has peered deep into her genealogy and soul and declared her to be Creole three generations back. She has accepted that identity with pride, and lived up to it. What you are comes down to how you feel, and how others see you, and Nina is African/African-American/Creole on both those counts.

He should have just been RISK. No author photo, no mention of his M.F.A. from NYU on the bio page, no mention of his grandfather in the promo packet. Then the fifty-bucks-a-book prick losers at the trade magazines wouldn't have had shit to say. They'd have assumed that Tris was black and just read the goddamn novel and written about it, instead of spending two-thirds of their little pussy-ass one-paragraph appraisals making snide references to his skin color, his education, the old man's comeback novel, and suggesting that those things made Tris some kind of clubfooted tourist, or starry-eyed anthropologist, or silver-spoon legacy case.

How dare they? What the fuck do they know about hip-hop, or him? Tris grew up with this music, this culture, these ever-diffusing cosmic b-boy energy ripples—hip-hop raised him as much as anything or anybody, so of course he wrote about it. These anonymous bottom-rung critics are the same people who made fun of him for sitting at the black table in high school—soulless dorks who'd shit themselves if they had to outrun 5-0 in a subway layup. Who clowned Tris because it was easier than contemplating their own stare-back-from-the-mirror lameness. They're the suck-ass hacks who graduated from M.F.A. programs five years ago with their own eager manuscripts clenched in their hands and got dissed by every publisher known to mankind, and now they drink their own stomach acid for dinner and rip books apart for spite. How the fuck can you review a novel about graffiti and not sign your goddamn name?

More to the point, how can you review two novels featuring graffiti artists, and like the one written by a septuagenarian better than the one penned by a true-school motherfucker who happens to be his grandson?

Tris's debut, *Contents Under Pressure*, has been in bookstores for three months now, long enough to burn through its paid-for face time on the New Fiction display shelf and then be escorted out of there, like a broke drunk from a pub, and abandoned to the catacombs of the literature section, wedged where no one will ever find it unless they happen to be browsing the *F* section. His grandfather's novel, meanwhile, *Rage Against It All*—a "sweeping, masterful panorama of late-century American malaise," according to the *New York Times Book Review* blurb gracing the front of the later editions, and "long-awaited, electrifying . . . a triumphant return to top form" in the words of the *Washington Post Book World* quote splashed across the back—dropped five months before *Contents*, and it's still sitting, thick and smug, right at the front of any bookstore Tris might fail to avert his eyes from as he walks by.

The old man's lead character is one Billy Vance, aka Rage, a time-bitten aerosolist estranged from his fertility-clinic-doctor ex-wife (as if any graff cat ever married so well) and precocious young son. Rage fritters away the days meandering through midwestern freight yards, painting whimsical, ironic "tributes" to such concepts as Christian fundamentalism and the Death of Jazz. He pines, lengthily, for the vanished New York subway era (for Oh, does it not represent the Lost Innocence of All?) and nurtures a wild dream of organizing the long-scattered graff community to descend on the transit yards en masse and bomb every car in the system, thus effecting a fleeting, glorious final victory.

Parts of the book are undeniably great, and parts reveal—to Tris, at any rate, if not the book reviewers of America—a glancing familiarity with the subject matter that threatens to unravel the whole enterprise at a cellular level. Certainly, the book is sweeping, almost aggressively large, and graffiti is only a part of it—*Rage Against It All* could kill a man if dropped onto his head from a second-story window, whereas Tris's novel would need six or seven stories to do any real damage—but whether it's the great cultural synthesis the critics claim, Tris is not sure. What he does know is that writers of a certain stature tend to get this kind of "brilliant observer" accolade heaped on them when they are ambitious, whether the work merits it or not.

That goes double if, as with Tristan, the tome in question ends a personal drought of more than twenty years. There is talk that the old man might finally win a Pulitzer, and whether *Rage Against It All* is genius or dog shit, he fucking deserves it: the recognition, the sales, the renewed interest in his backlist, all of it. On Tris's better days, he feels like part of his grandfather's comeback: without RISK, there could be no Rage, no Brodsky renaissance. The book is dedicated to him; what more can Tris ask? The old man didn't poach anything, not really, and it's not his fault that nobody gives a shit about *Contents Under Pressure*—not even his fault that his book dropped first, which probably wouldn't have made a difference anyway. He's shouted his grandson out in interviews, including one on National Public Radio that probably sold more copies of *Contents* than anything else.

There are better people to be angry at, like the folks at Frontier Press whose jobs are to make people give a shit about Tris's book, yet do not give a shit themselves. He has been assigned a twenty-two-year-old in-house publicist, salaried at about two-thirds of a living wage; she won't return his calls and cannot seem to operate a map or calendar without great difficulty. He's got a flustered, perpetually swamped young associate editor who returns his calls a week late, full of apologies, and has to appeal to some kind of mysterious, unsympathetic board of superiors for permission to do anything, from promotional postcards on up.

Tris's agent, Marty Hammerman, the guy who should be putting foot to ass on his behalf, is such a complete douchebag that it's actually comical. You'd think, to meet him, that Marty had hired a private acting coach to tutor him in the finer points of sounding, walking, even dressing like the kind of vulgar, all-about-the-money agent that some sour-smelling Marxist writer who disseminates his work by passing out poems on the subway and stapling short stories to telephone poles might conjure up to justify steering clear of The Industry. And as far as putting foot to ass, well, Marty does a lot of business with Frontier, and he's not about to jeopardize his next million-dollar celebrity memoir deal by raising a ruckus on behalf of a client whose advance was only $35,000. "They're doing a decent job for a thirty-five-grand book," is the kind of thing Marty says.

Tris has plenty of people to blame, but only himself to live with. He's carrying around an ugly, free-floating animosity that shoots out of his chest without warning and gloms onto strangers, relatives, friends. A girl he passed on the street last week in Union Square, so unbearably fine and stylish that she had to be a model, enraged him because he could not have her. He finds himself resenting Zone for going back to school to earn his M.B.A.—for knowing where his life is headed, standing on the verge of wealth. He tamps down bitterness toward Tristan on a daily basis, enumerates the reasons it's unfounded until they come to him with the ease of mantras.

This morning, as usual, Tris wakes up later than he'd like to, at 10:00 instead of 8:30, a problem he could rectify by plugging his alarm clock in, but has not. Instead, Tris coordinates his sleep habits with the sexual peccadilloes of Biggie and Pac, his downstairs neighbor's homosexual pit bulls, who never start humping and yelping in the garden apartment's postage stamp–size yard much after 9:30.

On a good day—meaning any day, until five months ago, weekends included—Tris would be dressed and cutting diagonally across the street by nine, past Fort Greene Park (a six-block sprawl of green that Biggie and Pac know nothing about) and toward the corner bodega where he scores a daily coffee so potent, the locals call it liquid crack. Five minutes' idle chatter with his boy Yuri, a gangly, perpetually unshaven Israeli realtor/actor/herb dealer, whose morning cigarette beneath the long awning of Realty on the Green coincides with Tris's caffeine run, and then back at his desk by ten past nine. Turn on the computer, turn off the phone, take a piss, fall blissfully to work. No interruptions, save a few more liquid crack expellations, until his hands start shaking and he breaks for lunch at 2:00 or 3:00.

That was how Tris wrote his first book, half his second. It was going to be a tetralogy, one novel for each of the four elements of hip-hop, all the stories subtly overlapped and eventually to be published together in one exultant, obscenely expensive collector's edition with cover art by some famous graffiti guy, FUTURA maybe.

That's not going to happen now. Novel two has gone untouched since the first review of novel one came out. Those two hundred words flash-melted Tris's jittery anticipation into a molten lump of dread, so heavy that he's barely moved since. How to deal with reviews: just one more thing they never taught him in grad school. What he did learn, though, in two years of workshops—perhaps the only thing, besides which of his classmates were on heroin—is how to sift through a dozen sets of disparate, contradictory opinions and decide what to take to heart, what to ignore.

At first, he'd judged the comment by the person, trusted the professors he liked, the kids whose writing he respected. But good writers weren't always good readers, and vice versa, and a better system soon imposed itself. The criticisms you had to pay attention to were those that made you feel as if you'd been kicked in the gut by a Budweiser Clydesdale. If it hurt, it was true. And when Tris opened the mailer from his agent and read the photocopied *Publishing Preview* review inside, the truth of it reached up and slapped him starry-eyed.

The pain was immediate, but just what had inflicted it proved harder to determine. There was the truth of *this book is not going to conquer the world*, the truth of *no PEN/Hemingway First Novel Award for me*, the truth of *I have just been publicly dismissed, and casually at that.* The truth of *Grandpa will see this*. And then there was the possible truth skulking just outside Tris's peripheral vision: that all of the above was instant, brain-generated spin control, intended to distract him from the review itself, from an opinion he could not discount and still be honest with himself.

That discomfiting suspicion has yet to be fully unpacked. Tris has been busy. He's given decently-to-sparsely attended readings in five East Coast cities and made sure to sign the store's entire stock each time, thus rendering the copies unreturnable. He's watched his

Amazon.com sales rank level off in the mid six figures, meaning there is literally a warehouse full of titles that have outsold his. He's read and reread his on-line reader reviews and waited in vain for somebody to post one besides Zone and his remaining grad-school buddy, Kat. Glowed for a whole day when a third review, complimentary, finally appeared, only to be sick to his stomach when a fourth, long and scathing, borderline vindictive, materialized out of cyberspace like an enemy battleship and neutralized the first three.

He's done a handful of radio phoners from his apartment, over the carnal woofing of the pit bulls. The questions never quite focus on his book: How did Tris get into hip-hop? Was it difficult to write African-American characters? Did he introduce his grandfather to the world of graffiti he writes about so masterfully in *Rage*? A mellifluous-toned black guy from a talk station in Baltimore is the only one who seems to have read past *Contents*' cover flaps and press kit.

The impotent fury of three months ago has dulled into a dreary, wounded stasis. In an effort to tap into the hard vein of comeback-kid resolve he can feel throbbing somewhere deep inside, Tris has decided a few things:

1. His book is not as good as he thought.
2. While it is far from perfect, the critical blows he's taken have mostly been unfair, caustic, and lazy. He's a victim of narrow-minded, complacent racists who think they're liberal, and their bullshit identity politics.
3. This is a war, and it's not over.
4. Writing three more books about hip-hop is not going to make him win—in fact, they may not even be published.

Marty Hammerman, when he punches up the sales figures, tells Tris as much. "It's not a disaster," he says in his dour, nasal voice. Marty's squeezing a stress ball in one pudgy fist and sporting a phone headset with a wraparound microphone, as if he's about to play Madison Square Garden and needs his hands free for the dance routines. This despite the fact that he told his latest almost-pretty blond assistant, as she ushered Tris into his office, to hold all calls. Perhaps he'll wear the thing to his lunch date later on. Marty has never taken Tris to lunch.

"You've sold about five thousand; call it four when the returns come in. Figure the same for the paperback, knock on wood, and . . ." Marty removes an oversized calculator from his desk drawer and taps at the keys. "Well, you're not gonna earn out." He shrugs. "Look, it was never a very commercial book. The reviews coulda been better, but hey, at least you got some. Even a bad review can sell books. Gotta have thick skin about it. Besides, most of them say something positive—even that obnoxious fuckin' *Times* short; there's a sentence we can use for the paperback."

Marty reclines in his ergonomic chair, crosses his little Tyrannosaurus rex arms behind his head. "So whatchu working on?"

"Well—"

"Ya gotta change direction. You know that."

"Okay. You're fired."

"Funny. Maybe that's it. You could do funny. You're a funny guy. But—" Marty points a finger at him—"no more hip-hop. That's dead in the water. Ya got burned, ya learned not to touch the stove. Right?"

"I could kill you right now," Tris says. "I could pull you across this desk and strangle you with the phone cord before anybody stopped me." The beauty of Marty, if any, is that you can say whatever you want to him. He doesn't give a shit.

"But you won't. Look, do something different. Take a risk. You're good with dialogue. Do a crime thing. Do the big epic family novel. You've got the talent for it. I can get you money for that, if there's enough sex."

"How's Scarsdale?"

Marty and his budding family have recently abandoned Carroll Gardens, Brooklyn, in favor of a return to the suburb from whence he and his wife came. It's like evolution in reverse. Tris imagines a prehistoric Marty Hammerman lizard turning around and slithering back into a sludgy ocean.

"You know what I did this weekend? Cleaned my gutters. Took both days. Home ownership's a pain in the freakin' ass, my friend."

"At least your kids will grow up around other WASPs."

The business part of the meeting is over, if it ever started. They will now insult each other for fifteen minutes, maybe talk some baseball. On the way out, Marty claps his client on the back and, unable to resist, tosses off his usual crass, half-assed come-on about Tris's grandfather.

"So how's the old man? He happy over there at Gromley? Thinking of moving at all? You tell him what a stand-up guy your agent is?"

"I tell my grandfather the truth." Tris steps aboard the idling elevator.

"Go do some work," Marty barks back as the doors close, aiming a little thumb-and-finger pistol at him. Tris nods, points one back. The doors close.

"Bang." He blows smoke from the barrel, holsters his gun.

Back home, the answering machine's message light is struggling to be seen through a thick blanket of dust. Speak of the devil: it's Tristan. Tristan never calls.

Unlike most members of his generation, the old man has no problem talking to machines; they allow him to soliloquize in private. "I call to present you with an opportunity of a singular nature," he says. "My old friend Albert needs some assistance this week, down at the Blue Note. I told him you might be available. His wife will call." A pause. "I strongly advise you to accept. Just what the doctor ordered."

Tris waits for more, but that's it. Dead air, then a beep, and then a woman with a strong Japanese accent is speaking.

"Hello, Tristan. This Mariko Van Horn. Grandfather tell me you can work this week. Fantastic! We see you no later than seven-fifteen, okay? Blue Note. Corner Sixth Avenue and Third Street. I see you seven-fifteen. Thank you, Tristan. Good-bye."

Tris sinks onto his bed. Well, there it is. Fait accompli. Seven-fifteen, yes ma'am. He's got no control over anything anyway, so he might as well be useful to somebody.

Just what the doctor ordered, huh? For what ailment? Failure? Lack of talent? Acute internal bleeding, hoof-shaped abdominal bruises?

This taking-inspiration-from-the-raw-black-stuff-of-life bullshit might have been acceptable in 1930-whatever, might have opened up the old man's eyes when he was some blank canvas of a kid, but that time is long gone. Screw Tristan and his Wise Negro Jazzman home remedies; why haven't the media come at *him* with snide insinuations that he's part of some tradition of awestruck voyeurism, savvy exploitation? Just thinking about that shit makes Tris want to rip out somebody's vocal cords and strum them like a banjo.

It is he, though, who's been rendered dumb. Kicking some self-justifying résumé, *I been down since I was eight, hip-hop flows through my fuckin' veins, I paid mad dues,* would only bring the case against him into sharper focus. Tris could have been standing behind the turntables with DJ Kool Herc in the 1520 Sedgwick Avenue community center in 1973, and it wouldn't matter. He'd still have to adorn his opinions with the same stupid disclaimer about how, sure, as a white boy there may be certain things he doesn't understand, can't understand, would never claim to understand. As soon as he says it, they've got him: he's invalidated himself. They get him every time, even in the arguments that play out in his head.

It's barely three o'clock, but there's no point in haunting the two rooms of his apartment, so Tris hoofs it back down Fulton Street and grabs the train. Everyone on board is reading; none of them is reading his book. He imagines what he'll do when it finally happens: sit down opposite the woman (it's a woman) and wait until she glances up, sees him, furrows her brow, flips the book over to check his face against the brooding author photo, flushes with excitement, comes over. He'll pretend it happens all the time. Whenever he rides the subway.

Jesus H. Christ, why is he even thinking this shit? Sometimes Tris wants to punch himself right in the fucking brain. How long is he going to pretend he hasn't failed? More to the point, when is he going to get his act together and do something to change the fact?

By 5:30, the Village is bereft of diversions. He's wandered in and out of record stores and head shops, avoided bookstores, copped a slice of pizza, lingered on the outskirts of the throng watching the basketball game through the chain-link fence around the court at Waverly. Thought too late of seeing a movie, walked by the theater anyway and confirmed that there is nothing he wants to see, just like there's nothing he wants to read, eat, listen to, or buy.

Finally, bored and cold and tired-footed, Tris pushes open the smoked-glass door of the Blue Note and steps into the long, high-ceilinged room. A crew of eight young waitresses in black stretch pants is setting chunky cut-glass candleholders on the dark wood tables. Tris asks one of them for a coffee, then strolls importantly through the room, pretending to be Albert's manager, passes the stage, and heads for the raised tier of tables in the rear. It seems like the best spot to set up shop: discreet but all-seeing, a perfect place to reinvent his career and ogle the staff. He pinpoints a four-top in the back corner, and makes for it.

Nobody's there, but it is clear the table's taken. Photographs and contact sheets are strewn about; a red wax pencil and a blue hardback borrowed from the Hunter College library perch atop the unintentional collage. Tris can't resist a closer look. He bends to peer at a partially obscured black-and-white image of a trombone player standing before a wide bathroom mirror, then slides the print out from the pile and rotates it right side up.

The room's geometry is elevated to perfection. The floor tiles, the gleaming fixtures of the sink, even the way the musician's horn meets his lips—everything comes together with seamless, casual grace, makes Tris wonder if life is always this elegant and he just fails to notice.

"Hey girl, you want another tea?"

"Yeah, I'd love one. Thanks, Stace."

Tris turns, to see a young woman climbing the stairs. He steps back from the table, but it's obvious that he's been poking through her shit; the look on her face says so. Whether she's annoyed or amused is harder to determine.

"Just looking, or do you want to buy something?"

The glint in her eye gives him permission to smile. "Sorry." Tris points at the trombonist. "I really like this one. Where was it taken?"

She's definitely amused now. "Here. You don't recognize the men's room?"

"Oh yeah," Tris says, unwilling to cop to his neophyte status. "No kidding. It's never looked so beautiful." The musician looks semifamiliar, enough so that Tris doesn't want to ask who it is and sound ignorant again.

"Thank you."

He can't be certain, in this light, what color her eyes are. Only that they're incredibly bright.

"You always hang around in men's rooms?"

"Yes."

A waitress appears at the top of the stairs. "One tea and one coffee." She deposits the drinks on a neighboring clutter-free two-top.

The photographer slides onto the couch seat, sours her drink with lemon. Tris takes the chair and sweetens his with two fake sugars. Few situations make him as comfortable as hunching over a table before a coffee. The way he holds the cup between a braced thumb and a finger looped through the handle, the slight wrist flick he employs when he tips it to his mouth, even the motion with which he stirs: these things gratify him. They may be all he does with elegance.

This girl, on the other hand, could not care less for form. She squeezes the lemon slice, drops it in her cup, submerges it with a stab of her long index finger, changes her mind, retrieves it with the spoon, and finally drapes it over the side of the saucer like some small expired fish. It doesn't matter, though. She's fucking beautiful.

They introduce themselves, and then she says, "What do you play?"

"Nothing." Tris switches to an overhand five-fingered grip on his cup and takes a quick sip, a technique he thinks of as *diner-style*. "I'm a novelist, actually."

He used to say *writer*—preferable for its workingman modesty, and also for the fact that the inevitable follow-up question, "What do you write?" allowed him to shed that modesty in equally modest fashion, as if the spectacular truth was being dragged from him. But no more; it's too much of a charade. Although *novelist* rings false, too, these days. More honest would be "I'm a guy who's written one novel."

"So, you're here because . . ."

"I'm helping Albert Van Horn. He's an old friend of my grandfather's."

"And your grandfather's . . ."

"A novelist, too."

"Huh. Literary family."

Tris shrugs. "Something like that."

"I guess it's the same as jazz." She gestures at the empty stage. "Everybody's second generation. Or third."

There's a hint of loneliness in her voice, Tris thinks. "What about you? Third-generation photographer?"

"Nope. First." The vulnerability he thought he heard is gone, if it was ever there. "So what are you doing for Albert?"

"I don't know. Whatever they need."

She nods. "Opening wine bottles and hanging out, probably. Mariko just likes to have someone on hand in case there's an emergency."

"You know them?"

"Only by reputation. But you've probably heard all that."

"Yeah, some." Tris takes a belt of coffee. "You shoot for the club?"

"I wish. A friend of mine is sitting in tonight. I'm trying to get some images of him and Albert."

"Is jazz your main subject?"

"It's what I get paid for." She fiddles with her spoon. Something in the gesture seems petulant—coy, in a girlish guess-what's-wrong kind of way, and so Tris takes a stab.

"It's a pretty male-dominated world, huh? What's that like?"

Her eyes dart up, a flash of green. "The whole world's a pretty male-dominated world, in case you haven't noticed."

He awards her the kind of deferential side nod you might give the person who outbids you at an auction. "Fair enough. I guess I'm just curious whether you ever run into any issues in documenting the culture, being who you are."

Nina stares at him over the lip of her teacup. "Being who I am."

The words, partially muffled by the porcelain, are both inflectionless and charged, and Tris feels compelled to elaborate, to implicate himself. "It's something I deal with all the time, personally. I write about hip-hop, so my race is always an issue. As it should be." Jesus, he thinks, there I go. It's become a damn reflex.

The cup clicks against the saucer, grinds as Nina gives it a quarter turn. "And who am I?" she asks, crossing her arms under her breasts and leaning forward until her elbows touch the table.

"You look like a nice Jewish girl to me." Tris smiles. "As they say."

She straightens so fast, it's as though his words have blown her back against the chair. "Who says?"

"I don't know, Jewish grandmothers, I guess. Although not mine."

"How did you know I'm Jewish?"

Tris thinks of CLOUD 9, and points a finger at a passing waitress. "How do you know she's black?"

"Nobody ever thinks I'm Jewish."

"Really? What do they think you are?"

"Creole. West Indian. Black."

"Get the fuck outta here. What do they say when you tell them?"

"I don't. I wasn't allowed to growing up, in Prague, and now, what's the point? I'm more black than Jewish anyway."

"What, in your soul?"

"Yeah," she says, deadpan. Tris waits a second, expecting her to undercut her answer somehow, but she doesn't.

"And nobody has a problem with that?"

"Who?"

"I don't know. Any of these jazz dudes you work for."

"Why should they? It's all about your conception, bruh. If you got a soulful type of vibe, you can understand the greatness and the sophistication of any tradition."

Tris wonders whether she realizes how dramatically she's just switched up her own vibe in the course of this pocket manifesto. "Maybe so," he says, "but that shit doesn't really fly in hip-hop. If I started talking about 'feeling black,' I'd get slayed. I'm barely allowed to be what I am in the first place."

"Then maybe you need to leave hip-hop alone. Don't get me wrong—I'm not trying to diss it. But name me one hip-hop dude who's dealin' with it like Albert Van Horn is dealin' with it. This is some profound historical shit, right here. This is *it*. And if motherfuckers can't accept that you know your shit when you know your shit because they're too caught up in trivial shit like how you look, then how could they be dealin' with anything profound? Art is supposed to be universal, bruh. We gotta deal with *that*."

Tris can't help but be impressed by the force of her conviction. And it's been a long time since anybody folded him into a *we*, especially a *we* like that. "Maybe I do need to leave hip-hop alone," he says. "Find something no one can deny." Even as he utters the words, Tris wonders whether he means *something no one can deny matters*, or *something no one can deny is mine*.

"Here you are." She nudges his hands, knuckle-to-knuckle. "You doin' it."

Tris looks up from the dregs of his coffee. Nina is waiting for him to meet her eyes, and when he does, their gazes lock. A staring contest. Tris hasn't had one of these since junior high.

"Here I am," he says.

At 7:14 and forty-five seconds, Tris excuses himself, lopes up the stairs, and double-taps the larger dressing room's door, wondering how he can dispense with whatever duties impend and get back to Nina. He's never had fantasies quite like the ones she inspires. Already, after an hour's conversation, he's imagining not a night in bed, but a life with her: the two of them locking together like Voltron robots to form an Artistic Power Couple. Tandem-grappling up the cliff face of success and walking solemnly, hand in hand, deeper and deeper down the mine shaft of creative commitment. Gliding through art openings, literary readings, jazz clubs. Living poetic, living fly. Living Brooklyn. Having each other's backs, viciously and without question. Buying a brownstone, filling it with art, books, music. Strapping huge cartoon-dynamite packs to the notion of race and blowing it sky-high, once and for all—producing work so searingly dope, so unassailably *dealing with it*, that nobody ever asks either one of them another dumb-ass identity question again.

"Open," calls the voice from his answering machine. Tris wonders for a moment whether Mariko is using the word as an adjective or a verb, then turns the knob.

A man who must be Albert is sitting in the only chair, one leg resting on the lap of the tiny woman on the couch across from him. The supple fabric of his suit pants is bunched above his knee. A long white scar runs down the visible length of his calf, stark and rough against the smooth brown of his skin.

"Howdy," he rumbles, punctuating the greeting by raising the drink in his hand. "Tristan number two. Last time I saw you, you were knee-high to a duck." He sets the glass on the floor, lowers his leg, drops both hands to the armrests, and begins to lift himself out of the chair.

"Hornsy, don't. You gotta rest." Mariko steps in front of him, and Albert aborts his effort, sinks back down. "Good to see you, Tristan.

You lifesaver." Mariko's skin is stretched taut over her face and hangs loose at the neck, like a rubber Halloween mask that's been yanked on and off too many times. Her lipstick matches her ankle-length burgundy dress, marks the near-odorless cigarette burning in her hand. "Albert recovering from arterial bypass," she explains, waving an arm at the appendage.

The saxophonist raises his eyebrows at Tris and grimaces. "Hard shit."

Mariko nods, resumes. "They open up whole leg. Doctor tell me, 'Your husband gotta stay in bed for three weeks, Mariko.' I tell him, 'That's okay, we booked at Blue Note in ten days.' He say, 'You crazy! No way he can recover that fast.' I tell him, 'You don't know my husband. He gotta play!' "

Tris grins, glances over at Albert to catch his reaction but finds none. His leg is crossed at the knee and he's kneading the muscle with both hands.

"So, this what I need, young man. You gotta get five waters and five towels and put onstage: one for everybody. And un–cover up the drums. When show start, you gotta stand by me—we cannot sit, Blue Note sold out, everybody wanna see Albert!—and go tell soundman if we need to make a change. I tell you the rest once show start. For now, you can visit with grandfather. I gotta go downstairs and talk to Mike about dinner for me and Albert. And Albert gotta go over set list with band—right, Hornsy?"

"Right," Albert grunts, dropping his leg. This time, Mariko lets him stand. He sets his weight down gingerly, limps to the door, and steps out.

"My grandfather? He's here?"

No sooner does Tris ask than a great happy roar of recognition fills the hall. "Brodsky the bodyguard!" Van Horn bellows. Tris steps into the corridor and, to his delight, finds his grandfather dangling six inches above the ground, locked in the musician's embrace, slapping Albert on the back. Tris looks at Mariko, waiting for the admonishment against overexertion he assumes will be forthcoming. Instead, he finds her gazing tenderly at them.

"I knew you'd bounce right back," says Tristan, regaining his feet.

Mariko slips into the hall, and the old man gives her a double hand squeeze and a peck on each cheek, then turns to his grandson. "I'm telling you—this man is a miracle of nature. Nothing can stop him."

Albert stares at Tristan, eyes grown wide. "The old mutual-appreciation society," he drawls, and then the two of them are laughing, harder and longer than Tris has ever seen his grandfather laugh before. And though the old man's delight at seeing his friend is obvious, equally clear is how hard he's straining to keep up his end of the moment. It's the kind of thing Tris wishes he didn't notice, and he turns away and lets himself remember Nina, sitting downstairs with her camera and her blazing eyes.

Albert departs into the second dressing room, where his musicians are; he opens the door to brotherly salutations, the thrum of an upright bass. Tris watches the band fold him into itself and feels a yen for the kind of creative fellowship writers never experience, then peeks at his grandfather and wonders if the old man is suffering the same pang. Mariko skitters down the stairs, and then the two of them are alone. They commandeer the dressing room, and Tristan takes the chair.

"Slip me a little of the grape, will you?" He indicates a bottle breaching the arctic surface of a bucket atop the minifridge.

"It's not open," Tris reports, lifting it.

"Change that."

"It's champagne." The reverence with which he says it sounds stupid even to him.

"In that case, have it bronzed and mounted."

Tris twists the metal wire and passes the old man a flute. "Will they mind if I have some? While I'm working, I mean?"

"I doubt it. Alcohol doesn't rank as a drug with Mariko." Tris pours himself a glass. They clink and drink.

"Nice suit."

"The very best," Tristan declares, pseudo-indignant. "Got it thanks to my old teacher, Peter Pendergast. I'm sure I've told you about him."

"A little." Pendergast's an enigmatic figure in the Brodsky oral canon; sometimes he's spoken of with derisive affection, sometimes outright contempt. All Tris knows for certain is that the professor kept his grandfather out of the war and helped him get published, and that there was a falling-out: unspecified, conclusive.

"Peter was one of these types with boundless energy. It was his undoing, in the end. Anyway, this exuberance was generally directed toward improving you. He liked to find some fault and then proceed to rectify it. Gave him satisfaction.

"Sometime in the late forties, he took me aside and let me know that he disapproved of my clothes. He told me that they didn't fit, that they lacked style, and that I simply didn't spend enough on them. 'Just once,' he said, 'you should go to a first-rate tailor and see what a real first-class suit is all about.'

"I, of course, paid no attention. After a few months of this private nudging, Pendergast began to rib me in public—to my great annoyance. I told him to cut the crap and take me to his suit man, and the next day, at about six in the morning, Pendergast turns up in his fancy motorcar and transports me to an establishment known to him as the best in Manhattan. The proprietor and head tailor, I'll never forget, was a man who was sort of an oily type but also managed to be very haughty. I disliked him immediately. Pendergast assured me that everyone disliked him immediately. So I leapt up on his box and let him take my measurements.

"The idea, I hasten to explain, was not to cut me a suit from whole cloth. That would have produced a cost equivalent to the gross national product of one of these small countries, say Bolivia. The idea was to take a suit off the rack and alter it. Which was not cheap either. So away we went, and three days later I returned, and the oily fellow gave me my suit."

Tristan pauses.

"And?"

"It did not fit me. But really, I didn't fit the suit. I'm of the lumpen proletariat. That's it for me. Can't blame the suit. I shoved it in the closet, and that was that. And then last fall I was poking around for something presentable to wear to your cousin Steven's wedding, and there it was. And the goddamn thing fit fine. What do you make of that?"

"Dunno. I'd have to see your tax return." Tris balances the glass atop his palm. "It's nice to see you and Albert together. You've known him forever, huh?"

"He started as a drummer. I used to haul around his trap kit when I was younger than you are now. We've never seen very much of each other, but when we do, it means something."

"So what is it I'm supposed to learn from him, exactly?"

"Whatever you can."

"What's he, like, your muse?" Tris says it just sharply enough to register, but not so sharply that he couldn't play innocent if he had to.

"Don't be a putz. You'll never get anything done if you believe in muses."

Tris decides he'd rather confide in the old man than take him half-assedly to task, and he flops onto the couch. "I'm not getting anything done anyway."

"Welcome to the club. What's your excuse?"

"General indifference of the world. I haven't written shit since *Contents* came out."

"That's nothing—what, a few months? Look at me: more than twenty years since my last book. They had me dead and buried." For an instant, the old man looks smug, or victorious, or something else Tris hasn't seen in him before. The look passes, and Tristan adds, "*I* had me dead and buried."

"But you already had a career, Grandpa. You could afford to take your time. Nobody's waiting for my next book, except maybe to slam me again."

Tristan waves off the complaint. "Fuck 'em. Everything moves in cycles. Do you know I just sold the movie rights to *Manacles*? Forty-six years later, people are finally ready for that book. Should have seen what I went through in '51."

"I don't have forty-six years, Grandpa. I gotta come up with something strong, or else apply to law school."

The old man levels a wine-hardened glare at him. "What do you want? A pep talk? How's this: be a lawyer. If that strikes you as a possibility, then by all means quit fucking around with something you're not serious about and do it." Tristan breaks off, shakes his head, and guzzles his champagne.

"Okay. Jesus. It was just a figure of speech. I mean, fuck law school." Tris stares into his glass, watches the bubbles hit the surface and explode.

The old man reaches over, and Tris feels his grandfather's cool, dry hand encircle his wrist. "Listen. I like *Contents*. Your sentences are beautiful. But it's too kind, Tris; there's no *fight* in it. You've got to push yourself if you're going to push anybody else. Whatever you love, you've got to stare it in the face until you find the dark part, the part you hate. And vice versa." There is excitement in his voice, but Tristan's face is grim. "It will take its toll," he adds. "I don't mean to make it sound romantic."

Tris lifts the glass to his mouth, feeling less like a writer than ever. There is something curdled in his grandfather—something stunted in the way writing and only writing can break him and heal him—that Tris is just beginning to understand. Or find the courage to see.

"I'm not sure I want to do it that way," he says, just louder than a whisper.

"You'd better decide."

"I met somebody," Nina says into the phone. She's pacing before the Brooklyn studio's one window, passing in and out of the harsh morning light.

One second of silence. Two. "Hello? You there?"

"Yeah," Marcus grunts, and clears his throat. "Good for you, babe. You like him?"

"Yeah," says Nina, bristling. She planned to do this gently, but if Marcus is going to play it cold and casual, dip into some kind of pimp routine, then she can be a motherfucker, too. "We talked until three in the morning. I think I'm in love."

"I'm happy for you." He sounds like he's reading the cereal box in front of him. "You deserve it."

Marcus can't be letting go so easily. This must be some cocksure can't-nobody-take-you-from-me bullshit.

"You meet him at school? He a college kid?"

"The Blue Note. He's a novelist. Why are you acting so weird?"

"What? How am I supposed to act?"

"Like you give a shit, maybe?"

"Look. You turn down every gig I'm on. You make time to see me maybe once a month. What—"

"And we have sex every time."

"If you like this guy, you should see him. I might be selfish, but I'm not that selfish."

"You're supposed to love me."

"I do love you. That's not gonna change."

Nina sighs, and the phone dissects her breath into static. "I love you, too, Marcus."

"But you can't do this anymore. Right?"

Famous last words. Without even meaning to, he's mocking her.

"Right." And as the first familiar pang of longing hits her, Nina knows that Marcus is going to get into his car and drive across the bridge and appear on her—his—doorstep, and they're going to make love on the thin mattress lying on the floor of the glorified darkroom she's been living in for almost nine years now.

"Hey. It's me." Nina is back on the phone, watching Marcus sweep the bottom of his overcoat aside as he prepares to slip behind the wheel of his 1974 Jaguar. He lifts his head and waves. Nina waves back, with a weak smile he can't see and she can't feel.

"Hey," Tris says brightly, on the other end of the line. "I was just thinking about you."

"Good. Me, too."

"Let's meet. Did you have lunch yet?"

"Listen, I don't want to sound crazy. I know we just met. But you know how I was telling you my apartment situation is kind of fucked-up?"

"Yeah. What's up?"

"Well, I need to clear out of here. Like as soon as possible. It's a long story. My landlord's an asshole, basically."

"Come stay with me," he says immediately.

"Really? Are you sure?"

"Absolutely. Want me to come and help you with your stuff?"

Nina looks around. Everything she has, aside from an armload of framed photos taken by her and by Marcus, fits in the two well-traveled suitcases Devon gave her as a first-year Christmas gift.

"That's okay. I'll call a car. Where are you, exactly?"

"Two oh nine Washington Park, corner of Dekalb. I'm on the parlor floor; it's buzzer number two."

"Okay. See you in a few. I can't thank you enough."

"Please. If I'd thought of it, I would have bribed homeboy to throw you out."

She laughs. "I promise it'll just be for a little while."

"Not if I can help it."

Tris tosses the phone onto the bed, crosses his arms over his chest, and stands in the middle of the room, grinning like an idiot, for a good five minutes. This feels completely right—brazen, crazy, and natural.

He snaps out of his reverie and appraises the shithole he calls home. Some guys spend weeks prepping the crib for their girlfriend's move-in. It's a standard rite of passage for the young bachelor, the kind of moment a beer commercial might immortalize. And here he is, half-assing it in an hour. Then again, Nina's not really his girlfriend, is she? All they've done is kiss. Usually, post–industrial revolution, the normal thing would be to sleep together first, discuss cohabitation second. Oh well. This is . . . passionate. Or maybe, he thinks—and then shakes free of the thought—it's . . . convenient.

Tris sweeps on a regular basis, because it's easy, but his apartment hasn't seen a mop in months. He doesn't have enough belongings for true clutter, but due to his reliance on what his mother calls a "piling system," the entire place looks as if it's in the early stages of being unpacked. At least there's no bad art of which to be embarrassed: no dorm-style posters of Tony Montana, no cheap Dalí prints. The walls are adorned only by a framed dust jacket of *Contents Under Pressure*—framed by Mom and Dad, naturally—and about thirty three-by-five notecards, indexing the various plot points of his now-abandoned second book. These are Scotch taped above his desk in long, uneven rows, and make his workspace look more writerly, to him and anybody who might chance to visit. Other than that, the cards are useless.

He snatches them down, shuffles them into a spiky stack, and shoves it in a drawer. His mop, nestled in the crevice between refrigerator and wall, is crusted with filth. He opens the front door and javelin-flings it straight into the trash can awaiting pickup at the curb, then soaks an old T-shirt in soapy water and slides it across the hardwood floor with his bare foot.

The buzzer sounds as Tris is staring into his lone closet, wondering how to clear some space and feeling increasingly as if he actually is a character in a beer commercial, the thought bubble above his head reading *Duh, girls got a lotta stuff*. He performs a last visual sweep as he jogs to the door: incense is burning, his one set of sheets is just back from the Laundromat, the stacks of books are clustered close enough to his desk to appear in use. Not bad. Besides, from what Nina told him last night, it's not as though she's been living in palatial splendor herself.

He swings open the door and they grin goofily and meet in a warm-chilly, indoors-meets-outdoors kiss right on the threshold. It's their most prolonged contact to date, so comfortable and hungry that Tris contemplates scrapping the no-pressure I'll-sleep-on-the-couch attitude he's decided would be prudent and just carrying Nina straight to bed, leaving her suitcases right there on the top step to be pillaged by the neighborhood's small nocturnal tribe of crack-rock enthusiasts.

That would be nice, in a way: to receive Nina baggage-free, with just the clothes on her back and the song in her heart, or whatever. Or maybe that's a fucked-up thing even to think, and why shouldn't her belongings mingle with his, her hair dryer befriend his bath towel, their CDs nuzzle together on cold Brooklyn nights?

"Come in, come in." He bends at the knees to heft a suitcase in each hand. Nina follows him, carrying her purse and an armful of frames bound up with twine. Tris shoulders the door shut behind her, and Nina slides the bundle onto the countertop that separates the kitchen from the living room and has a look around. What's she thinking? Tris wonders, following her gaze, trying to see the room through her eyes. Ten-foot windows, dirty on the outside and thus uncleanable, ceiling draped with spiderweb chandeliers, a low black leather couch that Tris has always loved but that suddenly seems as if maybe three minor characters from *Shaft* should be sitting on it, dudes in denim suits with black-fist Afro picks wedged in their hair. The blank walls shame him, and so it is with an instantly regretted zeal that he bounds over to Nina's stack of photos—as if the only reason he invited her was to get his hands on some art for the crib.

"Wow, this is great. Can we put these up?" He's looking through the twine at a picture taken from the orchestra pit of Detroit's Symphony Hall: the bowed heads of eight musicians, shot in such a way that the drum set's cymbals appear to hover over them like looming spaceships. The image conveys an odd mixture of humility and majesty. The servants of the music, bowing to it as the fans applaud.

Nina turns, and almost winces. It's a great shot, one of her favorites. One of his. "Sure," she hears herself say, and then wishes she hadn't. Why let Marcus follow her here? Why let Tris hang the work of her lover in his apartment? Already, in some vague way, she feels as if she's deceiving him, and it's the last thing Nina wants to do. But now he's rummaging for a hammer and a nail, and just like that, it's too late.

CHAPTER EIGHT

Amalia stubs out a cigarette and cocks her head at the ceiling. When Tristan can't write, he paces—sweeps across his study like a shark circling a caged diver, searching for an opening, a way to lunge in for the kill. He hunts failure relentlessly, never takes his mind off a problem until it's torn to shreds.

Her husband's ruthlessness, Amalia is on intimate terms with. The determination to solve problems, though, stops at his study door. They have squabbled during breakfast, needlessly, and footfalls are the only sound she's likely to get out of him today.

It began when she asked Tristan, again, if he'd decided which week in July would be best for the short vacation she wants them to take—a little diversion, a week by a lake in New Hampshire with Ben's family so nine-year-old Linda can swim and spend time with her cousins. As compensation for the solitude of only-childhood, Amalia tries to ensure that her daughter sees plenty of them.

She wanted to call Dora, make arrangements, book the cabin. Tristan still hadn't looked at a calendar, and he acted as if the whole matter, which would take thirty seconds of his time, was a hassle of Olympian proportions. She pressed, told him that if he didn't voice a preference, she'd just pick a week herself and he'd have to live with it, and Tristan exploded. Now she's violated the sanctity of his morning, derailed him with bullshit when all he wants, all he asks, is to drink his coffee in peace and get to work—as if she wants anything different, for him or for herself. She dropped it, *Fine, Tristan, fine*, and he stormed off.

The pacing stops, and Amalia squints in concentration, tracking the staircase creaks of her husband's descent until she hears his foot strike the deeper note of the downstairs landing. His steps will fade now, along the foyer's pale green carpeting, lighten in timbre as he reaches the tiled kitchen and heads for the snack cupboard. Its contents have been the same since the Brodskys moved here: tins of mixed nuts to sate Tristan's hunger-break cravings for salt and protein, boxes of instant oatmeal and jars of applesauce he sometimes fixes late at night, and Ashkenazi comfort foods, store-bought and bottled and thus stripped largely of their comfort—matzoh balls bobbing in broth, gefilte fish suspended in heavy translucent slime. Tristan has never so much as learned to boil an egg, and Amalia will be damned if she's going to cook him more than one hot meal a day.

Tristan's footfalls are not dwindling toward the kitchen after all. Amalia hears her doorknob turn halfway, then stop—her husband remembering, belatedly, that she, too, has rules.

His knock is chest-high. "Amalia?"

"Yes? Come in."

The door swings open. Tristan does not step inside.

"Have you got that letter from Herb Kaplan? I'd like to take another look at it."

"I think it's here somewhere." She stands and rifles through a pile of papers at the far corner of her desk. Why Tristan is willing to break his silence for the sake of a month-old piece of correspondence from a Chicago comedy writer they met on vacation in London last year, Amalia does not ask.

"Do you need it right now?" she says instead, the question an attempt to discern whether hostilities have truly ceased or just been momentarily suspended.

"No, no. Don't trouble yourself. It's nothing urgent."

"I'm sure I've got it somewhere." Seized by an eagerness to please, as if locating the letter will safeguard the peace, Amalia knocks over a bookend. Twenty volumes topple off the desk and onto the floor, taking a wooden music box with them. The introductory notes of its song wheeze forth: the first snatch of melody Amalia can remember hearing in her life, something her great-aunt played on Grandmother Elena's drawing room piano. Amalia hummed it for Tristan once, unable to name the tune, and months later he delivered it into her hands.

Her husband's coldness would not cut so deeply if he were not also capable of such fierce attention, of bestowing words and gifts that restore to Amalia things she doesn't even realize she's been missing. This room is full of books he's found her, by twelfth-century Sufi mystics and unknown wild-haired modern Greeks, poets whose troves were never excavated in the course of Amalia's classical education but whose words clang in her soul like church bells.

"Aha." She slides a sheet of paper from a stack of miscellany and holds it aloft.

Her husband takes it, frowns as he scans a few lines, then looks up. "I may have to go to California," he tells her. Before Amalia can respond, Tristan is on his way back up the stairs. He's neglected to close her door.

When he read the missive waiting for him in the mailbox, Tristan's first thought was that he was being bullshitted. The letterhead looks authentic, but only after he has held the typeface side by side with that produced by his various correspondents' machines and failed to find a match does Tristan allow his incredulity to fade, and accept that he is the Jewish Congress of America's 1961 Man of the Year.

It would be no more surprising to open his mail and find that he is *Car and Driver* magazine's top-rated luxury sedan. The Jewish Congress of America? He has never even heard of the bastards, as far as he can recall, but all these organizations are more or less the same, and none of them has reached out to him since *Manacles* except occasionally to request his money, or his time in some capacity that would allow them to alchemize it into cash.

And yet this letter, this invitation to speak at the awards banquet, this medium-size honorarium, has none of the feel of vindication. It is more like being asked to the birthday party of a kid who's bullied you on the playground every day since kindergarten, and so Tristan's thoughts turn to mischief, to revenge. What can he say up there behind that podium to shock them? To prove that he will no more give in to the Jewish community's veneration than its ire?

The notion that it is misdirected to thumb his nose at an organization that holds him in esteem flits through Tristan's mind, but he is able to talk himself past it. If they truly respect him—if this is about more than signing on to the success of his new novel—then they won't find the stunt he is already formulating outrageous in the least. In fact, they'll love it. As they should.

But if he is the Man of the Year only because Arthur Goldberg won in '60, and nobody is a big enough baseballnik to vote for Sandy Koufax, and Samuel Goldwyn hasn't made any decent movies this year, and Tony Curtis hasn't been Bernie Schwartz or Jack Benny Benjamin Kubelsky for a long time, then the Jewish Congress of America will likely crap their britches when Man of the Year Tristan Brodsky shows up with the Albert Van Horn Quartet in tow and reads an excerpt from his prizewinning novel to a raucous jazz accompaniment, Albert full-gale wailing on his tenor saxophone and Murray Higgins behind the drum kit, smashing the fuck out of everything in sight.

The money will cover plane fare and payment for Albert and his band, and the banquet is far enough away that perhaps Albert's wife and manager, Mariko, can even book them an additional gig in Los Angeles that weekend. Tristan cackles and sits down to compose a genteel letter of acceptance, thanking the Congress for this great honor and mentioning only in passing that, if possible, it would be splendid if arrangements could be made for a piano.

Not until he and Albert are sitting together on the flight to California, sipping cocktails rendered tasteless by the clouds of cigarette smoke filling the cabin, does it occur to Tristan that there is a sense in which he is exploiting his friend. That even if Albert, Higgins, Trey, and Devon are in on the joke, it does little to change the fact that Tristan is wielding blackness as a scare tactic, a shock technique, a weapon.

It is not so different from the way some of the Jews in his book wield it. *Blockbusters* tells the story of a small fictional Midwestern city in the throes of a present-day battle over who will live where—a battle that twists and turns and explodes, ultimately, into violence. On both sides, there are Jews: young northern civil rights activists determined to desegregate the white suburbs, one black family at a time, and unscrupulous realtors using the threat of black encroachment and plummeting property values to drive whites from their homes—which they then resell at a profit. Motives and allegiances grow mutable; the radicals and the profiteers prove less ideologically entrenched than they first appear. Double crosses, moral awakenings, and secret deals abound. Black community leaders and local white politicians scramble to hold on to their power bases; outside agitators find themselves dangerously entrenched in a struggle they begin to fear they cannot understand. Then the Ku Klux Klan shows up.

It is a fat, frenzied, polemical novel, broad-ranging and morally messy, and the critics have lauded or lambasted it on just these grounds. It has sold shitloads of copies—largely to young people and blacks, judging from the fan mail—and for the first time ever, Tristan's literary agent is fielding calls from Hollywood types interested in the film rights. The Jewish media has refrained from hyperventilating in disgust this time around, but neither have they opened their arms to welcome back the prodigal son. They still don't much like Tristan's Jews; they still don't much like Tristan.

This weekend is not likely to change that, he reflects as the captain dims the cabin lights. At first, Tristan tried to tell himself that his performance was intended to expand the minds of the Jewish Congress of America, those bandwagon-hopping sycophants, but now he's made peace with the truth. It is about conveying the message *I am not like you*. I am not like you, and here are the sound track and the visuals to prove it. Here I stand with those whom, let's be honest, many of you are only marginally ahead of the national curve in learning not to fear and despise despite all that has been done to you, a couple of dead freedom-riding kikes notwithstanding. Those whose holocaust, if one wishes to compare such things, and I do not, outhorribles even our own. Those who are more Other than we will ever be again, O universally shunned and crushed and banished Chosen People, O Sons of Abraham, forever persecuted for your differences, your clannishness, who have survived, and made it here, and by sweat and wit risen to become America's brain trust, Hollywood's finest, who continued to claw your way forever upward even as your families overseas were herded and destroyed like cattle. And I declare that I, too, am different. A tribe unto myself. And if I am to someday die for my differences, I pray that they will be my own goddamn differences, and not those I have been born into and tried to explore the richness and complexity of, only to have my efforts castigated by other members of my race. So thank you for the honor and the moolah, Jewish Congress of America, and if you're not all utterly crammed full of hypocrisy and horseshit, then maybe you'll enjoy the show. . . .

Albert leans over, into Tristan's thoughts. "I guess you're my new bodyguard," he says in the low, conspiratorial tone that makes Tristan feel as if all the musician does all day is tell secrets. It is Albert's casualness, more than anything, that is so wonderful. It implicates and embraces, makes Tristan feel as wise and down-home as the man himself.

The novelist shifts in the narrow seat, trying to arrange himself into a cool and confidential posture. The plane has leveled off now, and with the window shade drawn and the mind occupied and the alcohol inside him, Tristan can almost forget that they are miles in the air, cutting through the cumulus in an enormous, absurdly heavy metal bird powered by technology he couldn't hope to understand. He doesn't get nervous about it anymore, but there is still a gravity to Tristan when he flies, a feeling that any thought might be his last.

"I can't believe your former bodyguard gave up the job."

"Let's just say I put her on vacation." Albert opens his eyes wide. "Against her will." He stares at Tristan and laughs long and hard, and Tristan does the same because he wants to share anything with Albert that he can. But the laughter and the staring never end when they should; they go on and on, until they grow uncomfortable and almost scary. Eventually, Tristan always has to look away, or downshift into a grin, and Albert's laughter wanes reluctantly into a guttural sigh. If the silence goes on too long, or he has no glass in his hand from which to sip, he may start laughing and staring again, and Tristan will be right back where he started.

This time, the laughter dissipates more easily than usual, because Albert has more to say. He folds his lips into a kind of thoughtful frown and turns over the barely-breathable blue-gray air with an elegant gold-braceleted hand. "I told her the time had come for me to get out on my own. For her sake, much as mine. I told her there are ex-junkies and then there are nonpracticing junkies, and all I could ever be certain I was with her looking over my shoulder every second was non-practicing."

"And she accepted that?"

"Only because you were coming. If it was just me and the cats, forget it. She trusts you."

"Why?" asks Tristan, flattered and insulted.

Albert unfolds a finger for each of his friend's virtues. "You're not a musician. Not a dopehead. Not black. If only you weren't American, you'd be perfect."

"Well, I'll guard you with my life, and I can't tell you how much I appreciate your coming."

"Hell, I appreciate your paying me."

"You'd tell me if it wasn't enough."

"You better believe it. But money goes a long way when you don't shoot your paycheck in your arm."

Tristan smiles, marveling anew at the mystery of Albert's life in the years between the lapse and the renewal of their acquaintance, the years after Albert discovered dope and bebop and before Mariko discovered him. Van Horn speaks of those times accidentally but openly. He does not tell drug stories per se, but if some memory happens to intersect with those dark decades, he will relate it without censorship or hesitation. And yet, for all the lurid details Tristan has accumulated, he still cannot grasp the ravaging day-to-day reality of that struggle. He has elaborated the particulars into a sketch of a life, as he is trained to, but if the Albert of yesteryear were a character he was trying to write, Tristan would be tromping around his study and kicking over stacks of books by now, in frustration at being so masterfully eluded.

It is strange even to Tristan, but Albert's addiction provokes in him a kind of jealousy. There is a purity to the wrongness of it, a beautiful simplicity to Albert's battle to regain his life and to his victory. That affirmation of the strength of Albert's higher will underwrites everything he does, says, plays now. He is on the other side of the river, and Tristan envies him the way he envies war veterans and gangsters and Kurtz in Conrad's *Heart of Darkness:* men who have done something real, something clear in purpose and execution, whether right or wrong. Men whose wars are against tangible foes.

Clarity, in any form, mystifies Tristan—and the closer he comes to the world's easy navigators, the more incomprehensible the absence of ambiguity appears. Sometimes he suspects he simply missed the tutorial, that while he was slumped against a splintery wooden chair in an airless Hebrew school learning the story of Purim, they were gathered beneath the cool shade of a country-club oak, learning how to Do Things Right from teams of impeccably groomed, high-cheekboned tutors clad in tennis whites. It doesn't matter that Tristan's identity is predicated on his failure to catch up on those lost lessons. That wholeness of being, that unity of mind and heart and body he perceives in others, still fascinates and taunts him.

I should have brought my daughter on this trip, Tristan thinks as the plane hits a turbulent patch of air and the more inexperienced passengers gasp, clutching at armrests or spouses until the ride smoothes out. Linda is finally worth conversing with, and it is now or never. Either Tristan will continue to hover nearby as Amalia raises her—loiter with pocketed hands and observant eyes and an air of discomfort, just as he has since Linda was an infant and he an inept infant father, gaping in wonder as the baby mewled and squirmed and his wife bustled around Doing Things Right—or else he'll find it in himself to do more than offer Linda cashews and orange segments and offhand comments as she sits at the kitchen table after supper, bent over her homework, and he drifts into the room to find a snack. It is clear now that Linda will be Tristan's only child; he can no longer offer himself the excuse that women know best how to raise daughters and he'll do his share when the male heir arrives. Amalia is too well aware of her husband's priorities to have another child with him, and getting too old anyway.

Presiding over dinner had been involvement enough for Tristan's father, but expectations were different then. Fathers were supposed to be remote figures, their authority undiluted by familiarity. Old Yahweh hadn't gone around revealing His Divine Splendor to every schmuck and shepherd in Canaan, either; His voice hadn't thundered forth from burning bushes every five minutes to comment on the weather. Not that Tristan is a deity, or even a disciplinarian. Amalia handles all of that. It is another way he's failed her.

No one ever looks back on his life and says "I wish I'd worked more," Tristan's father told him—not his dying words, which, according to Benjamin, were, *Somebody please get me some lemon for this seltzer,* but certainly the last memorable thing Jacob Brodsky uttered to his elder son before deciding not to bother recovering from the influenza he contracted in the frigid fall of 1955. He succumbed to pneumonia six months later, a year after his wife died, but the real cause of his death, his children agree, was guilt. Some part of Jacob couldn't bear his own good fortune, could not reconcile his existence with his family's annihilation. As more details of the camps emerged, and the specifics of the horror became easier and easier to imagine, such knowledge grew harder and harder to live with.

Jacob didn't talk about it. Not to Tristan, anyway. Instead, he lectured his son on common deathbed regrets. *You know what people say, my boy?* he asked during what turned out to be their last visit. *They say "I wish I'd spent more time with my family."* Jacob spread his hands as if holding two grapefruit, and Tristan, face set to receive the peddler's platitudes, fingered the key in his pocket, darted his eyes at his parents' door. The landlord hadn't changed the locks since Tristan was a kid. Half the Hebraic world could probably access the building by now.

Your characters you write so beautifully. Such love you have for them. Such understanding. It wasn't quite proof that his father read his work, but it was close. *Why can't you treat your wife as well?*

Tristan didn't respond, though Jacob's opinion of his marriage was based almost entirely on one icy dinner, years before. He and Rachael had come to Connecticut for the weekend, and it had been the wrong weekend. Tristan had been pissed off at his wife, and in no mood to hide it—the reason why escaped him now, always escaped him after the fact. Some assault on his integrity, no doubt, his sense of himself and what he would and would not do, unintentional but met like any attack just the same, with lightning bolts hurled from the bag he kept strapped to his hip, then scorched-earth stillness: knowing himself was not the same as controlling himself. For the first time in Tristan's life, his mother had been quiet. A giant house filled with not-talking was so alien, she hadn't been able to get her bearings, and she never visited again.

Come, Jacob said, in the face of his son's silence, grabbing Tristan's hand across the kitchen table, nearly knocking over both their coffee mugs. *Pray with your father. Ask the Lord for wisdom.* He shut his eyes. *Shema Yisrael, Adonai Eloheinu, Adonai Echad.*

Tristan paused for a moment, stupefied, before he jerked away. *Are you kidding? What's gotten into you? Since when?* His father opened his eyes, regarded his son with a kind of mournful hostility, then got up and disappeared into the bathroom. When he returned, it was as if it hadn't happened; they discussed the Yankees' chances against the Dodgers in the upcoming World Series. Not until his father's death did Tristan stop worrying that Jacob would ask again. The possibility gripped him with a dread he couldn't explain.

He would have liked to tell Jacob that he found Amalia marvelous, still. So gifted and so calm, so capable, so present. That the knowledge that his wife sat each day in her office underneath his, writing her small, enormous, underappreciated poems, addressed a monumental need in him: to be part of something larger than himself. To understand that thing, and be understood by it, and still be bound together. She satisfied that need imperfectly, partially, but it was more than Tristan could imagine having with anyone else. He would have liked to tell his father that he kept a certain distance from his wife not because he didn't understand her, but because he did—well enough to know he was deficient, to know it was not in him to provide the kind of attention Amalia needed, or that he could not find and marshal it, if it was. That failing from a distance was better than approaching and failing and becoming furious with himself and her and retreating and approaching and failing again. Instead, Tristan stared at the dusty top of his parents' icebox and pictured himself in his final hour, regretting just what Jacob predicted he would.

It is a sad fate, but Tristan has resigned himself to it. He can imagine being struck with the agonizing realization that he has missed out on life, on marriage. The scene is so vivid in his mind that he can brace himself for it the way a devout sinner can brace himself for hell. Besides, everybody knows that you can't have it all. Look at Pendergast. Three fine-looking teenage kids with whom he spends vast scads of time, a stable marriage to a good woman, a nice writerly office overlooking Harvard Yard, a fine full head of silver hair. Martha's Vineyard every summer, seats on the boards of half a dozen well-meaning institutions thrilled to have an author in their midst. Two shipments of well-scrubbed freshmen each semester to romance into the life of the pen. Peter Pendergast is happy as a pig in shit and twice as venerated.

And every three years, marking time as dependably as the floor clock passed down to him by old Grandpappy Graham H. Pendergast, the man turns out another worthless book, looses another buzzing swarm of inane words on the already-overpopulated world. Not for anything would Tristan trade places with him.

The Man of the Year leans back in his seat, pulls up the window shade in defiance of his fear, and crosses his arms over his chest. Albert watches, and assumes a similarly ruminative pose. The plane cuts through the sky, and the two of them peer down awhile at the distant earth. The hum of the engine is loud and heavy, but every bit as lulling as silence.

It is such a relief to wake up alone, in an empty bed, that Amalia is ashamed of herself—for feeling so liberated now, and for accepting something less than freedom the rest of the time. She lies on her back in the warm bed, extends her arms and legs like a snow angel, and moves them against the warm flannel sheets. She has the sense that she has slept remarkably well, better than in ages. Her right hand traces a leisurely path over her breasts and the concave of her belly, then comes to rest between her legs.

Perhaps a short vacation from each other is just what she and Tristan need. When he comes back from Los Angeles, he will be relaxed and receptive, as he always is in the afterglow of so much adulation, and she will be strong and secure, the way she tends to be after so much time to work, so long a respite from conflict. They will find a way to approach each other. It is as good as done. Amalia feels more loving already.

She throws off the covers with first-day-of-school vigor, wraps a robe around herself, and walks to the kitchen down the narrow, steep back steps. Coffee. A cigarette lit on the stove. The blinds open onto clear early winter; weak sunlight cannot penetrate the ice crust of the backyard snow.

Amalia turns from the window to contemplate the clues spread over the breakfast table. They suggest what she would have surmised anyway. Linda has risen early, retrieved the newspaper from the driveway, and read the funny pages over a breakfast of toast, butter, and jam. Condiment effluvia now forms a ring revealing the former location of her plate. The dish itself rests in the sink, next to her half-full juice glass. Linda's definition of cleaning up after oneself is something she has learned from Daddy.

There are days when Amalia might be inclined to attribute Linda's carelessness to disregard for the feelings of others, but today she is too light on her feet for sighs or scolding. The deep, warm smell of coffee fills the room and she pours a mugful, then selects an apple from the bowl and peels it in a thin, unbroken strip. Her own silence, and the way it blends into the silence all around, is hugely pleasing.

She carries the meager breakfast through the dining room, the least-used chamber in the rambling house. It's filled with furniture from Amalia's childhood, opulent artifacts that harken back to a time when nothing was ambiguous and nobody felt guilty. When Jews like her father made and spent and gave away vast sums of money proudly, filled their homes with Turkish rugs and Russian tea sets, took their families on first-class cruises, feared nothing. When women like Natalie Farber, sharp, clever, fanciful beings in perpetual motion, rode chauffeured cars down to the Lower East Side to bargain with old-world vendors over chinchilla wraps, returned from trips to Palestine and contracted for Old Testament frescoes to be painted across the four walls of their sitting rooms. When the will of the matriarch and the dormant power of the patriarch constituted the balanced forces of the universe, and the dinner table now covered in dust and creaky with disuse was employed at full sixteen-seat capacity each Friday night.

Amalia trails a finger across it, remembering the portable gold basin that stood next to her father's place on Shabbos. It was Amalia's job to dry his hands with a special white towel after he washed them and before he commenced with the brief prayers, belting them out with operatic gusto and vaudevillian flair. Maurice's rendition evolved over the years, until any resemblance to the actual tune was mere coincidence. Natalie disapproved, but Maurice and Amalia considered the blessing an artistic vehicle, and his version a vast improvement. During the yearly seder, father and daughter played surreptitious chess games on a low stool situated between his head-of-the-table chair and her seat to his left; it was the only way either of them managed to behave through stern Uncle Yitzach's three-hour ceremony. The stool sits in a corner of the dining room now, obscured by a potted ficus dying of thirst.

Amalia eats at her desk while rereading the previous week's work and savoring her coffee. She drinks the stuff sparingly, once or twice a week, not wanting her body to grow accustomed to the drug. Tristan needs three strong cups these days to get started, and by the time his thoughts are flowing, he has to dam them every fifteen minutes, cross the hall, and pee. Often, caught up in his words, her husband ignores his body's needs until the last second, then dashes, near bursting, to the bathroom. From her study, the footfalls sound elephantine.

A few years ago, Amalia gave him an old-fashioned bedpan as a gag gift. Tristan keeps it atop a bookcase in his office, points it out whenever he gives a guest a house tour. Amalia wishes her single scatological joke had not developed so interminable a shelf life, so wide an audience. She wonders if the delight Tristan takes in her nod to vulgarity implies a belief that Amalia is generally prudish. It's possible; there is no accounting for some of the notions he takes up. But just as likely is that Tristan is happy to possess a totem attesting to the ferocity of his work ethic.

What a man you are, Tristan. What a strong, virile, unstoppable man.

And what are you, then? Amalia remonstrates herself. The patient coaxer of emotion? The weaker sex, too addled by sentiment to narrow your eyes and pound on toward greatness? Sometimes she feels as though the mutual knowledge that It Could Be Worse is what sustains their marriage. Worse for her, that is. In spite of all his shortcomings, they both know Tristan is a long evolutionary lope beyond most members of his gender. Many women just as capable as she are married to Company Men who scoff at any interests their wives have outside of cooking, cleaning, motherhood. And it isn't until such a man has wooed you and won you and shuttled you off to some sterile subdivision convenient to his office, where no one can hear you scream, that the mask comes off and you discover that your husband, the father of your child, is himself a little boy who wants you to be his mother. Who will turn into your father at his cruelest if his wishes are denied. And fifteen years down the suburban road, when and if you finally work up the courage to leave him, there you'll stand with no money, no skills, only the haziest idea who you are.

Amalia teaches more and more women like this at Southern Connecticut State: as old as she and back in college, their faces masks of fear and determination. They attend the first class in pearls, heels, and makeup, retaining some deliberate, coquettish aspect of the schoolgirls they remember being—they carry their books pressed against their chests, or search out just the kind of pencil box they used twenty years ago during the three semesters of college they completed before earning their so-called MRS degrees. Amalia is as kind and helpful to these women as can be. Not just out of there-but-for-the-grace-of-God-go-I empathy, but because they have few allies on a campus geared toward students half their age. The faculty is full of male professors who see the collapse of their own marriages and perhaps that of Western civilization foretold in these women, and are thus as mean to them as they can get away with being.

Amalia watches with pride as the women abandon first the pearls and then the heels and later, sometimes, half the makeup. The boys write blustery Hemingway knockoffs and the girls treacly, wafer-thin romance, but these women produce work that is honest, brutal, and reflective. Occasionally, one will get together with a college boy, and Amalia will watch the couple stroll the campus, arms tight around each other's waists, and not acknowledge that the feeling masquerading as well-good-for-her friendliness is mostly I-wish-somebody-would-touch-me-like-that jealousy.

Noon passes before she hunkers down to write. For once, Amalia is secure enough in the promise of the day and the state of her own mind to allow herself such leisure. Sure enough, as soon as she puts aside the upcoming week's student poems and the Rilke collection she keeps on her desk and opens at random anytime she needs a quick booster of inspiration, Amalia is able to reenter her poem. The decoding of a second-stanza implication—a previously hidden and now self-evident note to herself—spurs Amalia to insert a new third stanza, and soon the poem is finding its true shape, filling out, growing voluptuous. She works from 12:30 to 3:00, pausing only to approve Linda's request to go and play at Marcy's house around the block, and when she stops writing, Amalia is the proud mother of a beautiful baby poem, helpless but healthy.

Only upon pausing does Amalia realize she is famished. She walks to the kitchen feeling like her husband. But while Tristan would merely shovel a few handfuls of something down his gullet and move on, Amalia believes in paying attention to what she is doing. She slices a tomato and some cheddar, melts a pat of butter in a pan, and grills herself a sandwich. It is cooling on the table and the pan is filling with tap water when the telephone rings.

"Hello, Amalia?" It is Mariko Van Horn. She's never called before, but that accent is unmistakable. There's a slight flutter to her voice; Amalia identifies it as the wobbliness of the initial reach toward a potential friend. Exacerbated, naturally, by the fact that Mariko is reaching not just out but up. Amalia chastises herself for the thought, but facts are facts. She is ten years Mariko's senior, and has her own career, and the few times they have met, brought together by their husbands, Mariko has watched Amalia with an admiration she probably thinks is subtle. Amalia has been flattered, and amused, and treated her with sisterliness. Older sisterliness. She likes Mariko, but Amalia has never extended any invitation to a greater closeness.

Liking the little black-eyed beauty is easy enough. Deciding whether to respect her is harder. Mariko is brave and tough and cactus-sharp, and everybody knows that she saved Albert's life. But when Amalia looks at her, she can't help thinking of the sad, hollow divorcées she teaches. Composing an opinion is further complicated by the irksome fact that Mariko seems to consider the two of them, as the spouses of irascible geniuses, to be colleagues. Amalia would sooner commiserate with fellow poets, fellow artists, even fellow mothers, than with fellow mistreated wives.

"Mariko," Amalia replies, as if they chat daily, "so nice of you to call. How are you?"

"Fine, thank you," Mariko responds by rote. Then she sighs. "I not been away from Albert one day since we meet, Amalia. I wake up today, I don't know what to do with myself. I already miss."

Amalia sits before her sandwich, but she doesn't dare take a bite. "Do you miss him, Mariko? Or are you worried he won't be all right without you?"

There is a pause, and Amalia can feel her thinking it over. "You right. I more afraid than anything. I trust Albert now, much as I can. I know he gotta do. But I don't trust the world."

"It's out of your hands. Besides, I'm sure he'll be fine. Tristan will look after him. Just try to enjoy yourself. Doesn't it feel nice to be alone?"

As she speaks, Amalia wonders: is Mariko calling because Tristan is on the road with Albert, or because she has no one else to talk to?

"Nice, but strange. Before I think about it, I already make breakfast for Albert this morning. I think I probably gonna do the same tonight, so I wondered if maybe you want to come over for dinner." Mariko stops short, as if she hadn't expected to get it said so fast.

The invitation catches Amalia off-guard, with no excuse at hand. "Well, thank you, Mari. It's lovely of you to ask." And it is, thoughtful and sad. Solitude, it seems, is so distasteful to Mariko that she cannot fathom Amalia's not being lonely with her man gone. Here, too, is Amalia's out if she wants it: the fact that she is not alone. She has a daughter to look after, and it's not like popping into the city is easy—it's a commitment, a two-hour trip. But there are three more whole days until Tristan returns, and perhaps an evening is worth forfeiting for Mariko, who dared make this phone call. If nothing else, it will be interesting to see who she is in Albert's absence, although Amalia guesses that unless she herself directs it elsewhere, conversation will revolve around the men.

Amalia smirks as she imagines radicalizing Mariko, arriving at this meeting of the abandoned women's club with a big bottle of booze and working Mariko into an unrecognizable, man-hating frenzy, so that when Albert comes home, he'll find his protectress transmogrified into a fearsome virgin war goddess. Linda can stay the night at Marcy's.

"What can I bring?"

"Nothing," Mariko says happily.

New York City driving is not so bad when Tristan is beside her in the car, the two of them pointing out personal and joint landmarks and recounting their stories, but alone Amalia feels almost overmatched. Her skin prickles and her calves tense as she is funneled toward the massive arteries that are Manhattan's borders, and pumped through: another drop of lifeblood free to plot its course through the city's indifferent, blackened veins. Amalia flicks the radio off. The classical music she thought would soothe her infringes on her concentration, and she needs every bit for these next few minutes of navigation. Cars stream past her on the right and left. Amalia flinches with each honk.

The city she grew up in seems foreign now, threatening. She feels guilty over what it has become, as if by forsaking New York, she has doomed it to monstrosity. From time to time, Tristan still talks about moving back here. Threatens, really, since he knows it is the last thing she would ever want. Nor would he, but Tristan maintains a blustery reverence for New York's seething, compressed energy, its misery and hardness, its properties as a creative tonic. He speaks of it the way an ex-jock might speak of his high school football field, Amalia thinks, clicking her blinker and merging onto the West Side Highway.

Apartment buildings loom to her left, the Hudson shimmers to her right, and beyond it New Jersey glitters feebly. And here she is, speeding past the exits for Seventy-second Street, Fifty-sixth, Forty-second, alongside scores of others, suffused with an out-of-control sense that she is living in the future—that this accelerated, frenetic, largely unpleasant here and now is the tomorrow of her childhood, the future of the world into which she was born. It is not the kind of thought you can try for very long to explain to others. If they understand, they'll understand quickly, and if they don't, you'll only talk a rope of foolishness around yourself. Tristan would get it.

Amalia exits on Tenth Street, dodging potholes until she winds her way down to Third and MacDougal. She parks, double-checks to make sure all the doors are locked, and braces herself as she passes a convocation of rangy young people in woolen ski caps, their breath indistinguishable from their cigarette smoke, passing a fifth of Southern Comfort in front of Cafe Wha?

No one says a word to her. Why would they? Amalia reproaches herself as she continues up the block. Why would they take any note of me at all? Teaching seldom makes her feel old, but kids in their natural habitats have started to spook her. Before she knows it, she's turned the drinkers into the Arbiters of Art, the Grand High Council of Hipness, standing guard as if protecting the purity of The Scene against the invasion of the old, the moneyed, the unhappening. Amalia pictures them gathered in judgment inside their famed Village coffeehouse, pronouncing her poetry frail and aged, something their parents would probably read.

She brushes the image away, tries to laugh. Allen Ginsberg wants to meet *her,* she reminds herself. Not six months ago, Albert introduced him to Tristan at some Village party Amalia had declined to attend, and Ginsberg talked on and on about her work, knew it backward and forward. Tristan glowed as he told her the story late that night, half-drunk adoration beaming from his eyes. It is when others praise her that he remembers who Amalia really is.

She imagines telling the Arbiters about Ginsberg by way of validation—fisting her hands on her hips and invoking their gods as they sit slumped over their scarred wooden table and their dirty coffee cups, turning full young lips to one another and whispering, "Man, who is this old crone?" covering their mouths lest they laugh in her face.

The door to the Van Horns' building is ajar and so Amalia walks in, shuts it behind her, strides past a gust of pissy, heated air and a bank of mailboxes, and climbs the stairs to 2A. Mariko opens the door before Amalia can knock a second time.

"Hello-hello," she says, stepping back to let her guest enter. Amalia pays the toll before crossing the threshold: bends at the waist and presses her cheek against Mariko's in an exchange of air kisses. Mari's skin is softer than it looks, softer than Amalia's skin by far, and she is perfumed with a familiar, floral scent Amalia can't quite name. Her shoulder-length hair, though, smells like cigarettes—unavoidable if you smoke, and the reason Amalia keeps her own as short as fashion allows.

She hands Mariko a bottle of red wine and steps inside. A strange blend of excitement and apprehension washes over her, stronger emotions than an apartment usually has the power to provoke. Why, she wonders, has Tristan never mentioned that the Van Horns live in a home without walls? But no—it is more like the walls are invisible. There is a kitchen, a music room, a den. Everything is delineated, but nothing is enclosed. Even the bed, jutting from a far corner of the loft where two brick walls meet, is right out in the open. One Japanese screen rests flat against a row of windows and another stands unfurled between the dinner table and the sleeping area, segmenting the space but hiding nothing; it reaches less than halfway to the ceiling. The apartment is close enough to the ground to benefit from the glow of the down-turned streetlights, high enough to be impervious to their glare.

What an odd, honest way to live, Amalia thinks, eyes darting from the piano to the butcher-block peninsula, the paper blinds to the couch to the wardrobe by the bed. I would go crazy in a day.

Mariko stands with her arms folded, watching Amalia acclimate. "The house I grew up in so big, you never know where anybody is. Here, I always know where to find Albert, no problem."

"Mmm." Amalia drifts back toward the entryway. "But what if you want to lose him for a while? That must be quite difficult."

Mariko smiles. "You teasing me, Ama."

Amalia starts. No one has called her by that name in years. Her mother did not believe in nicknames for her daughter, and thus only Natalie's own mother—having endured the same insult when the former Natasha reinvented herself—had dared. Ama had sounded wonderfully delicate, deliciously illegal, when Grandma Elena said it. But the name died with the woman, almost fifteen years ago.

"Not at all, dear. I guess I just can't imagine what it's like never to want to be apart. You must be very much in love."

Mariko stares up at the track lighting. Her mane rustles against the back of her long-sleeved dress. She gathers it into a ponytail, then lets it fall.

"It got nothing to do with love." Mariko springs into motion, as if the conversation demands it: unsheathes the wine from its brown bag, sets it on the counter, plucks a corkscrew from a wall hook.

"I not love the man," she resumes matter-of-factly, leaning over the bottle and twisting the metal coil into the cork until her elbow stands perpendicular to the ceiling. Amalia watches Mari leverage, pull, pop, unscrew cork from coil, spin to snatch two glasses from a shelf she has to rock onto her toes to reach.

"I love the music," Mariko concludes as she tumbles wine into both glasses and sets down the bottle with a punctuation-marking clunk.

Amalia sidles to the counter. The combined effect of Mari's performance and her sentiment is manifesting as thirst. Without warning, the hostess launches into an athletic finale—lunges right, seizes a sponge, swipes it over a small red dribble, backhand-flicks it across her body and into the sink six feet away. Amalia suppresses applause.

Mariko hands her a glass, and finally looks Amalia in the eye. "Nobody understands. Not even my family. I don't expect. When I meet Albert, I never think, Do I love him? I just know he need me. What else can you do, Ama, when you find the person who need you most, and you know you can help him?"

"But does it make you happy?" Amalia takes a deep sip of her wine. "Helping Albert?"

"It makes me happy hearing him play." Her eyes light up at the thought. "He so pure, Ama! Albert never think of anything but music. Just like little kid. Even when he practice at home, he got so much emotion. Make me wanna cry." Mariko palms the wineglass, and the stem clicks against her wedding band. She gulps, sets down the drink, and dabs a finger to the corner of her lipstick.

"But what about you?" Amalia places her glass next to Mari's. "Who takes care of you?"

"I do. Men cannot take care of nobody. Especially genius." She picks up the bottle and another chute of wine splashes into Amalia's glass. Mari pours like a saloon keeper. "Tristan take care of you?"

She's made her point; Amalia doesn't even bother to respond. Instead, she thinks back to the fantasy of radicalizing Mariko that so amused her a few hours back, and wonders who is schooling whom.

Mari lifts her glass. "You right, Ama. It's good to lose them for a while." Amalia consents to clang it in a toast, and they both sip: Amalia deliberately, and Mariko fast, so she can talk on. "Everything I remember before I meet Albert like memory from different lifetime," she says, eyes trained on nothing. "Being single, going out with girlfriends, dancing on the beach all night. Things very different in Okinawa." She giggles. It is a strange sound, coming from Mariko, but very nice. "My first boyfriends American GIs."

As she listens, Amalia strips the intervening years from Mari's face as easily as peeling paper from a wall, and sees her teenaged and flirtatious, that tremendous energy not yet tethered to anything but the pursuit of fun. Mariko's bare tan legs glint in the moonlight as she dances, moving faster and faster, throwing back her head to challenge the night sky with her black eyes. When the image dissolves, the room has lost a little of its luster, and so Amalia dives again into the past, her own this time.

"Any boy who wanted to take me out had to have dinner at my parents' house first," she recounts, and a trill of laughter jumps from her mouth. She presses her fingertips to her lips, and the corners of her smile peek out from around them. "My father was so funny. Looking back, he was. At the time, I was mortified. My date would be sitting there, some poor sixteen-year-old in his best suit, as nervous as the dickens, and Daddy would be leaning into him and cracking jokes and elbowing him in the ribs, and then all of a sudden he'd sit up very straight and stern and start quizzing the boy on his plans for the future, as if it were a job interview.

" 'Just how do you intend to make a living, son?' " she booms in Maurice's baritone. " 'What kind of a noggin for business have you got?' " She presses her hand to her chest and giggles until tears rise to her eyes, looks over at Mariko and takes a deep breath and continues. "And then, if he thought he could get away with it, my father would switch over to math problems. He'd have the boy stammering about how he was hoping to study medicine, or law, and then Daddy would cut him right off and say, 'Yes, yes, very good. Now see here, lad. Let's say a train is traveling from Boston to Chicago, and at the first stop twenty men get on. . . .' "

Amalia breaks into hysterics and clutches Mariko's slim forearm. The instant she feels skin against her palm, Amalia's heart thrills as if it has been tickled with a feather. This happens now and again. Amalia will touch someone and only then realize how badly she has ached to. Sometimes she will also realize that she has employed some ruse or exaggeration in order to achieve her end: an imaginary fleck of lint, a not-really-so-tight squeeze through a party corridor, a laughing fit. These mini-crushes always vanish as soon as she becomes aware of them; Amalia tells herself she is a sensual person who needs more stimulation than she's getting, and thinks no more about it. But this is different. Touching Mariko is something she should have done sincerely, not under the guise of this semiauthentic laugh attack, which is now ending and leaving her winded and annoyed with herself.

"Oh." She sighs, letting go. "I'm sorry. I haven't thought of that in years. God, it must sound insane." Mariko grins, hands her a paper napkin. Amalia takes it, and as she dabs the corners of her eyes, Mariko turns away and lifts the lid of a stout blue pot sitting on the stove.

"It smells wonderful in here," Amalia says, a little louder than is necessary. She stands on tiptoe, bracing herself against the counter, and tries to peer over her hostess's shoulder from eight feet away. "Is there something I can do to help?"

As she utters what is so often a rhetorical offer, routinely dismissed, Amalia is sure Mariko will say yes. They are two women cooking together, not The Server and The Served. No men are cloistered in the living room as if the sight of uncooked food has been proven to cause impotence in the male of the species.

"You can make the salad." Mari opens the refrigerator, covers the peninsula with an array of produce. Amalia helps herself to a knife and a cutting board and carves a radish into thin translucent wafers. Saffron and cilantro spice the air, and Amalia breathes the bouquet greedily as she works. The background burble of Mariko's fish stew is the sound of excitement.

Soon everything is ready. "Can I light these?" Amalia calls over her shoulder, setting the wooden salad bowl on the table and noticing two orange taper candles standing in low iron holders on a bookshelf, wicks pristine.

Mariko is carrying the pot between two oven mitts, walking with the care of a pregnant woman. She gives her guest a quizzical smile. "Why not?"

Amalia strikes a match. "I thought maybe you were saving them for something."

Mariko sits down, folds her hands in her lap, and nods. "For you."

Amalia can't help blushing, but between the heat rising from the pot and the slight rosiness the wine has now imparted to them both, it hardly matters. She takes another sip as Mariko ladles the fragrant orange concoction onto a base of rice and lays a plate in front of her. There are chunks of haddock, shrimp, and scallops, small pieces of something that might be crabmeat or even lobster. Amalia thinks about her mother, the way Natalie always orders shellfish in restaurants because they are verboten in her kosher household. As if the Torah provides a loophole for Jews dining out.

"You know, I haven't been out dancing in years," Amalia remarks as they pick up their forks. The image of Mariko spinning between the sand and stars has lingered in her mind. In fact, now a summer storm is coming down and Mariko and her girlfriends are getting drenched, opening their mouths to taste the rain as great fast sheets of water spatter their clothes and stick them to their bodies. Soon they will escape into the ocean, calling one another's names.

Mariko shoots a bemused look over the top of her wineglass and Amalia feels ashamed, guileless, like a child hinting at what she wants for her birthday when the gift's been sitting in the closet, wrapped, for months.

"Me neither. So we go, then? After dinner?"

Amalia laughs, drops her eyes to the table, then raises them slowly. "We couldn't."

Mari spears a shrimp, holds it before her mouth. "Why not?"

Why not indeed? Amalia doesn't know whether she is rifling through her mind for an excuse or for the courage to say yes. Dancing has become a dare, and now Mari is watching her with those inscrutable dark eyes, waiting. It's too strange to dwell on just now, but this woman is acting awfully like the girlfriend Amalia used to wish for in college: someone to throw pebbles at her window, rouse her from her bed, and drag her out of doors and into trouble.

She leans back in her chair. "Where? Where could we go?"

"We find somewhere."

They go on eating. The stew tastes even better now. Richer, as if Amalia is ingesting every bit of energy that went into its preparation, from the walk to the market to the deveining of the shrimp to the chopping of the onions. For the next few minutes, her entire consciousness of food heightens and simplifies. These morsels she now places in her mouth are what will keep her alive until she eats again, what will sustain her through the night to come. It is how soldiers in the field must feel, tearing open their ration packets: newly cognizant of the obvious.

"I didn't make any dessert." Mariko is in the kitchen, opening a second bottle of wine. Amalia can't believe they polished off the first, any more than she can understand why she agreed when Mariko suggested uncorking another. She doesn't feel drunk. Perhaps her host drank more, but it doesn't seem likely. If Mari consumed the lion's share, she would be staggering by now, not dancing the bottle back into the dining room and humming. "I have some ice cream, if you want."

"I'm fine," Amalia says. "You have some."

Mari, standing over the table and pouring, shakes her head. "Usually, I never eat this much. When Albert around, I cannot relax. Cannot digest."

"You're a better woman than I, Mari," Amalia toasts, lifting her glass. "When I can't relax, I eat everything in sight."

Mari toasts back. "You very calm person, then. Else you not fit in that pretty dress. I wish I could wear." She gestures at herself, with a looseness of limbs that is Amalia's first indication that her host is tipsy. "I got no curves."

"Nonsense." Amalia can't help looking away, embarrassed. "You have a lovely figure."

"Please. I like stick figure." Mariko stands over her, the wineglass in one hand, the other resting on her hip. "Wind start blowing, I gotta run inside." Her cheeks are round with mirth, and when Amalia looks up, they both start to laugh. "Serious," Mariko persists. "Every time I buy dress, they gotta take in. I tell them, I should get discount. I only buying half!"

Five minutes later, bundled up and trudging arm in arm into the wind, Amalia realizes that she, too, is a good distance from sober. Given that and the weather and the fact that they have no idea where they're going, she finds herself willing Mari to call the whole thing off and invite her back to the apartment to warm up. She can already hear the lie they'll tell each other: We'll do it another night. Amalia squints and sets her jaw and shoves the thought aside. This is why you've never had a real partner in crime, she remonstrates herself. You have no stomach for adventure.

Even the Arbiters of Art have the sense to be inside now. Snowflakes are floating in the broad shafts of the streetlamps' light, weightless as dust particles caught in a sunbeam. Amalia squeezes

Mari's arm to get her attention, then nods upward to show her. They stand and stare at it awhile, the night grown suddenly warmer, the block deserted, the wind gone. Within a minute, the snow organizes itself, stops swirling, and begins to advance in ranks, like marching infantry. Amalia turns and watches Mariko instead. Big flakes glisten in her hair; her face is wet where snow has melted, and Amalia feels the wetness on her own face, too.

Mari turns and smiles. "Why you look at me like that, Ama?"

She says it kindly, and this time Amalia is not abashed to be caught staring. "You know," she ventures, unsure.

"I know nobody looked at me like that in long time." Mariko glances up and away.

"Looked at you how?"

She laughs and steps forward. More snow is landing on their faces than is falling through the space between them. "Okay, Ama, you gonna make me say it? Okay. Like you want to kiss me. Right?"

Amalia swallows. "Yes."

Mari's eyes shine through the blizzard. "So what you waiting for?"

"I don't know."

"Women always wait too long." Mariko looks left and right, then reaches up and places her palms on Amalia's cheeks and guides Amalia's mouth to hers.

The moment their lips meet, Amalia wants to cry. The softness of a woman is so familiar, and yet such a revelation. With a man, there is always something hard behind the gentleness: a force real or imagined, a drive he may slow or suppress but which is always beating in the depths. Mariko's kiss is the first of Amalia's life that feels like an act of lovemaking in itself, the first to take place wholly in the present. There is such freedom, such safety, in the absence of that unnegotiable male energy. Through their jackets, she can feel Mari's breasts pressing against her own, imagine the beating of her heart. Amalia pulls Mari to her, unafraid of being grateful, needy, weak or strong.

Tristan shoulders the door closed behind him, takes two steps, and drops his luggage on the hotel bed. The mattress jiggles, settles. He flicks open the latches of his ancient suitcase and unfolds a brown Brooks Brothers suit, lays the pants over the back of a chair and hangs the jacket in the bathroom to unwrinkle when he showers. Albert and the band are bunked two to a room three floors below, but Tristan is up here by himself on the Jewish Congress of America's dollar. The lousy bastards didn't even spring for a suite.

He flops onto the bed and stares at the gift basket on the desk for ten minutes before he can muster up the interest to walk over and unwrap it. He pokes through the assortment of California fruit, notes the absence of macadamia nuts with disappointment, and scowls at the bottle of dessert wine, then takes the card back to bed together with a kiwi he intends to play with, not consume.

The message Tristan extracts from the envelope is all the more infuriating because it is written not in the familiar hand of the sender but the buoyant block letters of some dictation-taking hotel-store employee:

Old Man,

I trust your flight was comfortable and this note finds you well. First off, congratulations on the splendid honor. No one deserves it more. If you feel up to a drink before dinner, ring me in room 718. Otherwise, I shall see you at the ceremony.

Ciao,
P.P.

P.S. I've taken the liberty of reserving us a noon tee time tomorrow. You have no prior obligations, I hope?

Tristan reads it twice, then flicks his wrist and watches the card sail across the room and hit the wall. He should have known that Pendergast, the great friend of the Jews, was behind this Man of the Year business somehow. Good old Peter: too impressed with himself to stop and wonder whether a favor is worth doing, or to keep one a secret. God forbid Tristan should believe he's won on merit. Better that Pendergast, the Puritan Pilgrim, make clear to his former pupil and greatest discovery that life's prizes continue to rain down upon him only because Lady Pete is still fluttering around up there on winged golden sandals, seeding the clouds.

Tristan turns onto his side, stares at the drawn drapes, and wonders what he'll say to the smug phony. How ridiculous that Pendergast is even here, that he holds any sway at all with this organization. Who votes on next year's winner, the Daughters of the American Revolution? Tristan mashes his feet into his shoes. He's not going to get any rest until he's spoken to the man.

A DO NOT DISTURB sign dangles from the doorknob of room 718, but Tristan knocks anyway, three short raps. The thought of breaking up Pendergast's nap is rather appealing, but Peter comes to the door clad in a white shirt and a Windsor tie, hair slicked back, healthy and tanned—tanned! It is December and Pendergast lives in goddamned Massachusetts.

"The Man of the Year!" he crows, clapping Tristan on the back. "Wonderful to see you, dear boy, wonderful to see you." Tristan is ushered into a room identical to his, except that manuscript pages are strewn over the desk instead of California oranges, and two pressed suits and a garment bag hang in the open closet. By the time Tristan completes his survey of the premises, Peter is in the bathroom, running the water. He returns with a freshly rinsed glass in each hand.

"How about a drink? I've got a bottle here somewhere. So, does noon tomorrow work? It was the latest decent time they had." The scotch is located. Peter sets the glasses on the desk and pours them three fingers apiece, hefts his drink to eye level and winks. "Always a bad idea to book an early golf game for a man who's being honored the night before."

Tristan takes his glass from the table and holds it at his waist. "What did you do, Peter? Did you make them give me this award?"

Pendergast contorts his brow, laughs, takes a nip of scotch. He's nervous, and hiding it. Tristan takes a step forward. Peter won't register him coming closer, but it may increase his agitation. The professor has probably never been in a fight. A simple punch in the nose would catch him completely by surprise, lay him out flat, scare him half to death. Six feet of bloodied white Anglo-Saxon Protestant writhing on the hotel floor, wondering what the hell happened, and Tristan towering above, daring him to move a muscle.

"What do you mean, make them give you this award? Who do you think I am? I'm not even Jewish."

No, Tristan thinks, and you never will be, no matter how many Heebs you manage to slip past the doors of your country club. Any more than you will ever know what it's like to be black, no matter how many angry black writers you broker book deals. You will only be the man holding open the door.

"But you did something," Tristan says, low.

Peter is already comfortable again. "I guested on the JCA's board last year. They always ask one Gentile. It's an honor." Pendergast leans against a bureau, crosses his ankles, and draws a semicircle in the air with his drink. "One meeting, a few months ago, they asked for nominations for Man of the Year. *Blockbusters* is a damn fine book, an important book, so I put your name down. Did I do something wrong?"

Tristan stares at him. Where to begin?

"Don't do me any more favors, Peter," he rumbles, speaking into the glass as he lifts it to his mouth. The scotch is irritatingly excellent. Only Pendergast would order a fifteen-year-old bottle of Glenfiddich from room service.

Peter's drink arm dangles to his side. "What ever do you mean?"

"It's quite a game, isn't it? First, you convince the goys some lucky Jew is all right, and then—and this is really where I have to hand it to you, Peter—then you have the audacity to go back and convince the Jews. Well, thanks. That's what I'm supposed to say, isn't it? That I can't possibly thank you enough?"

Tristan cuts himself off as his voice begins to climb in pitch, volume. For a long moment, Pendergast is quiet. "Tristan, I . . ." he starts, then gives up with a sigh and a wave of his hand. The gesture is baffling. It could mean I'm sorry, there's nothing I can say. Or: This is too absurd to merit a response.

"You know how the Jewish press has gone after me, Peter. What do you think it's like to finally be offered an olive branch and then find out that it's not real, just my guardian angel meddling again?" He sips his drink. "I *knew* it was something like this."

Pendergast stands straighter. "There were twelve of us who voted, Tristan. All I did was give your name."

"The WASP seal of approval. Best endorsement you can get."

"Ah. You're being ridiculous."

"The hell I am. And as a matter of fact, Peter, I never asked for a guardian angel. Don't you think it's time you found a new way to feel good about yourself?"

Pendergast drops his head and gives a little snorting laugh. "You're unbelievable, you know that? You could just take the goddamn olive branch. But no, you'd rather find a reason not to. You'd rather attack me for trying to get you the kind of credit you bloody well deserve. I think you're scared, Brodsky. You know the minute you accept that olive branch you won't have the foggiest idea who the hell you are."

"Spare me. All right? Just spare me. You can put us on the golf course, Peter. You can get us jobs. But don't you ever tell us who we are."

"Oh, it's 'us' now, is it? All of a sudden you speak for the Jews, Brodsky?"

Tristan throws back the rest of the scotch and sets the glass down. "Better me than you," he says before he walks out of the room.

But by that evening, there is nothing Tristan wants to say. He calls off the performance, accepts the award wordlessly, and goes back to his room.

Sun pours through the windows, saturating everything. It's almost noon when she wakes up, barely having slept, her breasts pressed against Mari's back and her hand draped over Mari's thigh, and every emotion Amalia possesses sits so close to the surface that she scarcely trusts herself to move. The slightest sweetness, the lightest touch, might summon tears. And Mariko has seen her cry enough already.

As she lies breathing shallow, stroking Mari's hair, Amalia has the strange and horrible thought that perhaps she is too feminine even for a woman to love—too sensitive, too vulnerable. All night, she vacillated between intuition and experience, between making love the way she wanted to, the way that felt right, and letting doubts and errant fears corral her. If she can't be herself, then what in God's name is the point?

Mariko slips out from under her arm and disappears into the bathroom. Amalia opens her eyes in time to see Mari emerge, hair falling down over her tiny bee-sting breasts, a yellow sarong knotted around her waist. She heads straight for the French press.

Amalia props her head against a pillow. This cannot end now with a cup of coffee, or in an hour at some restaurant where they will masquerade as friends meeting for brunch.

"Mari," she calls, "come home with me." She yawns and stretches her arms over her head, then adds by way of enticement, "I'll make you dinner."

Mari puts down her can of Folgers, picks her way across the clothing-littered floor, and sits down on the edge of the bed. She crosses her thighs, then reaches out and tucks a strand of hair behind Amalia's ear.

"If I come, Ama, I just have to leave again."

"I know." Amalia takes her hand. "But come."

"You got daughter at home. You gotta make dinner for her."

"I'll send her to a friend's," Amalia says, knowing it's Sunday and no parent allows it.

"Ama, honey . . ." Mariko stands and looks down at her. "No. You know is a bad idea."

"So when . . ." Amalia starts, but there's no point in asking. Mariko offers her a tissue from the nightstand and Amalia scowls, offended by the assumption that she will cry. But a moment later, it proves correct.

"Well then, I guess it's back to business." She permits herself to blow her nose. Mariko hands over another few tissues, and Amalia takes them without looking up, smears them over her face, and lets her hand fall to her lap. "Back to your husband and back to mine."

Mari moves to stroke her hair. Amalia flinches at the touch, then consents to it.

"What else, Ama?" Mari tilts her head, smiles. "Run away together?"

Amalia bursts into fresh tears. "You're making *fun* of me." With every sob, a bit more of her allure melts away forever, but the thought only makes her cry harder—and besides, she deserves to be disgraced. It's as though Mariko has been regressing her. Last night, Amalia was carefree and twenty; a few minutes ago, clumsy and fifteen. Now she is forlorn as only a five-year-old can be, in front of a woman who has no sympathy for children. Mariko—wife of a man she does not love, defender of a music she plays no part in creating—is a realist even in her passions. She offers nothing more than a few strokes of the hair as her lover goes to pieces on her bed. A bed that still smells like sex, like women, like things Amalia had never done before and doubts she will ever do again. The instant she is gone, the mattress will be stripped, the sheets washed. When Albert comes home, he will lie down on fresh linens.

"Ama." Amalia lets go of the pillow she's been weeping into and looks up through wide red eyes. Mari stares at her a moment, then cups a hand to Amalia's cheek and wipes a tear away with her thumb. "Have some coffee."

Amalia nods, lugs herself to the table, and sits down, still naked. Mariko rummages through a drawer, puts on a top, and joins her. The seats of the chairs are made of woven rope; the cords cut into Amalia's bare skin. They sit side by side and stare out at the street. Last night's snow didn't amount to much. Most of it melted when it hit the pavement, but there is still enough dusting cars and fire hydrants to bestow a little magic on the scene. Neither of them speaks. Eventually, Mariko gets up and begins washing last night's dishes. Amalia gathers her outfit together, glancing periodically into the kitchen. Soon she is almost dressed, and Mariko still has not bothered to steal a final glance at her body.

"You know, we still haven't danced," Amalia says as she buttons her sweater, loud enough to be heard over the running tap water, not at all sure why she says it. Mari smiles without looking up. Amalia crouches to hunt for her stockings.

They kiss good-bye at the door: a real, long, tender kiss. Amalia feels the whole time as if it's out of consolation, but when it ends and they stand staring at each other, it is Mariko who pulls Amalia back into another, harder than the first, this one both wonderful and cruel, a kiss Amalia knows must last her a long time.

She reaches the street dizzy. Bright light and cold air shock her awake. Cafe Wha? is packed; a blond folksinger sits on a stool with his back to the entrance, strumming a guitar, and Amalia, caught up in trying to listen through the door, slips on the ice-slick pavement and has to windmill her arms to keep from falling on her ass. She recovers, stalks across the street to her car and finds it gone—towed off for being parked in front of what was, unbeknownst to her, a church. Too much to deal with right now, just too much. She hails a cab and takes it all the way home to Connecticut, a hundred-dollar ride. The cabbie comes inside and she gives him a drink of water and pays him by check. As soon as he leaves, Amalia goes to bed, pretends to have the flu, and sleeps for the better part of a week.

II

CHAPTER NINE

"I must keep Albert's music alive," Mariko told Tris, her mouth hard and her dark eyes flooded with sincerity. It was the first fall of the new millennium, and after a lifetime of willful invisibility—after forty-five years of shielding her husband from the appetites that had once threatened to destroy him, and that continued to, at least in her mind, until the day he died—Mari was about to take the stage herself.

And so after two years' vacation from the road, Tris was back in his dress shoes and musician's suit, ready to reprise his role as drum setter, wine fetcher, dressing room confidant. He looked Mari over now—the spindly hand clutching its customary cigarette, the drawn mouth overembellished with pink lipstick, the eyes perpetually narrowed, as if staring down a foe—and saw the cost of eternal vigilance, the toll of decades spent holding a fragile world together and a demon at bay.

Even during those moments of respite when she'd sat backstage bending his ear, Mariko had always been listening to Albert through the door. Anticipating, with every synapse, the nightmare moment when his saxophone would caterwaul and cut out and she would run onstage and find him slumped facedown, or shaking uncontrollably, with the other musicians staring slack-faced as musicians always did. And just like that, it would be 1959 again, and Mariko would sling his ashy elbow around her neck and drag him out of there, frame buckling beneath his sweaty weight, Albert's legs knocking together as he underwater-walked.

That scene had never played and now it never would, but it was still as real as yesterday to her, much realer than tomorrow. She tapped her Dunhill against the glass ashtray and Tris thought, You don't have to do this, Mariko. You can go home and find yourself some peace.

But this dressing room in Amsterdam was home, as much so as a hotel in Nice or a nightclub in London or a restaurant in Chicago, and maybe more so than the mildewing loft on Third and MacDougal, where Albert and Mariko had never spent longer than six months at a stretch. All Mariko's domestic skills were geared toward travel; she kept an impeccable house in sixty cities around the globe, remembered what to order from room service at the Madrid Hilton and what not to at the chain's New Orleans branch. She could tell you how to pack for a fifteen-day, six-city swing versus a two-week string of one-nighters, where the best music shop in each city was located in case Albert needed reeds or Murray busted a drum head, how to fly with an upright bass in a hard case and a seven-piece trap set and never pay the airlines' extra-baggage fees.

"You know what Albert tell me one time?" she asked, smiling. Tris raised his eyebrows. "He say, 'Don't worry, baby. If you die before me, I'm gonna kill myself.' "

"Mmm." Tris said it with conviction, made the syllable an amen. This was a rare story, not in regular rotation. He believed it had happened—even Mariko wouldn't invent something like that—but Tris had never been convinced the saxophonist had meant what he'd said.

"I was so shocked, Tris! I never dared to bring it up again."

The irony was that it had been Mariko who'd ended up the subject of a suicide watch last month, when Albert passed away. Her stated purpose in life was to give the world the gift of Albert's music by keeping him alive and drug-free, taking care of anything that might distract him from his calling. Nobody had ever thought about what Mariko would do if Albert died, and so they assumed the worst.

But when he did, her instincts told her: Play. The watch disbanded within hours.

Mariko reached into her patent-leather purse and extracted another cigarette. The gig was scheduled to begin in ten minutes. In Albert's band, the guys would have been massing in the hallway to trade wisecracks, repeat the set list to each other, resolve minor song-structure confusions. Tris opened the door and peered out, but the untested young men who comprised the other two-thirds of the Mariko Van Horn Trio were nowhere to be seen.

"No one know Albert's music like me," Mariko said to herself, giving the vanity mirror a hennish nod. Tris didn't argue, though he could think of many who might. All the musicians who had played it with Albert over the years while Mariko sat in the wings muttering encouragement, for starters. Murray Higgins was off performing Van Horn's music right now, with an all-star lineup of their former bandmates, in a group dedicated to Albert. He'd invited Mariko to manage the tour, but she'd declined: *I tell him I not manager for hire. I only manage my husband.*

In Tris's time as a roadie—ten or fifteen short tours between '97 and '98, whenever the Van Horns were playing someplace too cool to pass up or he felt a hotel room might be a more conducive place to write than his and Nina's clutter-filled apartment—Mariko had never so much as fingered a piano. Sometimes she sang along, under her breath, to a Japanese folk song she'd arranged for the band; that was the closest to performing Tris had ever seen her come. How she'd even booked this handful of European gigs was a mystery. On the strength of her last name and her history with the club owners, presumably. Quite a chance they were taking. And on a woman whose unparalleled ball busting they'd spent the last forty years sniping over, at that.

"Are you nervous?" Tris asked, and instantly regretted it.

Mariko scowled, waving away the question the same way she did her own smoke.

"How your grandfather? I not seen since Albert's funeral."

"He's okay, I guess. Still working on his new book."

"Of course. Gotta keep working. What about you? When your book come out?"

"Four months."

"Fantastic. Your grandfather read yet?"

Tris felt his stomach pitch, and shook his head. "I've been too scared to give it to him."

Mariko clicked her tongue. "Nonsense. He gonna love. I can't wait read myself."

"You'll get the first one." At the reception after the funeral, he'd found *Contents Under Pressure* sitting atop the same pile of CDs on which she'd placed it four years earlier, when he'd presented them with a signed copy. It was for the best. The Van Horns had no respect for hip-hop, didn't consider it music, resented it for pushing jazz further toward the margins of financial viability. Tris had always been careful, in their presence, to disassociate himself from it. A *young painter,* he remembered telling Albert when the horn player asked what his book was about, declining to mention that the painter's canvases were New York City's slumbering subway trains, his medium shoplifted spray cans.

Mariko wagged her forearm, and the silver flecks in her slate-colored dress shimmered. "No, no. I buy. Never give nothing away, young man. Friends gotta support the artist. Not easy to make a living." She squeezed her eyes shut and shook her head once, and just like that, Mariko was speaking in reverie, in reruns. "I feel so bad for black musician. To be black man in America so hard! But Albert got his freedom! He overcome! Albert the last of the Mohicans." She shooed Tris without looking at him. "Tell band two minutes for me, please."

"Yes, ma'am." He crossed the hall, rapped at the door of the other dressing room. "Ready when you are, gentlemen."

Tris hustled down the stairs and took up position by the sound booth in the farthest corner of the club. The room was crowded, the vibe of the audience unlike any Tris had ever felt. They did not move with the ease of sophisticates out for a night on the town, and an expensive one, but with the formal gravity of funeral attendants filing into church pews. Tris saw his own doubts reflected in the jitteriness of their movements: the way they tapped their feet, glanced compulsively over their shoulders, worried their napkins, made geometric figures of the hard plastic stirrers garnishing their drinks. They didn't know whether to trust her, either.

"Ladies and gentlemen, please join us in welcoming the Mariko Van Horn Trio!" She marched to the piano on the left side of the stage, arms rigid at her sides. She sat down, twisted at the waist to bow to the audience, then dropped her head and stared at the keys, hands folded in her lap.

The noise faded, until only small rumblings persisted—the recrossing of women's nyloned legs, the clearing of male throats, the deliberate rise and fall of drink glasses. Even those died away, and there was true silence, odd forward-creeping silence that promised to deflate at any moment, punctured by delicate piano tinklings or authoritative drum strokes. The drummer and the bassist hunched over their instruments, faking cool reflection but really glancing over at Mariko in search of a cue. The pianist's hands stayed in her lap, and the room waited. A second round of rumblings erupted. Men scratched their temples, women leaned slightly toward them or away. More sips were taken, more glasses replaced.

Then a small noise from the piano bench perked up their ears and froze the crowd. Mariko was sobbing. Her back was turned, but the shaking of her thin torso was unmistakable. She sat and cried, growing no louder and no softer, and the club and the musicians and the soundman and the roadie watched, paralyzed. Tris caught a refracted fragment of her face in one of the decorative slivers of mirror hanging behind the bandstand. Makeup ran in streams down her cheeks. He found himself walking toward her.

Tris reached the stage and stood below it. He brought his hand up, almost placed it on Mariko's back, then changed his mind, recalled it to his side. Her sobs were like her singing voice, as clear and delicate as soap bubbles. Tris reached for her again, and this time laid his hand against the crushed velvet covering her spine.

Mariko jumped, and so did the room. Without turning toward him, she reached behind her and grabbed Tris by the wrist so hard he felt his pulse throbbing beneath her thumb. Mariko was strong enough to swing drum cases off an airport baggage belt herself if nobody else was paying attention.

He winced and leaned forward on tiptoe to whisper in her ear, trying to exercise what discretion he could. "Do you want me to take you upstairs, Mariko?"

Mariko shook her head, releasing his hand and turning far enough toward Tris for him to see the tears had stopped. "No. Thank you, Tris.

You good friend." She sighed through her nose and gave him a weak smile. "I cry for Albert plenty when he alive, but hardly at all since he gone."

"You don't have to play, Mariko. Everyone will understand."

"Bullshit. I gonna play Albert's music so fucking loud, he gonna hear me. Tell soundman to turn down monitors."

She turned back to the piano and held her left hand aloft, then brought her right up from her lap to meet it and dropped them both onto the keyboard, and a chord rang out and jolted the drummer's left foot back to life. His hi-hat pumped once, the first beat of a resuscitated heart. Tris stepped back, and Mariko brought her hands down again. *Doon*, another chord, and now the bass player was standing straight as a sunflower, his hands performing shiatsu on the big old double fiddle and his mouth moving along with his fingers, echoing each note he played in a soft, breathy baritone.

Mariko ratcheted her body up and down on the cushioned bench, long black hair already coming loose from its bun, frizzing into a mane, and a swell of sound rose up around her. Tris dropped into an empty stage-side seat, jutted his head and knit his brow and grimaced happily. That was what you did when somebody was swinging like a motherfucker.

A minute later, it hit him. Mariko was trying to play Albert's solo, the one on the record, and she was getting most of it, too. Every now and then she'd fork off, like a river diverging into a pair of streams, and play something of her own devising. The music would rush slower, shallower, and then when the time was right, she'd reconnect with Albert's notes and seize on their momentum and surge forward for a while more. How many of his solos had she committed to memory? Probably all of them, Tris decided. Probably every note he'd ever played. But how—when—had she learned to pound the keys like that?

An hour later, Mariko sat alone with a Campari and soda, and Tris stood outside the closed door of the dressing room, explaining to an anxious line of friends and well-wishers that Mariko was resting for a few minutes, would receive them shortly. The club's owner fronted the delegation, his face shiny with perspiration and his fist choking the equally sweaty neck of a champagne bottle. Just as Tris was tiring of the bouncer role, Mariko summoned him inside.

She had rebunned her hair and reapplied her makeup. Smoke willowed from a cigarette lying in the ashtray, and Mariko sat rifling through her purse.

"Tris, I don't wanna see nobody for 'nother ten minutes. Tell Rolf come back later. I gotta talk to friends first. I don't wanna insult! Some of these people I known thirty years!"

Rolf must have been the owner. Tris had shaken his hand earlier but hadn't bothered to register a name. "No problem, Mariko. You want me to let them in one at a time?"

"No, no, I can do. You gotta go on errand." Her hand emerged, and Mariko extended a Dutch bill. "Down the street, they got a place called Talking Blues." She bent toward the mirror and corrected her lipstick with a curled pinkie. "I need you pick up some hashish."

Tris stared at her in disbelief, then grinned. Mariko ignored him, occupied herself in rummaging.

"Any particular kind?"

"I have no idea. I never smoke in twenty years. Whatever you think."

Tris gangled down the stairs, laughing, and hit the street. Inside the club, it was easy to forget what country he was in, but now Tris stood in the middle of an iridescent midnight thoroughfare pungent with great rich clouds of herb smoke, thick with bicyclists, and multinational with barhoppers.

Not even Pleasure Central, though—with its rows of mood-lit hash bars and its twenty-four-hour money-changing stands, its pink-piped sex-shop windows and, most garish of all, its two-story McDonald's—could match the impact of listening to Mariko pull so much sound from that piano. Even the knowledge that around any corner might be a fully bonded and licensed whorehouse, with a near-naked woman standing behind the glass of each full-length window, flirting in mime language, was less discombobulating than the fact that Mariko was planning to sit in her dressing room and suck down a joint Tris would no doubt have to roll for her. Mariko—who fired cats for showing up fifteen minutes late to a sound check, who looked askance if Albert ordered anything stronger than wine, who'd taken young musicians publicly to task for sloppy table manners and muttered loud aspersions about their lack of home training. It was a brand-new day.

Talking Blues was a Jamaican-themed coffee shop built out of weather-beaten aluminum to evoke the charm of a Trenchtown hovel. A six-pack of obvious Americans, fresh off the train and more concerned with getting baked than finding lodging, was sunken into mismatched armchairs, mammoth backpacks by their feet. Aussies with blond ropes of dreadlocks winding down their backs bent forward over low tables, intent on rolling perfect cone spliffs. A trio of bored-looking Dutch waitresses, name tags still clipped to their blouses, sipped fruit smoothies and watched the tourists indulge.

Tris turned to the adjective-crammed menu posted on the wall, wondering what Mariko sought in a high. He couldn't picture her "giggly" or "mellow," didn't think he'd care to see her get "cerebral," was too cautious to bring a woman in her sixties any botanical described as "potent."

He settled on a "mild, relaxing" Chinese hash and got in the wind, eager to run interference between Mariko and the public before anybody's night got ruined. Years of shielding Albert from the drug dealers and lowlifes he'd once counted as his buddies had taught her to distrust strangers, to clutch grudges long past relevance, occasionally to abuse her power as gatekeeper. Tris had seen her slam doors in the faces of people she'd known half her life, for no other reason than to demonstrate that she could. Yesterday's misdemeanor was tomorrow's felony, and whether transgressors were permitted to plead their cases was, likewise, a matter of whim. Mariko might listen to a musician's five-minute dramatization of how he'd done some dumb shit like oversleep and miss sound check, nod, and let him off with *Next time, ask front desk for wake-up call.* And then a week later, when a cat tried to explain how he'd been trapped in an abandoned mine shaft without food or water and had only escaped by weaving his body hair into a rope, she'd glare and wave her arm. *I don't wanna hear! Musicians gotta be professional! You gotta think of Albert's reputation!*

Tris reached the club, still spangled with patrons, climbed the staircase to the dressing room, and knocked. The door swung open, revealing Mariko sitting just as he had left her: hands mufflered in her purse, cocktail gone watery on the table beside her.

"Ah." Rolf smiled, clutching the doorknob. "You see? There he is."

"Tris, where you been? I getting worried." Gauging travel time was not Mariko's forte.

"Sorry." Behind her, half-sitting on the waist-high lip of the counter, was a tall nineteenish blond girl with a lit cigarette cocked by her ear. There was a rangy, athletic restlessness to her, as if she were waiting to catch a fly ball or return a serve. A white hippie pullover billowed around her, sleeves pushed to the elbows to reveal thin, tanned forearms ringed with woven hemp bracelets. Automatically, Tris sized her up—she was a female in his field of vision—and his brain recorded the finding that she was fuckable, filed it away somewhere.

Rolf saw him looking. "My daughter, Saga."

"Hi," she said, then leaned toward her cigarette as though someone else were holding it, and took a drag without breaking eye contact. It was a profoundly goofy maneuver, but wholly original. Saga's whole full mouth relocated to the left side of her face and she blew the smoke behind her so as not to offend.

"Nice to meet you."

Mariko piped up right on cue, cock block at the ready. Among the band's alumni, she was famous for this. "How your girlfriend, Tris?" She turned to Saga with a sage nod. "Very lovely young woman. Photographer."

"She's fine." He glanced at Saga to see if she'd followed the logic of Mariko's seeming non sequitur, and found the girl's eyes roving around the room.

Rolf pushed off with his hands and rose from the low leather couch into which he'd eased a moment before. "I've got to take care of some paperwork. See you tomorrow night, Mari."

"Okay Rolf, thank you," Mariko singsonged, waving as he sidled out the door.

Tris waited for the owner's daughter to follow, but instead she reached for the champagne bottle and poured herself a refill, so he extracted the bag of hash from his pocket and offered it to Mariko.

She looked at it, then at him, and then at Saga. "Give to her. She look like she know how to make spliff."

Saga accepted the bag, expressionless, and went to work gutting a cigarette.

Mariko dropped her elbows onto the chair's armrests and crossed her legs. "So. When you gonna get married, Tris?"

He stooped to snatch a Heineken from the minifridge, tried and failed to twist the cap off, scanned the counter for a bottle opener. All of it was preferable to making eye contact with Mariko.

"I don't believe in marriage. We got a bottle opener?"

Saga, holding a low flame beneath the chunk of hash to soften it, looked up. "Give it to me." Tris passed her the beer. She popped the top with her lighter, handed the bottle back, and returned to her project.

"You grown man," Mariko continued, undeterred. "Your girlfriend gonna want commitment. I can tell." She cackled, eyes shining with wisdom, mirth, perverse delight.

Tris swung the bottle to his lips with an exaggerated looseness, as if this were a shooting-the-shit-on-the-stoop beer. "I dunno, Mari. I look around and I don't see too many married couples who seem like they've both really flourished, you know what I mean? Even if they love each other." He stopped short and eye-checked her. Mariko was impassive, but he decided to unimplicate her anyway, just in case. "I mean, look at my grandparents." Looking at his grandparents was a major part of what Tris had done for the last three years. The results were currently en route from Frontier's publicity department to book reviewers nationwide.

"Your grandparents a special case. Not everybody cut out to marry genius."

Tris shrugged. "The whole marriage-industrial complex just feels bourgeois and oppressive to me. People should be together because they wanna be, not because they're legally bound." He poured some beer down his throat. "I guess I'm too much of a romantic to get married."

"Too full of bullshit, you mean. You don't want to grow up, same as all men." Mariko smirked. "That's okay. She gonna make you."

"She feels the same way. Her parents' marriage was a train wreck."

"I know female mind, young man. Security very important, even if they don't wanna admit. Not me—I never have no security with Albert—but I don't think like a woman."

"Well then, I'm the wrong dude." He lifted his arms like a tightrope walker. "Working without a net, man. Anything could happen."

She grinned at him. "Asshole."

"Hey, I mean, we do live together. I'll have a kid or whatever. I just don't want to sign a contract. If Nina hadn't gotten into grad school, that would have been something else, but now her student visa's cool for like the next three years."

Mariko's smile faded, replaced by the deep furrows that surrounded her mouth at rest. "You ever been to INS, Tris?"

"Nah."

"Worst place on earth. Cannot bring nothing into the building—no food, no drinks. Cannot even go to bathroom, 'cause you don't know when they gonna call your name. Government make it as hard as possible, so people give up. I almost give up myself, but I know I gotta make it for Albert's sake. You know how it feels to try to make a life someplace, and be afraid you gonna get kicked out?"

"Okay," Saga proclaimed, and they both turned. A joint rested atop her palm.

She offered the masterpiece to Mariko, who crossed her arms. "You go ahead."

Saga glanced at each of them, then raised the joint to her lips, flicked her lighter, and expelled a lazy, lingering cloud. Tris took his turn, felt his head lighten, and passed the spliff to Mariko. She glared suspiciously at it, then scissored the thing between her fingers like a cigarette and dragged. Everything was fine for one second, two. Then Mariko erupted in a fit of coughing, rocking forward and slapping her palm against her chest.

"You okay?" Tris ventured for the second time in an hour.

She nodded, still hacking, and wiped away a single tear. "Last time I smoke hashish thirty years ago," she told Saga, looking up with wide eyes. "Albert have gig in D.C. Soon as we get to town, a blizzard hit us. Nobody come to the club except same six people, every night. So devoted! They feel power of the music, you know? By end of that week, we all best friends. For the last night, cooks and waitresses and band and customers have big party." She shook her head. "I got so fucked-up that Albert have to carry me home. I say to myself, I cannot do that no more. If I get fucked-up, who gonna watch Albert?"

Mariko remembered the joint idling in her hand and thrust it toward Saga, lipstick stains and all. "I gotta find new bass player, Tris.

You hear him tonight? He got no spirit." She clenched her fist, held it before her face. "You want to play Albert's music, you gotta have *spirit*."

"Smoke some more, Mariko," Tris urged. She shook her head, but that impish smile was in place. So seldom was Mariko teased that she truly seemed to enjoy it. "C'mon." He crouched by her chair with the spliff held between five bunched fingers like a tiny torch. "You deserve it. Besides, we're only a block from the hotel."

She uncrossed her legs and plucked the joint from its pedestal. "You funny, Tris. Okay. Sure. Why not."

Watching Mariko happy and animated was sadder, somehow, than watching her sit shuddering at the piano bench. How long could she do this? Did she intend to die on the road, alone in some hotel room after a gig, like so many of her jazz brethren? Tris couldn't bear the thought of her chasing such a fate, aspiring to it because going until you gave out was the most recognizable of the alternatives arrayed before her.

"Hey, listen, Mariko, before I forget. My grandparents told me to invite you to Thanksgiving at their house."

She narrow-eyed him. "I don't think so, young man. I think you deciding to invite me now."

"Why would you think that? They told me to make sure you'd come."

"Your grandfather said that?"

Tris was about to nod his head when something in her intonation stopped him. "No, actually, it was my grandmother. So you'll come?"

"What your grandmother say?"

" 'Tell Mariko we want her for Thanksgiving and don't take no for an answer. She should be with old friends now.' "

She pointed a finger at him. "Don't bullshit me, Tris." He raised his palms to his shoulders and gave a sputter of indignation at the very thought.

Mariko's glance held firm for another moment, then softened. "All right. If they want me, I will come. Thank you. Now, Tris, you gotta take me back to the hotel. I gotta sleep." She rose and patted Saga on the arm. "Good luck, young lady. Nice to meet you."

"Nice to meet you, too." Saga darted out of the way, gave Tris a half-smile good-bye, and picked the smoldering joint up from the ashtray. Tris took a last look at her, then chaperoned Mariko to the top of the staircase, spotting her from behind as she embarked on a methodical descent.

She took his arm when they reached the street. It was a good fifteen degrees cooler than in the club, and the air seemed to rejuvenate her.

"So, young man, what this new book about?" Mariko lurched slightly on her high heels, like a little girl playing dress-up.

Tris shrugged. "A man. A writer. His life. The title is *Pound Foolish*."

"Your grandfather?"

A sour feeling wormed through him. "Yes and no. I mean, there are . . . Yes and no. Partly." *Fuck*.

Tris had tried to be a benevolent and gentle god, breathe a unique vitality into his man of clay. A writer could understand a character only through the matrix of his own brain anyway, he told himself, could only inhabit a life if he imbued it with his own. Writing this book had been an act of great truth-telling and great lying, an endless discourse between revelation and obfuscation, invention and guesswork and life. Deep down, Tris knew he had shaved dangerously close to Tristan's history, allowed his imagination to run along a track that paralleled and crisscrossed with reality. He had taken risks, ambitious ones. The ramifications of the enterprise were huge and frightening, and it took only a simple question like Mariko's to bring them lumbering out of the shadows.

As *Pound Foolish* revealed itself, Tris had worked feverishly to build a prison maze clever enough to contain the ramifications—piled brick atop brick even as the ramifications howled, slavered, rammed their shoulders against the walls. He'd sent champion after champion into the labyrinth to slay them. Truth, crusading, sword held high, was supposed to blind the ramifications with pure white light, render them speechless. But they only bellowed louder. Art strolled in unarmed, intent on convincing them of its rightful ascendance and forcing the ramifications to submit to a life of servitude. Instead, Art staggered back outside half-dead.

Finally, Tris had simply tuned out the clamor, as if it were nothing more than the sodomitic coupling of the downstairs pit bulls. His grandfather was supposed to be invulnerable, Tris reasoned—his life like history itself. Unassailable, and thus public domain. Canonical, and therefore subject to reinterpretation, satire, general fuckery. Something he loved, and therefore had the right, the duty, to find darkness in. The supposition had allowed Tris to write as he had, but now it seemed flimsy, crass.

Pound Foolish, though, was neither. Irving Gold blazed from every one of its four hundred pages, thrashing and brooding and maintaining, throughout the seven decades of his existence, a fascination with the workings of his great gray brain that kept him floating just outside the world of human intercourse, like the man in the chair atop the hora dance—and like that man, Irving Gold was passed from one protector to another, barely noticing, until the arms and shoulders that supported him grew weary and he toppled down.

His life began and ended in the Bronx. There, Irving brawled in the streets until he learned to brawl with words, and there he returned when his wife finally tired of his self-obsession and his infidelities (always committed with his social betters, WASP women whom Irving fucked out of hostility toward his friends, their husbands) and the cannons blasting ceaselessly inside his mind. He exiled himself to the tenement house passed down to him when his father died, rather than extricating his finances from his wife's. And there, a desert of a man, fifteen years estranging him from his last novel, Irving tried to kill himself but, having decided to stick his head in the oven, could not get the flame to light. He resolved to asphyxiate on carbon dioxide; his car refused to start. There was no rope in the house, and Irving did not trust himself to locate an artery with a knife. He wandered into the war-torn streets—intoxicated by the fact that his failure to create art and sustain love had now become a failure even to destroy himself—thinking that if he presented himself with sufficient insouciance, one of the blocks' adolescent thugs would surely shoot him.

Instead, this being 1982, Irving Gold stumbled across ex–Savage Skulls gang members turned graffiti masters, and soon he was sucking the marrow from their lives, smoking angel dust with kids sixty years his junior, and writing again. It was not the first time a ghetto darker than Irving Gold's had vitalized him, though it would prove to be the last.

"Writers gotta write what they know," Mariko proclaimed, tapping Tris's forearm with the hand laced through it. "Cannot bullshit."

"Right." The hotel was just across the street. He could see the awning fluttering in the breeze.

"Just like music. Musicians gotta be honest, above all." She shook her head from side to side. "Albert so honest. Everything he do, Tris. He never bullshit. Albert care *so much.*"

"He was a great man, Mariko."

"Problem with young people, you all bullshit. America the culture of the cheeseburger."

Tris walked her across the lobby, to the elevator. When Mariko got going on this one, the only thing to do was nod.

"Everybody want fame, nobody want to study. Make me sick. Albert know whole *history* of music. Not just jazz; classical, African, everything! He never stop practicing. That what make the artist. Your grandfather, too. He know. He tell the *truth.*"

The doors opened and she stepped inside. "I'm on the ground floor," Tris said. "Can I take you upstairs, Mariko?"

"I'm fine. You can go, Tris, thank you." She regarded him across the elevator's threshold.

"Must sacrifice," Mariko said, pointing her finger as the doors pinged and began to slide. When they were only inches apart, her eyes fluttered closed, and Tris saw her wobble at the knees. He tried to hold the doors, but it was too late. Tris strode over to the stairwell, hauled himself up three flights, and made it to Mariko's floor in time to see her drifting toward her suite in stocking feet, one pump dangling loosely from each hand.

CHAPTER

TEN

Tristan sat at his desk, furious, staring into space. There was no getting around it: he wrote like an old man now. The simple slowing of his recall, the fact that the right word no longer bobbed straight to the surface of his mind but swam languorously upward and broke through gasping for air, was the least of it. More crippling by far was that his understanding of people had eroded. The world had grayed as he had. It was not the gray of complexity, but the gray of remoteness, the gray that faded to black. He questioned his footing with every step. Was he interpreting things right? Did people think the way he believed they did? Act for the thin reasons he gave them?

His characters noticed his unsteadiness and began to mistrust him. They looked at Tristan and saw an old man who would muddle or forget their secrets, and so they divulged nothing, humored him by making meaningless conversation. It was infuriating, trying to work with such people. Tristan had had reluctant characters in the past, but he'd overpowered them with persistence and wile, stalked them until he caught them in some moment of privacy or paradox and then blackmailed them for everything he needed. All he could do now was play the sympathetic geezer. Sit on a park bench, throwing crumbs to pigeons, and hope someone would shoulder in beside him and start telling his life story.

But Tristan was too fearsome, even in decline, to pull off such a ruse.

So for the past—what was it? Four years? Five? That seemed impossible, but they passed so quickly now, represented such a small percentage of his life. Let's see: he'd published *Rage Against It All* when he was seventy-six and he was eighty now, and he'd finished that a year before it pubbed, so yes, five years. For five years, he'd written chapter after chapter about the same goddamned asshole prick of a 1930s Bronx bookmaker and his cunt bitch Sicilian wife and his faggot rabbi brother and their fucking parents and their shithead kids.

The inspiration that had washed over him and midwifed *Rage* was gone. Tristan glimpsed it sometimes from a distance, the way a man hallucinates an oasis in the desert. Even the memory of *Rage* was disappearing, both the writing of the book and the vindicating swirl of celebration surrounding its publication, the feeling of being welcomed back from exile. The revelation that now that his absence had been bookended, it would be attributed to greatness, contribute to his mystique. As if it hadn't been hair-tearing frustration and self-censorship, but some heroic, cloistered discipline that had prevented him from publishing anything but the occasional short story since '73.

Rage might as well have been a dream. Here he was at work again, struggling his ass off, and past success, recent or distant, had no bearing on the matter.

Amalia would say that was precisely the problem—had said so, in fact, as recently as last week, when he'd moped downstairs for dinner, apologized in advance for his disinclination to make conversation, and then sat there immersed in his own blue thoughts, bringing fork to mouth.

Can't you derive any satisfaction from happy memories, Tristan? If nothing else, don't they provide some indication that things might work out again in the future?

No, he'd replied after chewing it over. *I guess I can't*.

Well then, how about pretending I'm someone worth faking a little sociability for? she'd said, laying her utensils against the edge of the plate and crossing her fingers beneath her chin.

Tristan had looked up reluctantly, the way a brontosaurus might lift its head out of the vegetation upon hearing a noise. Amalia had batted her eyelashes at him. Trying to lend the remark some levity, no doubt.

You're worth not *faking for,* he'd said, hoping that meant something to her. It did to him. But she had only sighed and reached for her fork. He'd wished he had a scene to show her, something so rich and right that she would look at him over the top of the page with that small I-know-a-wonderful-secret smile she used to get, and say, *Oh. Tristan. This is very good.* He'd wished she had a poem to show him. But Amalia didn't ask him to read her work anymore.

Now Tristan dropped his elbows onto the desk and rubbed his eyes, trying to clear away a sudden fatigue. There were three things he could do with this alleged book, these insufferable mounds of paper. He could dump everything in his editor's lap and tell him to make a novel of it; that was what would happen if Tristan were already dead. He could abandon the project to history's dustbin, as he had three before. Or he could soldier on until he located and told the story, which at this rate might be never. The prick's son was him, for Christ's sake, was essentially Tristan at age twelve, and he couldn't even write that. He'd had to call Benjamin last week and ask him what subway ran from Boston Road to the Lower East Side, something Tristan had known his entire life. Ben hadn't been able to remember, either, and the two of them had sat there on the phone, racking their brains. Finally, Ben had asked his wife, Dora, a girl—girl! he sounded like his mother; Dora was seventy-three now, and half-blind—from the old neighborhood, and she had told them.

Tristan heaved himself up out of the cracked leather chair, slammed his office door behind him, and grabbed hold of the staircase bannister as if it were an old friend's wrist. He dipped his left foot over the edge of the first step, then brought his weight down. Tristan's hand slid farther along the railing, and the right foot joined the left. He thought of a passage from one of his books, in which a man was described by his usurper: *He went from taking the steps two at a time to taking each step twice.* The words were jubilant and scornful in the young man's mouth.

Tristan was in the pantry, filching a cookie, when the doorbell rang. The sound was an anomaly. The Brodskys' home was never locked, for reasons of both hospitality and convenience, and everyone knew it. Guests admitted themselves, hollered greetings, followed the sounds of the replies until they located a resident.

"Who could that be?" he said aloud, on the off chance that his wife might be within earshot. Or his daughter; he could hear Linda and Abe bustling around in the kitchen, which was why he had steered clear of it.

Amalia appeared behind him. "It's Mariko."

He turned. "Van Horn? What is she doing here?"

"Your grandson invited her to Thanksgiving—you are aware that it's Thanksgiving, I hope. That was him on the phone."

"Well, let her in, let her in!" Tristan shuffled past her and Amalia followed him into the foyer, astounded by the simplicity of her husband's response. Did he not remember that she had just last month declined to accompany him to Albert's funeral so as to avoid this woman—Albert, whom she'd loved, whose death had prompted her to set aside the manuscript she had due so that she might compose an elegy for him? Did Tristan not recall or simply not care that Amalia had refused to invite Mariko into this house for decades, that the two of them had fought about it and she had held firm for once, told him, *I don't like the way she treats people, Tristan. Especially Albert*, and he had leaned forward, all chin, and said, *Who are you to judge?*

But what was there to say now, with Mari standing at the threshold? It was Amalia who'd squandered the hour since Tris's phone call, standing in the bathroom dolling herself up instead of walking down the hall and telling her husband who was coming to dinner. The only thing to do now was open the door and try to summon up some grace.

"Mari. Welcome." The way Tristan's hug engulfed the tiny woman reminded Amalia of a hawk descending on a field mouse.

"So good to see you, Tristan," Mari said when he released her. She reached back to grab the handle of her suitcase, still festooned with baggage-claim tickets. Tris had said she'd be coming straight from the airport. "I moving in," she joked, wheeling the mammoth thing over the welcome mat.

Tristan boomed a laugh. His public laugh. Amalia took a step forward and smiled. "Hello, Mariko."

"Ama!" Mariko shrugged free of her wrap and rushed over to embrace her. She still had her nimbleness, Amalia thought, her coiled, catlike energy. She was still the woman who'd heaved drum cases as big as she was into vans, the woman who'd carried Albert on her back. But my God, it was like hugging a dead sapling.

The two women pulled back, and Amalia wondered how she looked to Mari after all this time. Her eyes were not what they'd once been to look at; the pupils were cloudy, crossed with broken capillaries, and the flesh around them sagged away, so that, Amalia sometimes joked, she seemed to have regained her wide-eyed innocence.

Mariko's face, when Amalia got the chance to really look at it, was fascinating in its devastation. Her hair was still teased into the same black mane, but from the forehead down, Mari was bones and makeup. The black felt pantsuit hanging from her smelled of Albert: a rich, warm greasiness that conjured thoughts of a big southern meal. Amalia resolved to feed Mari, if Mari would let herself be fed. She had not expected to feel such sympathy, but how could you be angry at hardness when that hardness had so savaged its possessor?

"What are you drinking, Mariko?" asked Tristan from the fold-down wet bar built into the near wall of the living room.

"What you having, Amalia?" It was an odd gesture of deference, letting the hostess set the terms of consumption, but Amalia appreciated it.

"I'm going to have a very light gin and tonic," she said, unable to remember the last time she'd taken a drink so early in the day.

"Same for me, please."

Tristan passed the drinks over, hands slightly shaky, then raised his glass of Glenlivet, neat, chest-high.

"To old friends." The liquor's warmth trickled through him and the sensation, combined with Mariko's adoring gaze, carried Tristan back in time, reminded him of himself forty years ago, when the words had simply flowed onto the page. Before he knew it, he'd poured the whole glass of scotch down his throat. Amalia gave him a sharp look, *What do you think you're doing?*, and for a moment Tristan was cowed because he didn't know. Then he realized that his wife thought he was showing off for Mariko, proving he was still the man of violent intake and vicious insight she'd always considered him. All geniuses were crazy to Mariko, beginning with her husband. Sure enough, her face was lifted to his, lit with affectionate shock.

Tristan turned back to the bar and refilled his glass, more out of custom than desire, then joined the women on the living room couch. He crossed his legs, placed his drink on his thigh, and leaned over to tap Mariko on the knee.

"How are you holding up, old girl?"

She closed her eyes and nodded several times before she answered. "Better. Every day, better. I want to thank you again, Tristan. Your speech so beautiful." She smiled at Amalia. "When he finish, whole church crying. You gotta make a copy for me."

"It sounds like it was a beautiful service," said Amalia. "I'm so sorry I couldn't make it."

Why couldn't she? wondered Tristan. Had Amalia been ill? And then, as he sat and watched his wife and Albert's widow chat about the florist and the caterer, a long-forgotten string of words hit Tristan in the chest: *I will not have that woman in my house.*

"I don't know," Mariko was saying when Tristan tuned back in, returning to a present seemingly unrelated to that past. Amalia's face was tilted toward her guest's, trying to coax Mari's eyes up from her lap. "I so used to the road, I probably go crazy at home. And somebody gotta keep Albert's music alive. But you can see, Ama"—Mariko deposited her gin and tonic on the coffee table, then laid her arms out straight, as if about to donate blood—"I not young woman no more."

"Neither am I," Amalia said, and wondered what she meant. I'm older and wiser than I was the night you broke my heart? Age and time mean nothing; we are who we've always been? She willed Mariko to get it, and a flush of heat spread over her as Amalia remembered this sensation. She had felt it lying in Mari's bed that morning: an urgent desire to be understood better than she understood herself. And for the kindness that, surely, came with it. She had not received it then—or anytime since—but as soon as she recognized the longing, Amalia realized she felt it still.

"I don't think you have to worry, Mariko," said Tristan, and at the sound of his voice, Amalia started. During the few moments it had taken her to unravel her emotions, her husband had vanished from the world. "Albert's music will be here long after we're all dead and buried."

Mariko nodded. "Like your novels," she responded. "And your poems, Ama." She didn't quite seem to connect his comment to the question of her future. But that was Mariko; she could embrace both the belief that Albert's music was eternal and the notion that it was her obligation to work herself to death ensuring it lived on.

"I think it's nice that Tris went with you," Amalia offered, desperate to say something pedestrian. "I hope he was a comfort."

"Tris grow up into a man! Albert and I so proud of him. Second book supposed to be the hardest, no?"

"They're all the hardest," Tristan grunted. "It's a rotten business."

"Well," Amalia began, though it felt ridiculous somehow, grotesque, to have a prim domestic conversation, a little chat about family, in front of Mariko, "maybe we can do more to help him, this time."

Mariko's lipstick had left a perfect impression on her glass, Amalia noticed. It was the same bright stuff she'd always worn. The shade and viscosity would have overwhelmed Amalia's face, reduced her to constant self-consciousness, but on Mari it was garishly beautiful.

Amalia felt the sudden need to escape, and stood. "I think I'll see if I can help the kids cook." It occurred to her, too late, that Mari might offer to follow, that it would be the polite thing to do. But the moment passed and Mariko stayed where she was.

Abe was standing at the stove and Linda at the sink when Amalia crossed the threshold. "What can I do?" she announced herself.

"Nothing," said Linda, without looking up from the potato and the peeler in her hands. "We've got it all under control."

"I've no doubt. Come have a drink and say hello to Mariko, then—not that either of you drinks, but still."

"I'll be out in a minute," said Linda, true to form. Ever since her teenage years, she'd spent their parties in the kitchen, talking to the caterers and putting off entreaties to emerge, aggressively indifferent to her parents' world.

Abe stooped and peered into the oven, and Amalia glimpsed the pale, puckered skin of the turkey and looked away. A flash of dizziness came with the turning of her head, as if the liquid in which her brain floated had sloshed high and hard against the walls. It had been happening for several months now, and for minutes afterward her eardrums throbbed with a staccato pulse Amalia couldn't imagine was her heart. It felt more like the wing beating of a tiny insect trapped behind her cochlea.

Abe and Linda went on cooking as Amalia pulled a chair out and sank into it. She leaned forward, pressed her thumbs against the inner ridges of her ears to stop the thrumming. The kitchen's orange walls persisted in her field of vision even after Amalia closed her eyes, breaking into pinpricks and then fading to pale yellow.

"Mom?" Linda's voice, above her. "Are you all right?"

Amalia dropped her hands, opened her eyes, and looked up at her daughter. "What, sweetheart?"

"Are you all right?"

"I will be. Just a little dizzy."

"I'll get you some club soda."

Amalia cradled her head in the L of her thumb and forefinger. "That would be lovely," she said, in a voice so faint it startled her. The notion of club soda was alarming: ingesting something so cold, so effervescent, lifting such a heavy, thick glass to her mouth. Her hand, her arm, her tongue, tingled with apprehension.

Clunk. "Here. Have a sip, Mom. It will help." Linda brushed aside her mother's hair and pressed an inner wrist to Amalia's forehead. "You don't feel warm."

With great effort, Amalia reached forward and grasped the glass of club soda in both hands. She pulled it across the plastic wood-grained tabletop, and when it was aligned with her chin, she picked it up and brought it toward her lips. She felt the bubbles fizz beneath her nose, heard the sound of glass shattering against the floor, felt coldness in her lap. Then everything went black.

Nina made a beeline through Arrivals, dodging the reunions of strangers, and stepped into Tris's arms. "Welcome home," he whispered.

"You're my home," she told him. Which would make Marcus what, she wondered as they kissed. A vacation condo?

The first two or three times this had happened, Nina had feared, above and beyond all the guilt and shame and fury, that her actions were proof of impending insanity, heralded some disease of the brain in its early stages. That's how fucking demented it was to keep screwing Marcus.

Now she knew better. Nina wasn't deteriorating; she was simply flawed in this sector of life, weak for her manipulative jerk of a first lover. Her career happened to throw them together frequently, and always far from home, and so once or twice a year, Nina capitulated to history, under circumstances that could never lead to consequences. Some people went off their diets and devoured chocolate cakes at Christmas. Others got shit-faced, vowed never to drink again, and went barhopping the next weekend. Nina's vice was like that, only much less fun.

She needed to work on it, and she was. But no more autoflagellation; no more calling herself slut, whore, liar. Life was complicated, and such words were simple. Devon's voice sounded in her mind, *Keep it simple, Pigfoot. The most complicated thing is to keep it simple and keep it moving*, and she ignored it. Three hundred and sixty days a year, Nina was a blameless girlfriend. She and Tris had built something special together, something solid—the only solid thing she'd ever had. They were family, and she would never do anything to hurt him. Not *to* hurt him.

So when's your boyfriend gonna give me a tour of the hood? Marcus had asked her yesterday, naked in the hotel bed, apropos of nothing but his own assholishness. *I got all kinds of questions, you know? I wanna be a graffiti guy, yo. I wanna be down.*

Don't talk about him, Nina snapped. *You don't get to talk about him.* They'd been through this before.

Marcus lifted his hands in surrender. *My bad, my bad. Just being friendly.*

Well, don't be.

He stood up, trying to hide his smirk, and walked toward the bathroom palming his balls. She watched him go, seething at his arrogance and her stupidity. Why did she put herself through this, again and again? She and Marcus were family, too, Nina supposed. In the sense of can't-choose-yours, and with all the helpless get me-away-from-here connotations of her childhood.

Marcus must have felt her eyes. He turned in the doorway. *Yes? Can I help you?*

What was the most hurtful thing she could say to him right now? Words lacked credibility between them. Verbs of intent, anyway.

He's got a bigger dick than you. She crossed her arms over her breasts. *And he's a better lover.*

Marcus laughed. *So marry the white boy already. The two of you can raise some beautiful wanna-be-black babies together. Who knows, when they're old enough, maybe they can get through college on some bullshit scholarships of their own.*

Fuck you, Marcus. Shut up. And it's only five thousand a year.

As you wish, Pigfoot. As you wish. He closed the door and ran the shower. A moment later, the first lines of "My Funny Valentine" rose over the rush of water.

Nina pulled the covers to her chin, then kicked them off in frustration. Marcus never took a shot in the dark. When he wanted to do damage, he used an infrared scope, aimed carefully, and hit her with a tiny bullet of truth that penetrated precisely, burrowed, burned. It wasn't enough that they were living their own dirty secret. He had to bring up another, remind Nina that he knew something else her boyfriend didn't, wouldn't, couldn't.

If Tris found out she'd checked that box, taken that money, he'd be disgusted. She could see the whole conversation playing out in her mind: Nina explaining that blackness had truly been something she'd believed was hers to claim four years ago—he knew that, she'd said as much the night they met. Tris not buying it: *I never dreamed you'd actually act on that, that . . . entitlement.* Nina trying to make him believe she hadn't had the means, back then, to correlate blackness with disadvantage, or understand how fraught it was to claim it. All the black people she'd met in her life had been educated, glamorous, successful—she was from fucking Czechoslovakia, for God's sake, what did she know? Devon and the rest had given her permission to be black, to stand apart from the undifferentiated mainstream that they and she and all artists, she'd thought, were trying to—

Around there is where Tris would cut her off. *Even if that's true, why are you still taking the money? Why didn't you stop when you realized it was wrong?*

Checkmate. Fuck Marcus for making this the present when Nina had resigned it to the past, decided it was something she had done as a young, naïve, less principled, and much more desperate person, something regrettable but over, bricked up, forgotten. Now it would take her a month to banish it again.

"How was the festival?" Tris asked. He reached around Nina to grab the handle of her carry-on. She took his other hand in hers and they strode away from the gate, suitcase wheels clicking over linoleum and plastic.

"It was cool. Nothing special. Another T-shirt."

They stepped onto an escalator and Tris straddled two steps, leaned back against the handrail, eyed her. For a moment, Nina panicked—*he knows*—but then her boyfriend glanced left and right, reached inside her coat, slid his hand as far down the back of her jeans as he could, and squeezed her ass.

"How was your trip?" Nina asked when his body fell away from hers, back into its casual pose, the look on his face like a mischievous third grader's. "Could Mariko play?"

"Yup. Every night, she'd sit down at the piano, cry for about five minutes, and then swing her ass off."

"Wow."

"Right. And then we'd get high in the dressing room."

"Holy shit."

"She canned the bass player two nights in. He sounded fine to me. I think she did it just for old times' sake. Picked up a local Dutch cat and did Paris and Brussels with him. He didn't know half the tunes and he smelled like he hadn't showered in a decade, but Mariko loved him."

"Devon said his dad called a few weeks back to check on her, and Mariko told him that Albert had been talking to her. That he was in the apartment with her."

"Where else would he go?"

"She wasn't talking to him or anything, was she?"

"Not that I heard."

Nina's cell rang. She pulled it from her purse, looked at the incoming number, and rolled her eyes. "My father."

"At least he's calling at a decent hour." Miklos's typical, tearful phone call was at five or six in the morning. That was when the demons seemed to come.

"I really don't feel like dealing with him right now."

"Here, give it to me. Otherwise, he'll just keep calling." Tris took the phone. "Hi, Miklos. Nina's on the road right now. She left her phone by accident. I'll tell her you called. . . . Okay, happy Thanksgiving to you, too." He handed it back. "That ought to buy you a couple of days."

She dropped the phone in her purse. "I should call him more. But it's always the same horrible conversation."

They stepped into the parking garage, unlocked the car, pulled on their seat belts with mirror-image synchronization. A pang of suburban mundanity jolted through Tris and he had a counterurge to pull out without checking his mirrors, ram somebody's SUV with his rear bumper, and peel off at forty miles an hour. But he didn't.

Nina flipped down the vanity and scrutinized herself. For the last year, she'd been keeping a vigil on the three vertical lines running between her eyebrows, examining them in different kinds of light and at various times of day, as if hoping that under the right conditions their existence could be disproven.

Tris paid the attendant, wheeled the car into the daylight. "I'm bringing my grandparents *Pound Foolish*." He angled his chin at the glove compartment, where two bound galleys lay. "I get anxious even thinking about it."

"It'll be fine," Nina assured him for the thousandth time. "Your grandparents understand the concept of fiction."

Tris didn't respond.

"As long as you're proud of it, that's all that matters. And it's the baddest shit you've ever written. Right?"

He gave a derisive grunt and slapped his visor down. Nina studied him and felt her cheater's guilt turn inside out, become hostility. For months, she'd listened to Tris fret over his novel—not the story he'd penned, but its fate in the world. What his grandparents would think. How the critics would treat it. Whether it would sell. The shit was unbecoming.

She turned as far toward him as the seat belt would allow. "What do you want, Tris?"

He dangled his right wrist over the wheel and looked across his shoulder, eyes wary. "What do you mean?"

"I mean what do you want?" She took out a galley and thumbed through it. "To be famous? 'Oh, look, there goes Tris Freedman, the novelist! I'm gonna get his autograph'?"

Tris sucked his teeth. "Yes. Exactly."

She nodded. "Okay. I guess I didn't know that. Good luck."

He accelerated.

"No, seriously. If that's what you think will make you happy, I hope you get it."

"Thanks."

"How will you know when you're famous enough?"

"When I win a Pulitzer. Can we talk about something else, please?" He reached for the radio dial, cranked the jazz station up loud.

"I guess I'm just not accustomed to being around artists who want fame."

"That's because they already have it."

"No, it's because they do what they do out of a need to grapple with and stylize the human—"

Tris lifted his hand. "Please, baby. If I want to hear what Devon Marbury thinks, I'll turn on PBS."

Nina slouched in her seat and crossed her arms. They listened to the music. A pianist in a hard bop mode; Tris strained to dissect the technique and determine who it was, but he didn't have a clue—never did, unless he happened to own the record. There were too many cats. Nina was no better.

"I'm going to say Bobby Timmons," he declared after a few choruses. Always a safe, respectable guess.

"I was thinking Ahmad Jamal." Nina always went with Ahmad Jamal.

The tune ended and the DJ came on. It was Danilo Pérez; they were off by thirty years. Still a pair of dilettantes, Tris thought as the next song began.

He pulled into the Brodskys' driveway and Nina opened the passenger door. "That's weird. We beat your parents. I figured Linda would have been here cooking since dawn."

Tris frowned at the front door, loped toward it, and read the note taped there. Penned in a frantic hand were the words *Tris—Grandma blacked out & fell. We're at the hospital on Brayburn. Mom.*

They arrived at the emergency room, only to be directed upstairs to a private suite. A right turn off the elevator, then a left, and then his parents were rising from their chairs to greet him. Tristan remained seated, legs bowed, ankles crossed. He glanced up momentarily, nodded, then returned to his contemplation of the floor. Abe reached Tris first and wrapped his son in a tight, hard hug. Tris stepped out of it, impatient. "What happened? Where's Grandma?"

"She's in there." Linda pointed to the closed door of the room outside which they were clustered. "Sleeping. It's hypoglycemia. Low blood sugar. They gave her a shot in the ER and she revived. The good news is that she could easily have broken a hip when she fell, but she didn't. Just contusions."

Tris darted his eyes toward Tristan's slumped form and tapped his temple. "What about up here?"

"They don't know," the old man said, grimacing up at his grandson. "These sons of bitches don't know anything."

Linda glared at her father. "She should be fine. They're going to do some tests when she wakes up, but the doctor said there was no reason to worry."

Tris walked over and peered in through the high, small window. There his grandmother lay, melting into the sheets, with a tube snaking into her nose, a needle taped to her arm. At the bedside sat Mariko, a Styrofoam cup in one hand, leaning forward, her elbows on her knees.

Tris whirled. "Should she be in there?"

Linda shrugged. "The doctor said it can be soothing to hear a voice after a trauma. Mariko was the only one who didn't feel weird about talking to her."

Tris rested a hand on his grandfather's shoulder. "Hey, Gramps."

The old man didn't respond. He shook his head four or five times, as if trying to clear it, then raised his eyes and looked at each of them in turn. "If she doesn't recover, we're done for. I mean we're really through."

No one answered. The mingled odor of medicines and disinfectants hung stagnant in the air, and Tris inhaled it, hating the hospital more each moment. Nina sat next to him and held his hand. Abe sat next to Linda and looked as if he wanted to hold hers. Linda held a *People* magazine, rolled tight enough to breathe through underwater.

"Where the hell is the doctor?" Tristan demanded, turning to his daughter. "The man has vanished. She's been alone for hours."

Just then, Mariko opened the door. "Amalia waking up! She say your name, Tristan."

"She did?" He pushed against the arms of his chair, struggling to rise. Nina moved to spot him, palm hovering an inch from Tristan's back as he straightened. She, Tris, Abe, and Linda bottlenecked behind the old man, like cars waiting to pass a bicyclist on a narrow country road, as the patriarch advanced into the room.

"Tristan," Amalia whispered as the family fanned out around her bed. Her voice was scarcely audible and she stared straight ahead, not seeing him.

"Amalia, my dear." Tristan picked her hand up off the mattress. "Here I am." At the touch, she rolled her head toward him and blinked her husband into focus. Tristan tried to smile, in spite of the tube, the needle. "You gave us quite a fright."

"Tristan." She coughed, and her face crumpled with the exertion. They all winced. But coughing seemed to help. Amalia's voice, when next she spoke, had recovered a dram of strength. With great effort, she lifted her head an inch off the pillow.

"Tristan," she said, "I want a divorce."

He gaped at her, speechless, still holding her hand. The rest of them were gaping, too, but Amalia kept her eyes on Tristan, waited as he searched her face. "I'm sorry," she whispered, and now the softness of her voice seemed more a matter of intent than of necessity.

Tris had never seen anyone appear so broken as his grandfather did just then, looking up from his wife's bed and turning his ashen face out toward his family. "She's delirious," the old man said. He glanced down at his wife, then back at them. "She's in a bad way."

Finally, it was Linda who spoke.

"Mom? Can you tell me what year it is?"

Amalia cleared her throat. "It is the year 2000. I have been married to your father for fifty-seven years, Linda. And I have decided that I do not wish to die his wife. Does that sound like delirium to you?" She coughed again, and this time raised her intravenous-needled arm at the elbow, plucked a tissue from the box on the bed, and wiped it across her mouth, discreetly expelling a gob of mucus.

Linda looked from her mother to her father, and then back at her mother. "No," she said. "That—that sounds pretty rational to me."

Tristan laid his wife's hand on the bed, turned his back, and shuffled from the room. The door clicked shut, and the family watched him sink into a hallway chair.

Tris leaned forward into the narrow hallway until his knees were inches from his grandfather's. Tristan's head was thrown back, his eyes closed. Every few moments, a hard sigh shuddered through him. He looked so fragile that Tris hardly dared move; the slightest disruption to the old man's equilibrium seemed liable to send him toppling sideways onto the hospital floor.

The chair's hard molded plastic creaked beneath Tris, and his grandfather opened his eyes. "I've made some bad choices," he said after a moment, his voice pale and distant. "I don't know how to talk to her." Another head shake. "This is the goddamn end."

This is the goddamn end was exactly what had run through Irving Gold's mind when his wife tossed him out. Tris didn't know what to do with that.

"Talk to her now. Apologize. Tell her you'll change." There had been nobody around to say that to Irving Gold.

Tristan shut his eyes and squeezed the bridge of his nose with a thumb and forefinger. "Change," he muttered. "Who do you think I am? Change. I don't know a thing about that."

Tris cupped his right fist with his left hand. He wanted to stand up, to shout and throw his arms around, but he didn't dare. Nobody did.

"Things are going to change one way or another, Grandpa. If Grandma leaves you, it's going to be one hell of a change, so maybe you'd better give some thought to—"

Tristan winced, and raised his hand as if about to recite the Pledge of Allegiance. "Calm yourself. I thank you for coming after me, but you'd better go. I'd like some privacy." Tristan leaned back, resumed his half-dead pose.

"Grandpa?" The old man didn't respond.

"Hey, Grandpa!" Panic seized him, and Tris bent over his grandfather, only to hear a quiet wheeze of inhalation. His stomach unclenched. He straightened, stared down at the old man's fine white hair and through it to the pink, vulnerable scalp as his head lolled onto his left shoulder. Tristan was out cold; his body had shut down. Tris stood over him like a sentry, unsure what he was guarding.

CHAPTER ELEVEN

Tris's cell phone lay in the middle of the table, trapped amid water glasses, coffee mugs, the deep square plates containing his wild mushroom frittata, Zone's smoked salmon scramble, Nina's ginger-lemon pancakes. He reached for it, flipped the screen to check the time, and dropped it again, as he'd been doing every few minutes since they'd arrived.

"Dog, you're making *me* nervous," said Zone, fork in hand, looking anything but. "If you guys gotta go, just go. Otherwise, cool out and enjoy your fourteen-dollar eggs." He turned to Nina. "Of course he had to pick the most expensive place in the neighborhood. If I had won, we'd be at Academy Diner. You know that, right?"

Nina said she knew it well, and Tris smiled with the pleasure of having his girl and his best friend team up against him. Zone's protests were bullshit. His culinary standards had skyrocketed alongside his income, and this was the only brunch spot in Fort Greene that met with his approval.

Tris drank the last of his coffee, and immediately scanned the room for the waitress, the affront of an empty mug too much to bear. "Shoulda known better than to bet against me," he counseled. "I'm crazy hip-hop, son. Act like you know." The wager—stemming from a nerds' debate over the first song to use the "Substitution" breakbeat that had flared up when a car bumping "Don't Believe the Hype" rolled down Fulton Street while Tris and Zone were walking to the Cambodian take-out joint—had been decided weeks ago, minutes after it was made. The payoff had been delayed until now because Zone's much-reviled gig as a financial consultant stranded him anyplace there was a client, sometimes for months at a stretch. Paying Fort Greene rent to live here part-time seemed like a waste of money to Tris, but Zone could afford it as easily as he could these eggs.

"We should leave in fifteen minutes." Before Tris could check his phone again, it rang.

"Hello?" he said, pretending not to know it was his mother.

"Tris. Where are you?" Always her first question, whether she called him or he called her. Asked with a stiff urgency that suggested Linda was half-expecting the answer to be "Jail, Mom. I'm in jail."

"On my way. Just leaving Brooklyn now." He flagged the waitress with his free hand and attempted to make, in rapid sequence, the *check, please* and *more coffee* signs.

"You said you'd be here when your grandmother got discharged. I'm leaving to pick her up in five minutes."

"I'll be there as soon as I can."

"I can't be upstairs and downstairs at the same time, Tris."

"I'm on my way, Mom."

"All right. Hurry. But don't speed."

"Bye, Mom." Tris snapped the phone shut. "Jesus. Like the world is gonna end if we're not there for the grand reentry of Amalia the Destroyer."

Nina doused her last pancake in syrup and sliced it into strips. She ate each pancake separately, rather than cutting through the stack—so each one got an equal amount of syrup, she'd told Tris years ago, when he'd asked, looking at him as if he were an absolute moron.

Zone dropped his chin into his palm. "My boss, his mother died a week after his dad. Couldn't handle being alone. It happens all the time with old people."

"Nobody's gonna be alone. My grandmother's just pissed. It will pass."

Nina popped a doughy bite into her mouth. "Like Tristan said, he made certain choices. Maybe he's finally paying the price."

"It's not that simple, Nina. I'm sick of everybody just summing my grandfather up like 'Oh, he only cares about his work, he neglects everybody.' "

"Sounds familiar."

"Fuck you. I'm nowhere *near* as bad as he is."

"Oh yeah? When's the last time you took me out dancing? When's the last time you even took a day off?"

"Look, the point is, it's complicated. My great-uncle Ben told me once that Tristan never had to do chores when he was a kid. His family isolated *him*, because his brain was supposed to make him a fortune and lift everybody out of the ghetto. But instead, he decided to write books with it."

Zone slid his credit card onto the plastic tray the waitress had dropped off. Nina thrust a folded bill at him; he waved it away. "That's gotta be some Jewish shit or some immigrant shit or something. Black parents, they don't give a fuck how smart you are. 'But Mom, I'm a genius!' 'Oh yeah? Then bring your smart ass in here and do these dishes before I cut a switch, make your ass really smart.' "

"What the hell are you talking about, dude?" Tris beckoned the waitress back, still intent on a refill. "Your mom's a Buddhist. She never hit you in your life. 'Cut a switch?' What are you, from Alabama?"

Zone pushed the heels of his hands against his eyes, removed them, blinked the world back into focus. "You know what that was? That was the type of down-home bullshit I kick when I want a client to feel like I'm authentically black."

"I thought the idea was to make them forget you were black. Isn't that why you cut off your locks?"

"A little from column A, a little from column B. Corporate America's a bitch, boy."

Tris slung his arm over Nina's shoulder. "Well, you know Nina here is Creole three generations back." The boys laughed, as usual.

"I never should have told you that story."

"Don't sweat it," said Zone. "You're black enough for me."

"Gee, thanks, Malik."

"No doubt." He thumped his fist against his chest and pocketed his receipt.

Five minutes later, Tris and Nina were in their car, rolling through South Williamsburg's Hasidic enclave, en route to the Brooklyn-Queens Expressway. Tris peered out the windshield like a man on safari, distracted from his thoughts by the herds of bearded natives in black hats and bottle-bottom glasses scurrying alongside his car, shepherding identically costumed young. He drove slowly, considering the bits of trivia that comprised his knowledge of the people he regarded as real Jews. No man would touch a woman other than his spouse, not even to shake hands. If a woman was barren, her husband was obligated to divorce her. At certain times of the month, you had to fuck through a bedsheet to minimize bodily contact. Every aspect of an Orthodox life was prescribed; a man knew at all times where to be, what to be doing. Maybe there was something to that.

Tris could never simply wonder about the Hasidim. As he passed through their parts of town, his curiosity invariably turned inward, and he ached to know what they might think of him. Would a Hasid even acknowledge Tris as Jewish, or would he be considered an abomination, held at greater distance than an outright Gentile because he was of the Chosen and had turned away?

The bray of Nina's cell ended his speculation. She stared at the screen as the phone continued to fill the car with noise.

"You can turn the volume off, you know," said Tris. "Babe?"

Nina didn't look up. It was Marcus, calling from his reclaimed Brooklyn studio—on a day when there was no work to be done, and at an hour when he had no reason to believe she'd be alone. Probably thought he could convince her to come over, do some "developing." It was the second time he'd called since she'd been back. Marcus really didn't give a fuck.

She pressed a button with her thumb and stopped the ringing. "My father again. God."

The phone buzzed to indicate new voice mail, and Nina tossed it in her purse. "He asked me for my mother's number last time. Did I tell you that? What the fuck he thinks he'd say to her, I can't imagine. I almost gave it to him, just so he could call and Vasek could answer. But it's too mean. Plus, Mom would kill me."

"I wonder what his girlfriend has to say. You think she knows he calls you in the middle of the night?"

"I'm sure he sneaks away. Talk about something else."

Amalia left the hospital and returned to a house partitioned along venerable lines of territory. Her daughter got her settled on the living room couch, brought her a glass of water and a pill: the latest addition to her daily pharmacopoeia. Mariko adjusted the pillows behind Amalia's back, then declared her intention to fix some lunch and marched into the kitchen. Mari's big black suitcase stood in the hallway like a tombstone, right where she'd parked it yesterday. She'd spent the night at the hospital

"You and Mariko seem to have patched things up," said Linda.

Amalia nodded, unable to remember what she'd told her daughter about the source of their conflict. It didn't matter now. "I suppose we have." Her voice remained not quite her own, and the journey up the walkway had taken her longer than ever. Halfway to the door, she'd paused to light a crumpled cigarette she'd found in her coat pocket. That seemed to help.

"I'm sure she must be exhausted. I can drive her home after we eat."

"I don't think she intends to leave. She's very lonely without Albert, you know."

Linda's jaw clenched and released, clenched and released. Amalia wondered if her daughter thought the tic invisible. "Don't you think there's enough going on around here without a houseguest, Mom?"

"I can use the company." She flicked her eyes at the ceiling. "I doubt your father will be ready to talk to me for a week, at the very least."

Mariko burst from the kitchen carrying a sandwich on a plate, banked right, and climbed the staircase. "Besides," Amalia said as Mari's legs vanished from sight, "this way, he won't starve to death."

They heard her descend the back stairs, and a few minutes later Mariko reappeared in the living room and handed them their own mammoth turkey, relish, and stuffing sandwiches. Linda hefted hers in both hands. Amalia asked for a fork, removed the top piece of bread, and picked at the insides.

"Sorry," Mariko said, watching. "I used to Albert. He could eat two of these."

"What did my father say?" asked Linda.

"He's sleeping. At his desk." Mari lit herself a cigarette. "Tristan love you very much, Ama. One look and I can see that he in pain."

"I thought he was sleeping," said Linda, a little too sharply for her mother's taste.

"Don't matter," replied Mariko.

They were quiet for a long time before Amalia spoke. "Alfred Kazin once wrote something about someone else that I always thought summed Tristan up perfectly. He described the fellow—Delmore Schwartz, it might have been—as having 'the unmistakable look of the poet speaking from his own depths. He stood for something, and he knew it.' " Amalia's eyes sparkled briefly with the particular delight that pure eloquence gave her, and then her gaze fell to her lap. "Alfred died not long ago."

"What was it that Dad stood for?" From the look on Linda's face, it seemed she could not discern her father in Kazin's bold, certain phrases.

"I don't know that he ever entirely figured that out," Amalia said, feeling herself falter, the meaning of the words slipping away. "But he stood for something. And he knew it."

"That sounds like a problem."

"It is indeed." Amalia brought a bite of turkey to her lips. "I don't know what you did, Mari, but this sandwich is delicious."

"Some people born with the magic," Mariko declared. Amalia shot her a quizzical look, then realized she wasn't talking about sandwich preparation.

"But this country never support the artist." Mari pointed at the ceiling. "They don't want him to stand for anything. Especially black artist. Jewish artist, too. America the culture of the cheeseburger."

Tris opened the door on this familiar refrain. Linda heard, rose, met him in the foyer.

"The 'culture of the cheeseburger' routine, huh? Has she done 'last of the Mohicans' yet?"

"Yup. In the car." Linda shrugged on her coat. "I'm going for a walk. Do you think Mariko would like to come?"

"The concept of taking a walk just to take a walk would be utterly inconceivable to her. But you could ask."

They passed into the living room. Mariko rose as they entered, whisked the plates off the coffee table—leaving it barren except for the *Pound Foolish* bound galley lying there, its spine intact, the book apparently unopened—then stooped to grab the wastebasket sitting by Amalia's feet. Tris watched her spirit everything away, disquieted by the sight of Mariko acting on anyone's behalf but Albert's. *I not manager for hire*, she'd told Higgins, but how true was it?

Tris and Nina arranged themselves on either side of his grandmother.

"How are you feeling, Amalia?" Nina laid a hand on hers.

"Fine. Appearances to the contrary. Picked up an awful cough at the hospital. But I'm feeling . . . What's the word I want? Resolute."

"Hmm" was all Tris could muster.

"Strong word," said Nina almost to herself.

"I don't—" the old woman managed to say before she broke off, hacking. A pained expression crossed her face, as if she were choking down an overlarge pill. She winced and swallowed and her voice returned. "I don't want to burden you kids. And I'm sure your grandfather is eager to see you, Tris. Nina, maybe you and I could have a cup of tea? Would you mind putting on some water?"

"Not at all." She headed for the kitchen, Tris for the stairs. He reached the threshold of his grandfather's study and found the old man sprawled in his chair, asleep, a NYNEX White Pages from 1992 open before him. Not only did Tristan refuse to keep an address book, he didn't even bother to replace one year's directory with its successor. His cronies, the few who were left, tended to stay put until they died.

"Grandpa?" Nothing. Tris strolled over, stood behind the old man. He realized he'd never viewed the room from this perspective. There was only one photograph on the huge cluttered desk: the two of them in that dark freight yard, eleven years ago, a writer and his protégé. A feeling of heaviness filled Tris, and he looked away from the picture, only to find the copy of *Pound Foolish* he'd left yesterday. It was open, splayed over the lip of the desk.

Any thought of waking his grandfather vanished. Tris retreated to the high-backed purple velvet chair marooned in the room's opposite corner, the location and hideousness of which suggested that visitors were rare and barely tolerated. Tristan snorted, twitched, resettled. Tris's eyes roved up the stacks of fat manila folders that surrounded the desk, and set finally on the old man himself, alone in his kingdom, slumped forward on his throne, invisible crown slipping down his forehead.

Tris crossed his legs and watched him slumber.

Nina set the tray down on the coffee table and pulled up a chair. "So."

"So," Amalia returned.

"So should I just make conversation, or can we talk about your resoluteness? Is that a word, *resoluteness?*"

"Resolve, I think you'd say." Amalia sipped her tea. "I knew I liked you for a reason."

"I just thought someone ought to take you seriously enough to ask." Nina paused and swirled the murk of her tea. "This might sound awful, but hearing you say what you said moved me. I felt like I was watching you . . . I don't know, become yourself again, and I have nothing against Tristan, but to me it's, well, it's beautiful. That you could—"

She heard a moist snuffling sound, looked up, and found tears glittering on Amalia's face, the water ensconcing itself in the wrinkles of her cheeks like tiny jewels. Nina lurched from her chair, stepped over the coffee table, and wrapped an arm around her.

It had been years since she'd hugged an old person—really hugged one; the fingertips-to-shoulders greeting she usually gave Tris's grandparents didn't count. Not since she'd hugged her Deda, as a girl. The familiar thinness of the skin, hanging loosely from the bones. Its excruciating softness. Amalia's body gave instantly to the slight pressure of Nina's arm, and the old woman fell, shoulder to shoulder, against the young. Amalia weighed nothing, and the thought that people eased toward oblivion for years before they actually died crossed Nina's mind. Pounds melted away from bodies. Flesh began the work of baring skeletons.

Amalia's head rested on Nina's clavicle. Her feathery white hair grazed Nina's cheek. And then, with a sniff, the old woman righted herself, found Nina's hand, and squeezed it hard.

"Thank you." Amalia dabbed at the hollow caves beneath her eyes; a tissue had somehow materialized in her hand. "I'm glad you understand."

The old woman coughed—a sudden, fearsome sound—inhaled a draft of air, then coughed again. She closed her eyes and drew a long, calm breath, shook her head and tore apart her tissue. "This house might seem empty to you, but it's not." Her eyes darted to the ceiling. "It's full of his ambition, and the lies I told myself." Amalia stared into the room and smiled. "I never really fooled myself at all."

She covered Nina's hand with her own. "Thank God Tris has someone like you. You're braver than I was. You'll keep each other honest."

A dull shame rose in Nina, the sensation so familiar it dismayed and bored her. "I hope so," she said. "But I'm not so honest. Or so brave." She withdrew her hand, pulled her phone from the back pocket of her jeans and flipped it open, pretending she had a call. She didn't even have reception. "I'm sorry, Amalia. It's work. I should take this."

"Of course, dear."

Nina ducked into the old woman's office, closed the door behind her, sank into the swivel chair until her eyes were level with the desk. The shame was like a morphine drip: she could press a button and feel it surging ruinously through her, or she could spare herself and simply walk through life with a needle in her arm, wheeling an IV bag beside her and pretending she was fine and it wasn't there. She imagined Amalia sitting here just like this, her office a prison, searching for the courage to escape and finding it only now, with her life nearly gone.

Nina reached across the desk, grabbed the heavy old phone, brought it to her lap, and lifted the receiver. Her fingers hovered for an instant, then darted across the keypad. She closed her eyes, said "Ahhh," to ensure that her voice was in working order. The phone rang twice, three times, Nina's breath bouncing back off the mouthpiece hot and stale, her grip on the molded plastic tightening.

A pause in the rhythm of the tones told her she was getting voice mail. Nina couldn't tell if adrenaline was rushing into or out of her bloodstream. Whichever it was, the surge made her hands shake.

Marcus's outgoing message was the same as ever. "Yeah, bruh." Beep.

"Marcus." Her voice was an octave lower than usual. "It's over. It's really over. This isn't who I am, and I'm sick of not being who I am. That's all I've got to say. Don't call me. If you do, I'll tell your wife everything. I'm serious. Good-bye."

She placed the handset on its cradle and laced her fingers over it. For a moment, relief washed through her. Then Nina imagined Marcus listening to the message, chuckling, pressing whatever button on his phone erased it from the world. This was the same old bullshit. Everything she'd said, she'd said before. Only time could endow it with meaning, and that wasn't enough. An X-Acto knife sitting in a mug full of pens caught her attention, and Nina toyed with the idea of cutting herself—some pain to mark the moment, a scar to serve as a reminder. You needed scars in life.

Instead, her mind suddenly sharp and brutal, Nina dialed information, scribbled down the number to Hunter's admissions office, called, endured three rings before an answering machine picked up. Her heart thundered beneath her ribs, as if through sheer fury it might dissuade her from the ill-considered and hugely self-destructive display of morality she was about to make.

Beep.

"Hello. This is Nina Hricek, and I'm calling about my scholarship, the Dawes Black Achievement in Photography. The truth is that I'm . . . I'm not really black. I lied."

There was a click. "Hello? Nina? This is Dean Teasdale." A stern male voice. "Is this a joke?"

Nina could barely speak. "No joke."

Dead air. She almost slammed the phone down, ran away. "This is a very serious matter," Teasdale said at last. "I'm sure you know that."

"Yes."

"The disciplinary committee will have to discuss it. There will be consequences. You can be sure of that."

"Okay," she whispered. He started to say something else, but Nina was already replacing the phone on the cradle. She stood up, walked across the hall, locked herself in the bathroom. Bent over the sink and splashed herself with a handful of water, shockingly cold. She had to get herself together before Tris came back downstairs.

On her next turn, Amalia picked up the jack of spades, the very card she knew Mariko needed. She threw a seven, ran her free hand over the shawl covering her knees, and leaned back on the couch, pleased. She'd never been much of a game person—time to herself had been too rare to waste, except perhaps on chess—but in the past week, Mari had taught her how much fun a deck of cards could be. They sat in the living room for hours, drinking Mari's homemade ginger tea and smoking cigarettes and playing hand after hand. The storm that was her husband was still brewing; anytime now, it would gather strength and rumble down the staircase. Amalia felt wonderfully tranquil all the same. These were days of convalescence. Days she'd earned and would enjoy.

The house was warmer now than ever before. Tristan had always insisted that a chill kept the brain alert and warmth lulled it into fuzziness, so for almost fifty years the thermostat needle had never edged past sixty-two, even when snow blanketed the ground. On her second day of residence, Mariko had marched up to the small box and cranked it to a robust seventy, and Tristan had not done a thing. Perhaps he hadn't noticed, or perhaps his mind was already too lethargic for the extra degrees to make a difference.

On a normal week, Linda would have dropped in two or three times, but now she seemed to be keeping her distance. Perhaps she hoped the situation between her parents would settle on its own, but more likely she was deliberating like a judge in chambers, trying to decide whether her mother's behavior violated statutes on cruel and unusual punishment. In the meantime, since Linda did nothing in silence, she maintained a running commentary on peripheral matters. Mariko's presence baffled her. *Why is she still here, Mom?* Linda had asked yesterday, a note of restrained anger in her voice—a note that was almost always there, Amalia thought sadly, like a dog whistle that only Linda herself couldn't hear.

She's here for me, and she's a great comfort, Amalia had replied, bookmarking her grandson's galleys and staring at her daughter until Linda sighed and sucked her cheeks and went back to rearranging the contents of her parents' refrigerator.

There was nothing else to say. At first, Amalia had needed something to pass between herself and Mariko, wanted one of them to lay the past to rest, give it a eulogy. But the desire for words waned. Here they were: two old women, playing cards and drinking tea, noticing the nice things each did for the other, the little thoughtful gestures. When Mariko brought her a blanket because the evening had grown chilly, or asked what her favorite soup was, and then made it, that was an act of love.

They gave each other hand massages, cooked together, watched old movies. Amalia didn't want to kiss Mariko anymore. She didn't want to kiss anybody. Love wasn't that now. It was sitting quietly and moving tenderly and knowing that there had existed between you a moment of recognition, as real now as it had ever been. Being able to slice through all the layers of pain and pull out the warm marble of joy at the center and hold it in your hand. She couldn't do that with Tristan. Their pain didn't wrap around their joy but extended from it like tracks leaving a railroad station.

He could live upstairs forever. That was fine. Let the two of them shamble around and keep out of each other's way and remain cordial and go to weddings and funerals and family dinners together. Let him do just what he'd done all along, with nothing cut away but the pretense that this was a marriage. She would sit right here and play cards and be happy, and if he could be happy, too, so much the better, and if he couldn't, he could blame her for it. That, in itself, would probably be an improvement, since until now he'd had no one to blame but himself.

Mariko picked up the seven and laid down the six of clubs, and then the stairs creaked and they looked up to see Tristan in the midst of his descent to the kitchen. To Amalia's great surprise, he'd begun cooking for himself. Six straight meals prepared by his own hands had passed into his stomach. Three had been egg sandwiches, two hot dogs, and one oatmeal, but even Tristan's ability to boil water was a revelation. Each time, Mariko had met him in the kitchen and offered to fix something, and each time he had waved her off: *Don't trouble yourself*.

Amalia turned back to the game and tried to decide whether to pick up the six. She had one already, and doing so would mean shifting her strategy away from straights. She looked up only when she assumed Tristan was gone, and instead found her husband coming toward her, his face strained with rage.

She laid the cards on the couch, facedown, and turned.

"Hello, Tristan."

As slowly as he was walking, Tristan's halt still seemed abrupt, military. His arm swung up to fill the distance between them, a paperback clutched in his hand.

"Have you read it?"

Amalia arched her back and peered down her nose at the book, though she knew already that it was their grandson's novel. She had finished it yesterday afternoon, and made her peace with it last night. At first, Amalia had been devastated at the man her grandson had become, felt as she read that she was watching him pledge himself to a fate worse, even, than his grandfather's. Tristan's crimes were of neglect. He had cast real relationships underfoot in order to cultivate those he invented. Tris had shoveled the lives of two people who loved him as dearly as any on this earth into the furnace to fuel his art. She'd imagined him licking his wounds, growing bitter, weighing out revenge scenarios and comeback plans and deciding that such collateral damage as the loss of a grandparent or two was worth bearing if it meant unassailability, success. She'd almost closed the book.

But as Amalia had read on, the dread lying in the pit of her stomach dissolved, and she began to experience something entirely different: a soaring wonder shot through with a staggering, soul-deep relief—as if by reading she had unburdened herself—and finally an awed gratitude. He got it, she'd found herself thinking. This book is every true thing I have ever feared to say. She'd been a shitty Pandora, refusing to loose stinging things upon the world, accepting instead the misery that came with keeping the box closed. Tris had flung it open and the hordes had flown out, and now Pandora was free.

Amalia stared up at her husband, hoping Tristan noticed how untroubled she was by his rage.

"Of course."

The hand that held the galleys dropped to his side. "So you know what he's done."

She sighed at him. "What has he done, Tristan?"

"He's run our lives through the goddamned processor, Amalia! Right under our noses, he's been spying on us."

"You've never tried to kill yourself, Tristan. You've never moved back to the Bronx. You've never cheated, to my knowledge."

"It's still me. Anyone would know it. *Will* know it, I should say. Who the hell is going to tell *them* what's real?"

Amalia leaned against the firm curved back of the sofa. "I don't understand. You're angry because he made things up, or because he told the truth?"

"Both. It's both at once. Even the things he made up are true."

Amalia darted her eyes to Mariko, embarrassed to be having this conversation in front of her. But Mariko was gone, had flitted from the room without attracting so much as an errant glance.

"It's flat-out treachery, Amalia." He sounded helpless, hollow. "He used my life and made me out to be a monster."

"*Pound Foolish* doesn't have monsters, Tristan. There are elements of you. And me. But Tris's characters aren't that simple. If you want my signature on your declaration of war, you can forget it."

"Don't tell me," he boomed. "I've done this my whole life—it's all I've done, as your grandson has been kind enough to point out. I know how writers think. They change the facts but not the people. The people but not the facts. They take things a step further, a step to the left, a step to the right. They do the shit-ass hokeypokey. Especially the hacks."

"Like your first novel, about the other families living in your building?"

Tristan responded with a look no less infuriating for its familiarity, a grimace that meant, *Your lack of understanding is so profound that it is painful, tiring, to even speak to you.*

"That book was shit. But it's completely different. I didn't know those people. I had a few facts and I made up the rest."

"Just like Tris." Amalia realized she had clenched her jaw, just like her daughter, and relaxed it. "I didn't sit for any interviews. I never told him what it was like to be married to you. Tris imagined. He invented. And he nailed it. He nailed it and you know it. Some of it is my truth. Some of it is yours. But all of it is his. So goddamn it, Tristan, let him have it. Lord knows, others have done as much for you. Including Tris."

Tristan shook his head. "No. This is unforgivable. Our lives are known, Amalia. People will read this book and think I'm a drug addict. That I had an affair with Judy Pendergast, for Christ's sake. What kind of pseudo-Freudian bullshit is that?"

"Oh, come on, Tristan. The love scene in the country club bathroom? It's hilarious. There's no way that could be you—a hard-on for Judy? That scene *proves* the book is fiction."

"Only to you." He dropped his copy onto the coffee table and glowered down at it. "You know what our grandson is? He's a spoiled trust-fund brat with a fucking master's degree in fiction that we paid for, and nothing to write about except us and our lives. Some progress this family has made." His eyes met hers and anger blared from them, anger Amalia saw was covering for hurt. But if Tristan wouldn't own up to that hurt, he'd get no sympathy from her.

"What gives him the right? What in the hell does he know about anything?"

"A hell of a lot," Amalia snapped back. The dull tickle in her throat intensified. She swallowed hard against it, not wanting to cough. "If I had had the courage, I'd have written a book just like his—but instead I've got a desk drawer full of poems no one has ever seen." She waited for a response, but he said nothing, and just like that the secret ceased to be a secret and floated weightlessly away, like a balloon nobody cared about. Amalia watched it drift off, stunned, and then remembered she was furious.

"Is that the only reason you came down? To talk about the book?"

"Yes." His voice stiffened. "To talk about the book."

"Well then, I think you'd better go back upstairs." Amalia leaned forward and picked up her cards. Her husband stood before her, shocked, indignant, and Amalia pretended not to feel his eyes. Finally, he relented, turned, and disappeared.

By the time Tristan stood at the second-floor landing, with one hand clutching the bannister and the fingertips of the other splayed against the wall for balance, a sense of completion was settling over him. At long last, he was cut off from every other human being in the world. Unanimously betrayed. By his wife. His grandson. His daughter, who'd raised such a child—Tristan knew damn well what her agenda was. By the friends who had failed to provide better counsel, and the friends who'd been heartless enough to die. By the brain lollygagging in his head, the withered muscles of his body.

One way or another, everyone and everything had spoiled or faded, and now things were simple. He felt unburdened, and realized he had jettisoned two enormous weights he'd always carried: foreboding and hope. Things weren't going to get any worse or any better. Time had come to a standstill. Tristan could either struggle vainly as the resin encased him and hardened into amber or accept his fate and be still, perhaps spend the remaining time recalling happier occasions.

Perhaps this was why so many of the aged lost their minds. Capitulating to obsolescence was less painful if you couldn't tell your dick from a garden hose. But here he was intact, still full of anger at a time when anger was pathetic, useless. In eighty years, he'd neither earned the right to stand above the fray nor forfeited enough to fall below it. He had merely slowed down, and the other members of the pack had smelled his frailty and attacked. Soon they would fight over his bones, his legacy. But not before they'd gathered by his bedside to receive his benedictions.

Tristan sighed, dropped his hands from the wall and bannister, and considered his options. He could turn right and walk into his study, sit behind his desk and pretend that he might write, flanked by leaning skyscrapers of wasted paper, with a jar of gefilte fish and a plastic fork and a paper plate by his elbow and no horseradish with which to flavor the soggy morsels he'd been masticating mindlessly since youth. *Still Life with Manuscript Pages, Manischewitz Jar, and Bitter Old Fart.* Or he could turn left and stumble into bed and give himself over to sleep, wake only to eat and piss and shit, perhaps read something. There was pleasure there. Respite. A life of sleep had tempted him before, but he had always had the fortitude to forgo it. Some men coped with crisis by springing into action, purposeful or purposeless—by grabbing a rifle and marching straight toward the banditos or by grabbing a rake and marching straight into the yard. Others coped by deactivating, shutting down. Or by taking that same rifle and blowing out their brains.

Tristan had worked through wars, through illnesses, even through the seven days in 1980 that had passed between the removal of the polyps from his lymph nodes and the finding that they were benign. But now the notion of somnolence was too seductive to resist. A long, strong nap. Perhaps he'd wake up refreshed, with some of his rage leached away and his perspective realigned. Or perhaps he'd stir to consciousness groggy and disappointed, wanting only to return to dreams, and turn back over like a speck of flotsam in the ocean and submerge himself in them again.

Either way was fine. He pulled back the mothball-scented quilt of the guest room bed and lay down on the cool, soft sheets and closed his eyes, and time began to fall away.

That was what happened when you jettisoned hope and foreboding, he supposed; the hours and the days lost meaning. It was an opaqueness Tristan had always steeled himself against. Compared to most men, he had lived a timeless life, free from schedules and punch cards, and so Tristan had learned to impose such things upon himself. They called it self-discipline, but really it was just a way for him to feel part of the world. He got up when the businessmen rose to remind himself that what he did was work. To subdue any lurking self-indulgence, any fey capitulation to the whimsies of the Muse. Let the other bozos bitch and whine about how they didn't *feel* like writing today, how they weren't *inspired.* Lawyers probably didn't feel like lawyering every day, either, but they didn't stay in bed. Garbagemen manned garbage whether they were in the mood or not. The very act of consuming a mug of coffee at 7:30 A.M. was an affirmation, no less than imbibing a cocktail when the work was done.

But no more sensory Ping-Pong. No more ritual sharpening and dulling of the wits. Tristan slept. Not with abandon, but with diligence. Straight through the night, the morning, the beginning of the afternoon. When his body forced wakefulness upon him, Tristan dispensed with it as perfunctorily as he could, condescending only to a state of semiconsciousness as he stumbled to and from the bathroom, then returning to the business of slumber.

His stomach, rumbling, awakened him some hours later. He ignored it, turned onto his other side to fool it into shutting up, and dozed off. The next time he opened his eyes, it was to squint at the pale light behind the gauze curtains and wonder whether it was dawn or twilight. He spent a moment in speculation before deciding that it didn't matter, shutting his eyes again. He slept and he woke and it was dark and on the nightstand was a turkey sandwich. He ate it, drank the glass of milk beside it, considered getting up. But soon the food, and the promise of more dreams, won out. Tristan didn't remember his dreams during his brief bouts of consciousness, but he had the sense they were agreeable and mild.

In the days that followed, Tristan began to regard his new enterprise as elegant. For eighty years, sleep had merely been about refueling, and now at last he was granting this remarkable condition the kind of time and attention it deserved. In his reluctance to wake up, he found himself spending longer and longer each day suspended in a pleasant in-between state, with his eyes closed and his mind channeling both dream and thought. He had limited powers of control, and no desire to expand them. Bodily sensations, words, images, ideas, and essences swirled together, touching and eluding him. Each thing dancing through his brain was a liquid ribbon of color, and where they brushed or caromed off the walls, they left smudges, streaks, splatters.

Each time Tristan moved out of this limbo and into full awareness, he was left with an internal painting to admire and decode before it fell away. Often, some person he'd known seemed to be the subject. Most memorably, he'd awakened with a strong sense of Albert, a feeling of

Albert, an urge to listen to some of Van Horn's music. But the LPs were downstairs, in the living room, so that was that. He played them in his head instead, all he remembered, until they soothed him back to sleep.

Sandwiches and soup, water and tea continued to materialize. Only once was he awake when Mari entered with the tray. It was absurdly frightening: the sight of her, the anticipation of even the smallest interaction. Tristan shut his eyes and tried to mimic slumber, but he was too slow and she spoke.

"You have to get up, Tristan."

He regarded her through half-masted eyelids. "No," Tristan replied, his voice sludgy with disuse and surprisingly fearsome, "I don't." Mariko set down the tray and left without another word.

That, Tristan knew had happened. Whether Linda had banged on his door in a dream or in reality, or both, he couldn't be sure. In any case, he'd muttered *Go away* and heaved a box of tissues at the sound, and she'd obeyed. The box was back on the nightstand now, but that didn't prove anything. No one else had come around, not to his knowledge. Least of all the newest goddamned writer in the family. No fool he. The devious little shit was staying out of range.

CHAPTER TWELVE

Nina tore down the crisp autumn block, leaves crunching underfoot, arms pumping, cheeks red, ignoring the prurient glances thrown her way by every male over twelve as she passed in her T-shirt and track pants. This was why she never jogged anymore. Her tits jounced all over the fucking place, painfully, no matter what she wore. But she had to do something, and pushing herself to the brink of physical exhaustion was it. A week had passed, and nobody had called. Most likely, Hunter College was trying to figure out what to do with her, just as she was trying to figure out what to do with herself.

This much was certain: she was fucked. Hunter might or might not make her give the money back—and it was money she didn't have, so unless they planned to sue for it and garnish her wages, which seemed fairly ridiculous, they could chalk that one up, learn their lesson and make people prove they were what they claimed in the future. They might or might not expel her. Probably they would. She would if she were they. At a bare minimum, they'd put her on disciplinary probation and inform Columbia of what she'd done, and Columbia would revoke her acceptance to its graduate program. One way or another, her student visa was going to expire, rendering her illegal. As early as next week if they expelled her, in May if she were permitted to don a cap and gown.

That left two options, deportation and marriage. That was one option, really, and one option wasn't an option, but a necessity. The simplest thing would be to declare her situation openly, tell Tris she could stay in America only if they got engaged. She wouldn't even have to explain the lie and the scholarship and the consequences she'd brought tumbling down with that bout of truthfulness or moral reckoning or whatever it had been. She could just say she'd changed her mind about grad school and wanted to work instead, pay back her student loans.

But that was no good. If they were going to do it, they should do it for real. She couldn't have Tris feeling that he was rescuing her. That would give him too much power.

And really, Nina didn't feel as skeptical about marriage as she used to—didn't see its futility confirmed by the wreckage of her parents' union or Tris's grandparents', didn't consider it the ludicrous, doomed proposition she once had. Perhaps it was love, or age. More likely, it was the creeping exhaustion that mounted in her with each year of going it alone, in a foreign country, with no asylum and no money and Marcus still treating her like his personal concubine and Miklos bawling out his distant pitch-black woes. Marriage had started to seem like an increasingly nice, calm, sturdy idea as far back as two years ago—and this wasn't revisionism, Nina told herself, jogging in place as she waited for a red light to turn green. This wasn't tricking herself into believing what she had to. This was legit.

It would come as a shock to Tris, because his knee-jerk antipathy toward the institution had stopped her from ever divulging her own evolving opinion of it. That had been a mistake. She'd have to ease him into the idea quickly, convince him that it didn't mean what he thought it did, wasn't an agreement to live a boring life, or a finish line that marked the end of everything vital in a relationship. That it wouldn't turn them into his parents, grandparents, whatever suburban Hubby and Missus archetype he held in his mind. That it would be fun to have a big party, a public celebration of their love. Malik could DJ. It could be a hip-hop wedding. They'd get presents.

Nina turned onto Dekalb, the half-imagined seasonal aromas of pumpkin and hearth fire sharp in her nostrils, threw on a burst of speed, and crossed the street. Once more around the level rectangular route, three blocks long by five blocks wide, and then she'd go inside and shower and let Tris know she wanted him to marry her. No—she'd use *wife* as a verb, *wife me up*, the way he and Malik did. That would be nice and playful, convey the point that it was still her, that wanting to get hitched did not instantly transform her into some gross American sitcom harpie, waving her unadorned ring finger in the air and threatening to walk. The image made Nina think of the new wife her mother had conjured up for Miklos, the trashy, silicone-filled Californian broad. It was amazing how vividly Nina could still see the nonexistent woman in her mind.

How many hours have I just slept? Tristan wondered as he ruptured the surface of a bowl of minestrone with his spoon. He'd been awake now for an hour, mostly out of the desire to determine whether it was dusk or dawn. A hard urge to put down, that. He stirred only at ambiguous hours, it seemed to him. Or perhaps all light was beginning to take on the same wan hue. It was dusk, he had decided finally, and time he ate something. It had become a ritual of sorts—who knew why?—for Tristan to ignore the food left for him until he'd awakened to its company a second time. The spoon was halfway to his mouth when Linda barged through the door.

"Jesus, Dad, that's been sitting there since last night. I'll get you something fresh."

He chewed once and let the thick liquid slide down his throat. "Don't you knock?"

"What would be the point?" She sat on the edge of the bed, reached over and lifted the bowl out of his palm, then wrested the spoon from his grip and deposited both on the floor by her feet. He watched it happen, transfixed by his own inability to resist.

"Enough is enough, Dad. Time to get up. You've got a bris to attend."

He blinked at her. "I do?"

"Yup. Steven and Melissa had a boy. Nine pounds even. Kid's a fucking moose."

"Name?"

Linda dropped her chin and looked over her brow at him. "Prepare yourself. Thaddeus Carter Brodsky."

Tristan winced. "And they're having a *bris*? Really?"

"It would mean a tremendous amount to Steven, and his mother, and probably to your brother, if you went," said Linda, acting in her official capacity as liaison between the two branches of the family, a job she had inherited from Amalia.

"I don't think I'm up to it."

"Bullshit. Look, Dad, you are not going to spend the rest of your life asleep. You've got to deal. You know that."

Tristan threw back the covers, and the warm, stale odor of his body floated up from the bed. "I don't know anything," he said, lifting himself to his feet. He shuttled to the bathroom, closed the door, and took a weak, dribbling piss. For the first time in days, he glanced into the mirror over the sink. Stubble did not flatter an old man; he looked like a hobo with his patchy gray-white beard. His daughter was right. There was no dignity in this.

Linda rubbed the cuff of his desiccated bathrobe between two fingers as he climbed back into bed.

"Eisenhower administration?"

"Truman." He reclined against the headboard, one house-slippered foot on the floor and the other laid out straight in front of him. "You've read your son's book?"

"I don't read books written by relatives. Life is easier that way."

"I wasn't aware that you had such a policy. I seem to recall discussing some of my own books with you."

"Not since the one about the musician with all the women."

"It's pretty terrible."

Linda picked a piece of lint off his pajama top. "I'm sure it's brilliant. I just got sick of wondering which character thought what you thought and which didn't, and who was who, and which parts were real. The guy has all those affairs."

Her gaze meandered down the bedspread. "Sometimes I still read one of Mom's poems, if it's in *The New Yorker* or something. But I'm not going to read Tris's book. I'll buy twenty copies. I'll tell everyone I know to read it. But not me. I've learned my lesson."

"I never knew you felt this way."

"I never told you."

"Why not?"

"Because you would have waved your hand at me and said I didn't understand what you were doing. Which probably would've been true. And I would have felt even worse."

Tristan said nothing.

"He got a starred review from *Publishing Preview*," Linda offered. "They were hard on *Contents Under Pressure*, so it's a good sign. Mom's been raving about it, too."

"Because she thinks I've finally gotten my comeuppance." Tristan crossed his arms. "She's told you my opinion as well as her own?"

"She has, and it upset me so much, I've barely slept all week. That's the only reason I didn't drag you out of bed days ago—I was hoping rest might calm you down. Before you said something to your grandson that would break his heart."

"I don't intend to say anything to him. Ever."

"Don't be a schmuck. If you think Tris meant to hurt you, or expose you, or whatever it is you think, you're crazy. Everything isn't always about you, Dad, as hard as that may be to comprehend."

Tristan bowed his brow into a scowl, looked away. "You've said what you came to say. I'd like some privacy."

Linda stood. "Clean yourself up. I'll be here tomorrow at ten."

She left without waiting for a response. Tristan tried to fall asleep, but it was no good; that was over. His brain was back in gear, the memories flowing.

He gazed at the door Linda had just slammed, and remembered that a poster of John Lennon had once hung from it. And then it was 1969 and Linda was facedown on this bed, arm crooked above her head, body racking as she cried into her elbow, and Tristan was standing at the threshold with a gin and tonic in his hand and a professor of economics by his side—the man staring expectantly at him, at her, at him again.

Tristan hadn't done a thing, simply continued walking his guest through the house, as if a bawling teenager were part of the tour, a permanent exhibit. Downstairs, a cocktail party simmered: voices rising through the floor, filling the house. Minutes before, Tristan had watched his daughter race up the stairs, legs pumping, skirt flouncing around her thighs. And before that, he'd stood close enough to her, one conversational cluster away, to overhear the exchange that had routed her.

Hello, Mr. Andrews, Linda had said, entering the man's radius with two long, well-timed strides just as his previous conversation was concluding. In her right hand was a glass of white wine from which she had not sipped, from which she never would. *I just wanted to tell you how much I enjoyed your novel. I thought you did a wonderful job with Christine; I really felt like I knew her*. She raised her left hand to her temple, tucked a strand of hair behind her ear. *Is it true that it's going to be made into a movie? That's so exciting!*

Andrews drained his highball, staring around the glass at her as he brought it to his mouth, and then said, *Who are you again?*

She took the wineglass with her when she fled. It was sitting on her bedside table when Tristan passed her room and did nothing. Didn't excuse himself, slip inside, and lay a hand across her shuddering back. Didn't go downstairs and tell Andrews to get the hell out, or march him up there to apologize. He'd let her cry, let some prick humiliate his daughter in her own living room, and snuck past as if it wasn't his problem. Assumed Amalia would track her down, handle it. Convinced himself he wouldn't be able to help anyway.

The memory played on. Fifteen minutes later, he had turned, to see his wife guiding his daughter back down the stairs, an arm around her shoulders. Amalia was radiant—and realer to him, somehow, than she'd ever been. Whether this was what he'd felt then, Tristan did not know, but he felt it now. His daughter was the age his wife had been when they'd met, the same age Amalia had remained, in some ways, ever since. A part of her would always be that young, that beautiful, just blooming into brilliance. Tristan closed his eyes, and rivers of desire and regret gushed through him. He opened them and whispered his wife's name.

Tristan walked to the bathroom, found a razor in the cabinet, twisted the faucet until steaming water splashed into the sink. He didn't care about the world and how it would interpret the doppelgänger his grandson had devised, the old man realized as he wet his face, applied the shaving cream. He'd tested out that argument with Amalia, thought then that he cared, but it was clear to Tristan now that he did not. What could the world do to him that it hadn't already? He was ashamed, that was the truth. He was a selfish fuck, an absentee human being. All the battles he had fought had been for the wrong things, against the wrong people. And now all of it was set down in black and white, the essence of his failings abstracted, satirized, manipulated into goddamn art.

Tristan gripped the razor and slashed carelessly through the lather. The blade was dull, the bristles thick. Progress was slow and painful. Forgiveness was what he wanted, the old man thought as the basin filled up with hair. Even now, it was perhaps not out of reach—to be forgiven, to forgive—if only Tristan weren't so thoroughly himself, so beholden to the conviction that forgiveness would wipe him clean away, destroy whatever was left. He tried to tell himself that was a good thing, tried to think of forgiveness as rebirth. But it sounded distinctly New Testament, and besides, who the hell was he to be reborn? He'd only fuck things up worse if he bucked the cycle of birth and death, traded his dignity for a few breaths of golem life.

You had to bury a man to make a man, that was what Ellison had said. And he had lived too long, and Tris had tired of waiting and decided to make himself a man by throwing six cubic feet of words over his grandfather's shallow-breathing body. Perhaps Tristan would have done the same. He tried to sell himself on the idea. It didn't take, but Tristan plundered on, probed every nook and cranny of his mind, plausible and otherwise, looking for a loophole, a trapdoor, a crawl space: any semblance of a path that might open up on some kind of absolution, for himself or for his grandson. He suspected that the two were one.

The quest was as exhausting as it was unaccustomed, and soon Tristan stepped back from it. To die stoic and alienated and brimming with anguish, yes, that had long been part of the plan. To die in the grip of some horribly earnest attempt to set things right—to expire in the midst of a paroxysm of rectification, with your pants around your ankles and your thumb jammed up your ass—that was another story. A man should die the way he'd lived, not recant in his final hours. Addiction, as a cause of death, was respectable. Withdrawal was not.

"Tristan ready to go," Mariko reported, picking her way down the back stairs and joining Amalia at the sink. She took up a towel and rubbed it over one of the breakfast plates glistening on the drying rack. A perfectly functional dishwasher stood within arm's reach, and yet here Amalia was, despite everything else she had to attend to, doing the dishes manually.

There was something meditative about standing with your hands under the warm running water, something pure and useful to the act of cleaning. But Mariko was the real reason she labored so. The woman had never owned a dishwasher in her life, and she wasn't about to put her trust in one now, so after meals the two of them became a small assembly line, rinsing and drying. Tristan's dishes, Mariko did alone. The dishwasher was still full of the knives and spoons and bowls he'd used before he'd stopped coming downstairs. Mariko probably didn't realize they were in there, festering. Amalia was almost constantly aware of it, but she had no intention of running the machine herself.

She rinsed the last fork, turned it in her hands, and waited for Mariko's eyes to give up and flit elsewhere. The past few days had been like this: Mariko feinting and fluttering, looking for an opening, and Amalia refusing to give her one, shutting down the moment Mariko opened her mouth to plead Tristan's case.

Yesterday, things had come to a head. Mariko had been a hair more caustic, Amalia a hair more resistant, and that had been enough to make everything flare up, then curl and char and blacken.

Amalia, Mariko had said, walking into the living room wide-eyed and coltish, hands clasped in front of her, *your husband gonna wither away up there. He barely eats. You gotta do something.*

Amalia had squeezed her blanket and continued reading, forced herself not to reply. Only after Mariko had given up and returned to the kitchen, shaking her head, had it occurred to Amalia that she'd behaved just as Tristan would have. She finished her chapter, closed the book, and followed Mariko. Not to apologize, but to be fair.

Amalia found her sitting at the kitchen table, holding a mug of black tea, staring at her own reflection in the dusty television screen. Amalia stood to one side, out of Mariko's sight line, and rested part of her weight against the back of a chair. She was giving Mariko the opportunity to repay her rudeness by ignoring her back, but Mariko looked up immediately. She didn't know that game.

He'll come down when he's ready, said Amalia, softer than she meant it.

Mariko sat for a moment with her lips pinched tight. *Tristan a good man.*

The sentence hit Amalia like a bucket of ice water. It was a declaration of allegiance, a formal withdrawl of sympathy. How foolish she had been to ever believe this woman loyal. It didn't matter how many card games they played, how many dishes they cooked or cleaned together. Whatever existed between them was secondary. Mariko served genius. Male genius. She understood nothing. She was as cold as she'd ever been.

You marry him, then, Amalia said, and turned to leave—cheated out of a quick, angry exit by her own frailty. Nature's way of telling the aged that they shouldn't be embroiled in such drama, she supposed.

Why you so mad? Mariko said before Amalia had made it three feet. The younger woman's arm uncoiled, shot toward the ceiling like the body of an exclamation point. *What he ever do to you?* She let it fall back to her lap, clenched her hand into a fist like a period, and shook her head. *He don't deserve this.*

He deserves every second. That man has given me hell.

Mariko pushed back her chair, stood up as if she'd been waiting all week for this chance. *What hell? You want hell, try being married to Albert. My husband get high and then walk straight into the ocean! Until waves hitting him in the forehead, knocking him down! I have to rescue, Ama! My husband spend all our money on dope, and I gotta convince landlord not to throw us out into the street! Middle December! You hear me complain? Never! I take responsibility!*

She drew herself up, held out a palm as if checking the air for rain. *What you ever do for Tristan? What he ever do to hold you back? Nothing!*

So what, he got temper? He writer! You know that when you marry him. She threw up her arms. *This bullshit! You wanted to be poet, you fucking poet!*

Mariko's fists dropped to her hips and stayed there. The two of them stood for a moment gauging themselves and each other.

Oh, Mari, Amalia said at last, shaking her head. *You don't know the first thing about marriage, do you?*

I know the first thing. I know you don't abandon, Ama. That the first thing and the last. Mariko's face went blank, and she carried her teacup to the sink to empty, rinse, wash, dry it. Amalia stood and watched. Mariko moistened a sponge and wiped crumbs off the table, into a cupped palm. She pushed in chairs, shuffled newspaper sections into a neat stack. When there was nothing more to do, she strode out of the room, eyes trained on her path, and turned onto the back stairs. Amalia listened for a door to slam, but she got no such satisfaction.

Things she could have said to crush Mariko careened through Amalia's mind. You weren't a wife to Albert, she might have whispered. You were a manager, a bodyguard, and a groupie rolled into one, and he exploited you for forty-five years. And now he's gone, and what are you without him? Nothing. But what would have been the point? Mariko had made her peace ages ago, and each lie she'd told herself since then had glazed her like pottery, layer upon layer, until she was impervious to the winds of the world and trapped inside. Each lie Amalia had told herself had been a tiny tap against the sculptor's chisel boring its way into the crown of her skull, threatening to split her in two.

She'd nestled back into the couch and tried to read, and a few hours later, Mariko had walked into the living room and handed her an egg salad sandwich and a glass of orange juice. Amalia took them wordlessly, bewildered, and Mariko turned and walked away. Was this an act of self-assertion or negation? Apology or spite? It was as if with every gesture, Mariko wanted to prove she was the stronger of the two. That even her anger was not the master of her will.

Now, Amalia laid the fork on the dish rack and turned off the faucet. "I'll wait in my study," she said over her shoulder, as if speaking to a servant, and walked away from Mariko.

The new room was no less oppressive. Amalia slumped back in her work chair until her chest was level with the broad mahogany desk she'd inherited from her father, and found herself listening for Tristan's footsteps above her. Perhaps she would have done nothing without him, been nothing. Her best poems would not exist, that much was certain.

"So let me get this straight," said Tris, limbo-bending to check the knot of his tie. The mirror hung too low for such appraisals, but it provided a clear view of the queen-size bed abutting the opposite wall. Nina lay there now, vertically half-covered by a tan down comforter, listless and naked. "You're saying that if we get married, we can remake the concept of marriage into anything we want, and it doesn't have to be the same basically oppressive, deluded, mundane thing it's always been throughout history."

Nina cat-stretched, arms and legs going momentarily rigid, then crossed her hands behind her head and tried to summon patience. "Right."

"But why bother? Why don't we reinvent, say, slavery? Check it out, we'll sign some paperwork and officially you'll be my slave, but we'll reinvent the whole institution and make it what we want, and it'll be really cool." He frowned, undid the tie, and started over.

"Why do you have to be such a schmuck all the time?"

Nina had floated the idea of marriage yesterday, as planned. She'd traipsed into the bedroom and plopped herself down on his lap after her shower, dressed only in a towel, smiled and wrapped an arm around his neck and said, *I think you should wife me up*—light, playful, sexy.

Tris had stiffened instantly, smiled back but not really and said, *Oh yeah?* instead of what he was really thinking, what his body told her by clenching up—not the muscles, exactly, but something deeper in: the mind, soul, heart, whatever. One of those things, maybe all of them, had blared *Hell no!*, and Tris had tried to be polite, and blink at her as if she was sweet and he was happily surprised, but she could see his brain whirring. She imagined it as a computer screen, filled with number columns scrolling furiously down as he searched for some way to joke himself out of this, put her off gently, and then suspected that there was none and sighed inwardly, resigned to a failed gentleness and the likelihood of his day disappearing in an argument. And such an absurd, depressing thing to argue over.

Since when are you into marriage? he'd asked, touching her cheek, and for a moment Nina thrilled, thinking perhaps she'd read him all wrong and Tris meant *Me, too! I want it, too, but I've been scared to say so because I know how you feel!* But it wasn't that. It was a halting *Um, sorry, not interested* half apology, the other half not an apology at all, but passive-aggression. He was annoyed with her for putting him in the position of having to reject her, and for changing the rules, having an unsanctioned desire, one he couldn't—no, wouldn't—satisfy. It made Tris feel inadequate and at the same time in control, thought Nina; his refusal tipped the balance of power toward him, so far that it ceased to be a balance at all. She wanted something he'd denied, something perpetual that would stay wedged between them, keeping her on the high end of the seesaw, legs dangling in midair, and him on the heavy side, watching her flail for as long as he wanted. It even occurred to her that Tris knew more than he was letting on—had figured out, somehow, that she was in jeopardy and was punishing her for not telling him the truth. Or for something. Fuck.

She was on the verge of laying out the facts now, the visa part anyway, had almost reached that point of desperation. But after all this, how could she? More shame for her, more power for him. Plus, everything she'd said—every declaration of love, every argument about how marriage represented just the kind of intentionality their life together lacked—would be sullied, struck through with black ink like the censored letters her father had held under her nose as a child.

"Schmuck, huh?" Tris replied now, everything a game. "How you gonna speak Yiddish and be anticircumcision?" His knees creaked as he stooped to pull the cardboard shape-holders from a pair of shiny black split-toes he'd bought in Sicily while on tour with Albert. The guys in the band had all bought shoes, so Tris had, too. They'd sat at the back of the closet, unworn, for years, and then Nina had found them, told him they were slick. Now, they were his favorites.

"You've still got time to change your mind and come," he told her, crossing in front of the bed.

"Hell no. Fuck that barbaric shit. Poor little Thaddeus."

"Five thousand years of history, baby," Tris called from the bathroom. "Or six. Whatever. Abraham had to do his own with a sharp rock. You know what they say: ignorance is bris."

"It should be illegal. It's mutilation. Infants are extremely sensitive. I bet it's psychologically scarring, too."

He poked his head out. "Another theory to explain how fucked-up the Jews are?"

"You didn't have a bris."

"Yeah, but I was circumcised. Only difference is that nobody served lox and bagels afterward."

Nina hugged her knees to her chest as Tris rooted through the laundry strewn across the closet floor, looking for his belt. "If we had a son, would you want him circumcised?" she asked.

Tris shrugged. "Yeah, I guess so. It's like the most nonnegotiable, bare-minimum Jewish thing you can do."

Nina shook her head. "I'd never allow it."

He bent over the bed and kissed her forehead. "Then you'd better hope we have girls."

She propped herself up on her elbows, hands over her breasts. "I don't understand how you can talk about kids like it's nothing, and be so scared by marriage."

He fussed again with his tie, tightening, smoothing. She thought she caught the flicker of a smirk. "Yeah, I dunno. Just how it is, I guess." He buttoned the top of his shirt, then tried to ease the constriction by sliding two fingers inside the collar and tugging. "I didn't say I was scared. I ain't never scared."

More cavalier bullshit, Nina thought. More jokes. She pouted for a moment, then tried to be funny. "I don't think I'm so bad. Those Puerto Rican guys in front of the bodega all want to marry me."

He was back at the mirror now, preening. "Yeah?"

"Sure. I get proposals every week."

"I bet you do. What time is it?"

She slid halfway off the bed to peer at the ancient clock radio they kept underneath the frame because it was too ugly to look at. "Ten-fifteen."

"I gotta bounce." He kissed her on the small of the back before she could turn, then lingered there a moment, brushing his lips up her spine. Nina shivered.

"I love you. Don't marry the Puerto Ricans while I'm gone, okay?"

She flipped over, smiled, and gave him the finger as he walked toward the door. He smiled back, and for a moment Nina forgot why they were having this argument, and everything seemed casual and loose and normal. Then she remembered, and panic snapped at her with the force of a real living thing—a big-ass crab, an alligator. "I'm not making any promises," she called out as he slammed the door. She lay there awhile, staring at the ceiling, listening to Brooklyn breathe, then decided she needed to talk to someone, and picked up the phone.

The other guests rose from their chairs and drifted toward the dining room. Tristan sat still, too affected to stand, and hoped everyone would leave him be, allow him the few minutes he needed to shake off this remarkable, unexpected fragility. Then he would rise and find his brother, and seek to determine whether Benjamin had been similarly touched. Tristan suspected so. Ben had seemed on the verge of tears as he stood up there next to his grandson, hands folded in front of him, mouthing the Hebrew prayers along with the mohel. Tristan had been amazed that Benjamin remembered, but not as amazed as he'd been a moment later when he realized that he, too, was whispering along.

"Dad? Don't you want some lunch?"

"No, no." Tristan waved his daughter off. "I'm not hungry. Go ahead. I'll be with you in a minute."

"I'll fix you a plate," said Linda, and merged into the gregarious shuffle toward the buffet.

Tristan stared after her receding torso with unfocused eyes. Under his breath, almost against his will, he began to recite snippets of prayers he'd once memorized: great strange strings of syllables, faintly endowed with meaning, whose declamation required very little of his attention. The Sabbath blessing. The mourner's Kaddish. The Shema. They'd hidden themselves in the remotest caverns of his memory, and there they had remained for nearly seven decades. Now they ran toward the summons for which they'd always waited, and stood proudly at attention.

The sound of a body settling into the chair beside him brought the old man back.

"Pretty horrifying, huh?" his grandson said. He speared a length of asparagus, crammed half of it into his mouth.

Tristan bounced a glance off him. "I was quite moved. This is what millions have died for. The right to hold a simple ceremony."

Tris set his fork down, chewed, and swallowed.

"The Jews are less than one percent of the world's people," Tristan said. "Do you realize that? *Less than one percent*. Yet we've been blamed for everything, since the very beginning. Entire populations have been wiped out. There's never been anything like it in the history of the world. But here we are."

"Here we are. In Great Neck, Long Island."

"Yes." His grandfather fixed him with a scythe of a stare. "And you're lucky I'm speaking to you at all."

Tris frowned, hoping to evince innocence. His stomach took evasive action, curled into a ball. "Whoa—what?"

"That novel of yours, sonny. Why don't you tell me what it's about?"

Tris bit into his lower lip. "The struggles of a great man," he said after a moment.

"And who is that great man, pray tell?" Tristan asked, the old urge to combat mounting, unbidden, in him. This same trickle of adrenaline had been coursing in and out of his bloodstream for eighty years now, he thought. Why hadn't it gone stagnant, like standing water in a fountain?

"What do you mean? He's Irving Gold."

"Is he, for instance, your grandfather? Look at me, sonny. Is that loathsome, cowardly fool me?"

Guests were streaming past them now, en route to the tables set up in the next room. Abe and Amalia walked by, then Linda and Benjamin. Good, the old man thought. Keep your distance. He hoped his grandson noticed they were staying away, realized the family all knew what he had done.

Tris waited until they'd gone, then faced his grandfather. His tone was measured and cautious, like the footsteps of a man approaching a lion. "First of all," he said, "Irving Gold is not a coward or a fool, and if you think he is, you missed the point. I love Irving Gold. And yes, there are similarities. Many. But no, he's not you—not *just* you. He's me, too. A version of me. And you and I, whether we like it or not, have a lot of ugly shit in common."

Tristan narrowed his eyes to a wince. "You must have balls the size of watermelons. I mean, you must have to carry them around in a fucking wheelbarrow. Irving Gold is me with a raging hard-on, me in a funhouse mirror. He's my fucking age. He's married to my wife."

"On whom he cheats. And who—"

"Don't hide behind your goddamn facts! How *dare* you bullshit me!"

Tristan blinked and sighed and pinched the bridge of his nose, and for an instant Tris thought his grandfather would cry. But when the old man opened his eyes, they were dry.

"You're ambitious," he said. "Cop to it. You knew what you wanted to do, so you did it, and everyone else be damned—that, I can understand. There, you and I are similar. So stop conning me. Be a man and cop to it."

They stared at each other, oblivious of the noise and bustle all around. Finally, Tris bowed his head.

"You're right," he said, low. "I took what I wanted from your life without regard. I made things up without regard. I found all kinds of darkness—in you, in me—and I used it all. If I've hurt you, I'm sorry. But you have to believe me, Grandpa. It was never malicious. It just was."

Tristan looked sharply at him. "That's not a sentence. Just was *what*?"

Tris blinked. "True."

Tristan slid his hands down his thighs, clutched vaguely at his knees. The fight was draining from him; he felt a grim kind of relief. "Let's cut bait," he said. "I will forgive you for writing this character if you will forgive me for being this character."

"But Grandpa, he's—"

The old man raised his hand. "Leave it alone. I know who I am better than you do. I'm going to accept your apology on good faith, the same way you're going to accept mine. You can tell the rest to my tomb." He paused, shook his head the way he had outside Amalia's hospital door. "And if you really see yourself in Gold, you'd better make some changes, quick," he added gravely.

Tris shut his mouth and mulled that over. Both of them tracked the progress of a grinning two-year-old, a cream cheese–coated spoon clutched in her hand. She'd almost made it to the foyer when her mother caught up, swooped down, took her in her arms, and carried her back to the party. The toddler's face fell as soon as she was lifted, and the shrieking began. Her mother shot them a harried, apologetic glance as she passed. It went unacknowledged.

Tris picked up his plastic fork and snapped off the middle tines. "If you want, I'll have your name stricken from all my press stuff. Nobody who doesn't already know we're related will find out."

"I would say yes, but it's too late now. I've already had a message on my office telephone from some dame at the *Times* magazine. The word is out."

A balloon of excitement swelled in Tris's chest. His publicist's biggest long shot had come off: to convince a freelancer she'd played field hockey against in high school to pitch a grandfather and grandson piece to the *New York Times Magazine*, a dual profile of the literary giant and the young writer who had grown up in his shadow. An article like that was priceless, sat on millions of coffee tables for months. It made you, whether you deserved it or not.

"When was this?"

"Sometime last week. I only checked the machine yesterday." He eyed his grandson. "I don't imagine I'll call back."

Tris had forgotten what it was like to feel as young as he did now—this hideous with ambition, this single-minded in desire, this frantic in pursuit. This dependent on a decision utterly beyond his control.

"Isn't there any way you can, Grandpa? We can use the interview to set the record straight. I'll tell them Irving Gold's not you. We'll take that off the table forever."

"You can't control what they write. I learned that long ago. I'm sorry, I don't want anything to do with it."

Tris ground his teeth, trying to summon the grace to accept the answer. Instead, one thought blinked on and off, on and off, like the sign outside a bar. His grandfather was fucking him over.

Tris glanced over his shoulder at the clot of women bunched around

Melissa, cooing at the screeching, mutilated infant in her arms. He bent forward. "You know, Grandpa, I *could* tell them that Irving Gold *is* you. I could tell everybody that."

The astonishment slapped across the old man's face was as vivid as a handprint. "That, I would never forgive."

Tris made fists of his hands, dropped his chin to his chest. The treacly smell of noodle kugel wasn't what made him want to vomit, but it wasn't helping. "And I don't think I could forgive you if you didn't call the lady at the *Times* back."

Tris's skin crawled under the old man's glare, but he couldn't dodge it any longer. Their eyes met, and Tristan pounced.

"I'm not to be intimidated," he spat. "Not by the likes of you. I'm more important to them than you'll ever be. If I throw my weight around, they'll kill your story just like *that*." He snapped his fingers weakly, producing no sound. "Hell, I could call Meredith Rabinowitz at Frontier and scare her into putting your book through a complete legal vetting. I could threaten a lawsuit and tie you up forever." He leaned back, crossed his arms. "How *dare* you."

The venom of the old man's words burned Tris's shame away. Fuck begging and apologizing and weak, vile threats. There was a truth they shared that superseded all of this, and he would hold his grandfather to it.

"No. How dare *you*? This is my fucking story. *Mine*. Your life is part of who *I* am. *Everything* is part of who I am. That's how this *works*. Novels don't bend for the world—*you* taught me that. Now you wanna talk about prayer and survival and the history of the Jews, but you're the guy who put them at the helms of slave ships before the camps went cold. That's the story you needed to tell, and that's why it was great. You did whatever you had to do to survive, claimed what you needed, made it all yours—that's the fucking story of the Jews, of hip-hop, of everything. So don't you tell me I can't do the same." Tris could barely force himself to remain still; his body throbbed with the urge to punch something, kick something, throw a chair. He squeezed his hands into fists so tight they ached, and tried to breathe.

They sat and stared at each other. Tristan looked into his grandson's blazing, jittery eyes, took in his flushed, frightened face. If ever he was going to break with himself, the old man thought, now was the time.

What did he owe Tris? What did they owe each other? Were old men supposed to immolate themselves so young might prosper? Was that the way of the world, the way of family, the way of redemption? How could redemption come on the heels of betrayal; how could it come at the hands of this self-righteous, calculating putz?

"I'll do the interview," he said. "Not because I buy any of that bullshit. But because you're my grandson, you impudent little prick. And I owe you that much. For the good of this family. What's left of it."

Tris unclenched his fists. "Thank you."

"Don't you thank me." Tristan labored to his feet. "I thought you were willing to fuck me over for the sake of a book, but I was wrong. You'll do it for much less. For a few pages of publicity. A little taste of success. So have it your way, Tristan Freedman. I'll do the piece, and that's the last thing I will ever do for you. Good luck. I hope you take the best-seller list by storm."

And with that, the old man walked away.

CHAPTER THIRTEEN

Tris bounded up the stoop and swung open the tall wooden door.

"Babe? You home? Hello?"

"I'll call you back," Nina said into the phone. "Was it gross?" she shouted from the bed, turning toward his voice.

Tris appeared in the doorway, suit jacket slung over his shoulder. He leaned against the wall, crossed his ankles, and sheathed his free hand in the pocket of his pants.

Nina propped her head against her fist. "Well?"

"Well what, my love?"

"Well, why are you acting all cool and grinning like a lunatic, for starters?"

Tris shook out the jacket, folded it lengthwise, and tossed it at the bed. It slid onto the floor.

"Because I'm going to be in the fucking *New York Times Magazine*, that's why."

Nina threw her legs over the side of the bed. "No!"

"Yup."

"Holy shit! They went for it?"

"They did. It's a whole new ball game."

She jumped to her feet and pressed herself against him. "Tris, that's unbelievable. We have to celebrate."

"Yeah." He laid his palm against her cheek and Nina pulled back, beaming at him. "Absolutely."

"What do you wanna do?"

"I'm thinking we jump in the car, drive over to Atlantic City, and get married. How's that strike you?"

"Seriously?"

"Seriously. Right now. I mean, you should probably throw some pants on first. But after that."

She stared at him, the water rising to her eyes. "You'd do that for me?"

"I need you," Tris whispered.

"Do you?" She whispered, too, voice reverent and afraid.

"More than ever, Nina." He touched a finger to her chin and raised her mouth to his. They kissed.

"I need you, too," said Nina. "You're all I—all I want to need."

The phrase that had been sounding in his mind all the way home returned to Tris now: *Consecrate the lie*. He didn't know quite what it meant, had only theories about the words' persistence. In some obscure and awful way, he knew he would not be standing here with Nina, ready to bind himself to her in a ceremony he had until now disdained, if not for the anticipation of his grand public vindication, or the ferocious shame of his betrayal and the victory he had wrung from it, or the massive loneliness that lurked behind it all.

Tris understood the enormity and viciousness of his own will as never before. It was intoxicating and repellent. He felt like a murderer and an innocent, shapeless and rigid, an initiate to sacred rites and a thief in the temple. Full of love and empty of everything, words even.

He didn't know what the fuck he felt like. Whatever he and Nina had together would have to define and redeem and sustain him. That was, after all, what marriage was about, wasn't it?

"Let's go to New Jersey," he said.

Nina glanced at the Marcus Flanagan print hanging on the wall behind Tris, then took his hand in hers.

"Yeah," she said. "Let's go."

Tristan fit his worn key into the lock, opened the front door, and turned to wave at Linda. She waved back, shifted her vehicle, accelerated out of sight. Amalia had invited her in, but Linda had declined, explaining that she had to go home and tell everyone she knew that the *New York Times Magazine* was going to profile her son. It was all she'd talked about between Long Island and Connecticut, probably all she'd talk about for quite some time.

"What about a drink?" the old man said as he and his wife slung their jackets over the bannister.

For as long as Amalia had known him, the question had meant "what about fixing me one?" She would not play this moment the way she'd played so many others. She would not allow the public obligation to be civil to each other carry over into private, flattening a crisis by virtue of mere low-grade momentum.

"What *about* a drink, Tristan?"

He headed toward the bar. "I'm having scotch."

Amalia seated herself on the couch and toyed with the fringe of a blanket. "The same for me, then." Tristan handed it over, and Amalia studied the golden liquid through the beveled glass.

"I was proud of you today, with Tris." She owed him that much.

Tristan placed his own drink on the coffee table and backed into the chair across from her, balancing his weight against the armrests as he bent at the knees. The process was controlled and gradual at first, and then the old man's elbows buckled and he fell the last third of the way into the seat. He'd been sitting down this way for years now, but it still unnerved Amalia terribly.

"Don't be proud of me. I only did what I had to." A short sip, punctuated by a twitch of lips, as he recalled the way Tris had bounded over to the family table, not five minutes after Tristan had walked away from him and sat down at it, and asked, *Did Grandpa tell you the good news?* Smiling right at Tristan. Daring him to tell the truth. He hadn't.

The old man straightened in his chair. "Where's Mariko?"

"She went home for a bit."

"She'll be back, then?"

"I believe she will." Amalia thought about it, then added, "I hope so."

Tristan jiggled his drink. "Would it be accurate to say that Mariko now lives here?"

Amalia held her scotch in both hands, the way a little girl might hold her apple juice. "It would not be inaccurate. Am I to understand that you object?"

Tristan's palm floated up from his knee, hung in midair. "I didn't know we were running a refugee camp is all."

"It's Mariko who's running the camp, I'm afraid."

Tristan fell silent. Amalia watched the furrows of his brow compress and expand like the bellows of an accordion. He was laboring at something. Trying to locate the words, or the courage to say them. Or perhaps he was backtracking, regressing an idea to its point of origin and examining its parentage, so that when he finally elucidated it, he could begin at the beginning, as a storyteller ought.

"I want to say this right," he explained.

Amalia nodded, bemused and saddened at his need to account for himself. As if she didn't know him at all.

"I've been considering the notion of forgiveness," the old man said at last, crossing his legs, and Amalia knew his rumination had not yielded the approach he'd sought. Instead, Tristan had decided to come at the subject from a great distance, begin with lofty abstractions and rely on her to do most of the work for him. She was not surprised. She was not even disappointed.

She waited, but nothing more was forthcoming. "What about it?" Amalia asked, resolving that she would not prompt him again.

"Well, first in terms of our grandson. It was very liberating for me to forgive him for his book. . . ."

"I'm glad to hear it. Perhaps you're growing up." The words were out of her mouth before Amalia could help it. This was new to her, to pick on him when he was trying.

"Yes." The barb didn't seem to have registered. "I think that may be the single greatest mistake I've made in life, Amalia. Among thousands. To hold on to every insult, every offense, rather than forgive. Or ask forgiveness." He paused. "I've been terribly unfair, and I'd like to apologize to you. For everything."

He shut his mouth. Because he was finished? Amalia wondered. Or because he realized how much cowardice was packed into that word *everything*, how little content was contained in that stilted, swift apology, and how much presumption?

It was moving to see him struggle toward her, as overmatched as he was. But Tristan's words did not touch her. For the first time in Amalia's life, words seemed powerless, ignoble—mercenaries without honor, willing to serve any conceit.

"I appreciate that, Tristan. I never thought I'd hear it. But it's too late. It's just . . . too late."

He hadn't been expecting that, and she could see that it hit Tristan hard. His face sagged, and suddenly Amalia didn't feel cold anymore; she felt horrible.

"How can it be too late? We're still alive. We can still forgive each other." He pounded his fist against his bony knee. "Goddamn it, Amalia! If I can forgive Tris, you can forgive me!"

She reached forward and took his hand. It seemed like years since she'd last held it. "You have my forgiveness. As much of it as I can give."

She squeezed his hand, but before Tristan could squeeze back, or decide not to, Amalia pulled hers away and brought it to rest in her lap. "And if I wanted your forgiveness, Tristan, I would have asked for it."

Tristan slumped down in his seat, tried to formulate a reply and found that prayers filled his mind, blowing about like scraps of paper in the wind, hugely and ridiculously distracting. They had occupied him for the whole ride home and they were back now, pulsing quiet and insistent. The only way to shake free, he decided, was to say one aloud. Perhaps that was what the prayers wanted from him anyway: passage out into the world.

"Can you recall the Shema?" he asked his wife.

Amalia stopped herself from demanding to know what the hell this had to do with anything. It was the sort of question one just answered.

"Only the way my father sang it. The Broadway stage version."

"Would you say it with me, please?"

"Tristan—"

"Please."

Amalia tipped her face to the ceiling, straining in recall, then began to recite: uncertainly at first, but gaining resonance, fluidity, with every phrase. Tristan joined her, and with gazes locked on each other, the two of them made their way through the Hebrew prayer.

Hear, O Israel, the Lord is our God, the Lord is One.

Blessed be the Name of His glorious kingdom for ever and ever.

And you shall love the Lord your God with all your heart and with all your soul and with all your might.

And these words that I command you today shall be in your heart.

And you shall teach them diligently to your children, and you shall speak of them when you sit at home, and when you walk along the way, and when you lie down, and when you rise up.

And you shall bind them as a sign on your hand, and they shall be for frontlets between your eyes.

And you shall write them on the doorposts of your house and on your gates.

They sat in silence. After a moment, the old man sighed, deflating as the breath left him. "It seems like such a failure, to give up now. You'll say we gave up years ago. That may be so."

Amalia crossed her arms. "I have to reclaim something, Tristan. And you have to let me."

"I can't stop you."

"I want you to understand. I want you to agree. That's what I need."

The ice in Tristan's drink had melted. He lifted the glass until it was upside down and let the scotch-tinged water trickle down his throat.

"I suppose I do," he said at last. "I suppose you're right about it all, Amalia. I deserve this."

She opened her mouth to speak.

"And you deserve this," he added. She closed it.

The thermostat clicked. Heat hissed through the house. Amalia uttered her husband's name, and Tristan raised his eyebrows.

"Thank you," she said. The old man nodded.

Both of them were still, and then Tristan lifted himself to his feet and made his way upstairs. Amalia watched him go, listened until she heard him sink into his office chair. The wheels slid over the floor as he pulled himself closer to his desk. Amalia picked up her drink, and walked into her study.

ACKNOWLEDGMENTS

Thanks to my grandfather Benjamin Kaplan; my great-uncle and great-aunt, Philip and Esther Kaplan; Victor and Juliet Brudney; and Daniel and Pearl Bell for allowing me to pester them about such things as City College cafeterias, Bronx stickball rules, and 1930s subway routes. To Elvin and Keiko Jones for taking me on the road and giving me the chance to learn everything I know about jazz and opening wine bottles. To Andre C. Willis for facilitating that invaluable experience, and countless others. To Delfeayo Marsalis and Ashley Kahn for answering my esoteric questions about prebop trap sets. To KET for his continued expertise on all matters aerosol. To Professor David Goldberg for vetting the manuscript for historical accuracy. To Eddy Portnoy for providing 1930s Jewish slurs. To David and Lenka Siroky for fact-Czeching. Get it? Get it? To Daniel Alarcón and Vinnie Wilhelm for their invaluable comments on early drafts. To the Giants of Science for bringing violent retribution back to literature. To my cousin Matthew L. Kaplan, for brewing me many cups of extremely strong Brazilian coffee during one particularly grueling stretch of editing. To my father, Charlie Mansbach, for his newpaperman's ability to quote from memory the particulars of any news event concurrent with his lifetime, and my mother, Nancy Mansbach, whose zeal for researching truly random shit has not diminished despite a lengthy absence from the newsroom. To superagent Victoria Sanders, who bears no resemblance to the agent portrayed in this book. To everyone at Spiegel & Grau/Doubleday Broadway, and in particular my brilliant editor, Chris Jackson, for holding up his half of our endless and endlessly productive conversations. And to Victoria Häggblom for love, patience, editorial guidance, and putting up with me.